Rebellion

By Philip Yorke

mashiach publishing

First published in Great Britain: 2019
Reprinted: 2020

0012019

Copyright © Philip Yorke 2019

Mashiach Publishing

The Author asserts the moral right to
be identified as the author of this work

ISBN 9 78 169853 0734

Set in 12 point Baskerville and Baskerville SemiBold

Cover image: Shutterstock/Neil Roy Johnson
Internal images: courtesy of the Fairclough Collection
and The University of Leicester

philipyorke.org

Fought between 22 August 1642 and
3 September 1651, the English Civil Wars were the most brutal and murderous conflicts ever contested on British soil. More than five percent of the population died – and the fortunes of many families across the land were changed forever.
This book is dedicated to the many victims.

PROLOGUE

IT IS THE EIGHTEENTH DAY of October, in the year of our Lord, 1660, and I find myself shivering and fearful on this unseasonal autumnal eve.

My home is a hovel of a cell, a place from where there is no hope of earthly escape or clemency.

I have been incarcerated since the early summer, first in the Tower and now, for the last few days, in the stinking cesspit of Newgate gaol. Much has happened, not least my trial just three days ago, which declared me guilty of High Treason and decreed that my time in this world must come to an end. And on the morrow, a Friday, at nine in the morning, it most surely will when I climb on to the cart that will take me to my doom. Judgment Day.

I said little in my defence; there was no reason to have done so. I am no orator and never have been. I am a simple soldier, and fine words could not have saved me. My ruin was sealed the moment Charles Stuart returned to these lands and strutted into London on his thirtieth birthday, determined to execute his revenge. For among Kings, there can be no tolerance of regicide and no compassion shown to its perpetrators.

But my demise is not the source of my fear. I am told my death will be over in a few fleeting moments, once Squire Dun, the executioner, and his noose have set about their business at Tyburn Tree.

Do not misunderstand: I have no wish to die. I simply accept the inevitability of my fate. I do not fear my own life ending. After all, my end is more becoming than that of my friend, Daniel Axtell, who will join me in paradise tomorrow. Like me, he will be strung up in the morn. But he will be drawn and quartered too, suffering the same agonising fate as the others, whereas I will not. And for that, for sparing my loving wife, my children and my family this grievous state, I give thanks to my God.

No. My fears are for England and the living, and what will happen to her now a vengeful Prince has been restored to the throne. And I also fear for Isabel, my son, Francis, and my daughter, Anne. Upon my death, my estate is forfeit to the Crown and my wife and children will be left penniless, required to live off the charity of others. I feel powerless. Alone. I feel my principles and headstrong actions have betrayed them all. And at this late hour, as the sun sets one last time, I can do nothing to help the people I love the most in this brutal world to avoid the hardship and pain that awaits.

My determination to uphold my faith, protect the rights of the common man and hold a King accountable for his actions has led to my eternal disgrace. My country has also suffered most grievously. Two decades of war and turmoil, a time I thought was of liberation; that brought religious freedoms and tolerances; that replaced a tyrant with a Lord Protector; these years of bravery, courage and sacrifice now count for nought. And the deaths of so many, including the Monarch I played a part in condemning, as well as the untimely ends of so many friends and comrades, have all been in vain. In my final hours, I find myself contemplating these injustices and finding little comfort, except in my God. Death, I realise, will be a welcome release.

And I start to weep.

I have tried to lead an honest life; one that is just, one that is true. I have been a military commander of considerable repute, some would say. I have been elected a judge and I have represented my county in Parliament. Yet too many of my forty-two years have been committed to the slaughter of good men, women and children, whose only crime has been to be in the wrong place at the wrong time. Their faces – and their screams and pleas – have tormented me since the killing began. I have also prosecuted many men of the church whose views were not in accord with my own. Even though so many of these deeds were committed long ago, my conscience remains troubled. And soon I will be held to account.

I recognise the sin, pride and evil associated with my own deeds. I have condemned others when I had no right to do so. In my zeal, I have forgotten the need for tolerance, forbearance and compassion. Nay, even love. For even though my awakening has come late in my day, I now know there is a higher place, to which every man is called, regardless of their creed; where redemption can be found by all; where even the foulest of murderers and sinners – men like me – can be forgiven. And I thank my brothers and sisters in Christ for the strength they have given me, helping me find the peace I have needed to get through these dark months.

I have vilified too many for too long. And I have borne false witness for as long as I can remember. I wish it no more.

Foe and friends will find it hard to believe I, Francis Hacker, proclaim these things and, as I prepare to climb the scaffold, can so readily forgive the follies and devilry of those who call themselves my sworn enemy. But I now see the truth for what it is. For I know I have been forgiven for my many crimes and sins. And as I have been forgiven, I must also forgive those who have spoken falsely against me these past months, hurt my family deeply and preached a false gospel. This, I do freely. For a man has no right to judge any other. And for releasing me, and granting me my redemption as I await my fate, I give thanks and praise to my God, my Saviour.

My prayers and thoughts are interrupted by a harsh rasping noise. I look up just as the bolt that locks my cell is drawn back and the heavy, stud-encrusted door swings open.

"Hacker," bellows Clay, my spittle-flecked gaoler. "You have a visitor, someone who wants to help you unburden your damned soul before the morrow. Make yourself decent, man."

Out of the gloom emerges Hercules Sowerby, a friend, confidante and lawyer. He is based at Lincoln's Inn, where he has a thriving practice representing gentry and common folk alike. His nose wrinkles at the corrupting stench of decay and misery that shrouds this place. I am relieved to see his strong, unfashionably clean-shaven face.

"I didn't think you would come," I say.

"It wasn't easy," confesses Hercules, a man I have

known throughout the struggles. "There was opposition. Lots of it, as you can imagine. But I managed to convince the authorities there was validity in my visit. So here I am. At your service."

"You are a good man," I stutter, moved by the personal sacrifice Hercules has made to share these last few hours with me. At a later date, he will surely be held to account. "I thank you. You are indeed a friend. Now to business – you will need your quill and plenty of ink and parchment. This will be my only confession and testimony, so write it truly. There is much to say."

"Are you ready?" I ask.

Hercules eyes me through his hooded slits. I suspect this is how he looks when he is with a client, carrying out his lawyerly duties: proficient, to the point, patient.

He simply says: "Aye, when you are ready."

I take a deep breath and slowly start to recite the words that have been pounding in my head since before I became a condemned man. A traitor prosecuted for the foulest of treasons.

A regicide...

My dearest Isabel

I write this, my final letter to you, from Newgate gaol on the eve of the eighteenth of October, in the year of our Lord, 1660.

I have tried to be a true, loyal and loving husband and Father. And to know you are now suffering harshly grieves me dearly. For it is my sincerest wish that you find peace and contentment in the years ahead. That is why I have asked Hercules to take these last words from me. So you know the truth of my deeds, and I can correct the many falsehoods bestowed upon me by my accusers.

Be assured, you, Francis and Anne, are in my thoughts – and will be until the end. Know that I often think of our other darling children; of Isable and Barbara, who we lost so tragically; and Elizabeth and Mary, who passed away innocently in their infant years; these tragedies we were powerless to resist. I miss them dearly, as I know you do too. And as their Father, it comforts me to know, in a few brief hours, I will be reunited with them all.

In truth, my love, I have regrets that torment me. For the last eighteen years, I have been a poor father, soldiery and the nation's affairs always winning my favour above the needs of my bloodline. And the same can be said for the attention I have paid to you, particularly since the troubles flared again. In time, I pray you will forgive me for my selfishness, arrogance and stupidity.

I am a man of few words. You will know more than anyone that it has always been this way. For much of my life, my silence has served me well. Yet, I have rarely spoken openly of my love for you. Therefore have no doubt in your heart that you are mine. You always have been. My eternal regret is I have not told you this nearly enough.

My brothers always knew what to say and how to say it. Of the three of us, they were always more popular. I never resented this. I love them both dearly and await my heavenly reunion with Thomas with a sense of joy. I am asking Hercules to speak directly to Rowland about the estate. So there may be some hope in the weeks and months ahead. Hercules will do all that is necessary. Don't despair. Stay strong; what can be done will be done. I also urge you to call on Rowland if you are in need of support. Have no doubt you will be in need of his help. And I am sure you can rely on him. He continues to be my lov-

ing brother, despite all that has happened. And even though my name is disgraced, I know he will do all he can to see you restored.

You have often asked me what has driven my loyalty to the Parliamentarian and Commonwealth cause and men like Cromwell, Pym, Haselrig and Fairfax. Alas, I have rarely paid you the courtesy of answering your questions. Allow me to do so now.

The truth is, for as long as I can remember, I have always felt there has been a deep injustice in England, a place where the farmworker, blacksmith and servant have no voice; no control over their life; no right to practice the faith of their choice freely; and no right to speak out for justice. And to me, someone who has been born into privilege, I know this to be wrong. My failing has been to have been silent for too long and to put everyone I love at risk and all I own at the mercy of a monarch I know to be unjust.

You know I have tried to follow a true path of faith and conviction. You have been on the same journey. And I am fortunate to have found brothers with the same heart as my own. Try as I have, I cannot support a man who believes his rule is by divine appointment. A King bleeds, as do I. A King loves, as do I. A King feels pain, as do I. A King is mortal, as am I. To put oneself on the same pedestal as God is the ultimate sin. It is something I cannot condone.

My enemies say I am a regicide, a King killer without remorse.

This is not so.

It is true I am culpable, more so than most – but I did not actively seek the King's death. The manner of his ending pains me to this day. I was merely a soldier doing his duty. Infamy is my reward.

Because of my deeds, I fear life will be harsh for you, Francis and Anne in the weeks and years ahead. And this grieves me; I would not have wished this for you. But it will not be forever. And my prayer is you will soon be restored, in wealth and in honour. Our God is a loving and nurturing Father.

I now urge you to follow the path that is true for you, and you alone. For too long, we have disagreed about religion. It has put a barrier between us that should never have existed. I was wrong to try and impose my views and ways on you. I implore you to follow your conscience in this regard. You are a strong and godly woman, and this is a matter for you alone — and our Father. Know that whatever course you take you have my blessing and love.

Finally, I ask you not to dwell on the events of this week. You acted kindly, truly, with my best interests at heart. You were not to know the Court would distort your words; your actions willfully misinterpreted; and the Warrant you bore used to condemn me, and others, out of hand. I know you did everything out of your deep and unselfish love for me, and your desire to see my innocence proven.

But, my dearest, that was an outcome that could never happen; I think you know that now. So please, do not torment yourself. It is my time. I am called to a higher place. That is all.

I leave this world comforted in the knowledge our children could not have wished for a more devoted mother. And I thank you for being a true and loving Wife.

In the days that come, always remember that I have the highest esteem, respect and love for you. I hope you find happiness once again. And I long for the day when we will be reunited.

Your loving, devoted and faithful husband, Francis

I look up and see Hercules looking at me through the gloom with an intensity I have rarely seen in all the years we have known each other.

"Is that everything?" he asks softly.

"A few inadequate words are all I can offer her," I splutter. "Best I tell Isabel all I can, even though, in honesty, I find words of the heart hard to come by. Feelings have never been something I have found easy to convey. Be sure to tell her of my love and devotion. And tell her she was in my heart until the end.

"Promise me also that you will take this letter and testimony to Isabel with due haste when we are done. Ask her to share it with Rowland and our children. I fear for her health; I fear for her mind; I fear enmity and shame will tear at her soul, and the life she has left will be hard."

Hercules scrutinises me for what seems an eternity, his penetrating eyes reaching into my inner recesses.

"You have my word, my friend," he whispers at last, wiping away a tear that has swelled in the corner of his eye. "You need not worry. With all speed, I will take this to Stathern and offer as much comfort as I can to your good lady."

I offer a rueful nod of the head. And I smile.

"Thank you," I say. "Now let us consider the events of yonder years that have been the cause of so much pain for so many…"

"A few honest men are better than numbers… If you choose godly, honest men to be captains of horse, honest men will follow them… I had rather have a plain russet-coated captain that knows what he fights for, and loves what he knows, than that which you call a gentleman and is nothing else."

Oliver Cromwell

ONE

LIFE. DEATH. I AM SOMEONE who holds the power to give one and take the other. And I revel in it.

Since the troubles started, I have seen men, some little more than children, slain at my command. Occasionally, they have been brave and faced their fates boldly, unafraid, with their eyes wide open. But more often than I care to remember, they have pleaded for their lives before they have been put to the sword, or our muskets have barked fire. As the blade has cut forth, or the lead shot has bitten deep, their terror has been released, and they have pissed and soiled themselves before succumbing to the after-life. For the end is nearly always brutal and demeaning. It is rarely kind.

I have to tell you that I have not felt guilt, shame or remorse at these moments of lust. I have watched my enemies die and, to my eternal shame, rejoiced at their pain and suffering. My men and I are at war. We are battle-hardened warriors fighting for a holy cause. And we will not let any puppet of the King stand in our way.

But it hasn't all been bloodshed and gore.

I can recall many times when we have behaved with honour and compassion, when we have reunited our foe with their families and set them free. We have done this knowing they would soon be rallying under the Royalist banner, with husbands, fathers and sons returning to the fray in the hope of making a Parliamentarian kill. That knowledge hasn't mattered. At these moments, we have been simple men once again – not assassins.

Right now, I am looking at more than a hundred unruly souls. They are my brothers in arms.

It is late. There is a chill in the air. Most are drunk. Like me, all are filthy and stink. Yet I feel a unique bond with these men branded renegades and rebels by the King. Our loyalty is borne out of the God and cause we serve, the slaughter we have inflicted on our enemy, the pain we have endured as a group, and the pure joy we draw every day from the simple pleasure of being alive. It's these things that are forging our identities, ensuring we become one of the most feared militias in the land.

Out of the corner of my eye, I can see Smith. Fat, bald and missing most of his teeth, he is a man of contrasting ugliness and beauty. On one level, he is a supreme killer, fearing nobody – least of all me. Skilled with sword, cleaver and musket, he is the one soldier you want by your side in the heat of battle. Yet he also has the most melodious voice I have ever heard. At this moment, he is singing a song – lamenting one of his many long lost loves and a lifetime of regrets – and it sounds like an angel is in our midst.

My men, those sober enough to retain some sense

and reason, have smiles etched on their faces. Huddled around the campfires, they are swaying to Smith's wistful lullabies, hooked on every word; and they are as close to earthly heaven a tormented soul can be. They want to escape from their world of death, pain and futility, even if it's just for a fleeting moment.

And, I confess, so do I.

Smith's wondrous, tortured melodies, help us forget everything that has passed and embolden us for what is about to come.

We embrace moments of tranquillity and joy with a vengeance and zest, and we heartily sing along.

Until men like me give the order to break camp.

"It's almost time," I say to Abijah Swan, my ever-loyal Subaltern. "Prepare the men. Tell them to be quiet. And let's make sure the horses have been fed and watered, so they are ready for the long day ahead."

A nod of the head and an impish grin is all I get back in reply. And that's all I need.

Swan is my brother in everything other than flesh; the man I trust most in this murderous world. He's got my back – and, in ten long months, he's already saved my life many times. And my men love him. He's one of them: tough, ruthless and seemingly without weakness. But he also possesses raw intelligence and is a natural leader. In truth, I tell you, there is not a better man alive with whom to share my fears, joys and pains.

With the click of Swan's tongue, the angelic singing stops abruptly. Smith looks up and his left eye twitches. In the silence, dozing men stir. Drunken heads clear.

"Make ready," says Abijah.

"Check your muskets and your gunpowder; make

sure they're dry. Check your swords and daggers; they had better be sharp. And make sure you wear your helmets. They will save your life one day, but they will only do their job if you lump heads happen to be wearing them!"

As one, my men rise and go about their business with the precision of disciplined veterans. And I smile as I see many of them heeding Swan's words, reaching for their ungainly and heavy helmets.

Many seem too young to be consumed in this pitiless bloodshed. Rather than cleaning daggers and counting their lead musket balls, they should be tucked up in their pallets and mattresses, with their loved ones around them. Old-timers like Lambert, Hill and Hipwell, should have hung up their scabbards and muskets years ago. But they can't. None of us can. They, like me, feel called to teach our King the lesson he deserves.

This cursed, uncivil war has scarred England's rich and verdant lands, ever since the King and his allies sought to crush the voice of Parliament. If the truth is known, the struggle against the Crown has been raging ever since the days of James, late King and father to Charles. That's more than thirty long years. Yet it's only in recent times that bloodshed became inevitable.

The decisive moment came in January when the King sought to arrest five Parliamentarians: the figure-heads opposing the excesses of his rule. Among them were John Pym and Sir Arthur Haselrig. Thankfully, they were forewarned and escaped before Charles could have them thrown in the Tower. But a critical line had been crossed, and the countdown to the inevitable military conflict had started. That became a reality eight months later, in

August when Charles raised his royal standard at Nottingham. It was an unambiguous declaration of war.

The fighting was supposed to be short-lived: one major battle would decide all, or so we all thought and hoped. Edgehill, an unremarkable place in Warwickshire, would be the fight to settle everything and restore the balance. Kill many it did, with thousands more maimed and injured. Yet it settled nothing. So here we are, almost a year later. And still, there is no end in sight to the madness that consumes our weary country.

Our foe has held the upper hand throughout much of this cursed conflict, soundly beating our troops in pitched battles in Cornwall and the south. Many thousands of Parliamentary soldiers have died needlessly while our leaders have stood by, unable to stem the flow of defeats and a growing sense of doom. Our minor successes are quickly forgotten. Much blood has been spilt, so many good men lost, because of incompetence, negligence and sheer damned lies.

Too often, we have been out-thought. But rarely have we been out-fought. And that knowledge continues to give us hope, enabling us to believe our cause is just and God remains by our side. I, for one, know this to be true. Aylesbury, in its way, proved it. So, too, did Edgehill, Turnham Green and Hopton Heath. We may not have won decisive victories, but our men bloodied the tyrant's nose at these battles, as we have at others since.

And that's why the Cavaliers fear us.

Right now, we may lack their discipline and order. But they can see we are getting stronger by the day: tactically, strategically and in sheer weight of number. Their generals and King know that unless they destroy us in the very near future, the tide will surely turn.

Until then, the men of the militias, drawn from the fifteen counties under the control of Parliament, have to find a way of staying alive. Our struggle must continue to flourish; until the moment we are strong enough to seize overall control.

For us, the men of the Leicestershire Militia and the Midlands Association, that means killing as many of our enemies as we can before they have a chance to stab, cleave or shoot us. And we will; for when we are not preaching, praying or reading our Bibles, we are experts in dishing out death.

On this morn on the thirtieth day of June, in the year of our Lord, 1643, we have a chance to gain some precious, long overdue respite for the people of the north.

It is four o'clock. We are less than five miles away from Bradford. And even in the midst of summer, Yorkshire's early morning air has a chill to it that forces the Tawny Owls and foxes that roam this land to seek the warmth of a nest, or a covet. Oh, how I miss a welcoming mattress, my loving wife, Isabel, and my beloved children.

My Militia is garrisoned on the borders of Nottinghamshire, Leicestershire and Rutlandshire, close to my home in Stathern, where we continue to make life hard for those Royalists foolish enough to stray south of the Trent and actively seek to test our strength. Among them are my brothers Thomas and Rowland, ever-loyal champions of our tainted King.

Alas, we are one of the few parts of England that hold the upper hand. Everywhere else, Charles's forces are in the ascendency.

For us, at least, there has been a lull in the fighting in our fields, towns and pasturelands. We have been away for four long weeks, and now my men and I have been tasked with bringing some valuable Cavalier prisoners north, for an exchange.

The meeting and bartering took place two days ago, by Parliamentary decree, no less.

The names of the restored I have already forgotten – but their intolerable arrogance is not. While I question the wisdom of such exchanges, having looked the defeated enemy in the eye on numerous occasions during our journey, my comfort is my growing belief there will be a day of reckoning. After all, God is always good.

Knowing of the reputation of my men, the Commander of the Parliamentary forces in the north, General Ferdinando Lord Fairfax, has pleaded with me to stay for a few days. He wants to discover more about the fight in the Midlands, and how we are keeping the foe at bay.

The General is particularly eager for my men to help his inadequately trained forces gain a better understanding of the tactics associated with fighting a successful campaign on foot, and horse. Good men are hard to come by. When an opportunity presents itself, you grab it with both hands. Fairfax has done so. And knowing how poorly prepared our brothers in the north of England really are, and how successful the Bohemian mercenary, Prince Rupert, the scourge of our forces, has been of late, we have willingly shared what we know. I can only pray it will be enough.

My scouts return to camp with news that a small Royalist

force, comprising some two hundred light cavalry and dragoons, is camped just outside Adwalton Moor, less than a couple of miles from our encampment. They are soundly asleep, seemingly without a care in the world.

"How many sentries? Have you seen any of their scouts?" I ask Longbone, who led the party.

"Three sentries; certainly no more than four, Captain, and there were no sightings of any of the enemy's scouts," he replies. "We circled the camp and counted just three men. But another could have been having a crafty piss. From our position, they looked like they were there for the taking."

"That's precisely why I am concerned," I retort.

I glance up at the ruddy face of Harold Longbone, a young farmer from Cottingham, a disease-filled village in East Yorkshire, who signed up for the Parliamentarian cause at the turn of the year. The man has a youthful face and is barely into his twentieth year.

His village, located close to Hull, has been overrun once already; his family at the beck and call of the enemy when a large Royalist force, led by the King himself, camped there while they besieged the walled fort and garrison. That was almost a year ago. Eleven months on, the threat remains, for the tyrant will be back: it's just a matter of time.

Despite these fears, Longbone, who commands five of my best men, is one of the Militia's finest and most able servants.

"These dandies are either the most stupid men we are ever likely to face, or they are trying to set a trap for us because they believe us to be reckless braggarts," I say.

I turn away from the young man. I need to think

through what I now know and act wisely. Eventually, it is clear what I must do.

"Leave it with me, Longbone," I instruct. "I need to speak to Lord Fairfax and relay the main details of your report before we decide what our immediate course of action will be. I am mindful to advise caution. In the meantime, take your men and feed them. There's some good stew left over from last night, and you have certainly earned all you can eat."

Two hours have passed since Longbone and his scouts returned to camp, and the sun is already starting to beat down on the hills. The blackbirds and magpies have barely had time to yawn. Yet here we are, all ready for the kind of exhilaration only battle brings.

Soon the thin mist that has acted as our shield will start to rise.

I relay the news of the enemy force to Fairfax and, as my superior officer, he has decided we should take the fight to the enemy.

"Our troops need their morale boosting, my dear Francis," he decrees. "We need a decisive victory, and you and your men will do all you can to win a memorable day for us."

My protests and concerns are ignored, not for the first time during this conflict. Fairfax is unmoved by my protestations; his mind set on a course of action I believe to be fraught with danger; bordering on the rash and reckless. How I wish I was more than a Captain of Horse and had a sharper, more decisive tongue.

In fairness, Fairfax has become aware a Royalist army, similar in size to his own and commanded by the

Earl of Newcastle, is in close proximity.

Details are sparse. We don't know how many foot or horse they have. And we have no information about the strength of their artillery.

Nonetheless, regardless of the risk, Fairfax is eager for battle. His blood is up, even though defeat would leave the north defenceless to the retribution of the Cavaliers. But at these pivotal times, sense and reasoning rarely win the day as the potential for glory beckons.

Experience has told me that this is a time when we should be on our guard when we are at our most vulnerable. But it is a rare day indeed when a General heeds the words and caution of a subordinate officer.

My only hope now is that my fears and uneasiness are proven wrong, and the reckless optimism of his Lordship is well placed and ultimately wins the day.

At the head of our small column is Swan; as alert as ever; leading the way.

I am struggling to focus. I am uneasy, even though the men are in good spirits and humour.

Smith is sitting directly behind me. Strict orders have been issued to everyone to maintain absolute silence as we make our way to the enemy encampment. Yet I can hear the faintest of melodies coming out of his mouth, as he builds-up his personal blood lust. I find myself distracted, no longer able to control myself; I laugh aloud.

"Quiet there, you blithering idiot!" barks Sergeant Farndon, without being able to identify the offender. "Are you trying to get us all killed?"

As my eyes adjust, the fields and trees emerge from the fog and visibility of the terrain gets better by the minute.

We make good time to East Bierley, close to a ridge known as Wiskett Hill. And as we approach the village from the north, we hear the horses of our enemy. They are restless and alarmed. I should know the telltale signs, for I am, too!

Suddenly, I become aware of how close we are to the Royalist encampment. A sense of dread threatens to engulf me. My jaw tightens.

"Over there, sir," whispers Longbone, pointing downhill to the left. "They still appear to be fast asleep."

In the distance, I quickly make out several pitched lines of tents, picketed alongside a dense row of Hawthorn trees. Some braziers are alight at the front of the camp, and I can see what appears to be a handful of men talking as daylight continues to emerge out of the darkness.

And just as Longbone reported, the bulk of the camp appears to be still.

The trace of a smile starts to stretch across my face. Fate looks like it has been kind, and I start to say a prayer for the soon to be departed.

Seconds seem like hours as we wait. Only the rousing birds keep our wits occupied, their incessant chattering amplified by the silence of the early morning.

I can feel my heart thumping against my doublet. It always does, just before the moment of battle. I prepare myself to be unleashed. My fears are banished. God is by my side; I am confident we will prevail this morn.

I look to my left and can see the men fanning out, daggers and swords drawn. In the dim light, I can see Smith making practice thrusts with his cleaver: this is no fight for the Doglock.

The time for prayer and regrets will follow afterwards.

We edge forward. Closer; nearer; crouching; tense; within earshot of the camp and any sentries who may be alert enough to hear a hundred desperate rebels descending on them.

The morning dew soaks our boots and breeches. A few of my men start to piss themselves; such is the exhilaration and terror the imminence of battle invokes in a man's soul and his bladder.

"You disgusting sods," growls Stanton, just a few yards away. "Can't you whores of Babylon control yourselves?"

Knowing, nervous sniggers ripple down the line.

Suddenly there is a cacophony of noise. A trumpet blasts on my left flank. I hear harsh shouts coming from straight ahead, and in the dawn, I see puffs of smoke signalling musket fire to our right.

Then chaos descends.

We are not prepared for what comes, and I suddenly realise how exposed we are. We have been fooled. And my good men, my brothers, start to fall.

Within a blink of the eye, our enemy is upon us.

I see Abijah parry one blade; he blocks another aimed at his throat, and then I lose sight of my closest friend. However, within seconds, I am too preoccupied to be worried about anything other than my own survival. I start to stab and slash my way forward as enemy troops appear from nowhere.

A few feet away, Smith is battling desperately as three advancing Royalists, who have emerged out of the shadows, threaten his flank. But his rage, skill and ferocity are more than a match for these ill-equipped adversaries. Slowly, and surely, he starts to overpower them, and I rest easy. Soon fresh blood drips from the edge of his cleaver as it slices into tissue and bone.

But others are less fortunate.

I see the veterans Hipwell and Lambert disembowelled by the hacking cuts of boys barely in their teens; their teeth gleaming in the light; their confidence soaring as they ruthlessly cut down my two faithful bulldogs. Shock and disbelief are etched on the faces of both men as they fall. The melee consumes them. Then they are dust.

The fighting has been raging for what seems like an eternity but is really less than twenty minutes. All around me, men are emitting the keening rattle of death, their struggles at an end. Pitiful cries well up; the noise is unbearable.

We have been surprised; we are outnumbered; we will soon be surrounded. My head is spinning, and I know we must withdraw if we are not going to be annihilated.

"Tell the men to fall back," I yell at Swan.

"Fall back. Fall back," I shout above the maelstrom.

At first, we edge away in a disciplined wedge, our rearguard rallying magnificently to the defence of the remnants of our main body. I call on the men closest to me to cover our backs. My plea is tantamount to an execution warrant. They know it. So do I. But such is the ferocity and precision of the ambush that I have little choice: either a few souls pay the ultimate price, or soon we will all be embracing the after-life.

The valiant efforts of Shawe, Montague, Taylor, Hardaker and Morrice, the men I have ordered to form a rearguard, save the day. The reward for four of them is death. They are cut down where they stand.

Only Shawe survives, and he hangs on to life by a thread after a lead musket ball slices into his left shoulder. He will be lucky to survive the loss of blood, shock and the surgeon's cut. And even if he does get through the next few days, the cursed gangrene awaits; and many of us know, after losing too many friends and comrades to this cruellest of afflictions, it is in no hurry to claim its prey.

I don't know how many of my men have fallen. But it is too many. The ground where we fought is littered with the bodies of the Militia as we make our way out of the bloody killing ground.

An hour earlier, there had been a hundred of us. But not any more; we have been routed.

Even so, fortune continues to be our companion this day, for there would surely have been slaughter aplenty had the Cavaliers not suddenly been ordered to rejoin Newcastle's main force, just at the point when their absolute victory was assured.

Instead of killing us where we stand, they are disengaging from the fight, regrouping and rejoining the Royalist army's main host, dug in close to the village of Adwalton, where, it seems, a far greater and more important battle now rages.

And I thank my God and Saviour: our Deliverer, this terrible day.

The Militia regroups on Swan; I quickly order five of the survivors to stay behind, so they can tend to the bodies of the fallen. I leave them with instructions to return to Stathern after they have completed the burials, giving the names of all the dead to the guardhouse, before they return home to their families and lick their wounds.

I walk to the top of the rise, watching the last of the

Royalist riders disappear. I fall to my knees and pray. I then take what's left of our depleted force and follow the enemy's trail.

We hear the noise of a great battle long before we can see it.

And as we arrive at that jagged, barren place, where even the hardiest of Yorkshire sheep struggle to find shelter and solace, we see the hopes of Parliament being dealt a crushing blow.

The scene that confronts us at Adwalton Moor is one of slaughter, capitulation and total panic.

Newcastle's army, more numerous than Fairfax had realised, has surrounded the General and his commanders. The Royalist cavalry is leading the slaughter, hacking and slashing indiscriminately. I can see some pockets of resistance, but they are fleeting.

Rather than stand their ground and fight, our men are fleeing for their lives. And that is their fatal mistake.

Only minutes before, Fairfax's smaller force had appeared to be in the ascendency, thwarting Newcastle's attempts to surround them. Indeed, the enemy appeared to be losing heart; seemingly buckling in the middle of its line of pike. And that was Parliament's undoing. Our men chased after their wilting foe, only to discover the Cavaliers were far stronger than they appeared; and far more cunning.

No matter how big the enemy's force, Fairfax's troops would take some beating if they had stuck together and fought with a semblance of organisation and discipline. But on their own, as our gallant men now are, with their backs to the foe and running for their lives, they are ripe for butchering. And this morning, the killing knives have been sharpened.

I watch on as crimson torrents of Parliamentarian blood wash the fields as far as the naked eye can see.

The Battle of Adwalton Moor
Parliament was dealt a devastating blow when Royalist
forces overwhelmed its northern army

TWO

THE NEXT TWO DAYS ARE lost to me.

As we left the battlefield, a Royalist musket ball creased my temple, knocking me cold. If the marksman had aimed his shot two inches to the left of my right ear, the leaden ball would have shattered my skull, penetrating deep between my eyes. And I would be no more.

But luck must have been with me that day, for I am alive, and my guardian angel would appear to have been protecting me once again.

Yet despite my good fortune, my mood is as dark as it can be as I come round in the Militia's makeshift encampment.

Abijah informs me forty-nine of my best men, my friends, my brothers, were carried from the field. Still. Cold. Never again will they savour Smith's soulful and melodious voice. They have been laid to rest in an unmarked mass grave many miles away from their homes and families.

I run my hand through my hair. I feel despair. This

is not how the end should be.

It breaks my heart to lose men like these, so many in the prime of their youth. Selfless they were in life; heroes they are in death. Yet soon their sacrifices will be forgotten. What a pitiful, shameful waste.

But my losses compare nothing to those suffered by Lord Fairfax and Parliament's main northern army.

Abijah informs me that up to two thousand of our men were either slain or captured. And of the two thousand that survived, many have now returned to their homes, Flintlocks, sabres, and their continuing will to fight, now buried deep in Yorkshire's peaty soil.

Parliament's cause has been dealt a crushing blow.

"Generals and Lords," I shout, my tongue loosened by the scale of our losses and my grief. "My God, they are a curse to honest soldiery, to every man seeking to rid this land of a tyrant King. This butchery was unnecessary. We didn't need to engage in this ridiculous fight. Caution was needed. But vanity prevailed. And now far too many have perished for no gain."

I am angry. My rage is swelling. And, in truth, I forget much as I spit out slanders against Fairfax and his son, Thomas.

For long months, these two men have fought a remarkable nomadic war against the Earl of Newcastle's superior forces, striking at the enemy wherever they can throughout the deteriorating northern theatre.

The gallantry of Fairfax and his son has bought Parliament precious, much-needed time; their quick-witted tactics achieving much, albeit they may have only ever been an irritation, never strong enough to deal a major blow against superior forces. Nonetheless, they regularly pricked Newcastle's skin, forcing him to keep his forces in the north, unable to join up with the roving Cavalier, Prince Rupert.

And everything was continuing to go according to plan, until the calamitous day of the thirtieth of June!

Shame-faced, I turn to my friend.

"Forgive me. I speak out of turn," I say. "Fairfax is a good commander. So, too, is Thomas. Both are loyal and true. A superior host has bested us. That is the simple truth of the matter. Yet it pains me so. And I cannot but help think it may be the end of us all."

Swan takes a deep breath. "I am afraid that's not the only dire news I have to tell you," he confides. "The other matter concerns your brother, Thomas. We must talk…"

Thomas Hacker is the most sensible of my brothers. Next to me, Rowland is the most headstrong. I have a sister, too. Anne is her name. She is measured, calm and wonderful company. And despite our many differences, I have a deep affection for all three of my siblings.

I am the black sheep of my family. My Faith – I am a staunch Presbertaryian – has been an issue for as long as I dare to remember.

My parents have always been devout Churchgoers and have renounced the evils of the Church of England, and Popists like Archbishop Laud, as vocally as I have. Unlike me, however, they have never expressed their views publically.

Now only my father lives. But he remains a staunch Puritan, seemingly opposing much of what I believe to be true. His sympathies, and those of my brothers, are with the King and not Parliament. And that is the crux of it.

Charles Stuart has the support of my bloodline, and I struggle to understand why, for I believe Charles to be a cur; an abuser of power; a corrupt man who, if he could, would rewrite history for his own ends and force his subjects to recognise him as a divine entity.

During these past few turbulent years, I have committed my body and soul to stopping him, and those who support his cause. I believe my God is by my side, not theirs, in this holiest of quests.

When I have tried to explain my opinions and thoughts to my family, particularly Thomas and Rowland, it has always led to disagreement, bitterness and recrimination. Now I am outcast, misunderstood at best; a rebel rejected by my own flesh and blood.

Since the outset of war, I have championed the cause of the people and Parliament, while my brothers have taken commissions in the King's army. We are now sworn enemies.

But Abijah's despondency leaves me reeling.

"I am so sorry to have to tell you of this. I wish it were not so, but Thomas is dead, killed at Colston Bassett, when he and your brother, Rowland, engaged with a company of the Leicestershire Militia," he reports, his voice cold, matter of fact.

"He was buried some six weeks ago."

I look at my friend, and I shake my head. I cannot comprehend what I have just been told: Thomas is dead? Buried?

"How?" is all I dare say, fearing my emotions and sudden grief will overwhelm me.

"He and Rowland were on patrol with a small Royalist cavalry force from Ashby Castle, when they ran into our men," reveals Abijah. "They were surprised, and our troops simply did what we have trained them to do: they struck hard and fast. You know the lay of the land at Colston Bassett? Your brother was exposed. Sorely isolated. He fought bravely but to no avail.

"The fight, if you can call it that, lasted less than ten minutes. Most of the Cavaliers were killed shortly after the initial ambush. Thomas was one of them.

"Rowland escaped with his life. He fought valiantly and was injured. He is now in our custody. Our men didn't realise who they had set upon until they checked the bodies. It was then that our men recognised Thomas. More details came from Rowland and two other prisoners. All three were unhorsed.

"I only found out what had happened when we returned from Adwalton. You were unconscious, and I didn't think we should try to awaken you. You did not look well.

"A rider spent weeks looking for us. It seems our whereabouts are not generally known by the Committee in Leicester, so they have been unable to get the news to you any sooner, even though they have seemingly been trying to find us for a month."

Tears well up and I cannot speak. I feel nauseous, and I suddenly understand what guilt feels like when it torments your soul. I turn away from Swan. I feel a heavy weight on my heart.

"Leave me, my friend," I request. "I need to compose myself. And I need to pray for my brothers and my family."

I have spent an hour reflecting and praying. My tears have

dried. My head has cleared. But the guilt I bear is unbearable.

The death of Thomas has left me cold. There was always a chance one of us would kill the other. But I never thought this ever likely to happen. We had a pact, an accord, which now counts for nought. The reality of the situation feels abhorrent. Even though I know it to be true, I cannot believe my men have slain my own flesh and blood: an errant brother, who I loved, despite our differences.

And it could have been worse; Rowland, too, could have been taken from me. I never thought it would come to this. Am I damned? A Jonah?

I open my eyes and focus. It is a warm day. The sun is shining. We are on our own. Yet I am drowning in this cold world at war.

Abijah strides over to where I am kneeling.

"Are you able to ride?" he asks, as he lowers his hand and offers to help me stand. "We need to get away from here. Newcastle's men are still rounding up stragglers, and a large enemy force is not far away."

I grip his wrist firmly and rise.

"I have a sore head and a grieving heart, but nothing that will stop me getting into the saddle. Where are we heading?" I enquire.

My second in command draws a crude map in the dirt. He pats a section on the right with some urgency.

"We need to get to Hull," he barks "It's the only stronghold Parliament holds in the north. Now the northern army has been crushed, the towns and cities are all surrendering or falling. Going south is not an option; the Royalists are strong for at least thirty miles, putting our men in serious peril if we seek to return home.

"Only Hull stands firm and loyal, albeit Royalists are roaming the countryside between here and the city. If we can get there, we can regroup and plan our escape. Fairfax has already left by boat to try and reach the East Ridings. And, with God's speed, he will. But we will need to be cautious. Our lives depend on it. There are spies and Cavaliers in every village, so we need to tread carefully until we meet the man who will guide us to safety.

"There is a price on all Parliamentarian heads, particularly those of officers, and we don't want every Royalist in Yorkshire scouring the countryside; looking for us; keen to hunt us down like dogs."

The East Ridings of Yorkshire are desolate and flat. Even at the height of summer, the breeze blowing in from the North Sea and Humber ensures there is an uncomfortable chill in the air.

Our passage from the west of the county is fraught with danger, and we often have to take flight. Cavaliers are our scourges; death our reward if we are discovered.

We make our way to an unremarkable place called Gilberdyke, just twenty miles from Hull. Such is the peril we face; it has taken us four days and nights to negotiate a meagre fifty miles. Stealth and caution have dictated our course. They will continue to do so until we have reached safety.

Hull has been at the forefront of the conflict with the King, enduring Royalist molestation long before the formal onset of war. It is an important city and is, among many things, the major armoury in the whole of England. Vaults teeming with more than twenty thousand muskets and seven thousand barrels of gunpowder make it a notable prize both sides want for themselves.

Mercifully, it is now a haven for many of Fairfax's defeated army; soon, a further fifty-one souls will be granted sanctuary in this walled Jerusalem.

Gilberdyke was founded in the time of the Dane Law. It consists of nothing remarkable, just a water well, a couple of decent-sized abodes, the properties of the local magistrate and a wealthy landowner no doubt, and a further two score and ten tightly packed dwellings that house the local workers who attend the crops grown in the North, South and Middle Fields. No matter where we go in this land, it is ever thus.

"The last time I heard, these places in the Ridings held Royalist sympathies," says Swan, his eyes scrutinising an unfamiliar landscape encrusted with uneven, rustic rooftops and where roaming dogs are rife.

"With Cavaliers at every juncture, until we reach the outskirts of Hull, I cannot guarantee our safety if we stay here too long. It's hard to keep more than fifty men hidden and out of harm's way."

"We had best find the house of Lazenby quickly then, had we not?" I retort.

I speak brusquely. Harshly. Aloof. My sorrows have turned me to stone. I am angry. I am alone with my sorrow.

"Longbone, where is the place we seek? Are you sure you can vouch for this man and his family?"

Harold Longbone walks forward; chin raised, exuding confidence. He has grown in stature since Adwalton Moor, one of the very few of my men to do so.

"Aye, Captain," he says assuredly. "They are my

family; my mother's brother no less, and they as true as you and I, sir. Righteous is the son, a good, devout lad. He will guide us through to the garrison, of that I am sure. And he'll do it quickly."

It is the fourth day of July when we leave Gilberdyke.

Righteous Lazenby proves to be a good man, just as his cousin promised. He is an able guide with a true heart for God and Parliament.

We travel for much of the day. Our wits need to be sharp to avoid Cavalier patrols that become more numerous the closer we get to our destination. Thankfully, they are not vigilant, nor are they inquisitive. But they hold us up, ensuring our progress is slow.

We only dismount when we approach the western side of the city – where the Beverley road dissects the main thoroughfare to Cottingham. It has taken us most of the day to get this far. We still have three miles to negotiate before we are safe.

Our horses are blowing; they can't go much further. The sun and heat have been unrelenting. From here, we march cautiously, for many in this northern city would happily see the King regain his absolute authority, and leave his enemies, men like us, dangling from the branches of the scores of Sycamore trees that populate the local woodlands.

So many still believe us to be nothing more than rebels, brigands and felons. And many resent the hardships and deprivations brought on by the garrison holding out against the King.

It takes us two more hours, and a series of snickets and paths, before we find ourselves within the walls of the stronghold. We visibly relax as we make our way to the fort's main administrative block.

It is now four o'clock in the afternoon. Hull is teeming with defeated Parliamentarian soldiers. And its governor, Sir John Hotham, is feeling the pressure.

My relief at reaching this haven is overwhelming. I have a physical reaction to this newfound refuge, which, much to my shame, I am unable to hide from my men.

"Here. Take this, Captain." Lazenby hands me the remnants of some ripped hose after my guts have spilt out on to the cobbled road. I thank him and wipe down my beard and leather jerkin.

The stench of puke continues to pollute my nostrils and is a timely reminder that I suffer the same weaknesses as my men. Rank and breeding offer no defence; like them, fear is my constant companion.

"It is a pleasure to meet you, Captain, albeit under rather unfortunate circumstances," says Sir John Hotham, from behind his large and ostentatious desk. "How can I be of help to you and your men?"

Powerfully built, friendly and charming, Sir John is an impressive man: a baronet, no less.

It may be one score years and more since he passed the first flushes of his youth, but he still carries with him a distinguished air of authority, albeit he looks more of a dandy than he does soldier.

He has just spent three hours with a host of senior officers from the defeated northern army, who are still licking their wounds and cursing their bad luck after the catastrophe of Adwalton Moor. Understandably, he appears somewhat tired and tetchy.

"I am honoured to meet you," I say to my host, eager to get to the point. "It has been a long and arduous journey to safety. My men are exhausted and hungry. Yet it is important we return to the Midlands as soon as is practicable. So I hope you may be able and willing to aid us in this regard, Sir John?

"The Militia in Leicestershire and Nottinghamshire has only junior officers leading it at the present time, and they are inexperienced and highly vulnerable in the face of the near-daily confrontations they experience with Royalist squadrons commanded by the rogue, Henry Hastings.

"Sir, while we are with you, we are at your service. But I would seek to leave your walls within the week, so we can return home, and once again take the fight to the enemy."

I was granted an audience by Sir John and his son upon my immediate arrival in the city. Not everyone receives such preferment.

Perhaps my reputation has preceded me, for the younger Hotham eyes me with keen interest. He secured Hull's walled fortress upon the instructions of Parliament some eighteen long months ago, long before the first musket was fired in anger.

His reward was to win the enmity of the King for himself and Sir John; both men were branded as "traitors" and promised the vilest of deaths should they ever fall into Royalist hands.

Since then, times have been hard for everyone in the city: camp fever has swept through the garrison, killing, or incapacitating, three out of every ten men; the plague is festering too, and food is in short supply, the Cavaliers' blockades throughout the north ensuring only a meagre amount finds its way through to the defenders. If that isn't enough, there is also the constant threat that the King's forces will return at any time, eager to secure the stronghold and reclaim the military riches of the Royal Armoury.

It is with little wonder then that the son looks at me with a combination of anger, hostility and curiosity etched across his face.

"Are the conditions here not to your liking, Captain?" asks the younger Hotham, from his seat in the corner of his father's study. "Are you already missing your roast beef and the comforts of your homely mattress and wife?"

He laughs at his own quip. But I also detect a trace of menace lurking beneath.

The Hothams have already seen their depleted supplies ravaged by the many hundreds of survivors of Fairfax's army fortunate enough to have found their way to the city. They have also heard stories aplenty of the cowardice that contaminated the ranks of the Parliamentarian force as it fled the battlefield after being routed by Newcastle.

Clearly, the younger Hotham doubts my honour and integrity also.

Had I not been exhausted, I would have found his light-hearted slur easy to ignore, even to laugh off. But today I am weak, not thinking clearly.

I try to suppress the rage that is simmering within me. But the sheer impudence and arrogance of this young dolt gets the better of my usual good nature. So I succumb to temptation.

"No, sir. Far from it," I retort. "But as you'll appreciate, I have a duty to take the fight to the enemy, and continuing to hide behind these walls will not help the cause of Parliament. It will only aid the Cavaliers."

My words have an immediate impact. The weight of the insult infuriates both father and son.

"Good heavens, man, do you take us for idlers, for cowardly laggards?" The voice is that of Sir John. "Do you think we have sat on our arses this past year and a half without taking the fight to the King and Newcastle's men?"

I realise the magnitude of my mistake and rashness immediately.

"Sir John," I start to say. "I meant no offence. My words were clumsily said. And I am grateful for your willingness to offer myself, and my men, a safe roof."

But it's not enough; the damage is done. My riposte to the son has bitten deeply. I am a lily-livered imbecile.

I have humiliated two of Parliament's most highly esteemed soldiers, men who have thwarted a King's ambition for so long. And I should have known better than to rise to a bit of light-hearted jest and provocation. Alas, I am unable to find a way to appease my hosts.

"We can offer accommodation and food for you and your men, and stabling for your horses, for one day and one night only," states a frigid Sir John. "Then you can return to your precious Leicestershire. I wish you God's speed. And make sure you pay your bills. Food and drink are scarce. We take a dim view of folk who try not to pay their way."

A brisk shake of a ring-encrusted hand, fingers cupped in the direction of the study's ornately panelled door, leaves me in no doubt the meeting is over. I am free to leave.

Swan, our men and myself depart Hull before breakfast the following morning. Getting back to our home is our priority, not loitering in a place that doesn't want us. We will eat when we are well on our way, I decide.

Righteous Lazenby has long since returned to the familiar trappings of Gilberdyke, so a detachment of half a dozen garrison men escort us to the city's west gate, and help us plot a route that should keep us safe for twenty-five miles, or more; until we have passed the Minster town of Howden.

All that matters to me right now is that my men and horses are well rested and fed, and I am delighted to discover that less than a handful have fallen prey to the city's whorehouses and inns.

By lunchtime, with the Humber and Hull far behind us, and no visible sign of Cavaliers blocking our way, I turn my thoughts to my estate at Stathern, the war on my own doorstep and the welfare of Isabel and the children.

I am thankful the Hothams and Adwalton Moor are already a fading memory.

Stathern is my rock, a tranquil place, surrounded by gentle, rolling hills that provide rich pastureland for the plentiful numbers of cattle, sheep and horse that inhabit this idyllic part of England. Even in the midst of this brutal, unrelenting civil war, this place is somewhere I am able to find true peace and solace.

My estate covers more than three hundred acres of green, fertile land and forest.

Located in an area known as the Vale of Belvoir,

which borders the counties of Leicestershire, Rutlandshire and Nottinghamshire, the Hall has been owned by my family for more than seventy years, ever since my father's father left Somerset, in the age of Queen Elizabeth, and resettled in the Midlands.

In years to come, it is my hope the estate, and a house and land I own in Colston Bassett will be passed down to my son. Today, it is my refuge; a place where I can forget about politics and war and be Francis – husband, father and friend – once again. How I miss it when I am on active duty. The morrow, I hope it will be a haven for future generations of Hackers.

Bucephalus, my trusted horse, knows the lie of the land well. He is named after Alexander the Great's famous war steed.

While I am certainly no Alexander, he more than lives up to his title, for he is a majestic beast: loyal, strong, fast, sensitive and intelligent. And he loves his home, as do I.

His nostrils flare and his ears prick up when he senses his stables are close by. And I am sure I sense an extra spring in his step this day, as the lure of Isabel's loving embrace gets ever closer. For my wife adores this horse as much as I do and, I confess, I am sometimes uncertain what place I occupy in her affections when I see the sheer happiness and joy my thoroughbred invokes in her.

We are a mile away from the Hall when Peter Harrington, one of my trusted men from the estate, approaches our ragged column.

"Sir, it is so good to see you," he shouts as he nears our tired, drawn-out band. "We have been fearful these past few weeks, Master Francis. Our concerns have grown in recent days after we heard the news about the northern army's defeat. We have been praying you and the Militia have been kept safe. So it is wonderful to see you back in these parts, sir. Home at last."

Harrington looks at my demoralised and exhausted men, and I recognise the pain and concern on his face as I see him desperately scan our ranks. He is looking for Stephen, his son, one of our trusted number.

"Fear not," I say, reassuringly. "He is safe and unharmed. He is but four miles away, carrying out an important errand on my behalf. He will be returning to Harby in good time. You need not worry; you will be seeing your son very soon."

Tears well up in the sockets of this loyal man, who has served my family faithfully for the past thirty-five years.

"Bless you, sir. His mother will be overjoyed. She worries and I can do little to stop her fretting," is all Peter will allow himself to reveal about his anxieties before he recovers his composure.

"The Mistress was told you were close by and asked me to reach you before you return home," he continues. "She sends her love and deepest esteem. She also sends you urgent word about your brother, Rowland."

My joy at returning home after so many weeks away on the campaign trail is suddenly replaced with concern and wariness. "What is it, Peter?" I bark. "Is everything okay? Is my cad of Cavalier brother well?"

"Rowland is at the Hall, sir, and he is as well as can be expected considering the circumstances," replies Harrington. "He was badly hurt in the fight that took the life of young Thomas, may God rest his soul. He was shot and badly cut on the shoulder and arm. He has lost a lot of blood. He is weak, but he is recovering.

"The Mistress is doing all she can to keep him out of harm's way. She is concerned there may still be enmity and bitterness between the two of you. That's why she sent me to meet you. To warn you, if a warning is needed?"

I turn and face my men.

"Make haste, your homes and families beckon," I say. "I have received word from Stathern. I am needed and must go directly. Unless there is an emergency, we will muster the day after tomorrow. Thank you for your many sacrifices these past few weeks. I do not underestimate the cost to so many of our families. May God bless you all."

I look directly at Swan. He knows what is coming.

"Take command of the men, my friend," I say. "I will visit you when I know how things are at home. And thank you. I am lucky to have you alongside me, a constant source of support. It gives me great comfort to know I have you watching my back."

Then I ride for home.

I haven't seen Isabel for almost two months. The time has passed by so slowly. Oh, how I have missed her, the children, too. It is two long days since we left Hull, yet by the time we reach Stathern, it feels like I have been in the saddle for an eternity.

Bucephalus is first to sense her presence.

He tosses his head high, snorts and stops abruptly in the courtyard, his ears alert. He paws the ground, and I sense my steed's excitement and anticipation. Then I see my wife, strolling across the emerald green lawn, her dark hair shimmering as the summer sunshine bathes her in light.

Suddenly she is running. And then beauty is standing before me.

"Francis. My love" is all she can say before I embrace the most wonderful and loving person I know.

My response is equally short. "I have missed you so," is all I can manage.

Following closely behind are Francis, Anne, Isable, Barbara, Elizabeth and Mary. My heart swells as I watch them scamper after their mother; tears of joy trickle down my cheeks. My goodness, it feels so good to be back home, away from the madness of the battlefield.

"Tell me," says my wife, her opal green eyes searching my face. "Tell me all. Leave nothing unsaid. Nothing untold. Tell me of the horrors; tell me all you can of these past few weeks. And when you have done that, I will tell you of everything that has come to pass while you have been away."

We walk to the Hall arm in arm, our children dancing at our feet. And I start to tell Isabel of the slaughter, of the folly and meaningless of war, and how I wish it could all come to an end.

THREE

HOME IS AS I REMEMBER: quiet; spacious; sweet-smelling. It is a happy place; my castle, if you like, albeit there are no turrets, giant keep or drawbridge to be found at Stathern.

Isabel is the one who makes everything possible. She is cheerful and energetic. She doesn't shirk hard work. And she speaks with a warmth, radiance and intelligence rarely found in a man, or woman. I ask myself, how did I, a dullard who is often lost for words, manage to capture the heart and loyalty of such a wonderful creature? I have been posing the same question for more than eleven years, and I am still waiting for an answer.

It is the morn of the ninth day of July. It is some two days since I made my return, and my aches and blisters are, at last, starting to fade. Good food and company, the occasional balm for my painful saddle sores, and the love of my wife – all these offer fast-working restorative powers. And they need to. For my brother's presence has unlocked some deeply buried emotions.

I visit Rowland, after digesting a dispatch from Leicester, informing me I have been appointed to the Committee responsible for governing the city. The appointment is effective from the morrow.

Initially, I am unsure how to react to the news. Upon reflection, I decide family matters are more pressing at the present time; my own personal concerns can wait.

When I arrive, Rowland is resting. The loss of so much blood has left him weak. But his wounds are on the mend. And his eyes reveal there is still spirit and fight in a man who is five years my junior and is devoted to his tyrant King as much as I am to my Parliamentary masters.

"It is good to see you, brother," he says as I enter the chamber, which is nestled in a worker's cottage hidden in the woods. He is propped up on a mattress, supported by three of the fattest goose down pillows I have ever seen. "There is much to discuss, is there not, Francis?"

I take in my surroundings, and I can sense my brother wishes to confide in me. He looks troubled. So I pull up a crude, wooden chair.

I am ready to talk.

"Rowland. I thank the Lord that you are well," I tell him. "It grieves me to see you here. Wounded. Hurting. I wish it were not so. Tell me, brother, how did this happen? Did we not agree, among the three of us, we would at all costs stay away from each other's territory? Did we not agree this? Wasn't it this very situation we were trying to avoid?"

"Aye, we did so," responds my youngest sibling. "But it was taken out of our control, Francis. It seems word of our arrangement may have found its way to my superiors in Newark.

"An aide to the Earl of Essex sent a dispatch, instructing Thomas and myself to start patrolling the Vale of Belvoir area. We were told that failure to do so would be regarded as an abandoning of our duties to the King. We would have been court-martialed for insubordination and cowardice if we had ignored our orders.

"How this has happened, I do not know, brother," he continues. "All I know is our senior officers believed we were not prosecuting the King's case with the utmost vigour. And there is truth in this. We both know it to be so. But I am at a loss to know how they found out."

We look at each other. The hopelessness of war! Is death going to be the only winner in all of this madness?

"I understand," I say softly. "Tell me, brother, tell me of Thomas: what happened that fateful day?"

Rowland looks away. I see his shoulders sag. His head tilts forward. There is a sob.

"It all happened so quickly," he says. "One minute we were riding, close to the trees, just three miles from where I now sit. We were close to Colston Bassett, but mindful your men could be patrolling.

"It was peaceful. There was no reason to suspect the Militia may have seen us and we were under threat. Then all hell broke out. We were fighting for our lives. The ambush achieved complete surprise, and my men were cut down all around me.

"I saw Thomas surrounded by three of your cavalry; I recognised their colours and tried to alert them to who we were, but I could not be heard above the melee.

"Our brother was fighting valiantly. But he could not prevail, not against such overwhelming odds. I saw him get slashed across the back, and then get stabbed in the chest. As he lowered his guard, a Flintlock finished him.

"It all happened so quickly. Yet I remember every detail. I tried to cut my way through to him. But I was attacked also. I deflected blow after blow. But a thrust caught my arm just above the elbow, and I then felt a hot, searing pain in my chest. And then I can remember no more. Not until I came round and found myself looking into the face of your beloved Isabel."

I walk to the side of the mattress and sit next to my brother. I lean forward and put my arms around his shoulders. I feel him tense, relax, then fold into my embrace. We both weep, remembering a brother we have lost in his prime. Consoling ourselves as brothers should: in prayer and unity.

"My dearest Rowland; my brother; I will always love thee," I say after a while. "Thy will always be my blood first, as long as there is breath in my lungs. We may believe in different paths for our country, but we are kin first. And we must have peace between us. To not do so will lead to more destruction and heartache. And I do not wish this to be so."

"Aye, Francis," he replies, holding on to me tightly. "Forgive me. We must not let others, of selfish intent, damage our family any more than has already been done so. There must be no enmity between us. We must find a way to win through this war intact, to emerge stronger. For our real quarrels are not with each other."

At a time of such pain, I smile.

A fresh seed of hope has been planted in Stathern. And I, for one, will do all I can to see it flourish.

Over the next few days, Rowland continues to recover his strength and spirit. He stays hidden in the cottage. Isabel tends him daily, and I visit him regularly. We pray for an end to the killing and for our lost brother. And we talk. We discuss the garrison at Trent Bridge that Rowland commands; we remember happier days; and we map out our hopes for a united England, once the fighting is over.

For the time being, we forget about politics and the rights and wrongs that have plunged our country so close to the abyss these past thirty years, or more. We are brothers, no more, no less. And we have a right to enjoy the blood bond that exists between us.

But while my relationship with Rowland grows stronger by the day, I become increasingly aware of a barrier that exists between Isabel and myself. In the decade we have been married, we have never truly quarrelled. But I know something is amiss, and I am increasingly aware the source of our disquiet is likely to be our faith.

On the last Sunday of July, as we eat breakfast before attending prayers at Saint Guthlacs, and an audience with William Norwich, our King-loving Minister, I bring up the subject of our increasingly differing views about Puritanism.

I try to speak openly about things. Little did I know I would be unlocking such fury.

"My dear," I say, as we both eat bread and cheese at the kitchen table. "I am growing concerned that we seem to share contrasting views on the Church. That is all well and good. But in public, we must be in accord. And we plainly are not. Tell me, what is the source of your agitation?"

Isabel stills herself. Her lips are pursed; her body stiffens; I see her hands tighten, white patches gleam around her petite knuckles. Then she speaks with an intensity I have not detected in many a year:

"Francis, I am not sure this is the right time or the right place to be discussing such things," she says. "My faith is as important to me as you are. It is not something I treat lightly. Yet, as you have raised the subject, I have to tell you I am struggling to come to terms with the faith you, and others like you, are prosecuting. Its harsh ways are no better than those advocated by the King.

"When the war started, and Parliament chose to stand up to Charles, we did so, because I believed we sought justice and fairness for all. Scripture inspired the deeds of the cause we serve. Or so I thought, for malice and greed were the hallmarks of our King, not of our number.

"Yet I have seen such a change in you and our men in recent months, and I do not like what I witness. In all honesty, I can no longer tell the difference between Cavalier and Parliamentarian. Your goals are seemingly the same: to win power at all costs. And the means with which you are prepared to achieve your goals are also the same: you will do so at all costs.

"My love, where is our Lord in your deeds? For I most certainly do not see the compelling evidence that shows me He is continuing to guide and lead you and your men.

"I am sorry to speak of these things now," she continues. "But there is never a good time to raise a subject like this.

"We are in dispute because of our differences about faith. I certainly want no discord with you, the man I love.

"But I urge you to examine your conscience and

read your Bible. I fear you are in danger of wandering from the path God has chosen for us. And if you wander too far, my dear, my fear is He will abandon you."

I struggle to respond in a measured way to Isabel's outburst, for my fury has been uncorked, fuelled by a false sense of righteousness.

"My God, woman," I shout. "How can you say these things, to me? I am your devoted husband. I am a God-fearing man. A sinner, I most certainly am, as is any man. But I also seek repentance daily. And leading a true and faithful life, devoted to you and Him, is something I strive to do every day. So I do not understand what you mean. And I know not why you have waited until now to tell me of these things?"

"Husband," says Isabel. "The life of being a follower of Christ is not an easy one. But you are making harder than it need be. You are not a talker. You lock things inside that remain hidden from me; concealed from all.

"Because you refuse to talk, it is impossible for me to tell you how I really feel about anything, particularly matters of importance. And my God, the Church and the way we are leading our daily lives, is of significant concern to me. Yet I must remain silent, anguished and lost.

"All I wish is for you and I to grow stronger together, doing what we have been commissioned to do. I have no wish to abuse the trust God has placed in us, and the authority we have been given in our community. Yet I see abuses now taking place all around me. And we are the abusers. That cannot be right."

I look away. She is right; of course she is, and about so many things. Our people are going hungry. Killings and reprisals are happening on a daily occurrence in our towns; quarter is not being given on the battlefield; and Parliament is stripping the Churches of all plate, brass and valuables, purging them of idolatry images in the name of the people and God. I know it to be true.

I have forgotten much about the reasons I chose to stand behind Parliament and reject the King. But I know upholding God's Law has been at the heart of everything I have done these past few months, even if on occasion I have failed in my duties.

So I try to reason with my wife.

"Admit it, you no longer know why you are supporting the cause of Parliament," she says, interrupting me as I am about to speak. "Battle and death are shaping you. Accept this, Francis; do not deny what we can all see. Husband, seek your Saviour before you are lost to Him and me."

Suddenly there is a knock on the kitchen door. Without waiting for an answer, young Francis walks into the room. He is wearing his Sunday best and urges Isabel and I to take him and his sisters to Church.

Isabel composes herself. Within a few seconds, she mellows.

"We will talk later on this, Francis," she says. "Now, we need to go to Church and make our peace. And please be civil to the reverend Norwich. He may sympathise with the King, but remember he is a man of God above all things. Forgive him for his weakness, as I am sure he forgives you."

We leave the Hall together. Our arms are linked. We look every bit the happy family, with our children walking ahead of us, resplendent in their finest clothes.

Yet there is a distance between us. I am aware of it.

I can tell Isabel is too.

We don't speak again that morning.

I have a lot to ponder. Some truths bite deeper than others. And right now, I am wounded.

FOUR

I HAVE ONLY GOT TO know Oliver Cromwell during the last five years, ever since the rumblings in the Long Parliament first started to surface about the King's conduct and his excessive demands at the time of the calamitous Bishops' Wars.

As a Member of the House, he has been something of an anonymous figure. But the onset of the war has been the making of him.

On the few occasions I have been in his company, I have found Oliver to be a principled man – someone who has a genuine concern for the plight and welfare of the people of England and the upholding of the law. He is a godly scholar, preacher, servant and soldier all rolled into one; a man I believe is quite without equal.

Several times my family has visited the Cromwell home in Ely. On the last occasion, we spent three idyllic summer days with Oliver and his wife, Elizabeth, and their children, who are considerably older than my own, letting the days drift by talking about literature, hunting and the array of problems and injustices associated with being gentlemen of limited means and minor social importance.

We laughed, shared wine and tobacco, and on one notable occasion, drank far too much ale at The Falcon Inn, located conveniently in nearby Huntingdon. On that notable evening, Oliver swore me to secrecy.

"I was a drunkard once, many years ago," he confided as he extracted my pledge. "I was at University; I didn't fit in. But I changed my ways when the Lord entered my life. I still have an occasional weakness for the ale. And I think it best that Elizabeth doesn't hear of it, my friend. What say you?"

I promise to keep my word.

And that is as much as that can be said for the depth of our association.

I am certainly no confidante. We share no great friendship or family intimacies; after all, there are some nineteen years in age between us. We have a warm acquaintance. And that is all.

So I have to confess to being slightly alarmed when Oliver rode into the grounds of the Hall unannounced on the afternoon of the twenty-fourth day of July.

He brought a large retinue of armed men with him, as befits his status as a Colonel and the second in command of the Eastern Association Army in Cambridgeshire and Huntingdonshire, two of the fifteen counties now under Parliamentarian control. And the friendly, avuncular face I recall from our previous engagements a few years ago has been replaced with hawkish features that are most notable for an intelligent alertness I find slightly unnerving.

"Greetings, Francis. It is a fine summer's day, is it not?" calls Cromwell, his distinctive, deep and commanding voice as powerful as I remember it. "I apologise for not informing you of this visit. But there was no time to get a messenger to you before I left Huntingdonshire. I do hope I don't put you and your family to any great inconvenience?"

I smile warmly, as the man, who is gaining more and more renown as a military commander and politician, leaps off Black Jack, his muscular horse, and clasps my outstretched hand.

"Oliver, it is good to see you. A surprise it most certainly is. But it is always a pleasure to greet you. Allow me to offer you and your men some refreshment. Then we can talk if indeed talking is something in which you wish to partake?"

Peter Harrington is in the far corner of the courtyard. I call out to him, and he lays down the scythe he is carrying and scurries over.

"Fetch bread and cheese, as much as you can muster for these fine men," I request. "Any ham shanks you can find in the kitchen will, I am sure, be appreciated. And, Peter, ask some of the estate workers to help Colonel Cromwell's men with stabling and finding adequate provisions for their horses. For at least a couple of hours, we are going to need as much help as you can muster."

Oliver clearly appreciates the hospitality I am affording his men. He takes me by the arm and guides me into the garden, where, I am pleased to say, peace and tranquillity are resident.

"You must be wondering why I am here, my young friend?" he enquires while guiding me effortlessly towards the summerhouse that stands in the far corner.

I squirm at the reference to my age. I am twenty-five-years-old. Green. Wet behind the ears. Inexperienced. And, most certainly, ill-prepared for any conversations of note with a man of Cromwell's growing stature.

An embarrassed nod of my head is all he requires to continue.

"First, I am here to congratulate you on your appointment as a Member of the Leicester Committee. You are young, and you have done well," he says. "Your elevation is good news for Parliament. In these parts, for far too long, there has been much weakness and division between the Mayor, the city's Aldermen and Lord Grey of Groby. With your appointment, you can do something about this sorry state of affairs.

"As you well know, the war is not going as well as we envisaged. We have had some notable successes. But Adwalton Moor was a blow that has left us reeling. I believe you know all too well, through your own losses, just what a sorry state our forces are in at this present time?

"Myself, and some of the other Members, particularly John Pym, believe this defeat has left Parliament sorely exposed. And, I have to confess, we are deeply worried about what the future may hold for us all."

Oliver lets me ponder the significance of his words. Surprisingly, he then changes the subject.

"You may not yet be aware, but Parliament has had cause to arrest Sir John Hotham and his son," he says. "I believe you met both men during your recent stay in Hull?

"We have uncovered an elaborate plot, involving both of them, which would have seen that city, and its armoury, being surrendered to the King.

"We only found out by chance, when correspondence between the son, and a Royalist Colonel, was found on a rider we captured near Ripon. The evidence was clear and damning. Both men have confessed and thrown themselves at Parliament's mercy. But there will be none. We cannot be seen to be condoning treachery; the Hothams need to receive just punishment. And they will."

I look at the man standing before me, full of vigour, purpose and zeal. And there is something else; I can't put my finger on it, but I sense there is a newfound hardness lurking deep within the soul of Oliver. He tries to hide it well. But it's there, not far from the surface.

Talk of the Hothams forces me to reflect on my meeting with both men just a few weeks earlier when they were still the toast of the Parliamentarian cause. Cromwell's words cut through the fog of nostalgia threatening to engulf me. If what I have been told is true, then I have little sympathy for their treachery, which would have certainly led to hundreds of wanton and unnecessary deaths. The scaffold is what they deserve. And the scaffold is what they will get if Parliament gets its way.

Having revealed the undoing of the two traitors, Cromwell returns to the main topic of the conversation – and the reason for this unscheduled visit.

"Pym has conferred in earnest with myself and others of greater importance these past few weeks, and these discussions have resulted in Parliament sending an envoy to Scotland in an attempt to secure the Scots support," he continues. "Protracted negotiations continue, and we are hopeful an agreement will be reached, which will see a large host enter the war, on our side, and help us turn the tide decisively in our favour. Are you taking all this in, Francis? Pray, tell me to stop if I am proceeding too quickly."

My head is starting to spin. There is a lot to comprehend. But I am in-step with Cromwell. I clearly understand the implications of everything being revealed to me.

He waits a few seconds before continuing.

"We can expect up to twenty thousand foot, pike and horse to join our forces in the near future," he says. "In principle, all is agreed; all that is outstanding is to agree on a price and confirm our overall campaign plan.

"Our Scottish friends have indicated they will be willing to muster their men before the end of October. I am less confident. The reality is their host may not be ready to enter the fray until well into the New Year. And that is a setback. But our armies are not yet equipped to win this war. And in Newcastle and Rupert, we have cunning and devilish foes, who are all too aware of our weaknesses.

"One significant reversal in the field has the potential to inflict a serious blow to our cause. So we need to adopt an alternative strategy; one that we can control; one that can start to work quickly; and one that can bring about the conclusion we seek.

"And that's where we need your help, Francis. I believe we have a task for you that is vital for the future of our imperilled nation."

My conversation with Cromwell has left me lost for words.

As I sit in my study, a dull ache spreads across the lower part of my head. These occur from time to time, usually when I am at home, forced to deal with a particular conundrum. Strangely, I never experience this sensation in battle. Then, I am fit and in my element. Yet I am rarely to be found so when tasked to deal with statesmen, politicians and Isabel. At these times, I find my tongue is tied, and I am unable to find adequate words to make a meaningful contribution to a conversation. And so it has proved yet again today. All men have limitations. And I am now acutely aware of mine.

Right now, I feel I have again been outmanoeuvred and played like the simpleton I occasionally and convincingly appear to be.

I have agreed to a course of action that now puts me under an obligation to do the direct bidding of the Parliamentary faction, controlled by Pym and supported by Cromwell, in secret, with a degree of risk that puts my family in peril should anything go wrong.

Nobody must know about what I have been tasked to undertake. Such is the sensitivity of the matter, Cromwell has made me pledge, on pain of death, that I will not divulge the plan Pym has hatched to anyone, particularly Isabel or Abijah. He is adamant.

"Wives have loose tongues," he declared. "Friends have loose tongues. And a loose tongue has the potential to get us all condemned and hanged as traitors."

Cromwell told me about the Parliamentary war effort. But much of it I didn't hear. I was lost in the mental fog that always descends when I feel helpless; I was staring, offering little in the way of conversation, and I was grateful Oliver was content to do all of the talking. For I would have been found wanting, should I have been required to make a substantial contribution in any way.

I simply could not comprehend the magnitude of the task I had been asked to undertake.

Cromwell departed for Westminster at six o'clock, but only after securing the pledge from me that he required. He needs to make haste as Pym has an illness that is causing great concern. Doctors fear the worst. So too does the man we call "King Pym". Yet he continues to work at a pace that would put a man half his age to shame.

I thank God for the life of John Pym, for without him, our cause would most surely be lost. Of that, I am certain.

"I bid you a good evening, Francis," Cromwell said as we shook hands. "I will send word shortly. Think hard on what we have discussed. You must play a pivotal role in the affairs of our nation. Much depends on a successful outcome."

And with that, he and his men spurred their horses forward and thundered down the main street of Stathern.

As I sit in my study, my head in my hands, I now find myself ruing my impotence and pride. What a foolish and feckless man I am.

An Eastern Association messenger arrives at the doors of the Hall less than a week after my meeting with Cromwell. The man is drenched, his skins providing little protection to the torrential rain that has been falling since early evening. He has been riding for the last three days, swapping horses every thirty miles, or so, on his long journey from Ely.

Stathern is the seventh Parliamentary outpost he has visited since leaving the safety of his home, and he looks like he has barely slept or fed himself. Such has been his determination to do his Master's bidding.

"The Colonel wishes to express his gratitude and sincerest best wishes to you, sir, and has asked me to relay this message with the utmost urgency," he says.

There is a keenness and alertness in the young man's

eyes that reveal a devotion I know from my own men. He passes me an envelope. It bears a simple red wax seal, and I immediately recognise Cromwell's distinctive hand.

"Thank you," I say appreciatively to the rider. "You look tired, nay exhausted. And you look as though you haven't eaten in a month. Allow my servants to clean your clothes and offer you some food. And please stay for the evening. We have more than enough spare mattresses to ensure you can sleep off some of your aches. What is your name?"

"I am Isaac Threadmorton, sir," responds the messenger. "Colonel Cromwell retains my family. And I have instructions from my Master to immediately return to Ely, with your reply. So, if I may, I must decline your kind offer."

I look coolly at Isaac; the man has not realised my words are an order rather than mere advice.

"My good man, I admire your devotion to your Master," I say. "And I am sure he is in need of your services. But it is past ten in the evening, it is wet and cold, and you are in dire need of some sleep and food. It is plain to see. Otherwise, you will not make it back to your Master. Instead, you will find yourself occupying a wooden box buried in some quickly forgotten field.

"Please make yourself comfortable in my house, allow me to read the message in a degree of comfort and prepare an appropriate response. You can be about your business once again at first light. How say you?"

There is no meaningful protest to my suggestion. So I show young Threadmorton to the kitchens, leave him with Else, our wonderful cook, who has catered for our needs for longer than I care to remember after joining my family from the royal court at Whitehall almost thirty years ago.

I make my way to the Hall and the welcome lure of a full fire. Even though it is still high summer, it is a cold place in the evening. But I set these thoughts aside. For now, it's time to read what Cromwell's plans are for me:

"*My dear Francis,*

"*Make your way to the town of Chipping Norton. Find the Blue Boar Inn. A room will have been reserved for you in the name of Maxwell Threadmorton. Be sure to be there on the eve of the twenty-ninth of July.*

"*Someone sharing our common heart will make themselves known to you at nine o'clock. They will carry my seal, and you can trust them with your life. Heed their advice. Make haste. And be sure to stay safe.*

"*I will pray for your success.*

"*Your friend and truthful servant, Oliver Cromwell.*"

It is a brief message, communicating everything I need to know.

I have four days to get to the market town, which lies some twenty-five miles away from Oxford and is, at worst, a journey requiring three days in the saddle. It is close to where the King has set up his court, but far enough away to avoid the most concentrated of Cavalier patrols. The area is sympathetic to the Royalists, as are so many, but like all of England's towns, there will be large pockets of resistance; sympathisers; men like me. And I certainly don't fear whatever lies ahead.

It is time to get my affairs in order. I need to speak to Abijah. He must be told what I am doing, even though he has to be spared much of the detail.

I received a dispatch order yesterday, ordering the

Militia to Nottingham, to carry out some important duties in support of the governor, Colonel John Hutchinson. I had intended to lead the men, who are now mostly recovered after the sufferings of Yorkshire, against the forces of the infamous Hastings, the scourge of the Parliamentarian war effort throughout the Midlands.

Hastings, Lieutenant-General of the King's forces in Leicestershire, Nottinghamshire, Rutlandshire and Derbyshire, is garrisoned at Ashby Castle with a two-thousand-strong force, many of them Irish Catholics. The Royalists are located some eighteen miles away from Stathern, from where they have been harassing Parliament's supply columns, which hail from Manchester and beyond, on a near-daily basis.

But affairs of the state now require me to be elsewhere, so Swan will have to fill the void. And I am confident he will do so with aplomb, particularly when he is required to liaise with Colonel Hutchinson's prickly wife, Lucy. As for Hastings, he can wait. Teaching the Royalist commander a lesson or two will give me something to look forward to when I return.

It is past midnight. Even at this late hour, I know my second-in-command will be awake and welcome a visit. So I make the short journey to his cottage, avoiding the worst of the mud and the rain, which continues to hammer down rhythmically on the slate and thatched roofs of Stathern.

A torrent pulses down the raised banks of the hill and, on several occasions, I have to be at my most vigilant to avoid tumbling over. But while I manage to stay on my feet, I am wet, filthy and cold.

Thankfully, as I reach my destination, its front door is swung open, and the strong hands of Abijah Swan reach out and pull me inside. I suddenly find myself thrust into a world of warmth and peace.

"How did you know I was out there?" I ask, after shaking off the water that's glued to my cape and settling into a chair by the blazing fire. "I thought I had been quiet; the rain is beating down, making such a commotion. How do you do it? Where do you get that sixth sense from?"

My friend looks at me, mocking me with those piercing eyes.

"I think I must have known you were on your way here even before you did," he snorts. "The dog started barking some ten minutes ago, which put me on alert. I have been outside to see what is happening, and I have constantly been looking out of the windows. I saw you heading this way from yonder. You were quite easy to see in the full light of the moon."

I look around at the darkened room, the only light coming from the glow of the candles burning brightly on the mantelpiece, fanned by a gentle breeze. I know this room well, having been a frequent visitor over the years. Yet tonight something is not quite right. I say nothing. I just gaze into the room, where I soak up the tranquillity of the evening, and the rhythmical breathing of Abijah's dog, Prudence, a renowned collie among the many farmers who live and work in these parts.

The beast is stretched out across the hearth; her black legs are extended as far as they will go, soaking up the heat. She remains undisturbed by my presence.

My eyes quickly adjust to the light of the room, and

I suddenly realise what has put me into this state of alert: I see two half-full wine glasses on the mantelpiece. I then see other telltale signs of a recent visitor – the indentations in the seat cushions of both chairs, and the clearly visible footprints of a stranger. I would have missed them had my suspicions not been aroused.

A smile begins to form on my mouth. So Abijah does have a life outside of the war after all?

I choose to say nothing. If my friend wants me to know what he is doing, I will find out in good stead. And, when he tells me, I will be happy for him. After all, Abijah is a man who is in sore need of the love of a wife and, in time, a family. So instead of questioning my friend about his personal affairs, I tilt the glass of ale I have just been poured in the direction of Swan in acknowledgement of our long-standing friendship. I take a hearty sip. The impact is immediate as it glides down my throat; how I love the beer made from the sweet hops of Kent.

I take another sip and then another; until, at last, I start to relax.

"Abijah," I say, "I have been ordered away on important Parliamentarian business, and I need to leave on the morrow. That means, with immediate effect, you will be taking over command of the Militia."

Swan looks up. Surprised, he puts his tankard on the floor. There is no smile, just a frown.

"I am flattered," he says, his eyes betraying his true feelings about his elevation. "But where are you going? And why am I and other members of the Militia not accompanying you?"

I look away. Through the window, the moon is bright. Its full, golden orb is basking the world outside in something akin to celestial light. How I love this place, it reminds me of the night I proposed to Isabel.

Ours had not been an arranged wedding. We were young; I was barely a man; Isabel, six years my senior. We were betrothed through a common longing in our hearts. Yet I do not know how it came to pass. I can only surmise; it was meant to be, part of God's grand plan.

It was on a night such as this, with the rain sweeping the land, puckering those half bent trees that swayed in honour of the ascendant full moon, that I plucked up the courage to ask for her hand. Miraculously she agreed to be my wife. And, to this day, I wake up wondering how I snared the loveliest creature I have ever known.

Our wedding took place in July, in the year of our Lord, 1632. It was the fifth day of the month, and it was a gloriously happy day.

All these years later, our union remains strong, as it was that July day. Yet how our world has changed beyond all recognition. Peace has been replaced with war. Brother is now locked in war with brother. And all I can wonder is how we have descended into the pit of Hades so quickly?

"Francis! Francis!"

I become aware of Swan calling to me. His urgency draws me out of my stupor.

"Forgive me, Abijah," I say. "It has been a long, long day. A lot has happened, and I am tired. Fatigue is in my bones. Give me a sniff of ale, and it doesn't take much for sleep to engulf my body and my mind to stray into the comfort of blackness.

"That will all have to wait, for there is a lot to tell you. And pray, I need your assurance that what I say you will go no further? It is between you and me. Lives depend on it, my own included."

Abijah's brow creases. I sense his agitation and deep concern.

"I don't understand, Francis. What do you mean?" he enquires. "What do you speak of? Say it plainly, please."

So I tell the man I trust with my life, everything about what Cromwell has asked of me. I unburden my soul. And afterwards, I feel safer and better for doing so.

"Why you?" asks Abijah.

It is a good question, one I cannot answer. So I do not try.

"You are a soldier, a damned fine one. But you are not a man who hides in the shadows and plays these kinds of narcissistic games. It makes no sense."

I have to confess; I do not profess to understand why my betters have chosen me for this task. And I am as confused as Swan. But I am trained not to question my orders. My role is to do as I am told, to do my utmost to ensure that my men and I succeed.

"I feel very uncomfortable with everything I am being asked to do," I admit. "I do not know the world of intrigue and mistrust that I am being asked to enter. But I do know that Pym is desperate. Cromwell has told me so. And we are no closer to winning this damnable war than we were last August. So we must take risks.

"We cannot allow ourselves to be defeated every time we take to the field in battle. If we do, all will be lost. And then there will be repercussions. Charles is a vengeful man. He will not forgive easily. Many will be required to pay the ultimate price for standing up to him. Estates will become forfeit; families of good standing will become destitute, and our King will think he is God. And I, for one, do not wish to see any of that come to pass.

"So, given a choice, I would prefer to try and support this plan, no matter how low the chances are of it succeeding. For the alternative doesn't bear thinking about, regardless of the personal cost to me."

I look at my Subaltern, and I see defiance in his face. He is angry. Fearful. He knows I will be a lucky man to escape with my life. As do I. And if I am at risk, then those closest to me are too.

"What about Isabel. What will you tell her?" he asks, flicking a dying ember in the fireplace with the poker and igniting some sparks from the inner recesses of the pyre. "She is in grave danger. So are the children. She has a right to know everything, Francis. You must tell her all. It is only right and proper."

I shake my head violently.

"No. She cannot know any of this," I reply. "Isabel must not learn about what is required from me, not from you, or anyone. You know that. Only you are aware of my quest. That is how it must remain.

"I have told you these things so you can plan and prepare. If I fail, you will need to protect her, the children and yourself. And I know I can rely on you more than anyone to do the things that are right and necessary."

I leave Swan's cottage at two o'clock in the morning. I give my friend an embrace. We recite the Lord's Prayer – pausing at the sentence "thy will be done" – and we wish each other well.

With Abijah in charge, I know the Militia is in safe hands and that, at least, brings me some considerable comfort. In truth, I suspect taking the men to Nottingham, and warding off the cutting remarks and scorn of Lucy Hutchinson, will be something of a welcome distraction for him.

For now, Abijah knows my true intentions, and he will be as haunted as I am until I return.

I feel guilty. I am troubled and remorseful. Could I, should I have spared Abijah from knowing the truth, from carrying this burden? I return home as the deluge continues to fall, contemplating this question.

And the future is far less certain than it was just twenty-four hours earlier.

It is ten o'clock in the morning and time to make my excuses to Isabel.

"I have been called away by Fairfax to give counsel to the Eastern Association forces Cromwell is mustering for a counteroffensive," I lie to her.

I am a poor deceiver, so my words lack conviction.

"I will be gone for about a week, my dear. No longer. In my absence, when he gets back from Nottingham, Abijah will help you with the estate, should you need support. He will only be gone for a couple of days.

"When I return, we will have a celebration. There has been too much woe since our return from Yorkshire. We need to put the past behind us and start to look to the future once again. So let us invite all the families from Stathern and the surrounding villages, and the kin of the Militia, to the Hall. Can you prepare things in my absence?"

Isabel is crying. She is a perceptive woman. She knows I am keeping something from her. But she also knows it is futile to press me, as I will not give up my secrets. I never do.

"My love, I sense there is more to say on the matter of your departure?" she probes me. Her kindly voice and smile mask her true feelings. "But I realise you must have a good reason for keeping matters to yourself. So I will ask no more. I will wait for you to tell me in your own good time. Until then, I will continue to be a good mistress of this home, a good, faithful wife and a devoted mother.

"Be assured we will organise a banquet that will be the talk of the Vale and serve to unite our people. Take care, my dearest. And come home to us alive and well. That is the only thing I ask of you."

I am relieved.

I comfort Isabel, kiss her forehead and run my fingers through her silken hair. I am blessed to be wedded to this strong and beautiful woman. Even in her distress, I can only marvel at her magnificence. I wish I were a stronger husband and better father; that I was a more deserving man. For if I were, we would not be facing the danger in which we are now embroiled; I would not be required to deceive my wife.

I give her a final embrace and then leave her in the Hall. Sobbing. I go to the back of the house and say goodbye to the housemaids, labourers and grooms. They smile at me, not realising the magnitude of the sinister game I have now entered, and they wish me a safe and prosperous journey.

Else emerges from the kitchen, dusts down her smock, climbs on her tiptoes and gently kisses me on the cheek.

"Stay safe, Master Francis," she whispers. "I will be

praying for you. May our Heavenly Father protect you at all times."

This is her ritual whenever I am required to go away. On this occasion, I am more thankful than I have ever been before.

I walk to the stables. Bucephalus has been saddled and is ready. Although my mind is preoccupied this morning, his excitement and eagerness do not escape my attention.

I take a last wistful look at my home. I turn my horse around and start to canter away from everything I hold dear.

I am beginning my journey.

God willing, in some way, it will lead to the downfall of a tyrant.

FIVE

IT TAKES ME THE BEST part of the day to reach the outskirts of the small Leicestershire town called Hinckley. This place has chosen to retain its neutrality in the war, although some of the more notable townsfolk are known to have strong Parliamentarian sympathies. But bloodshed is something they do not wish to countenance. So it serves the two sides equally well. Neither can have any complaints about the accommodation that has been reached, which allows Royalist and Parliamentarian troops to secure food and supplies on alternate days of the week, without any threat of conflict.

Leading away from this place is the main artery to the south of England: the old Roman thoroughfare known as the Fosse.

It usually takes less than three hours, at a gentle canter, to reach Hinckley, which is close to places like Nuneaton and Coventry.

Unfortunately, Hastings has sent men out in force from Ashby seeking to locate the supply trains that keep towns loyal to Parliament alive.

Today, Cavalier patrols are more numerous than normal, and knowing they are close by, and potential capture, or worse, awaits me at every twist of the road, I decide to be doubly cautious; nervous even. I am known in these parts and would be a prize to many who wear the colours of the King, particularly the likes of Hastings, who would like nothing more than to spend a day, or so, interrogating me in one of his dungeons.

So I have decided to ride to the Royalist garrison town of Ashby de la Zouch, rather than take the more direct route. Some may consider it a foolhardy move to ride into the lair of my enemy. Under different circumstances, I would most likely agree. But we live in times when the usual rules no longer apply. Cunning and deviousness are required. And I intend to be as unpredictable as I can be.

My rationale for entering the lair of my enemy is simple: the Royalists won't be expecting it, and I desperately need to find out more about the intentions and whereabouts of my enemies. This knowledge will aid my endeavours in Oxfordshire greatly.

Travelling to the burgeoning market town is something of a detour and adds a significant delay to my journey. Its Royalist garrison is stationed at the magnificent Norman castle located in the heart of Ashby and easily identified by the stone ramparts of the Keep that towers above the roofs of the humble dwellings that are so numerous.

Thankfully the King's troops are overconfident and lax and have been since the troubles first flared. And I am unmolested as I enter Hasting's stronghold.

A likeable knave called Isham Perkins, who holds the

rank of Colonel, governs the town. He and I have been known one another for many years and, before the war, we were on cordial terms. But that is the past. Right now, I am thankful his men are complacent and overconfident; this negligence serves me well.

It is in Ashby, I learn of news there have been several skirmishes between the two sides during the last few hours.

Tensions are running high in the area. There are credible rumours the Royalists are preparing for another large-scale assault.

But if they know where, the townsfolk are unwilling to tell me, a stranger asking questions, the intended location. So I depart watered and fed, but none the wiser.

I make slow progress the rest of the day, finding a place to rest and sleep in the hollow of a tree at a place called Watery Gate, notable only for the lush green fields that straddle the River Soar as it oozes through the fertile countryside. It is five miles north of Hinckley and close to the villages of Earl Shilton, Thurlaston and Huncote.

A hill, rich in wildlife at a place I later learn is called Croft, gazes down at me, as the early evening sunshine becomes the dark of night.

I suffer a broken night's sleep as an attentive owl lets me know it is keeping a watchful eye on me. In my stupor, I smile. My prayers have been answered for my Lord and Master would seem to be protecting me.

While I love the warmth of home, on occasion I also seek the tranquillity only expeditions like the one I am pursuing can offer. I have time to think; I am afforded the opportunity to plan, something denied to me so frequently when I am at Stathern, consumed by my responsibilities to my family and men.

Soaking up my surroundings while cooking crayfish, caught in the nearby river, on an open fire, I am also able to forget the horrors I am responsible for perpetrating.

Right now, I can live; I can breathe, and I can openly thank my heavenly guardian for everything He continues to provide a worthless wretch such as me.

The following day takes me as far as Warwick. It is another slow thirty miles of trekking with Bucephalus. The larks, swallows and the occasional deer are our only companions throughout much of the day.

As we stroll for long periods, I marvel at the engineering skills of the conquering legionnaires more than eleven hundred years earlier, as the stonework of the ancient Fosse rises through the mud and dust.

Fellow travellers eye me with suspicion when they see the quality of my sword hilt, and they do everything they can to avoid contact, so I enjoy a day free of conversation. But remain vigilant I must.

Alongside me, Bucephalus is playful, nudging me repeatedly as I refuse to give him more than a couple of apples every couple of hours. He gets his water and oats, but I will not succumb to his greed. If Isabel were accompanying me, she would ensure his every need is met. I chuckle to myself. What a harsh man I am!

It isn't until the evening of Tuesday the twenty-eighth day of July that I see the thatched roofs of Chipping Norton and hear the bells of Saint Mary's.

Many a mile has been travelled. Thankfully my destination is now gratifyingly close.

Although I have never visited this corner of

Oxfordshire, I have met the town's minister, Stephen Norwood. He is a decent man, with excellent Puritan credentials and a dry sense of humour.

Several years before the war started, I recall attending a landowners meeting in Banbury. The Reverend Norwood was also present. Indeed, I recall him delivering a powerful sermon attacking greed and the love of money shortly before he tucked into a lavish banquet, paid for by a member of a minor member of the King's court.

Among the many things he said, which received a mixed response from the hundred, or so, gentry, farmers and merchants in attendance, was a direct and open challenge to the King's policies of the day, which included the disastrous attempt by Archbishop Laud to impose a Common Prayer Book on congregations throughout the land. Such was the disgust this move met in Scotland, Bishops, and other members of the clergy were forced to seek protection from armed guards. Many were locked into their own Churches for protection, with armed guards posted outside, such was the strength of feeling about Archbishop Laud's proposals.

Afterwards, over a draught of beer, Norwood and I spoke openly about these matters, and I found myself agreeing with everything he said. A rapport and friendship quickly developed that has served us both to this very day.

As I walk the last mile, or so, to the Blue Boar Inn, I find myself wondering if Stephen is Cromwell's man, the agent he says I can "trust with my life?" I don't fail to recognise the irony of a priest so opposed to the Stuart cause living in the midst of Royalists and presiding over a flourishing parish. In truth, I applaud his bravery.

I am tempted to stop at Saint Mary's and reacquaint

myself with the good minister. But I think better of it. It is best to let events take their course. After all, I will know the identity of my ally in less than twenty-four hours, when all is revealed.

The Blue Boar looks resplendent as it dominates the lesser dwellings of Goddards Lane. It is a narrow street, typical of so many found in towns like Chipping Norton. It is noisy; dogs and children crowd its paths, even at this time of the evening; and piss and shit runs freely down the central gutter of the street. The smell is overwhelming. Even the sweet perfumes of the roses that adorn a number of the dwellings can't mask the stench.

I find myself thinking of the tranquillity of my home and thanking my God for everything He has given me, particularly the freshness of the air I breathe.

I remain alert, not least because a score of Cavaliers are propped up against the Inn's walls as I approach its unwelcoming entrance. They have a swagger and aura that would suggest they have already won the war. Or maybe I have it all wrong? Perhaps they are drowning their sorrows, aware that the likes of Pym and Cromwell, are plotting their downfall? Either way, it matters little. I simply need to get past them so I can claim my room, a much-needed meal and some long-overdue rest.

"Hey, cumberwold. Watch where you're going," one of the soldiers yells at me, as my tired limbs collide with one of his outstretched legs. He is squatting, and he is angry. "Are you blind, stupid, or both?"

The voice is slurred, and I can see the soldier's doublet is stained around the neck and chest. As I get closer, I smell the rancid stench of stale ale on his breath. I am hungry, thirsty, impatient, and this puppy is an obstacle I must quickly overcome.

"I am sorry, sir," I utter unconvincingly. "I was not looking. Please forgive my clumsiness."

I look at the loiter-sack stretched out before me. He belches. A loud fart follows. He then twists his trunk and stands up, swaying before steadying himself. His audience is appreciative of the efforts he has made to put on a performance. I sense this is not the first time this act has been played out.

"You tell him, Hind," calls out one of the entourage. "Sort this sop out. How dare he assault one of the King's finest."

Extended to his full height, Hind stands at just over six feet tall. He is well built, and I suspect his torso packs considerably more muscle than it does fat. But I more than match him. He lurches towards me, looking menacing.

With his acolytes hanging on every word, he says: "How say you, sir. Was this a cowardly assault on one of the heroes of Braddock Down?"

He looks at one of his fellow conspirators and enquires: "What say you, Thomas. How should I deal with this insolent stranger?"

I eye the drunkard standing in front of me. The truth is I have killed many a dolt like him: brash; arrogant; overconfident; and inferior. And I believe I have the measure of this fool. But to strike would be madness.

In his stupor, Hind is playing a dangerous game. I am on edge, my surroundings unfamiliar, and I realise the futility of rising to the bait.

"Sir, this claim of assault is a gross misunderstanding," I reply evenly. "Please accept my apologies. And as adequate recompense, please allow me to buy you and your good men a round of ale, so we can toast the good fortunes of the King."

A roar of approval greets my words. Hind grins. He looks at Thomas, his accomplice, and winks. The acknowledgement is instant, and then I understand. He reaches out his hand to shake mine.

"You are a gentleman, sir," he says. "It would be a pleasure to drink some fine English beer with a man of quality like yourself."

We retire to the bar where I proceed to spend the next hour and a half listening to James Hind as he regales me with tales of heroism that are beyond the call of duty. He has no love for the Parliamentarian cause, of that he leaves me in no doubt. But, underneath his gruff and boorish demeanour, there is a man who seems genuinely convicted to do what he can for the King he follows.

I respect that.

Moments earlier, I could have opened this man's throat with a flick of my sword, yet I find myself developing a liking for him. I look across and see his men gradually falling silent as the rigours of an afternoon and evening of sipping the Blue Boar's cheapest liquid refreshments finally takes its toll.

As I prepare to take my leave, Hind opens his eyes and looks at me with a sobriety I hitherto failed to see in the man.

"Are you a fighter, sir?" he asks. "By the quality of your sword, and the width of your shoulders, I would wager a Laurel, or two, that you know how to swing that blade of yours?"

Then the void reclaims him. His eyes close. His head

falls to the side, and he starts to snore.

I awake to the sound of a cockerel unleashing its early Wednesday morning musings on the good people of Chipping Norton. Looking out of my window, I can see they are as delighted as I am: several are throwing stones at the unfortunate bird, while another seeks to scare it off by hurling a bucket of water in its direction.

Thankfully, I have had a good night's rest, the ale partially helping me to recover from the rigours of my travels. I dress quickly, pray and then go downstairs, where Gillian, the scullery girl, escorts me to a quiet corner of the Inn.

Within a few minutes, I am eating pottage and some impenetrable freshly baked bread. A warm flagon of ale also finds its way to my table. I start to unwind.

"Are you enjoying yourself?"

I look up, taken by surprise. The question appears to be directed at me.

The sun's dazzling rays are arrowing through the Blue Boar's shutters, and I have difficulty making out the features of the man standing at my table.

"Sir, you have me at a disadvantage," I say, as I shield my eyes. "Do I know you?"

As I speak, I take in as much as I can. I see fine clothing; polished, buckled shoes; clean, pressed breeches; and no sword at his side. My tension eases; I continue to eat my breakfast, waiting for a response.

"I believe you may be expecting me?" says a cultivated accent. "We are not acquainted. But we do serve common masters, men who are in sore need of our loyal service. Allow me to introduce myself. My name is Henry

Cornish, and these are my credentials."

Pushing aside my tankard, he lays down a round, solid mound of wax. It is the seal of Cromwell.

"Do I have your attention, sir?"

Cornish steps to the side, out of the direct glare of the sunlight that is arrowing into the tavern, and I start to note his features. He stands at around five feet eight inches tall; he is carrying a gut; his doublet is strained at the waist, and he looks to be at least fifty years of age. In truth, he is unremarkable. But I do not underestimate him. For, if he is Cromwell's man, he most certainly has hidden talents and cunning aplenty.

I push a chair out from under the table with my feet and invite my guest to join me.

"Gillian," I call. "Another flagon of ale if you please, and some more pottage, bread and cheese."

I extend my hand in greeting and wait a few seconds before speaking further. "And what do you know of my business, sir?" I eventually ask.

"I have been told very little," admits Cornish, looking around the Inn, probing the darkened corners for eavesdroppers. "I have had a profitable association with Colonel Cromwell these past few years, one that has served both of us well. I have also had occasional instructions from John Pym.

"While a staunch Parliamentarian, my leanings are not commonly known in these parts, so I have enjoyed the luxury of being able to live a life free of scrutiny and suspicion. My wealth and rank allow me certain freedoms and patronage, which I can put to good use. And, although I do not know the specifics of your task, I do know I have been ordered to support your endeavours at any cost to myself, and my family. This has never been requested of me before, so I assume your adventure has a higher level of importance that I am usually required to deal with.

"Please don't be offended when I say I am naturally eager to achieve what needs to be done and see you on your way. And, quite frankly, the less I know about what you are here to do, the better for all concerned."

I look keenly at Henry Cornish. He strikes me as being a truthful man.

"And what of our meeting here, this morning?" I ask. "I was told I would be meeting an agent of Parliament this evening, not while I break my fast. Tell me, what has happened to change the arrangement?"

"Have you not heard the news?" enquires Cornish, looking surprised.

I shake my head. "No," I say.

"Prince Rupert has marched with the King's army and is besieging Bristol," he reveals. "After the loss at Roundway Down, and this latest news, Pym is desperate for a change in fortune. I received a messenger last night from London, carrying new instructions and ordering me to bring our meeting forward.

"Cromwell is away with the Eastern Association, so I am to tell you to proceed to Oxford with all due haste. Whatever you have been ordered to do, I am afraid you will need to do it far quicker than you expected. Much depends on it."

I have been caught off-guard. Unprepared. I am exposed. I didn't expect this, and I don't like it one bit.

"Have you made the preparations?" I quiz my ally. "Is everything ready?"

"Everything is in place," reassures Cornish. "Getting

you into the city is not a problem. But when you get there, I am afraid you will be on your own. Your wits will need to be your guard."

Henry Cornish stays with me for another hour, briefing me on what I must do, and where I must go, in order to gain access to the city where the King's standard has flown since November. He also passes me an official-looking warrant.

"Your destination will be easy enough to find," he states. "Use this document to gain access at the gate. And use it also if you are stopped by a patrol. It should see you through any difficulties."

I look at the paper I have been handed. It is dated the twenty-fifth day of July and reads:

"To whom it may concern.

"The bearer of this document is on official business for myself and Charles Rex, King of England. He is to be allowed passage to, and from, Oxford (including the King's Court at Christ Church College). Under no circumstances is he to suffer detention, or questioning about his affairs.

"Any soldier of the King's army who disobeys this Order will be subject to an immediate, summary court-martial."

The document bears the seal of Prince Rupert, the King's nephew and the Royalist army's most formidable commander.

SIX

THE TOWER OF CHRIST CHURCH emerges out of the dense afternoon fog that has shrouded Oxford for the last two hours. It is a beacon, guiding me towards the city.

On the roads leading to the Royalist capital, I have seen thickset columns of troops for the last hour. At one point I think I recognise James Hind and the men I shared ale with at the Blue Boar Inn the night before. They pass me in jovial mood, their armour gleaming; their Matchlocks poised; Gloucestershire and the West Country awaiting them.

My destination is the North Gate, the strongest remaining part of Oxford's perimeter wall. It is heavily guarded, and the quality of my credentials will most surely be put to the test. I pray to God I have not come this far to be captured tamely at the city gates.

Considering I am a man who is in control of nothing, I am as confident I can be.

A sergeant bars my way as I seek to pass through the city's defences. He looks resplendent in his uniform, the

King's bright colours unmistakable in the hazy afternoon gloom.

"State your business, sir," he barks. "And let's be quick about it."

I produce the warrant given to me by Cornish. A twitch develops in the corner of my left eye.

"I see," says the guard. He ponders briefly. "Are you aware Typhus fever is rife inside the city?"

I shake my head. "No. This is the first I have heard of it," I say truthfully.

"Be careful then," he whispers. "Be sure to avoid the parishes of Saint Mary Magdalen's and Saint Michael's. It's at its worst there. I bid you a pleasant and safe day, sir."

"Thank you," I retort, my smile betraying the concern I have at mention of the killer disease we also know as Morbus Campestris.

"A favour, if you please," I ask of the sergeant. "Could you point me in the direction of the High Street?"

It takes me twenty minutes to follow my instructions and find my destination.

The fetid, sweet smell of death and decay is everywhere. I have arrived in a city that is in the midst of a major outbreak of one of the most feared diseases in Europe. In every nook and cranny, I see signs of festering corruption.

I speak to a tradesman, selling some roast chestnuts, who tells me as many as forty burials are taking place every week.

It seems the Devil himself has made his home in this part of England.

While most of Oxford's inhabitants have had to

absorb the influx of thousands of troops and their families, which has led to chronic overcrowding, Charles has set up his court and military council at Christ Church, the university's most prestigious and wealthy college.

The King and Queen Henrietta Maria have taken over the Deanery, while the Privy Council meet in the canonical lodgings. Meanwhile, other members of the court have taken more modest accommodation, ensuring they are kept well away from the city's unwashed and diseased masses.

The princes, Rupert and Maurice, have chosen to take up residence at the outlandish home of Oxford's Town Clerk. This keeps them out of immediate scrutiny of the Stuart household, enabling them to live lavish, semi-independent lives while remaining close enough to the King and Queen, should they ever be called upon.

I thank my Lord. This arrangement serves my purpose perfectly.

My rendezvous is scheduled to be six o'clock and, now I have found my bearings, it is highly unlikely I will forget how to find 10 High Street.

With less than four hours to spare, I meander through the streets of this once-thriving city, which are now enveloped in contamination and fear.

Bucephalus remains close by my side as we negotiate the streets. I find stabling for him in Fish Street and a straw mattress and room for myself at the Spotted Cow Inn. Rather appropriately, my abode for the night is located next to Hell's Passage.

With death stalking the streets, few visitors wish to spend too much time in this place. Yet life goes on. The streets teem with town, gown (the name given to the many university students still resident in the city) and soldiery all mingling in the main, cobbled arteries close to The Cornmarket.

I walk to Christ Church Meadow, where I intend to pass the next few hours on my own and where I hope the air is clean. Unobserved. Invisible.

With Bucephalus looked after for the evening, I need to prepare for a meeting that could change so much in this country, which is ripping itself apart. Am I truly the best person for this task? Have Cromwell and Pym taken leave of their senses? Self-doubt starts to creep in. I need to regain my composure.

At all costs, I need to avoid contact with the areas infected by Typhus.

The bells of Christ Church, and those of Saint Aldgate's, announce the appointed hour: at last, it is six o'clock.

I have spent the last forty-five minutes easing my way to the rear of 10 High Street, keeping as far away from the most populated sections of the city as I can; making sure I am unobserved; working out the various permutations.

I have been told to find a gate that is ajar. It doesn't take long before I find it.

I walk into an empty walled courtyard. A lawned area and ornate hedgerows guide me to the house. Some hundred yards away, I see a servant standing outside, beckoning me onwards. He is wearing the livery of the royal household. Warily I approach.

"Good evening, sir. You are expected," he says to me, no trace of fear or concern in his voice. "I have been asked to escort you to the parlour. Please follow me."

The house is among the finest I have ever seen, full

of the latest French paintings, the finest Belgian fabrics and types of furniture I have never seen before. No expense is spared. My, how an Oxford Town Clerk lives; I am sure he was delighted to be forced to give up his home so the princes could reside here!

We walk through a maze of corridors until we reach a set of lavishly carved double doors.

"In here, sir," instructs my chaperone. "You will find their royal highnesses waiting for you."

I stride purposefully into the room. Three gaily-painted faces turn as one to face me. Two are men. One is a woman. A black poodle barks a greeting. Their expressions are neutral. Or so I think.

"By rights, I should have you hanged, drawn and quartered, man," shouts a resplendent young man, who looks like a bejewelled peacock. I am under attack before I have barely stepped into the room. The fierceness, sincerity and threat are undeniable.

Although there is a strong European accent, the English is impeccable. The tone, however, is formal and cold. And the authority is unmistakable.

"You are a traitor in open revolt against your King," he continues. "I am meeting you today only because those closest to me have advised me to hear what you have to say. But understand this, it is against my better instincts. If I suspect this is another trick of Pym's, I will have you flayed alive. Test me, if you dare."

I must look stunned because the woman, a combination of strength and beauty, glides over to me. She looks me up and down, appraising my substance.

She smiles and says: "Please forgive the Prince's outburst. Events of recent days have been extremely testing for us all. But for Rupert, the demands have been rather excessive, and he is somewhat testy. Nonetheless, allow me to introduce ourselves to you more formally and, hopefully, less brutally."

She points to the man whose tirade I have just been subjected to. He is no more than twenty-four years of age, I would guess. He is tall, broad-shouldered, standing at well over six feet. He's confident and striking. And at this moment, he is stroking the dog affectionately, never taking his gaze away from me. Rumours about his romantic dalliances are the talk of Parliament and the King's court. And, if true, I can appreciate why he is so popular with female courtiers.

"This is Prince Rupert, Commander of the King's Cavalry; third son to Frederick the Fifth, Elector of the Palatinate," states the statuesque woman.

I bow my head in acknowledgement.

"A pleasure, I am sure," he spits in my direction, before directing his attention back to the dog at his feet. "Boye, go to your mattress."

The dog does as he is instructed. I now have the master's undivided attention.

I look at one of the most renowned cavalrymen in Europe and wonder why, beyond the opportunity for personal enrichment, he has chosen to support an uncle, whose family betrayed his own so coldly and dispassionately? If James the First had not been so weak in his negotiations with the Spanish more than twenty years yonder, the Palatinate, in all probability, would still be under the control of Frederick, or his lineage, and Rupert would not be leading the nomadic existence he is forced to ensure as a mercenary.

But my thoughts matter little, for fate decrees the paths we all take. And it has been ordained by a higher authority that I should be pleading Parliament's case with a man renowned for his unpredictability, as much as he is for his prowess with sword, flintlock and horse.

Leaning on a windowsill, close to Rupert, is an equally imposing young man, albeit he has gentler, less abrasive features. If anything, he is more striking than the hothead he is standing next to. He is also dressed in expensive clothing and looks every inch a gentleman.

"And this is Prince Maurice, the fourth son of King Frederick," adds the woman. "As I am sure you already know, Maurice is also a senior commander in the King's army. He is Rupert's younger brother."

Maurice says nothing. He just stares at me, his intelligent brown eyes boring into my very soul. There is no hint of hostility, just interest and curiosity. There are no obvious signs of malice. Not at the moment. But that may come as our talks progress.

Right now, I am sure he is wondering why a Roundhead has made an audacious visit to the heart of Royalist England, potentially forfeiting his life in the process. What could be so important?

I suddenly find my voice.

"Thank you. At another time in another place, I am sure it would be a pleasure to meet you both," I say, surprising myself with my boldness. "But, for now, I must thank you for granting me this audience. I am sure I have much to say that will be of interest, particularly to you, your Highness."

I realise I am talking directly to Prince Rupert. Quickly remembering my manners, I turn my attention elsewhere.

"And you, my Lady, to whom do I have the pleasure of addressing?"

"Why, sir, I am the Countess of Carlisle, Lady Lucy Hay," she says, with a calm and understated assurance. "I am a friend and confidante to Queen Henrietta Maria and King Charles, and I am here, this evening, as a guest of the princes."

The Countess continues to look directly at me.

"Perhaps you would like to sit?" she invites.

Involuntarily, I mop my brow. I am sweating. It is little wonder. I am in esteemed company. Two Princes. And now I discover, the woman standing in front of me, commanding my attention, is one of the most famed courtiers of the land; a renowned seductress, who, if gossipers are to be believed, has captured the heart of many a famed poet and Lord.

If I hadn't fully realised it before, I now know the stakes of my mission are the highest they can be.

Lady Lucy indicates a seat, close to the empty fireplace, enabling me to address my audience in its entirety, without the need to strain my neck or raise my voice. I am thankful. My nerves are strained. And I fear my voice will be no louder than a whisper. So I sit, trying my best to look an authoritative and composed figure. Who am I trying to fool? I am neither. Yet I am here on vital business. So talk, I must.

"I am here in a bid to try and avert more bloodshed and to attempt to bring this senseless war to an end," I say.

My voice is clear and strong, even if I am not.

"I speak with the full authority of Parliament, although what I am about to discuss with you is only known to a few. I appreciate my presence here may present you with some difficulties, so I will try to keep this as simple as it needs to be. For my hope is I can leave Oxford on the morrow and let Parliament know whether there is any hope of peace between us."

I am about to start outlining Parliament's proposal when Rupert throws down the gauntlet.

"That's all well and good, man, but so far you have said nothing that justifies my brother, the countess and myself risking our necks by meeting with you," he quips. "Who the hell are you, and what is your business with us? Speak plainly, man, or begone from here."

I take a deep breath. I understand the Prince's impatience. I suspect I would be just as irksome if an enemy stood before me, saying much but offering nought.

I find myself in a near trance, speaking slowly and deliberately.

"Your Highness," I state as calmly as I can. "I am here to petition you to accept the Crown of England; I am here to tell you Parliament will end its opposition and cease this bloody war if you accept its offer to become our sovereign King."

Silence greets my words. Nobody moves. Twenty seconds feels like twenty long minutes. Then Prince Rupert raises his head. He looks at his brother for guidance. None is forthcoming. He turns to Lady Lucy. She smiles demurely, but remains tight-lipped, averting her gaze from everyone in the room. Eventually, the Bohemian mercenary, the scourge of the Parliamentarian army, turns towards me, his face and neck a mottled red in colour.

"You have a nerve. I'll give you that," he bellows. "I

am a loyal officer serving in the King's army, his nephew no less, and you come crawling to me, just days after we have laid siege to Gloucester and Bristol has fallen, pleading that I accept my Uncle's throne, a crown that isn't yours to offer; a crown that will be fully restored in the fullness of time.

"You Roundheads must be desperate men? You have no honour and even less courage on the battlefield. Sir, quite frankly, you repulse me."

"Your Highness," I stammer in response. "It is not my intention to insult you or waste your time. I am merely a messenger. I am here to tell you Parliament has never sought war with the King. But now we are in armed conflict, we will prosecute it with all the available means at our disposal. There will be no compromise while Charles Stuart is on the throne of England. There cannot be.

"But warfare is not our preferred option. And surely it cannot be yours either? Too many innocents are being slaughtered. The country is almost bankrupt. We are on our knees; all of us, not just the Parliament. I can see with my own eyes the deprivations your Royalist forces are being required to endure here in Oxford. Nobody is winning, with the exception of Charles, who lives in opulence; King of a broken and divided realm.

"If you would be prepared to consider our proposal, then England can start the business of repairing itself and restoring order. That is what we hope for: compromise; reason; and an end to folly and ruin. A change is what we seek, not the end of the Stuart line. Nothing more.

"I beg you to give our proposal serious consideration so we can begin the task of meaningful negotiation."

Rupert glowers, struggling to control his infamous

and unpredictable temper.

"I would rather consort with the Devil himself than Parliament," he shouts. "You are close to defeat. Your troops are poorly disciplined; your generals are poor battlefield strategists. We have you where we want you, and this is the best you can do?

"I have to tell you, sir, your proposal offends me to the core. I am no usurper. I am no traitor. I have sworn allegiance to my Uncle, your King, and I will do all in my power to crush you and the Parliamentary rebels. Tell that to your paymasters. And be sure to leave Oxford by the morning, for if you are here by midday, I will have you arrested and hanged, drawn and quartered."

I walk back to the Spotted Cow looking every inch the forlorn figure I am. I have failed. Miserably.

The meeting with the Prince lasted barely fifteen minutes. I didn't even have the opportunity to tell him my full name and rank, so shambolic was my performance. How right I was to question Pym's decision to send me on this quest. How wrong they were to put their faith in me.

What future beckons now for Francis Hacker?

The streets of Oxford are deserted. I see a church. The door of Saint Ebbe's is open. I need to confess my sins and weakness to my God. So I walk into the empty main chamber, sparkling in the torchlight, and drop to my knees. I read from the first book of John in the New Testament and urgently seek forgiveness and mercy. I quickly lose myself. Peace and calm descend.

I repent. And I am renewed as re-energising powers course through my veins.

I re-emerge onto the city thoroughfare just before

ten o'clock. It is dark. I walk briskly to the Inn; my stomach is cramped due to a lack of sustenance. I realise I haven't eaten since breakfast, some fifteen hours earlier. I no longer care what I consume or drink. I just need food.

The pub is a haven for many who still attend the university. It is found at the end of a narrow winding alley, located between Holywell Street and New College Lane.

I talk to a couple of scholars as I order cheese and flatbreads, and a tankard of ale. They tell me the place is popular because the landlord allows after-hours gambling to take place. And the ale is cheaper than anywhere within ten miles of the city. I wonder what my friend, the Reverend Norwood, would make of this place, and I find myself laughing aloud. If he were here, the words "Hell" and "Damnation" would soon be flowing from his lips.

Shortly after my meal arrives, a shadow approaches my table.

"Francis? Francis Hacker? Follow me."

I look up, but the figure, a woman, is already leaving the Inn. I fasten my cloak, grab some bread and a hunk of cheese and set off in pursuit.

"Wait," I call. "Wait. I am coming."

My visitor is waiting for me at the entrance to Hell's Passage. A hood shields her face. I can only make out a strong jawbone and a petite mouth. My guide reminds me of Isabel.

"Come," says the woman. "Stay behind me. Do as I say. Someone important wishes to speak to you."

We walk for twenty minutes, or so, hugging the walls as we skirt through the winding streets. I do not know how far we have travelled. I only know it is in a direction away from Christ Church, as I can see the glow from its braziers in the sky. Eventually, the woman stops at a large house that has two guards standing outside. She waves her hand.

"Inside. Quickly," she urges.

I do as I am instructed and find myself in another richly decorated home. It is sparser than that occupied by the princes but just as rich. It is a large building, and we make our way to its rear, past the kitchen, and outside into the garden. I see two candles burning brightly. They play the role of two erect sentinels guiding me through the night.

A lone figure sits at a table, sipping from a goblet. The flames silhouette the face of my host.

"Over there. Go now," pleads my escort. "You don't have much time."

I walk the short distance to the table. A woman looks up, putting her glass on the table.

"Francis Hacker. It is good to see you again," says Lady Lucy Hay. "May I pour you some wine?"

Without waiting for a reply, a goblet of fine claret is pushed towards me.

"I am glad I managed to get to you before you departed Oxford," comments the Countess. "You are a hard man to find. I have had my people looking all over the city trying to discover your whereabouts. Wherever have you been hiding?"

My surprise at seeing the Countess again, particularly under these circumstances, quickly evaporates. I tell her about my disquiet following Prince Rupert's outright rejection of Parliament's proposal. I also tell her about my visit to the Church and my search for some inner peace.

"So you are a pious, Godly man, are you, Francis?" she asks.

Her question is genuine. Her soothing voice betrays no hint of mockery.

"Aye. I am," I say. "Pious, no, not that. But I do have faith in our Saviour. I have conviction. And I do believe He is now needed more than ever."

"If God does exist, we surely do need Him," she concurs. "And I truly hope your prayers are answered. But we can discuss spiritual matters any time we care. Right now, I need to talk to you about a more earthly pursuit: the matter you brought before Prince Rupert this evening. I think you will agree; this is something of the utmost urgency?"

I am alert again. My hunger and fatigue are quickly forgotten.

"Of course, my Lady. Of that, I am sure," I say. "Tell me, how can I be of service?"

For the next two hours, Lady Lucy Hay and I talk animatedly about England's future and what can be done to bring peace to our shores. And when I leave her home, just after midnight, I depart with a genuine belief we may have found a way to reconcile our broken and bleeding nation.

Lord Fairfax, Parliamentarian Commander
Fairfax and his son frustrated the King's army in the
north – before defeat at the Battle of Adwalton Moor

SEVEN

I LEFT OXFORD SOME TWO hours ago, having departed the Spotted Cow after enjoying another of its hearty breakfasts. After the breakthrough of last night and a good six hours of sleep, I can honestly say simple oatmeal and honey has never tasted so good. My bill of half a crown could yet prove to be one of the best investments I am ever likely to make.

Riding at an even pace, I estimate it will take the best part of two days to return to Stathern. And that means being in the saddle for long hours. I plan to rest for the night just outside Hinckley, at the Blue Pig Inn located in a small village called Wolvey.

If fate is kind to me, I should be at the Hall by sunset on Saturday the fifteenth day of August.

I am looking forward to seeing my children and my men. But, most of all, it will be good to be reunited with Isabel.

Before then, I am going to need to have my wits about me, for the heavens have decided to open their doors. I am sodden. Not an inch of me is dry. And the unrelenting rain, and the conditions it is creating, is a curse for any rider. So I will now need to keep an eye out for the many hazards I will encounter on the path towards home, which could lead to Bucephalus suffering an injury, as well as the patrols of Hastings, and his men, which I know are active in the area.

One blessing of this unrelenting downpour is it's helping to keep my steed cool as his fulsome stride eats up the mud and grass of Oxfordshire, Warwickshire and Leicestershire. It also gives me the opportunity to think about the detail of the plan I have hatched with Lady Lucy. The more I digest its intricacies, I realise it could have a realistic chance of working. But for it to succeed, so much that is beyond the control of myself and Parliament must fall neatly into place.

I realise that it represents a significant risk to anyone who is involved. For if a confidence is betrayed, or one piece of the jigsaw does not fit correctly, then I am doomed. So is the plot. And in all likelihood, so too, is Pym and Cromwell.

But thoughts of destiny are for another time.

Right now, as Bucephalus and I pick our way through the sodden countryside, which is glistening as the rain beats down on the long grasses and branches, I pray for my family, Parliament – and for Lady Lucy Hay.

Father, if you are listening, I beg you heed my pleas.

I arrive home late on Saturday evening. Seeing the distinctive ironstone buildings of Stathern always brings a smile to my face. And tonight is no exception.

I find Isabel and the children sound asleep. The

only signs of life come from the kitchen, where Else is hard at work, preparing fare for the morrow, the Sabbath. The fire is ablaze. And the smell of the smoked hams and mutton pies she is preparing is intoxicating.

"Master, you gave me a fair fright. I didn't see you standing there," says Else, as she notices me for the first time. I am wet and cold.

She stops preparing another tray of pies and walks over to me. She stands on her tiptoes and gives me a welcoming kiss on the cheek.

"It is wonderful to see you back at the Hall. I trust your business was satisfactory?"

A quick nod of my head and a smile is all Else needs to continue.

"It has been an eventful time while you have been away, Master Francis" she confides. "The Militia has been called out by Lord Grey and has been seeking Cavaliers attempting to disrupt our supply columns from Manchester. I am sure Abijah will tell you all when you see him in the morning.

"And the plague has struck several villages. Thrussington, Upper Broughton, Upper Clawson and Willoughby have all been affected these past few days. There have been deaths. The people are fearful."

The news is not what I hoped for. Peace is what I sought. It looks as though my Maker has chosen to torment me by sending death in its place.

"It is late, Else. I cannot comprehend all you tell me at this hour," I say. "But I thank you for reporting these things to me immediately on my return. I needed to know.

"Be sure, I will look into the matter of the plague, and the steps Stathern and the local villages are taking to ensure the infection does not spread. And I will get a full report from Abijah first thing in the morning. But before then, is there anything I can eat? I am famished."

After devouring some bread and cheese, I retire to the chamber I share with Isabel. The room is dark, a sliver of light creeps through the closed shutters and lights up the face of my wife. She is thirty-one years old and, in eleven years of wedlock, has given me six wonderful children.

Tonight she is as beautiful as she was on the day I first met her. Time has been kind to my beloved. My hope is it will continue to be so.

I lie down beside her on the mattress we share and listen to her slow, rhythmic breathing. She is enjoying a deep sleep. I do not disturb her. I cannot. With my eyes adjusted to the darkness, I simply look at her and thank God for the treasure He has placed in my life. And it is not long before I also succumb to the welcoming embrace of darkness.

The following morning, I find Swan in my kitchen, waiting for me. It is eight o'clock. We embrace. It is good to greet my closest friend. We have a good two hours to catch up on events of recent days before the bells of Saint Guthlacs call us to Sunday prayers and another of William Norwich's excruciating sermons. And I need every minute to digest all that has happened.

"It is good to see you back home safe and sound," says Abijah. "We missed you. I trust all is good and matters are proceeding as you had hoped?"

I am touched by my friend's concern.

"You could say that," I state a bit too tetchily than I

intended. "My friend, if the truth is told, I thought my quest to be all over inside less than fifteen minutes of meeting the Prince, for he gave me the poorest of receptions.

"Whatever discussions had taken place with others, and whatever ambitions he had declared to them, he was adamant he was the King's man. No sooner had I arrived, I was shown the door and threatened with execution if I didn't leave Oxford immediately. So there was nought doing as far as my plan was concerned. I feared all was lost.

"Yet, as I prepared for my departure, a sorely defeated envoy, the door of opportunity swung wide open. And now it is possible I can report a solution to Pym that will win Parliament's approval."

For the next few minutes, I proceed to reveal to Swan the extraordinary conversation I had with Lady Lucy Hay. But before he can ask me any questions, I clap my hands, something I am prone to doing when I wish to change the topic of conversation.

"Pray, tell me, my friend," I command. "Tell me of the plague arriving in these parts yet again. And tell me of the work of the Militia. For I hear you and the men have been busy harrying the Rob Carriers while I have been away."

Swan pauses to collect his thoughts. He then reveals six villagers, two of them children, have fallen victim to the plague. Most are from Thrussington, a small village located some ten miles away from Stathern. The others who have died are from Upper Broughton. Villagers in Willoughby and Upper Clawson have been confined to their homes. The prospect of them surviving does not look promising. Pickets have been placed on the outskirts of all villages in the Vale, controlling the flow of people in, and out. Thankfully, for the last two days, there have been no reports of new outbreaks of the disease.

"Well done," I say appreciatively. "You have acted with decisiveness and speed. I pray that we have contained things, and this period will soon be over. One question, though: how have you disposed of the bodies?"

Abijah passes me a sheet of folded parchment that is in one of the pockets of his jerkin.

"Plague pits have been dug in both villages, and the victims have been placed in these," confirms Swan. "Only the gravediggers have been permitted into the affected areas. And they have not been allowed to return to their homes, for fear they may now be carriers themselves. Instead, the Ministers of the churches have provided these men with accommodation and will continue to do so until all is well and the worst has passed.

"Everything you need to know is in the report I have just given you."

I am satisfied. I congratulate Abijah again.

"All is in order," I say. "I could not have done any better. I thank you, my friend. Now to the business of the Militia: what of the threat from the Cavaliers to our supply columns? What is the risk? What are we doing to counter any threat?"

Some five hours later, at one o'clock on the afternoon of Sunday, the sixteenth day of August, Swan, myself, and a detachment of the Leicestershire Militia set out to hunt down the Royalist forces who are a thorn in our side.

In the end, I have to make my excuses to Isabel for

my absence from morning prayers. In truth, I am quietly relieved at missing the King-loving minister's weasel words.

William Norwich is a man I will have to deal with in the very near future. His Royalist sympathies are plain for all to see, and they are increasingly influencing his ministry, and undermining my position as squire. It will undoubtedly become a problem for Isabel when I do make my move. But I will have to find a way of dealing with this matter, and the issues it will undoubtedly create for my wife and I, at the appropriate time.

But thoughts of the reverend are for the morrow. Today, it is military matters that must take priority.

Abijah has it on good authority, from one of our informants in Ashby, a large Cavalier force of horse and dragoons is set to attack a supply column that set out from Manchester three days ago.

For the last few months, I have been seeking an appropriate opportunity to confront the Ashby garrison and curb its growing ambitions. And I sense the moment may have arrived.

The Royalists have become a problem in recent months, frequently capturing essential supplies and generally frustrating Parliament's war effort.

Thanks to our growing network of informers in the area, this is the first time we have received advance knowledge of an intended attack. Therefore it is time to teach our foe a long overdue and very painful lesson.

I take one hundred and fifty-strong detachment of dragoons with me. We ride to Copt Oak, a small village located in the north of the county and one of the highest points in all of Leicestershire, where a small

Parliamentarian garrison is based.

From this vantage point, I can see much of the Leicestershire and Nottinghamshire border. The view is breathtaking. Woods and forests stretch far and wide. And there is an abundance of livestock. Some locals say it is possible to see as far as Lincolnshire. But I won't be required to see that far today. Clear vision for just a couple of miles is all I need until I catch sight of the supply column and its guard.

Thankfully, I am not left waiting for too long.

After thirty relatively short minutes, a dark line, a mass of horses, men and munitions, comes into sight. I am relieved to see all is calm and as it should be.

We ride to meet our comrades. The ground is firm, despite the soaking it has received in recent days. I am greeted by the commanding officer, one Subaltern Carshaw.

"Good afternoon, Captain. I didn't expect to see you this afternoon," he says. "Is there reason to be alarmed?"

I apprise the officer of the situation and explain why we have ridden out to greet him and his column. Carshaw appears to be of a similar age to myself; whether he has the stomach for a fight remains to be seen.

"We have seen nothing of the enemy, sir," he reports. "My scouts have been active ever since we left Manchester. We know of the reputation Hastings and his horse have in these parts, so we have been vigilant ever since we crossed the county border into Nottinghamshire. But we have sighted nought."

"That is most welcome news," I reply. "Very welcome, indeed."

I think for a moment. I now have two hundred and fifty men and horse at my disposal. Many are hungry to avenge our grievous loss at Adwalton Moor that saw so many young, vibrant lives taken. I make my mind up quickly.

"Officers on me," I shout down the line. "Subaltern Carshaw, keep forty of your men with the column and send the remainder over to me. Instruct your officers to accompany you and come directly to me. I will be giving you your orders. This afternoon, we are going on the offensive."

I now have a mobile fighting force comprising more than two hundred men. And we are all eager to teach our unsuspecting and over-confident enemy a harsh lesson they will remember for a long time.

After an hour of waiting patiently, we catch sight of Hastings' men on open ground near to Loughborough. And we give chase.

The Royalists are a smaller force, perhaps just over a hundred men in total, and we outnumber them by more than two-to-one; I like fights offering odds stacked in my favour.

We track the enemy to the outskirts of Ashby, where their garrison is based. It is the largest of the King's forces outside of Newark. They make good speed. But less than two miles away from their destination, they have an unwelcome surprise: they encounter eighty of my best men who I have sent on ahead, via a separate, more direct route. Their passage to the safety of Ashby's safe walls is blocked.

I had guessed they would seek to return to the

Hastings stronghold. I could have been wrong; there are many places where a detachment of horse can hide. But I was praying the enemy's commander would behave in a predictable manner. And he did.

Out-thinking an opponent is just as important as besting them on the battlefield. In some situations, it is more important. And so I hope it will prove today.

By splitting my forces, I am able to force the Cavaliers to turn away from Ashby. Soon they are in full flight, heading towards the sanctuary offered by Bagworth House.

I know of this place. Having travelled close to the walled manor house only a few days earlier when I returned from Oxford, I know the terrain and locality. It is not easily defended. And there are not nearly enough men to thwart a force the size of mine.

I feel the surge of elation. My blood lust starts to grow. I pray aloud, thanking my God.

We catch up with our enemy on the heathland and copse that surrounds Bagworth, less than a mile away from the enemy's final destination. And the fight doesn't last long.

My men tear into our ill-disciplined and terrified foe with a savagery I barely believe they are capable of. Before I can reach the confrontation, I see a Cavalier decapitated by Smith's expert hand. The butcher is quickly into his stride, sword and cleaver working in unison, a blur of motion and destruction. And he is singing once again.

Elsewhere, panic starts to grip Hastings' men, not least because their commander has been attacked and is clearly in difficulty. Blood drips from the corner of his left eye, and his armour is in a sore state, having suffered a succession of blows from the cleavers and muskets my men have used to bludgeon him. To yield now would mean certain death. Somehow he remains in his saddle, displaying strength and determination I can scarce believe.

The last I see of the officer is when he turns tail and flees the scene, but only after three of his men have offered themselves as sacrifices to save him.

I survey the scene being played out on the grasses of Bagworth. My men are in the ascendency; the battle, if it can be called that, is going our way.

More of the enemy's cavalry fall, wounded or killed, while many others throw their swords and muskets to the ground, indicating they wish to surrender. Then suddenly it's all over. Our foe is defeated; my men have barely suffered a scratch.

It is hard to describe my feelings immediately after battle: I am elated; I am happy; I feel a deep sense of guilt; all in equal measure. But there's so much more than mere words can ever convey.

There is nothing more exciting than surviving a fight and seeing the terror on the face of a vanquished opponent just before he is sent to Hades. But there is nothing worse in this world than being responsible for the wanton death and destruction of another human being. Unfortunately, compassion will not surface until the lust has started to dilute. Until then, you are feral. A killer. Nothing more.

"Captain. Captain Hacker?" The voice of Subaltern Carshaw snaps me out of my euphoria.

"We have killed at least six of their men and captured sixty," he says elatedly, his voice breathless. "We have also taken their horses, ammunition and weapons.

"A Captain, Subaltern and a Sergeant Major are among the prisoners, sir. And there are many wounded."

I focus on the pup sitting astride his white mare.

Carshaw has suffered a deep gash just under his left eye socket, the blood staining his starched breeches and tunic. He is jubilant. His blue eyes are shining. I sense it is his first taste of action.

I congratulate my subordinate.

"Is this your first time?" I enquire.

"Yes, sir," he responds. "It is. I can't believe it was this easy."

I look directly at him. Oh, the arrogance of the virgin soldier.

"Don't worry," I say, pronouncing my words slowly and deliberately. "Most Royalists will be far harder to defeat than this bunch. Our enemy is a formidable opponent. Remember that. Underestimate them at your peril. Next time, I am confident you and your men will have to work far harder to win the day than on this memorable occasion."

Several days after the fight I discover it was Hastings himself I saw fleeing the field at Bagworth Heath. He was sorely hurt, yet he still had the strength and heart to resist the thrusts of some of my best men.

Hastings lost an eye and was shot at least three times as he fought for his life.

And when he was close to defeat, three of his troopers sacrificed their own lives to save him. Would my men do that for me?

Even though I do not wish it to be so, I find myself holding a new and grudging respect for the brave enemy commander.

And I curse my bad luck.

Opportunity had presented itself that day and rather than prosecute my advantage fully, I played the part of the merciful victor.

I hope I do not live to regret my mistake.

EIGHT

OUR RECENT VICTORY HAS DONE wonders for morale among the men. Memories of the Parliamentarian defeats of recent times have now been replaced with new-found hope. I pray this is a sign of things to come.

In an age when a day seems like a lifetime, Oxford now feels like an eternity ago. And, in many ways, this is a blessing.

As time has passed, I have become less anxious. I have been able to be the husband and father I am called to be, much to the delight of Isabel and the children. In truth, I feel more like the man I was before my country came calling and secrecy took over my life.

Isabel is preoccupied for long periods mothering the children while Rowland, his strength much improved, has at last returned to his garrison, some ten miles away at Trent Bridge. I pray he will not face Colonel Hutchinson's men again, just in case his luck runs out.

We parted this week as friends; brothers indeed once again; agreeing to meet on occasion, particularly if either of us receives orders that threaten the peace of the other. Perversely, war and death is helping us heal our differences and appreciate the unbreakable blood bond that exists between us. God truly is good.

News from other parts of the country filters through occasionally, usually when a messenger arrives at Stathern with orders for the Militia. These I increasingly pass on to Abijah. But I like to digest the reports of the fortunes of other militias around the country. And for the Parliamentarian cause, it is grim tidings in the pages of the pamphlets published by both sides in an attempt to control what the populace thinks.

It would seem the Royalists continue to make gains, seemingly holding the upper hand outside of the Midlands. Morale is at a low-ebb everywhere, with our men deserting in droves all over the country.

Our generals haven't learned a thing these past few months as our soldiers prepare for defeat and a return to the evil ways of the King.

Strangely, I have heard nothing from Cromwell and Pym since I sent my dispatch some twelve days ago, informing them of what was achieved in Oxford.

I can only assume their silence is because Parliament continues to be embroiled in protracted negotiations with the Scots over the proposed military alliance. For our friends north of the border are now pivotal players in this make or break game of chess.

On Friday the twenty-eighth day of August, a messenger arrives at lunchtime wearing the distinctive colours of Cromwell. He has ridden from Cambridgeshire, where his master is reputed to be working on the development of a new military strategy for Parliament's armies.

"Captain Hacker, I bring you an important dispatch from Colonel Cromwell," says the soldier, wearing the colours of the Eastern Association, encrusted in dust and mud from his lengthy ride. "The Colonel sends you his warmest regards and asks you to respond immediately. I need to be on my way within the hour."

"Are you serious, man?" I ask, incredulous at the punishment the rider is willing to inflict on his horse and body. "Surely, you can at least take some refreshment and wash yourself?"

"I am sorry, sir," he says. "The Colonel expects me back with all due haste. If I may, I would be grateful if I could leave my horse with you and take anything you are able to offer that is fleet of foot and sturdy? My own beast is a good animal. He just needs some rest. I have ridden him hard and far these past few days."

I look at the man. It is plain to see he is suffering from fatigue and hunger, yet he strives to serve Cromwell as faithfully as he can, without complaint or regard for his own wellbeing. What strength and determination. I wish Lord Grey's forces had more men like this. Perhaps then, we would not be struggling to win this fight.

"It is the least we can do for you," I say reassuringly. "Speak to my men in the stables. They will arrange for you to take one of our finest and most reliable steeds. And be sure to get yourself something to eat before you attend to these other matters. While you attend to your affairs, I will read Colonel Cromwell's orders, and write my reply."

I retire to my study, a place where I enjoy being completely alone. I open Cromwell's letter. I groan as I read the Colonel's words. It seems I am again required elsewhere and I have little time to make my preparations, or say my goodbyes.

"*My dear Francis.*

"*I have received and read your dispatch of the thirteenth of August with considerable interest and optimism. What you report is a most welcome development, one I feared would be beyond you. I congratulate your courage and enterprise. Please proceed with the proposed arrangement cautiously. Discretion is of the utmost importance.*

"*Our friend, John Pym, is unwell and is unable to travel. He is also struggling to complete many of his Parliamentary duties. So I must support him as best I can. This means I cannot join you at the present time.*

"*I require you to attend a further meeting in Chipping Norton. Be there by the third of September.*

"*A trusted friend will make contact upon your arrival. For the time being, you have full authority to lead talks on behalf of Parliament. But you have no mandate to offer assurances on anything. Your role is to reach an agreement in principle. Nothing more.*

"*May God bless your endeavours.*

"*Your faithful servant and friend, Oliver*"

A rueful smile crosses my mouth.

So, once again, I am required to enter the fray with wolves that have a far greater bite than myself. I am getting used to being alone. Fear is now my only companion.

Seven days after I have received Cromwell's instructions, I arrive at Banbury Castle, a stronghold recently taken by the King's forces after the Battle of Edgehill. Its motte and bailey structure, a common feature in so many strongholds, dominates the landscape; its imposing walls shimmering in the sunshine.

The castle is sited at the top of a hill that overlooks miles and miles of rich Oxfordshire and Northamptonshire countryside. It is the perfect outpost for an army; little wonder it was drawn to the attention of Charles immediately after the inconclusive, first major battle of the war. If nothing else, it ensures the King can control a town that is renowned for its Parliamentarian sympathies.

Within days of his success, the King decreed a garrison, under the command and supervision of William Compton, should hold Banbury. A hundred men – only a handful of them cavalry – are now under his command. And they are under orders to hold on to the stronghold at all costs. And I can see why.

At two o'clock in the afternoon, on this late summer's day on the fourth day of September, it is William I am now being escorted to after approaching the castle flying a banner indicating I come in peace.

Although I have slept well enough these past two nights at the Blue Boar, and I have regained my strength after a lengthy journey that lasted almost three days, I am nervous. My plans have been unexpectedly altered. And I feel exposed.

Henry Cornish informed me, upon my arrival in Chipping Norton, that I would be required to ride to Banbury, where arrangements for a meeting where hastily being made.

It would appear that prying eyes are everywhere at Court, and the Prince is concerned about keeping his dialogue with Pym and myself a closely guarded secret.

Banbury, some thirty miles away from the new royal

capital at Oxford, and a remote location, serves our mutual purposes much better.

"So you are Hacker? I have been expecting you," exclaims a strong voice.

I look up. The gatehouse, where Bucephalus and I have been waiting, is a cavernous place, with stairs and ladders leading to the second floor of the castle. Soldiers are busy with their duties. Ten well-groomed cavalry horses are tethered to a pole, while they munch nonchalantly on some hay. Looking down at me from the highest stairwell is a well-dressed and confident young man, who, by all appearances, would seem to be younger than myself. He has a strong, genial face, emphasised by his pointed beard. And he is smiling at me.

"Come," he beckons. "Up here. I am just eating and there is plenty for two to share. You have been vouched for, so I know the garrison is safe with you in it!"

And with that, he turns on his heels and disappears through the oak door that separates the Governor's private chambers from the hustle and bustle of castle life. I follow. But I am unsettled by this unexpected bout of friendliness in the lair of one of the King's most trusted servants.

"Sit here. You must be famished?" My host pushes some bread in my direction. "If you care for them, there are some excellent smoked cheeses and cold meats?"

I nod encouragingly. And soon, with the grease of the hams dribbling down my chin, I start to relax and converse as openly as I can with a man whom I am at war with.

I have to confess, I find William Compton a likeable adversary; indeed, some would say he is a charmer. I quickly discover he is just eighteen years of age, some seven years my junior; and he is the second son of the Earl of Northampton. Despite his youth, he has distinguished himself on the battlefield on more than one occasion. As I have found out myself, through the valour of men like Harold Longbone, it is wrong to judge a man merely on his age. Compton is, I am sure, as formidable and intelligent a foe as a man twice his age.

"So, tell me Francis, why are you here? What chicanery is this?" he asks. Compton doesn't believe in small talk. He likes to get to the point, and quickly so.

"Two days ago, I received notification from Oxford that I am to play host to a Parliamentarian. Not just any Roundhead. Nay. Francis Hacker, one of the commanders of the Leicestershire Militia, and a renowned cavalry officer.

"I am ordered not to speak to anyone about this intrigue and I am told to hold my tongue and not to ask any questions. I am ordered to show you the utmost respect and hospitality. And that, I hope you will agree, Francis, is precisely what I am doing?

"I am also told to expect other guests, who will arrive this evening. Their identities are not revealed to me. So I check who has issued the order and discover it has come from the House of Prince Rupert. When I asked the name of the issuing officer, I was told to mind my own business and prepare a room and appropriate amenities to host a conference of some kind.

"So, sir, will you kindly tell me what is going on in my castle, and what this great mystery is all about?"

I look directly at the governor.

Unlike me, he is just an honest soldier. He isn't seeking to get enmeshed in games of brinksmanship or politics;

I feel sympathy for the man. But, alas, there is nothing I can do. I have my orders, directly from Pym. I am to tell nobody about my mission, or its ultimate purpose.

"I am sorry, sir," I say. "I am not at liberty to tell you anything, other than what you already know. There will be a meeting, here, this evening. You need to keep the area secure and ensure as few of your men know about it. Should your senior officers in Oxford wish you to know more, I am sure they will tell you.

"I wish I could say more. But that is as far as I can go. I am truly sorry."

Irritation flashes across the eyes of my host. Then it is gone. A smile returns to the friendly features of the young Compton.

"I understand," he says. "Well, one has to try."

My host shrugs his shoulders.

"Be assured I will ask no more of you, other than to tell you you're fighting for the wrong side," he continues. "I have met both of your brothers; fine men they are. We have fought alongside each other on several occaisons. They are good soldiers. And, after now meeting you in person, I have no reason to believe you are anything other than a decent man yourself, albeit seriously misguided.

"My father has brought me up to treat people as I find them, regardless of their creed or the reputation that precedes them. And that is how I try to conduct myself at all times, Captain Hacker. So while you are my guest, you will be treated with the utmost respect. If, however, we were to meet on the field, I am afraid I may not be so accommodating."

The warmth of these words takes me by surprise. And I join in as Compton laughs aloud.

How can I regard a man such as this as my avowed enemy? He has displayed kindness, courtesy and respect. Yet I must deceive him. My future depends on maintaining his ignorance. So, too, does England's.

I do despise this game I am being forced to play.

"Thomas is dead," I declare, in a voice devoid of emotion. "He fell towards the end of May, in battle. Rowland was injured, but is recovering. As far as I know, he has now rejoined his garrison on the Trent. Their suffering has been hard for me to accept.

"We made conscious decisions to support different sides in this war, and harsh words have been said between us, they are my blood, and to lose Thomas grieves me deeply."

William clasps me on the shoulder. He, too, has suffered grievous loss. His father, the Earl of Northampton, was killed at the Battle of Hopton Heath just six months ago. The Earl was a renowned soldier. His loss has been a serious blow to the King.

"This damnable war," he says. "Too many good men, on both sides, are being slaughtered for naught gain. The vanity of man is a curse on this land. Yet men such as us are powerless to do aught about it, Francis. That is the truth of the matter. We are pawns. Disposable commodities. Naught else. And it breaks my heart too."

What a strange place to find a soul mate, someone who shares my views, values and frustrations. I do hope I will have the opportunity to reacquaint myself with the honourable and likeable William Compton under happier circumstances.

Sunset passes and I am yet to hear news of any visitors

arriving at Banbury. The gates to the castle are now closed. The watch is on duty.

In the quiet of the evening, any arrival will be betrayed by the cobblestones of the courtyard, the hooves of horses echoing throughout the castle. I take a sip of ale from the tankard I have been given by William's steward. I am in a room comprising a mattress, a table and a threadbare chair.

A resolute candle licks at the wall in the corner, its flames fanned by the cool breeze flowing from my open window. I should be happy to find some tranquility. But I am unable to do so.

I must have drifted off into a deep sleep. Almost an hour later, I am awoken by the sound of the braying of horses and the clatter of hooves. The guards' voices are raised. I am groggy. Confused. I wipe the crusts of sleep from corner of my left eye and I hear the word "Highness" barked out into the night, but I can't distinguish what is being said, or by whom, as the thick walls muffle the conversation.

Suddenly there is a knock on my door and the dense, studded, wooden panel swings open. One of the guards steps in to the dim glow of the candlelight.

"The Governor sends his respects, sir, and requests you join him and his guests in the main hall as quickly as you can."

"I am on my way," I say.

The soldier bows, takes a step backwards and is then lost to the shadows. I find my cloak and strap it on. I reach for my sword, and then think again. I wash my face in the basin, the cold water stinging my flesh. I feel refreshed. With mixed emotions, I walk out of my room and take another step towards an uncertain destiny.

I reach the castle's main hall to be met by William, who is walking in the opposite direction. He looks ill at ease. Two guards, wearing royal colours, stand outside the main doorway.

"There is something not right about this," the Governor hisses to me as he passes. "I fear I am being used in some subterfuge and I do not like it one bit. I hope for your sake, Francis, you do not drink from the same cup as that viper?"

I look at my host and acknowledge him. I feel alarmed. Dread starts to encircle me. But there is naught to be done, except what I have been commanded to do by Pym. So I enter the brightly lit room, shutting the door firmly behind me.

I immediately see Lady Lucy sitting on a chair, close to the fire. She is still wearing her riding clothes, and she looks radiant.

"Francis," the countess calls out to me. "It is good to see you. We have just arrived after our journey from Oxford. Tell me, are you well? Is all as agreed?"

I walk over to the Countess and greet her cordially and respectfully.

"My lady, I am well and everything is as I promised it would be," I say. "With the exception of one thing: Cromwell and Pym are unable to attend. Pym is unwell and is confined to his bedchamber. But be assured I have full authority to discuss all relevant matters and take things as far as we would like them to go. I hope that will be acceptable to you and the Prince?"

Her ladyship turns her head and looks to the far end

of the hall, where a library occupies a considerable area. An impeccably dressed man makes an appearance, holding a copy of the King James Bible, a book his great uncle commissioned during his tempestuous reign.

"Maurice," she calls. "You can join us now."

I barely spoke to Prince Maurice, son of King Frederick of Bohemia, at our first meeting in Oxford, in July. Yet I recall him having a good command of English and an assured, confident manner. Unlike his brother, the unpredictable, firebrand, Maurice listened to reason and displayed wit, intelligence and wisdom beyond his years.

So I am delighted to see him here at the Castle. I was unsure whether he would attend. The Countess reassured me he was a man of his word, and so he has proven to be. And I don't underestimate the personal danger he has put himself in.

"Your Highness, I am delighted we are able to meet again," I say as confidently as I can.

"I appreciate this meeting creates a significant amount of personal risk for you. I am hopeful the outcome will now be more beneficial to both sides. So I hope you will believe me when I say only a handful of people are aware it is taking place. We have kept to our side of the bargain. Secrecy has been of paramount concern."

The Prince smiles and says: "I am delighted to hear it, Hacker. I would expect nothing less. If you did not have my confidence and interest in the matter at hand, I would not be here.

"The King would find it very intriguing to discover why I am meeting an infamous Roundhead, a man who is thwarting our forces in the Midlands. And he would not rest until I told him why. And that would most certainly be the undoing of us all, would it not?"

I laugh nervously. Lady Lucy glances at Prince Maurice and they exchange a knowing look. No more words need be said; we all recognise the dangers we face if we are discovered. For, beneath our expensive clothing and impeccable manners, we are conspirators. Nothing less. And, if exposed, we will pay the ultimate price.

A silent pause enables me to regain my composure. But before I can speak further, I am put to the test.

"When we last met, Hacker, you proceeded to offer my brother, the man who is laying siege to your cities, seizing your strongholds and defeating your armies, the Crown of England," says the Prince.

"You did this, even though it is not yours to give. For the King, my uncle, is in rude health and has no intention of losing this war. And the last time I spoke to him, which was yesterday morning, he led me to believe he is determined to remain England's sovereign. Under these circumstances, how can your proposal work?"

I look at the Prince. His face betrays no emotion. And why should it, for he is no fool.

Considering the seriousness of this meeting, and the radical steps that will surely follow, if a common consensus can be agreed, I would also seek some assurances before negotiating the details with an enemy officer. So I answer the only way I can.

"Prince Maurice, your army has hurt the Parliamentarian army, of that there is no doubt. The south-west is bowing to you; so, too, the north. But you have not mortally wounded us.

"Our forces remain committed. And with every

reversal we become more determined, capable and stronger."

I look at the Prince and I can see I have his attention.

"As we speak, our envoys are negotiating with the Scots," I continue. "A Scottish host, some twenty thousand strong, will soon join this war. This influx of men will enable us to retake the northern territories you have occupied in recent months. It is not a matter of 'if', but 'when'. Parliament is also spending more money on arms and supplies.

"In a short period of time, we will not only be your match on the battlefield, we will be your superiors. And when that happens, there can only be one conclusion: the destruction of Royalist forces and the defeat of the King."

I pause for breath. I look up. I continue to have the full attention of the Prince.

"But, we do not wish to walk this path," I concede. "Unlike the King, who will willingly wage war on his own people without counting the cost, we fight on reluctantly, not because we seek to rule at any cost. Many of us will gladly accept the monarchy, as long as we have a new sovereign who is willing to work with Parliament, not rule it like a tyrant. Pym will ensure all of the sides within Parliament adopts the new King, of that I am certain. But it has to be the right man. Without him, this plan is worthless."

The Prince's brow creases. He looks troubled.

"What say you, Lucy?" he asks the Countess. "What do you make of all this?"

Maurice looks directly at the bejeweled woman sitting next to him, and it becomes evident she is playing a leading role as this high-stakes drama unfolds.

"Your Highness knows my views, very well," she says. Her fingers toy with the glass she is holding, betraying the nervousness she is feeling. She takes a sip of wine and continues: "I have heard nothing from Francis that suggests the dangers have grown. Nor have our agents detected anything is awry. We all know the risks are still significant. But this plan can work. And change in our country is needed.

"Charles is destroying England. He is a weak King; he is an unlucky King. And more and more people, particularly among the nobility, don't think he is fit to rule.

"Should you accept this invitation, dear Prince, there are many who will think your accession is justified, considering the role played by James in ensuring your father lost the Palatinate. So I say we must proceed; with vigour."

Prince Maurice's face is flushed. He paces down the hall, to the library, turns around, and then marches back to where we patiently await him. He clearly is not comfortable with the topic of the conversation.

"Before I say 'yes' or 'no' to anything," he says, "I want to know what will happen to my uncle if this plot succeeds?"

He looks genuinely concerned; he is demanding assurances.

"He may be perceived as a misguided King; even a tyrant by some of your side. But he is a loving husband, father and uncle," adds Maurice. "If I bind myself to this plan, no ill can befall him. That is something Pym must promise. There can be no negotiation on this point."

I relax.

The conversation is going better than I thought it

would; I understand the Prince's concerns. And I have the authority to make a binding pledge.

"Parliament will not seek to harm the King, Queen or Prince of Wales in any way, your Highness," I say convincingly. It is the truth. Pym, via Cromwell, has told me so.

"But the King and his family will not be allowed to live within this realm, or Scotland or Ireland. For the sake of England, and you, this cannot be so. He will be banished to France. Queen Henrietta Maria is still a very popular figure in her home country. Being reunited with his sister will present no difficulties to King Louis. And we would not be ungenerous in terms of compensating the King. Bloodshed, at this time, is not an option we are actively considering."

Maurice walks over to the window. He opens the shutter and gazes out into the night, looking at the constellations as they glitter in the darkened skies. He is still for a long time. Contemplating. Considering. Reaching a decision.

After what seems like an age, he makes up his mind.

"It will be so," he says decisively. "Providing you keep your promises, I agree to become your King."

It is almost three o'clock in the morning before I am able to retire to my room. Much has been discussed, many things have been agreed and several tankards of ale have been consumed.

England is to have a new monarch.

Having spent more than four hours talking to Prince Maurice, I believe he has the makings of a good and fair ruler. All that is now required is for Pym to influence the will of Parliament and it can be ratified, thereby paving the way for Charles Stuart to be removed from the throne peaceably.

I undress, folding my doublet, shirt and breeches over the chair. I lay my cloak carefully on the table. It was a gift from Isabel. And it is my treasure. I fall onto my mattress. My whole body is aching.

Such is my fatigue. I start to fall asleep. I am drifting into the world of unconsciousness when I become aware of a soft tapping noise at my door. Within a few seconds I am wide-awake.

"Who is it?" I say, as I stand behind the wooden frame of the door.

"Francis, it is me: Lucy," comes the reply. "I must talk to you."

I open the door. Standing before me is Lady Lucy. And I struggle to speak. For her nightdress barely conceals her modesty.

"Francis, can I come in?" she asks.

I usher her inside the small room. I light the candle and offer her my cloak. But she waves it aside, preferring instead to sit on the edge of the mattress that is raised off the floor on a crudely fashioned pallet.

"I'd like to discuss some matters of importance with you," she says provocatively. "I think it is time we agreed one or two things. But before we talk in earnest, we need to learn to trust each other. Come. Sit beside me. Tell me something of yourself; tell me of your hopes for England."

"My lady," I start to say. "This is highly improper. Can it not wait till the morn? What is so urgent? Why this hour?"

"Come here, Francis," she commands. "Relax. I simply want to get to know you better, that is all."

I wake at nine o'clock in the morning. I am racked with guilt. I feel lost. Unaccustomed feelings are devouring me.

I climb out of my mattress and open the window. The fresh air rushes in. My heart gets heavier as my head starts to clear. I suddenly remember it all. I kneel and I pray, seeking strength, forgiveness and God's grace. Wretched soul that I am, I deserve none of these things.

An hour later, I am breakfasting. The porridge fills my stomach, but I am empty inside. I cannot settle so I decide to walk over to the stables. It is nearly time to prepare Bucephalus for our journey home. Out of the corner of my eye, I see Lady Lucy emerge from the other side of the castle. She looks directly at me.

I walk up to the countess. "Good morning, my Lady," I say to her quietly. "I trust you are well?" Before she has an opportunity to respond, I continue: "Last night…"

Lucy Hay smiles. She is a handsome woman; of that there can be no doubt. But there is something insincere about her words this morning.

"There's no need for us to talk of such matters right now, my dear Francis," she says soothingly. "That can be saved for another time. Oxford and the Court beckon. And I must make haste. I am in no doubt we will see each other again; affairs of the state will see to that, I am certain. Until then, be vigilant and watchful, for we live in the most dangerous of times."

No sooner has she finished speaking then she is gone, the pleats of her skirts clinging to her heels as she makes directly for her armed escorts at the far end of the gatehouse. It will be their job to ensure she returns to the safety of the Royalist citadel speedily and securely. And I can't help but feel a tinge of regret at our parting.

I watch as she climbs onto her mount, a striking chestnut mare. Lucy sits in the preferred style of a Lady, and trots calmly out of the gatehouse, followed by the men of the royal household, their chests puffed out in unison while hands rest on the sword hilts at their sides.

As I continue to watch the party disappear into the afternoon sunshine, the emotions I feel as I think of Isabel, my loyal and faithful wife, threaten to consume me. I reach for the wall as giddiness takes control of my senses temporarily. I am light-headed. My legs feel leaden. I am suddenly aware of everything I have done these past few hours; my dishonour. And it is overwhelming. Yet, I must somehow find a way of seeking to redeem myself, for I cannot fail in my quest to make right such a wrong.

"I have a feeling you are going to live to regret becoming entwined with that woman!"

The voice is commanding; it is coming from behind me. I look around. I am still in the stables of the castle, ensuring Bucephalus has eaten ample food, and there is enough water in the skins we will be carrying to sustain him for up to seven hours, until we are halfway home once again. William Compton is standing just a few feet away. His hands are on his hips. He is looking concerned, his expression grave.

"Don't deny it, my reckless young friend," he says, wagging a finger in my direction. "One of my men reported to me first thing this morning that the countess visited your room during the early hours of the morning. And she wasn't bringing you early morning porridge and your prayer book. Of that I am sure? My man tells me the good lady was with you for well over an hour."

My host pauses and looks around to make sure none of the guards are listening. When he is reassured, he continues: "I wasn't spying on you, my impetuous Francis; far from it. But experience has taught me that when it comes to Lady Lucy Hay, it is best to keep a watchful eye on that woman, lest one finds one's life turned upside down and powerless to do aught about it."

The look on my face is a combination of confession and confusion. There is no point denying anything; I would not be believed. After all, William appears to be aware of at least one key fact. Nonetheless, I believe it important he knows some of the truth. "Please be assured she was not invited," I say limply and defensively. And then my tongue is quietened.

"My good man, what you got up to with the Countess is a matter for you and your conscience. And our Lord," brays the Governor. "Your relations with that woman are of little concern to me.

"No, I am here for two reasons. Most importantly, I want to wish you a safe return to Leicestershire. It has been a pleasure to make your acquaintance, and I hope we have the chance to meet again, when times are happier and our country is more secure. Let's hope that is sooner rather than later. But I also feel it is my duty to warn you about Lady Lucy Hay. Be in no doubt, she is a serpent. She is well connected; indeed she is a striking woman; but a user of men for her own ends and desires, she most certainly is. Understand this: she is poison. And she will destroy you if she has to."

I am taken aback at the strength of William's warning. And I know he speaks truthfully; for I now have some personal knowledge of the Countess. In my room, her ladyship revealed some remarkable things to me, including the disclosure that John Pym, among others, is her current lover, replacing the odious Earl of Strafford.

Without naming them, she also intimated prominent members of the royal household were also known to her.

Her desire for dangerous liaisons is only matched by her quest for secrets. For I discovered the Countess is an accomplished trader in information, which she provides to Royalists and Parliamentarians alike. The more sensitive and important the intrigue, the more she desires it; and the higher the price her paymasters are prepared to offer.

Quite frankly, it is a world that repulses me. Yet, I am now entwined in its unseemly tentacles. And I don't know if I will ever be able to break free. Thankfully, men like William Compton keep me sane and thankful.

"I thank you for your generous hospitality and friendship," I say to William. "You have been a gentleman that has shown me, an avowed enemy, true kindness and courtesy. These past two days, you have earned my respect and esteem. And I hope, one day, to be able to repay your kindness in a fitting way. Be also assured, I will heed your words."

"Aye," adds William, as we clasp hands and say our farewells in the Romanesque way, as soldiers often do. "Be wary, Captain Hacker. Lady Lucy is a woman of influence who likes nothing more than to play games.

"She is intimately connected to the most powerful men in England, who sit on either side of the fence. I think that makes her someone to be feared."

Sir John Hotham, Governor of Hull
Sir John, and his son, denied the King access to the royal
armoury in Hull for eighteen long months

NINE

I HAVE BEEN HOME FOR several days and relations between Isabel an myself have been strained since my return from Banbury.

We have barely talked to each other; it is as if Isabel knows something, but is unwilling to say. We are pleasant enough in front of the children and the estate workers. But when we are on our own, there is a gulf between us for the first time in our marriage. I sense it acutely and both of us seem powerless, or unwilling, to bridge the divide.

My guilt is weighing me down. I want to confess all, yet I also wish to protect my wife from the pain of my recklessness and foolishness.

Isabel is strong, much stronger than am I. If she were to learn of my recent actions, she will be deeply hurt and angry. Yet it is not her wrath I fear; it is her pity I do not wish to be exposed to. For, while she is all too aware of my weaknesses and indecisiveness, she is willing to forego these fallibilities because she believes me to be a true and loyal husband. But I am not:

I am a weakling: undeserving, brazen and false.

I fear telling Isabel everything that has happened these past days will cause much hurt and damage to our marriage. I wish to avoid this at all costs. But fate is unkind. Again I find I am to be put to the test.

While I have been away, a dispatch rider has left orders for me to apprehend the Reverend William Norwich and take him to Leicester, where he is expected to swear his allegiance to the county Committee and the Commonwealth. If he fails to do so, he will be forced to forfeit his ministry in Stathern. Worse could also happen: he could be imprisoned; and he could also face the gallows. Regardless of whether I want to, or not, I will be unable to help him if he refuses to listen to sense.

"The man is a Royalist and he openly defies my will, and the will of Parliament." My face is flushed. My voice is cold. I can feel anger rising within me. And I am shouting at my wife.

"I cannot ignore his defiance any longer. And neither can the Committee. He has to go to Leicester and explain himself. There is no other course of action open to him."

Isabel is as piqued as I am.

"Francis, you are a better man than this," she bellows at me. "What you are proposing is wrong. Wrong. It is not the right thing to be doing, of that I am certain. My darling, I urge you to reconsider this matter. This is not a good thing. You are talking and proposing a course of action that makes you look like you do not have an ounce of sympathy in your soul. I have to confess, right now I do not recognise the man who is speaking. He sounds like a despot, not my husband.

"The man I love tolerates many things. He displays love and compassion to our people and our enemies, in equal measure. He is a faithful servant. And when he can, he seeks to do good deeds; much of it at a personal cost to himself. But everything that has been said about William conflicts with these things. It shows a darker side of your character that I cannot and will not accept. That's why I oppose you. What you are proposing is so wrong. Can you not see the truth of the matter?"

Isabel and I have been arguing at the kitchen table for more than an hour. I had wanted to talk to her about events at Banbury Castle, but that moment has passed.

Else and the kitchen maids have long since disappeared.

When our passions are inflamed, others in the household know to stay out of the way. For neither of us will give way. We are both certain we are right.

Earlier in proceedings, there was no indication the conversation we were having about ecclesiastical matters of Saint Guthlacs would degenerate into a bitter confrontation. But I made the fatal error of introducing the name of William Norwich into the debate.

As the local Constable, I have to take a view on matters that affect the governship of the local area. I take my responsibilities seriously. And the rector of Stathern, who took up his position less than two years ago, continues to openly support the King's cause. This means his actions have now come to the attention of the most senior Parliamentarian figures in the county, and they have expressed their concerns directly to me about his activities.

Since eleven fifteen on the morning of Tuesday the

fifteenth day of September, there has been deadlock and much disquiet between my wife and I, as we discuss the future of the loose-tongued and disloyal clergyman.

I draw in my breath and seek to compromise.

"My dear, I know this is not a pleasant business. It is not something I wish to be doing, but we must face up to the fact we are living in dark times," I say. "Because of the present circumstances afflicting our country, we cannot permit people like William to whip up opposition to the Parliamentarian cause.

"If the man kept his prejudices to himself, then that would be a different matter. But he doesn't. Every Sunday, he uses his pulpit and sermon as an opportunity to proclaim his love, and that of the Church, for Charles. And people are starting to listen to him.

"I cannot allow this state of affairs to continue. And neither can Parliament. And I have to confess I have very little sympathy for the man. He has brought this on himself and his family. And, if he has to leave Stathern, then so be it."

Isabel, when she is in full flow, is an equally magnificent and terrifying sight. She has a warrior's heart, an intelligence that is razor sharp and a tongue that can do more damage than a dozen muskets. I have learned from experience she is a woman to be treated with the utmost respect; it is a fool that takes her on in a fight.

Today, I am that fool.

A plate containing the remnants of her breakfast crashes to the floor as her delicate fist slams on to the table. The porcelain breaks into three pieces, scattering bread, sweetmeats and cheese in all directions. I have to move quickly to stop two glasses from crashing to the floor and shattering on the slates in similar fashion.

"My goodness, Francis, you are the most stubborn and frustrating of men," she shrieks while continuing to pound the oak surface. "Can you really not see the errors of your ways?"

I look straight at her. I am unable to respond quickly enough.

"Let's get one thing straight: if you and the Committee oust William from Saint Guthlacs, and consign him and his family to poverty and a hardship that none of you can comprehend, then I will no longer be your wife," she continues.

"In name, and publicly, I will be that woman. And I will, of course, look after our children lovingly and diligently.

"But be in no doubt, you will become a stranger to me. We will have separate rooms and we will no longer share the same mattress. The main bonds of our marriage will no longer exist. That is what will happen if you choose to play a part in removing William from his ministry. Now decide what you want. And be quick about it."

I have no doubt Isabel means what she says. In her own way, she is considerably more stubborn, compassionate and determined than I will ever be.

She has been a loving spouse all these years. But you push her to her limits at your peril. She means what she speaks. And I know when I am beaten.

I remain silent for a long time, staring out of the window; licking my wounds.

Outside, it is a beautiful day; inside the Hall there is a coldness I am struggling to comprehend. I briefly think of the Countess and I instantly regret it. Thoughts of the corruption contaminating my soul weigh heavily on my heart. And I cannot escape the conclusion that the problems I am experiencing with Isabel are of my own making.

I walk to the window and look out across the fields and pasturelands, up to the woodlands that encroach the walled garden.

The cattle are nowhere to be seen. So I gaze at the men, women and children in the fields, bringing in what is left of the harvest. They are smiling and laughing as two young boys run around, throwing straw over each other while darting across the golden field. I smile too. I look to the sky and I suddenly find joy in the incredible beauty and awe of the world we inhabit. And once again, I seek forgiveness and solace from my Creator; and I promise to resolve matters with my wife.

After more than half an hour has passed, I feel rational and in control of my speech once again. I turn towards Isabel.

"My love," I say. "I will not allow this matter to come between us any more. Believe me when I say I will do all I can to ensure William is allowed to stay. But I beg you, please talk to him and urge him to desist with his Royalist rhetoric. If he continues to promote the King's cause in Stathern, or anywhere else for that matter, I fear he will be a lost cause. Nobody will be able to save him."

She looks at me; a satisfied smile greets my announcement. It is as much as I will get from Isabel this day. I seek the strength to discuss the events at Donning Castle, but I waiver at the crucial moment. Tackling the Devil within may prove harder than I thought.

Four days later, on Saturday the nineteenth of September,

I learn that the King's war effort has received a significant boost.

I am in Leicester, carrying out Militia duties at the Guildhall, situated adjacent to Saint Martin's church, when a messenger arrives from Lord Grey of Groby. The rider carries some important news for some the city's Committee members: his dispatch is addressed to Thomas Haselrig, John Browne, Francis Smalley, Will Stanley, Edmund Cradoc, Valentine Goodman and John Swinfen.

All seven men are engaged in an animated conversation about an inconsequential municipal conundrum when Grey's messenger strides in and hands Haselrig the communiqué.

I am sitting in an adjacent room, pouring over the city's defensive plan, which I have been asked to assess, when I witness everything that unfolds.

"Sir, I am instructed to ask you to read this and share the news with your commanders," says the messenger, as the dispatch is handed over. "But His Lordship urges you to be discreet. He urges you to exercise some caution. There is no need to share this news far and wide."

"Thank you," replies Haselrig, frowning. He is the younger brother of Sir Arthur, the highly regarded Member of Parliament for Leicester and, alongside Pym, was one of the five leading figures King Charles tried to arrest in January 1642.

"What is it with all your undue haste, man?" he adds. "Do you bring us good, or bad, tidings?"

There is no reply so Haselrig rips the wax seal from the back of the letter and scans its contents.

In an instant, the colour from his ruddy, expressive face disappears.

"These are indeed unfortunate tidings. I wish it were not so," he says. "Gentlemen, if you will allow me to read the document's contents to you:

"My dear brothers of the Leicester Committee.

"Parliament has today learned the Marquis of Ormond has signed a ceasefire with the Irish Confederates, which comes into force with immediate effect. This arrangement will allow the King's forces in Ireland to return to England and support the Royalist army. I am sure you will agree, this is a most unfortunate and inopportune development.

"Parliament's negotiations with the Scottish Covenanters continue and we are confident a military alliance will be brokered in the very near future. When signed, this Act will boost the Commonwealth army by at least twenty thousand men and horse and give us a significant advantage in the North and the Midlands.

"Be assured, I will keep you informed about all developments.

"May God continue to bless you and the townsfolk of Leicester as you stay vigilant in the name of the people.

"Your most humble servant, John Pym."

An audible despair greets the news.

"When was the message sent," asks Swinfen, a wiry man whose best years are long behind him. "Do you have a date?"

Haselrig scans the document.

"It is dated the sixteenth of September," he states. "That means the news is already three days old and the Cavaliers who have been fighting in Ireland could, by now, be back in England. It takes less than a day to sail to the mainland, if the weather is set fair. I know, for I myself have done it."

I watch as the Committee members start arguing and bickering about the adequacy of the city's defences, and the readiness of the garrison to repel a Royalist onslaught. I detect panic and fear in several voices.

But I care little for these men who have neglected their duties for too long; my thoughts are already far away.

I am thinking about my meeting with Prince Maurice only days before, when we talked openly about Parliament's attempts to persuade the Scots to form a military alliance. At no point did the Prince mention anything about the Royalists undertaking negotiations with the Irish Confederates, and being close to an agreement.

I realise he may not be as trustworthy as I originally thought. Nor, too, is the Countess. For she, also, must have known a treaty was close to being concluded, one that potentially gives Charles a significant advantage. Yet she chose to say nothing.

I feel I have been outmaneuvered and out-thought. Again. Whatever will Cromwell and Pym think of me?

I decide to speak to the Committee members for the first time. My fears and anxieties about the Prince and Lady Lucy will have to wait until later. Right now, I need to intervene. And having watched proceedings from my vantage point, and seeing the conversation degenerate, I decide now is an appropriate moment to step in.

"Gentlemen," I say in as commanding a voice as possible. "Fear not. We are in no immediate danger from the Cavaliers in Ireland, for it will take them much longer than three days to mobilise their forces. Ships will need to be requisitioned, supplies will need to be found. Moving an army is a major exercise. And this means we have some time to prepare ourselves and, God willing, for Pym to secure the military alliance we are seeking with the Scots.

"But we are in danger. That is a fact.

"What should be concerning us more than anything else right now is the state of Leicester's defences, not what is happening across the Irish Sea."

As one, all seven turn to look directly at me. I have their attention.

"Gentlemen, I am afraid the greatest risk we face is from the Royalist forces that are already in England," I say. "For Leicester is not equipped to withstand an assault of any scale; far from it.

"We have ramparts we need to build from anew, ditches that need to be dug and fortifications we need to bolster and strengthen. Our walls, in their present state, will not protect the townsfolk or the garrison. And time is of the essence. A month of hard work will make a huge difference. Are you able and willing to commit to such a programme?"

Haselrig looks at Smalley and Stanley. "What say you?" he enquires of them both. "What do you make of what our friend Hacker has to say?"

The two men avert their gaze, preferring to study their leather boots and the quality of their breeches, rather than answer his question.

"See what I have to put up with?" Haselrig is speaking directly to me now. "Young man, I fear, in the short term, we will not have the resources to be able to do much about our situation. Prince Rupert took five hundred pounds from the Corporation's coffers only last year and the costs of running a garrison out of the city means we have little money to pay for the cost of such works, even though they are essential to our survival.

"And, as you can see, among some of us, there is little heart for the fight. So make of that what you can."

I leave the city later that afternoon, close to despair.

The Committee is just like so many others dotted around England: impotent, incompetent and divided. It is little wonder the men and women of our divided country are continuing to desert our armies and increasingly pledge their allegiance to the King. I shake my head. I need to see things more clearly. I have work I need to do that affects much more than a single city. And I need to be in the right frame of mind to have any chance of succeeding.

I make my way to the stables that adjoin the Guildhall, where I have left Bucephalus in the capable hands of a team of grooms. When I see him, he is a picture of power and majesty. A far cry from the men I have left to continue their petty squabbling.

I climb up on to his huge frame. He raises his head in expectation.

"Come on boy," I say. "Let's get home to the people who matter most."

It is late. I have eaten Else's delicious fare several hours ago. I am full and content.

Like all simple men, if my belly is full, a smile will often be found on my face. And, for the moment, relations between Isabel and myself have been restored. While we occasionally fight like cat and dog, there are long periods in between when we are blissfully happy. And I sense we are returning to one of those periods now.

A major factor in my jovial mood is the conversation I have had this evening with my wife shortly after I returned from Leicester.

While I have had a fruitless day with the Committee, Isabel has had an altogether more successful day visiting William Norwich. And it seems she has been able to get the rebel Minister to see some sense at last.

"Are you sure he will comply?" I ask her one last time. "It is critical he does. For his sake, and that of his family. Parliament is now issuing decrees against all ministers who are preaching Popist ways, or are supporting the King's cause.

"There is no room for compromise. He either complies, or he will lose the Church and his income. And the Committee's will is final in this matter."

Isabel looks at me coolly and then her face brightens.

"Francis, everything is in order," she reassures me. "I have had a very productive afternoon with William, and he is willing to stop undermining you and Parliament. Immediately. I have his word.

"In fact, he has asked me to thank you for giving him an opportunity to amend his ways. He knows the risk he has been taking. He just needed somebody like me to explain to him the consequences of his actions, so he can comprehend the scale of the hardship that would befall on him and his family. He now understands what will happen and has promised me he will no longer draw attention to himself, or embarrass you."

This is timely news indeed.

While Isabel was meeting the minister, I received a direct order from Lord Grey, just before I left Leicester this afternoon, specifically requesting me to "silence William Norwich by whatever means are the most expeditious".

Thankfully, Norwich's silence has been gained without the need for formal action, as my faithful wife has come to the rescue of us all. In thanks, I say a prayer thanking my Lord for interceding.

Isabel, myself, and the children, dine together that evening, devouring one of Else's fine mutton pies.

I look at my wife, as I am often prone to doing. She is a bonny woman and a loving mother. And I see once again the overwhelming goodness in her that is prevalent in everything she does. Her defence of William Norwich is just one of many examples of Isabel fighting for what she considers to be the right thing.

Thankfully, it is the first time I have experienced such an immense clash of loyalties and feelings. And I pray it is the last.

Once again, I smile to myself. There is no doubt about it: I am a lucky man to be bonded to such a woman.

Whether Isabel will share these feelings, once I have told her about my encounter with the Countess of Carlisle, waits to be seen.

But find the strength to address this matter, I must.

William Compton, Governor of Banbury Castle
The son of the Earl of Northampton and a man destined
to become known as "the godly Cavalier"

TEN

THERE IS A CHILL IN the air and my bones and head are aching. Summer and autumn have come and gone, replaced with the darkness and unwelcoming embrace of winter. How I dread this time of year.

Several weeks have passed since I last visited Oxfordshire. And there has been an unerring silence from Colonel Cromwell since I sent my last report.

Not knowing how my report has been received fuels fears burning inside me that all may not be well within Parliamentarian circles. In my experience, such periods nearly always indicate a problem. For the war has seen many of the Committees and militias under Parliament's control struggling to restrain the enemy.

I am aware John Pym's state of health is becoming more of a concern, as his body continues to deteriorate, the cancer biting deeper every day. The thought of losing Pym, a man who has spent much of his lifetime seeking to restrain the excesses of Charles and his father, James the First, is hard to comprehend.

So there is much for our military and political leaders to contemplate. And this is the most plausible explanation why I have not yet heard anything. Thankfully, Scotland has formally backed the Solemn League and Covenant. As of yet, however, there is no sign of its twenty thousand men coming south of the border and joining in common cause with us.

In the areas I can directly influence – Leicestershire, Rutlandshire and Nottinghamshire – the war is faring as well as can be hoped for. But while all appears to be under control here – even though my errant brother, Rowland, is proving a thorn in the side of Colonel Hutchinson, and the garrison of Nottingham – I am conscious all things could change in an instant, such is the uncertainty and unpredictability of the times we now live in.

My fellow Militia officers and I do not underestimate the challenge facing us. Much is going to be asked of us in order for the tide of this great conflict to be turned in our favour. We must be prepared for greater sacrifices; we must accept there will be significant loss and deprivation on both sides; and we must pray vigilantly for victory on a daily basis.

Until that moment comes, men like me have been tasked with continuing to take the fight to the tyrant's forces and raising the defences of places like Leicester, cities critical to our cause, yet highly vulnerable to attack from the enemy.

Thus far, the Committee has poorly managed the city's fortifications and defences; bickering between the men charged with governing is common, effective decision-making proving to be beyond their limited means. This has already led to a stalemate at all levels for twelve long months. But it cannot be allowed to continue. And it is my job to get the men of authority in this place to see sense and start doing the right things. Before it is too late. "Tell me again, Captain Hacker, what we must do in order to safeguard the city."

The question is posed impatiently by Thomas Haselrig; a man for whom I have a growing sense of respect. He sees the irritation on my face and tries again in a more conciliatory voice. "In simple terms, what must be done, Francis, and by when?"

I move to the side of the large, dark table that dominates the Guildhall's main meeting room. It is a new building, constructed just five years before the King raised his standard and declared war. From here, the Committee, comprising more than thirty leading dignitaries, goes about its business.

Just Thomas and myself are present this Wednesday morn. This is a deliberate ploy. We have no desire to talk to the others, not even to my confidante, Sir Arthur Haselrig, brother of Thomas, not until we have agreed a credible and compelling way forward.

I open my leather satchel. It contains official documents I have been assembling these past few weeks, ever since I was handed my commission to oversee the rebuilding of Leicester's defences. A quick search enables me to locate the large map I possess. This identifies all the walls, ramparts and cannon sites that will be required for Leicester to withstand a major Royalist attack, or siege.

"Look for yourself," I say calmly, pointing to the various areas I have marked with red wax. "The city is severely exposed. Its crumbling walls cannot be defended effectively in many locations; there are simply too many places where the enemy can gain entry. In our current state, if an attack were to be forthcoming today, there is little prospect of the garrison being able to mount anything resembling a meaningful defence. And Charles will come. You can be sure of that.

"The only reason the Royalists have not descended on us yet is they have more pressing matters to concern themselves with, at places like Newark. But they will come, of that I am sure. If nothing else, they will want to break our control of the heart of England and add the city to their growing list of conquests.

"We must put the time we have, and the resources that are at our disposal, to good use. So Thomas, I implore you and the Committee to act now. You have to find a way to remove the impasse that so threatens this city."

I have known Haselrig for little more than three months. In that time, he has impressed me with his wisdom and calm manner. I have not seen him overly worried by anything. Until today!

"It cannot be done," he says, the sparkle and determination gone from his grey-blue eyes. "What you are proposing will take six months at least, and that's if we get the agreement of a majority of the Committee and can find enough money to pay for such a venture.

"The city is in a sore state. Our vaults are bare of money. We can fund some of the work, but not nearly enough. To our eternal shame, I fear we have failed our townspeople and Parliament."

I look at the man who stands before me. He is nothing like his elder brother.

The redoubtable Sir Arthur, one of the country's most notable politicians, would never allow the city to be so vulnerable to attack. His personality and sheer determination would force the Committee to act appropriately, regardless of the cost or the divisions that exist between its members, aldermen and the Mayor.

Alas, Sir Arthur is rarely in these parts, London is where he spends much of his time. So it requires men like Thomas to lead from the front. But he is a very different creature. In fairness, I judge him to be a good man. I like him. But he is a lone voice on the Committee. And without the clear support of a majority, he is impotent.

"Your response does not surprise me, Thomas," I say. "I expected as much. That's why I have been working on a contingency. My alternative proposal will take three months to deliver, from the point it is approved. It will also cost considerably less than any full-scale plan. If put to the test, I fear it will not, in itself, be enough to repel a prolonged siege. But I am confident it will ensure the city can withstand the kind of attack Prince Rupert and his cavalry prefer to mount. What say you: are you happy for me to tell you more?"

Haselrig nods his assent.

I roll up the map and return it to the satchel. I open the side pocket and extract a single piece of paper, which contains the details of a plan I hope, and pray, will save this city from the vengeful Royalists, who are likely to show the people of Leicester little mercy.

I pull up a chair, and urge Thomas to sit next to me. He uncorks a sherry bottle and pours us both a glass. Even at this early hour, I am inclined to accept this hospitable gesture.

In increasingly good humour, and with a warm glow spreading throughout my body, I proceed to explain for the next few hours how the city can, and must, be saved.

It is the twenty-seventh day of November, a Friday, in the year of our Lord, 1643. The sunrise is yet to make itself known. But this dark winter morn requires me to be in the saddle and on my way to the market town of Melton Mowbray.

After our private meeting at the Guildhall, Haselrig and myself finally believe we have formulated enough of a plan to be able to present it to the Committee, and gain its approval and assent.

Before we do this, we have agreed to ride to the north east of the county, to meet with Arthur Staveley, the only other Committee member Haselrig is prepared to reveal his hand to.

Staveley, Haselrig and a detachment of three hundred dragoons made the journey from Leicester overnight, preferring the comfort of an unfamiliar pallet and mattress to travelling in the early morning, the mist and the odd scavenging fox the only company a traveler can look forward to at such an ungodly hour.

I don't blame either man. If I didn't have my wife to keep me warm I may have made the same decision myself. But I am a luckier soul than my two Committee colleagues, who are both batchelors. But I must make haste. We have arranged an important meeting that will enable Haselrig and myself to tell Staveley of our plans for Leicester's defences, and hopefully elicit his support.

With Staveley prepared to back us, we can move on confidently to addressing the rest of the Committee, or cabal, as I prefer to call them.

Melton is a mere ten miles away from Stathern.

Even in the dark, with just the moon to guide us, it is less than an hour's ride, particularly when Bucephalus gets into full stride, as he is prone to doing when given the opportunity to stretch his legs on the fertile lands of Leicestershire.

Because I know the route, and there is seldom any threat in these parts from enemy forces at such a time, I choose to travel on my own, much to the annoyance of Isabel, who accuses me of being "an irresponsible man who over estimates his own capabilities".

Even though it's a cold morning, the Vale looks to be at its majestic best. Its gentle, undulating hills shimmer as the glow of the moon lights them up. And the slivers of early day mist give the setting an ethereal dimension that takes my breath away. I have witnessed the scene many times, but it is one I never tire in seeing.

At this moment, as Bucephalus thunders through field after field of dew-crusted grass, his nostrils exhaling vast plumes of steam and his ears pricked skywards, the sheer beauty and immensity of this world I am part of is something to behold.

It's hard to believe the world in which I live is being torn apart by the cruelty of men determined to win power at any cost.

I hear the bells of Saint Mary's long before I can see any physical signs of the town of Melton on the horizon.

It is almost eight o'clock in the morning and the church is calling parishioners to the first of its three daily services, where they will hear God's word spoken in English, by a good and faithful Puritan minister, not a Royalist sympathiser like Norwich, the man I am forced to endure at my own place of worship.

I look to the skies and find myself saying a prayer for the souls of Martin Luther and King Henry. No sooner have I uttered my thoughts to my Maker, I become aware of the irony and contradiction. And I laugh aloud.

I head towards the centre of the town, in the direction of the Square, near to where Parliament's garrison is stationed.

As Bucephalus and I amble along the cobbled streets, we pass Glebe Fields. Just a short distance away from me, I see a line of six men with matchlocks. The visibility is good, albeit there is a distinct chill in the air.

In turn, each of the soliders is firing at a wooden shield, positioned less than a hundred yards away. I dismount from my horse; I am eager to watch and discover what is going on.

After a few minutes of witnessing a particularly poor exercise in marksmanship, I call to the nearest man: "What goes on here. Pray, can you tell me, private?"

A youth of no more than eighteen years saunters over to me. At a distance he looks a picture of health and vitality. Yet the closer he gets, the more I can see the physical ravages of war etched on this face and body. His right cheekbone is heavily scarred and it is clear he is blind in his left eye. I am also conscious his left shoulder sags, as if, in the not too distant past, it has been clubbed, or worse. It is a common battlefield injury. I have seen many, affecting friend and foe alike.

"We have been told to improve our marksmanship," he reports. "Colonel Rossiter is keen to see all of the troops under his command become better acquainted with the long barrel Matchlock. So we have been ordered to come here at least twice a week, before breakfast, and spend an hour improving ourselves."

I smile encouragingly.

"And what are you firing at, young friend," I enquire, using my most encouraging voice. "It doesn't look to be much of a target?"

The soldier chuckles; he coughs violently and is forced to clear his throat before attempting to answer.

"That," he says, pointing in the direction of the rust-coloured wooden shield, "that is the King's coat of arms. It was removed from the church and we were told it would come in handy for our practice. And so it has proven these past few weeks. It is now peppered with holes having absorbed much of our lead. I doubt whether it will be able to withstand the lead shot for much longer."

"I am delighted to hear it," I say, masking my disbelief at the youthful boast. Even from this distance, I can see the shield is not badly damaged, the colours of the King sparkling in the winter sun. I change the subject.

"Your shoulder appears to be hurting," I say. "How so?"

The young fighter glances to his left. He winces, no doubt remembering vividly how he received his painful injuries.

"I was at Edgehill," he explains. "As you can see, I got away with my life. But my injuries are a daily reminder of the price I was required to pay. My brother was less fortunate."

I tip my hat in the direction of the soldier, in appreciation of his time and sacrifice. He need offer no more of an explanation.

"Do you know if the good Colonel Rossiter can be

found at the garrison today?" I press the young man. "I have official business in the town, but it would be good to see him, if he is not engaged in governorship or military matters."

"Can't rightly say, sir," comes back the friendly reply. "I saw him go out with a few men as we set out from the garrison to come here. But I know not what time he will return."

It is three years since I last saw Edward Rossiter. We used to be reasonably closely acquainted. But families, and war, have put a distance between us that has been difficult to bridge. Hopefully, he will return and we can renew our association.

I make my excuses and leave the Edgehill veteran to his exercises; an important meeting with Haselrig and Staveley beckons. But before we get down to the weighty subject of the day, Bucephalus and myself need re-energising. Food is our immediate priority; we are both famished.

The garrison is full. The three hundred troops that have accompanied Staveley are busy rising from their impromptu pallets and resting places, making their way to the stables to ensure their horses have adequate food and water.

Many have chosen to draw breath, say their prayers and break bread with each other. I think of Cromwell; this scene would certainly meet with his enthusiastic approval.

The troops have been posted to Melton in a bid to aid Parliament as it seeks to take the fight to the Royalists in Lincolnshire, while also bolstering the local area, so it can minimise the threat of attacks from the Cavalier strongholds of Newark-on-Trent and Belvoir Castle.

I find Haselrig and Staveley in a room set aside for

officers, clerks and officials. They are eating a hearty breakfast and appear to be in a jovial mood. Their lips are stained with the rouge of a good claret they must have enjoyed the previous evening.

"Greetings," I say, as I stride into the oak paneled room. "It is good to see you both in such good spirits. I trust you had good journeys?"

"Good morning, Francis," responds Haselrig. "Yes, the ride from Leicester was very agreeable, albeit there was a bitterly cold winter's wind blowing for much of the journey. I was just explaining to Arthur what our hopes are in relation to the…"

From outside, an alarmed shout pierces the tranquility. It silences Haselrig mid sentence.

"Cavaliers," bellows a voice outside the room where we are sitting. "We are under attack. Man the walls. Close the…"

The crack of a musket volley and cries of "For the King" drown out the rest of the defender's urgent appeal.

As one, the three of us stand.

"Stay here," I command both men. "You must stay safe until I find out what is going on. Do not leave this room. Until I come back and report everything is okay, assume it is not safe for you outside. Both of you will be prime targets."

I turn to Haselrig, unable to hide the urgency in my voice.

"Thomas, please do all you can to hide the satchel," I urge the Committee man. "We do not want the proposals we are here to discuss falling into the hands of the enemy. If necessary, and there is no other option, find a way of destroying them. I have made copies we can retrieve from Stathern, if needs be."

I stride from the room leaving both men looking bewildered. Immediately the noise of close quarter fighting engulfs the peace and quiet. Above the grunts and exertions of men fighting for their lives, I can hear the occasional crack of muskets being fired and steel clashing against steel. What I don't know is which side is winning.

I run through the passageway that leads directly into the Melton garrison's courtyard. Three bodies lie still on the cobblestones. One is that of an officer. He is still. Dead. The others belong to the two guards I spoke to earlier, upon my arrival. Thankfully both are still breathing; but both are incapacitated; unmoving; incapable of defending their positions. I look beyond the gate and see a swarm of men with their hands by their sides; motionless; subdued. They are our men. I become aware of the relative quiet now descending all around me.

Authorative voices barking orders puncture the early morning gloom. Suddenly, I comprehend what has happened. In mere minutes, we have been defeated; we have capitulated.

And not only have we given up the fight, we have also surrendered our honour.

"So who am I lucky enough to have standing before me?"

I turn around to see the gloating face of Gervase Lucas, Royalist governor of Belvoir Castle, looking down at me. He is astride a fine Chestnut gelding and is clearly enjoying his moment of victory.

"Just as I thought, it is Captain Francis Hacker," continues Lucas, reveling in my obvious discomfort and state of alarm. "Unbuckle your sword belt, Captain, and unsheathe any knives you may be carrying. You are my prisoner now, as are Haselrig, Staveley and a few hundred of your men. And please make haste.

"We have accomplished much already this morning, such is the complete surprise we have achieved. But I don't wish to be detained for long, lest our luck changes and we meet some of your reinforcements."

I do as I am instructed and place my sword by my feet. I also retrieve a prized dagger from underneath my leather jerkin and slowly put it on the ground. Isabel gave it to me on my twenty-first birthday; I doubt whether I will see it again.

The limpness of my surrender amuses my captor, who laughs aloud at my meekness. I grit my teeth, accepting my humiliation. For it would be an act of folly to resist such overwhelming odds. I must remain pragmatic. By succumbing peacefully, I will live to fight another day.

As my hands are tightly bound, and a Cavalier roughly searches my body for any valuables, weapons and documents I may be attempting to hide, I pray my betters in London do not forget me; I hope Haselrig and Staveley have found a safe-haven for the plans of Leicester; and I ask God to protect Isabel and our children.

I still have much to do in prosecuting the war on behalf of Parliament – and being the husband and father I am called to be. And being a prisoner of war is not part of the plan I have for myself.

In my twenty-five years of life, I have never been imprisoned, or lost my liberty. So I do not know what to expect from a period of enforced confinement.

The reality is a shock.

My cell is small, and it is bitterly cold. A candle is all I have for light and heat, and my mattress is ridden with lice; having been incarcerated for only a few hours, I can already feel them biting at my flesh. I don't wish for any sympathy or favour from my host. But neither do I expect to be left to freeze all night, and to squirm in my own filth and piss. Yet this is the reality of my newly found situation.

My fellow inmates are equally discomforted.

There are far too many of us for the dungeons of the castle to be able to accommodate us all. We are imprisoned all over the stronghold. Some hundred men, or so, are housed close to me. I can hear them talking among themselves; I can hear them coughing; I sense their unease and discomfort; and I also hear the occasional anguished cry, as a nightmare invades the peace of an unfortunate comrade's slumber. Something will have to be done about the situation, for the sake of the castle garrison as well as the large number of prisoners that are now detained.

I have been able to speak to Haselrig and Staveley. They are in the cells adjacent to my own; they are as uncomfortable as I am. But at least they bear a piece of good news, if indeed our current predicament allows this to be possible.

Just before they were captured, Haselrig was able to hide the satchel, containing the plans for the defence of Leicester, behind the ornately decorated wooden panels that surround the main fireplace in the officer's mess room. There is a secret chamber located to the side of the hearth, seemingly created for such emergencies.

In their growing panic and desperation, the two Committeemen discovered its existence by pure chance. This is significant news. And although it doesn't improve my mood, I am reassured. Knowing our enemy has not become aware of Leicester's true state of weakness is indeed a blessing.

I am not aware of the moment I succumb to the lure of the night. But I do not enjoy much sleep before I am awoken at first light by the unforgiving hands and voice of one of my gaolers.

"Get up, Roundhead scum," he roars in my ear, as he pulls me up from the straw bedding I share with the lice. "The Governor wishes to speak to you. God knows why? If it was down to me, I'd be cutting your throat, not wasting precious time exchanging words with a vile turd like you."

I am tetchy. A fog grips my mind. I start to protest at my treatment. Then I am on my feet, not quite sure how I managed to achieve this feat. A bowl of cold water is thrown over me. The shock awakens me from my stupor. I start to shiver uncontrollably. My head is throbbing, like it always does when I have had little rest and peace. And my throat is dry. Suddenly I remember I have not eaten anything for more than twenty-four long hours.

"Where are you taking me?" I ask through my cracked lips, my body aching. "Why the need to get me up so early?"

There is no response. My captor simply drags me by my shackles through a catacomb of dimly lit passages. I stumble along, unable to avoid crashing into a myriad of obstacles that line the way. I can see very little, as my eyes struggle to become accustomed to the darkness, the only light coming from the torches that adorn the castle's crudely chiseled underground walls.

After a few minutes, I emerge into the early morning

daylight. I am outside, in a large courtyard. It is dusk. And in the gloom, I can see there are at least twenty guards and soldiers performing a variety of duties in this walled area in a bid to stay warm.

Two men dressed in fading Earl of Rutland colours guard the entrance to the main castle building. The castle was the Earl's until a few months ago, when Lucas and his men captured it in the name of the King. It is now a major Royalist outpost causing much disruption to Parliament's affairs.

The guards are cold and irritated; the steam of their breath leaves a plume for all to see, even in this dim light.

"State your business," the guard stationed on the left of the door barks at my gaoler irritably. "What is so important at this early hour, man?"

The response is matter of fact. "The governor wishes to interrogate this fellow," states my captor. "He's a Roundhead officer, the brother of our very own Captain Hacker. That's all I know."

The door swings open and we are waved through.

For an instant, the warmth threatens to overwhelm me. I feel faint. Nausea and unsteadiness grip my stomach and legs simultaneously. Then my body starts to acclimatise. A tingling sensation pulses in my feet and hands as I climb the stairs to the governor's quarters, which are located on the first floor.

By the time I reach my destination, my wits have partly returned. Once again I start to feel alert and I am able to exercise a degree of control over my body. I am ready to meet my tormentor.

Sitting at a large, rectangular table in the Governor's study is Gervase Lucas. My foe is clearly continuing to enjoy my discomfort. I know him to be a decent enough man, albeit he is not universally liked or respected by many Royalists, including the likes of Henry Hastings.

As I wait, I watch Lucas picking at his breakfast, chasing a piece of meat around an ornate, silver bowl with a knife. If I were a free man, I would find myself laughing at the comedy of the situation. But I am not at liberty. So I choose to remain silent. I look straight ahead, seeing nothing but acutely aware of everything that is happening around me.

Gervase dismisses the gaoler and the guard that have accompanied me into the study.

"Leave us, please. Pray, leave us alone," he orders. "The Captain is hardly a threat to myself and the King in his present predicament."

With only the two of us in the room, the governor adopts a more friendly tone.

"I hope your night was not too uncomfortable?" he enquires. "I am afraid the accommodation here for gentlemen like yourself is pretty basic. But, once we have decided what to do with your men, things should become more comfortable. By tonight, Haselrig, Staveley and yourself will be allocated secure rooms that, at the very least, are warm and clean."

I say nothing. My eyes are fixed on Lucas's breakfast bowl. And my stomach betrays my hunger.

"If I am not mistaken, you appear to be in need of some sustenance, sir?" comments Gervase Lucas. "Come. Join me. Let's eat and talk of the situation we find ourselves facing. You know me to be a reasonable man. You have nothing to fear."

I pull out the chair opposite my captor and sit down. As soon as I do so, my stomach reminds me just how hungry I am. Although I have not eaten for a day, it is more than forty-eight hours since I last ate a full meal. And my belly is empty.

"Thank you. Your hospitality is most welcome," I say appreciatively, as I chew on a chunk of fresh bread.

After two more mouthfuls my tongue gets the better of me.

"Tell me, Gervase," I say, "how did you get into Melton so easily, and without being seen; and what are your plans now you have taken us as your prisoners?"

My adversary looks at me appraisingly.

"It is well known in these parts that the Melton garrison is complacent, particularly in the early morning when the watches are changing," he says. "We decided to put Colonel Rossiter's troops to the test. In truth, we expected to be detected long before we rode into the town. But at no point did any of your militiamen challenge us. It was as if the garrison's sentries were all asleep on duty.

"Initially, I thought our task would be beyond us; that the information we held was flawed in some way. But I was assured all would be well. And so it proved to be. I still cannot believe how easy it was."

I forget the call of my stomach. I am alarmed.

"So, are you telling me you were on a mission; this was not an unplanned, opportunist raid," I splutter. "Whatever were you looking for?"

Gervase Lucas explodes into a fit of laughter. He pushes back his chair and steps toward the large window that affords panoramic views of the castle's magnificent grounds and the open expanses of the tree-lined lands beyond. I start to wonder if this is the same window used by Lucas ten months earlier, in January, when he stole into the castle and bravely opened its doors to his assembled troops, who then proceeded to claim it as a citadel for the King?

"My goodness, Francis, your wits have clearly been left behind in your cell," he says, shaking his head. "You are clearly addled by all this excitement. Do you really expect me to believe you have no idea?"

I shake my head. I am confused.

"No, I cannot see any reason why you would execute such a reckless action, unless there was a significant prize to be had," I reply. "And although three Committee members, some officers, three hundred soldiers and their horses and arms, is clearly some kind of success, it is hardly the grandest of prizes. Our capture certainly does not justify the risks you took. Right now, I would guess we are more of a liability?"

My considered response allows my host to roar once again. His mirth is such; all thoughts of breakfast are quickly forgotten.

"You really are slow on the uptake this morning, my dear Francis," states the governor. "Our mission was very straightforward, For Francis, it was you we were seeking; and you alone; nobody and nothing else. And here you are, my prisoner. We have taken the others to disguise our intentions.

"Consider that, will you. And while you do, you also need to know that quite soon, once some important guests arrive, you will be asked some questions. Depending on how you respond to your interrogation, you will be allowed to live, or you will be executed.

"Now, man, fill your belly and try to enjoy the good company you are blessed to share this fine morning. Right now, everything else is unimportant."

ELEVEN

I DO NOT SEE GERVASE Lucas again until Monday the thirtieth day of November, by which time Haselrig, Staveley and myself have all been allocated secure accommodation in different parts of this vast stronghold. This makes communication between us now quite impossible.

True to his word, the governor has released all of the troops captured in the attack on Melton, minus their horses, swords, knives, muskets and lead shot.

The men have been freed, on the promise they will not take up the fight against the King upon their return. Lucas and the garrison at Belvoir Castle know the pledge that has been extracted is meaningless, and the men will be manning the walls and mounting patrols within hours of their return. But pragmatism and sense have thankfully prevailed; now there are three hundred fewer mouths to feed.

Yet while the men have been released, an uncertain future awaits the three of us who remain prisoners.

I have been told nothing about what the future

holds, other than I am going to be questioned. Neither have the others, as far as I know. It is my own fate that weighs heavily on my mind.

For two days, I have been praying for some kind of assurance. And, as of yet, I am still waiting for an answer.

At eleven o'clock in the morning, my cell door opens unexpectedly. Fresh, warm water is brought into my room; so too, a razor. My ageing gaoler, whose ambivalence towards me is becoming increasingly evident, provides me with newly laundered clothing.

"Let's be having you, Roundhead," he shouts. "There's no time for slacking."

As the man leaves, Gervase Lucas steps into my enforced abode. My surprise at seeing him is quickly brought under control.

"You will be required this afternoon," his staccato voice bounces off the cell walls. "I hope the breeches and doublet fit. They are mine. We are of a similar build, are we not?

"I do not know what will be required of you, or why, but you are going to need to answer some questions and account for yourself, on pain of death. I would not have it this way. But believe me when I say I am powerless in this matter. I have no influence on these events, or with your interrogators."

Gervase looks at me keenly. I can see his curiosity is raised, but for some reason he is not prepared to ask me what I have done to provoke such interest among Royalist circles. Perhaps he fears knowing the truth? Perhaps he already knows what fate awaits me?

"Three people are coming to see you," continues the governor. "At this moment, I do not know who they are. But I do know I will not be allowed to remain anywhere near the room when you are questioned. Such are my orders, I am afraid that is all I can tell you. So, please, prepare yourself. A lot depends on what you say this afternoon, not least your life."

After a long pause, he adds: "Francis, I wish you well."

At precisely three o'clock in the afternoon, my door is opened and four guards escort me down several flights of stairs to the ground floor of the castle.

We meet nobody on our brief journey until we reach the entrance to what I presume is the main hall. Standing outside, two guards are wearing the colours of Prince Rupert. They do not look particularly pleased to see me.

"Wait here," bellows a portly sergeant major, a man full of authority, pomp and self-importance. "I will see if they are ready for you."

Within a few seconds, he returns and instructs my guards to unlock my shackles. Once free, I am allowed to enter the hall without molestation.

"Ah, Hacker. How good of you to join us." I identify the distinctive voice immediately: flawless English with just a hint of a native Germanic-speaking tongue. And, for the first time, it is heavily laced with something I recognise as loathing; perhaps worse.

"I had such high hopes that something good was going to come out of our relationship," continues Prince Maurice. "But it seems you have been playing me for an idiot. Is that so?"

I am pushed towards a heavily built chair in the centre of the room.

As well as the Prince, I can see Lady Lucy Hay watching me intently. And there is a third person; a man; someone I do not know. His black, unblinking eyes have followed me from one end of the hall to another. A sense from deep within tells me he is a man to be feared.

All three are sitting on settees laid out in a horseshoe formation around the chair from which I presume I will endure my inquisition.

"I ask you again, Hacker, have you played me for a fool?"

There is no mistaking the Prince's tone.

He is struggling to contain his impatience, anger and frustration.

"Highness, I know of no reason why you ask me that question," I reply honestly. "I have done nothing to merit such an accusation. That is the complete truth."

The Prince looks at me. I see distrust and hostility in his eyes. He waits a minute, contemplating what he should say next.

"When we met at Banbury Castle, we agreed to a certain course of action. Did we not?" Prince Maurice's question is rhetorical. "Yet, these past few weeks, my agents have revealed to me that the heart of Pym and his confidantes have changed. No longer do they seek an alliance with myself. My understanding is Parliament no longer wishes to offer me the throne. If my men are to be believed, forcing the King to bow to the might of Parliament would now seem to be the preferred option. As a result, none of what was pledged between us is likely to happen. What say you of this, man?"

Whatever my face betrays, it forces the Maurice to look at Lady Lucy and seek some sort of affirmation.

"You look surprised by what the Prince has just revealed," says the Countess. "Is this so, or are you simply playing games with us, Francis? I hope for your sake, and that of your family, that you are being honest. For there can be no second chances. If you have betrayed our confidences, we will find out, sir."

I hear her words. But as she speaks, I continue to find myself drawn to the man sitting next to Lady Lucy. He is muscular, with a cruel fighter's face. His dark, black hair hangs limply to the base of his shoulders. His weathered features betray no sign of emotion or feeling. He is dressed like the killer I presume he is. And his inquisitive and suspicious eyes have scrutinised me from the moment I entered the room.

"Allow me to introduce our friend," says Lady Lucy, noticing how I am watching the man perched alongside her. "This is Feldhauptmann Gustav Holck. He is a Bohemian officer loyal to Prince Maurice. He fought alongside the prince and his brother against the Spanish, as they attempted to prevent the Catholics from seizing the Palatinate. He is a loyal servant and he is proving to be particularly valuable at the present time. He serves Royalist interests at the present time.

"You should know he has been watching you, and your family, ever since you returned from our first meeting in Oxford. You won't have been aware he has been observing you. But, these past three months, he's done a thorough job in learning all there is to know about you, your wife and your children. It was he who learned you were travelling to Melton.

"Should you prove to be unworthy of our trust, he will be ordered to bring your family here, where he will kill them in front of your very eyes. And be assured, he will. He will then garrote you. So, Francis, please be very careful with what you tell us. And make sure everything you say is truthful."

My head is spinning. I want to shout out at the injustice of my situation. But I am unable to make a sound. My throat is dry. My heart is beating wildly. I don't know what to say, or do. Any protest would be futile; meaningless; an indication of the weakness that is paralysing me.

My agitation does not escape the attention of the Royalist trio.

"So, Hacker, do we have your attention? Can you be trusted?"

The voice is Prince Maurice's. Normally, under most circumstances, I would acknowledge the speaker. But today, in the predicament I find myself, I am struggling to concentrate. The wave of panic that is engulfing me is controlling my every thought.

Suddenly my left cheek stings, struck by a hammer of a fist. Holck's face appears a few inches from my own. I can smell his rank breath. He moves effortlessly, as assassins do. He makes to strike me again. But, as he raises his hand, the mercenary thinks better of it.

"Show the Prince the respect he deserves," snarls the German. "Answer your superior. Now."

I try to focus and look directly at Prince Maurice. I remonstrate once again: "Sir, I do not understand why these events are happening. I am not guilty of conspiring against you, far from it.

"Everything I have promised to do, in our united cause, I have done, at great personal risk. I have heard nothing from Pym, since I returned from Banbury Castle.

I sent my report and have received no new orders.

"As far as I am concerned, we are continuing to pursue our plan with vigour. Our desire is to see you crowned as King and Charles banished from these lands. Nothing has changed. I swear it."

Maurice's steely eyes continue to probe me, watching everything I do, every facial twitch I make.

"Do you realise what I have had to do in order to attend this meeting?" he asks softly. "I have had to withdraw from the siege of Plymouth, under the pretence of illness, to discover what is going on. My absence from the field threatens to slow down our army and seriously undermine the King's attempts to reclaim Devon, at a time when our forces are in the ascendency.

"All this I have done simply to comprehend the extent of your treachery. Too much is at stake. And be assured, one way or another, we will discover the game you have been playing."

The Prince pauses, he is seemingly lost for words.

In recent weeks, the Royalist pamphleteers have been writing about his campaigning prowess in Exeter and Dartmouth, where town after town has fallen. But I also know Parliament's strength in the southwest lies in the people of Plymouth.

If Maurice's efforts are going to be frustrated anywhere in the region, then this town is certainly one place where his army could start to be frustrated.

I am suddenly brought back to the reality of my situation when the Prince shouts at Holck in his native tongue: "Bihnd ihn. Dicht."

Translation: "Bind him. Quick."

With one enormous stride, Holck is again on me. His

strength is overwhelming. With an iron grip he holds me down, quickly lashing both of my wrists to the armrests of my chair, my palms facing down. Next, my ankles are secured, tied together.

I am immobile. Discomforted. I look up; awaiting whatever is to come.

"Hacker, it pains me to do this to you, but it seems there is no other way to get the truth out of you." The Prince is talking without a trace of emotion. Cold. Aloof. Practiced.

He turns to Holck and issues another order: "Fange an, seine nä gel herauszuziehen. Langsam. Hör auf, wenn es sich anhört, als würde er etwas nützliches sagen."

Translation: "Start extracting his nails. Slowly. Stop if it sounds like he's saying something useful."

Before the killer can do his Master's bidding, the Prince holds up his hand and turns to the Countess.

"My dearest Lucy, you may wish to leave us now," he says. "No lady should be forced to witness what is about to happen in this place."

As instructed, Lady Lucy Hay hastily departs what will soon become a butcher's parlour.

I am drenched in sweat. My eyes are stinging. And I feel Holck's brutal strength, as he uses all his might to restrain me. Then I feel a piercing, agonising pain. I look down at my right hand. Blood is oozing from my thumb. Where once there was a fingernail, now there is just gore.

My torturer's pliers grip the remnants of the nail. He is laughing; quietly congratulating himself, as he examines his crude handiwork.

The Prince is also smiling, unconcerned by my pain. Abruptly he barks out yet another order: "Gute arbeit.

Nun zum nä chsten."

Translation: "Good work. Now to the next."

I don't need an interpreter to know what is coming.

This time, the agony is more intense as the nail of my index finger is ripped from my hand. I try to suppress a scream, but it's too late. My weakness has escaped. I am hurting.

Holck turns to me. "That was number two. There are another eight to go. And then there are your toes," he says in his heavily accented English.

"You decide if we go any further with this. If you want it to stop, tell the Prince everything he needs to know."

I remain mute.

Nothing I can say will change anything.

I have been wounded in battle and in the field. By musket ball and sword. Yet I have never experienced such pain as was inflicted on my body on Monday, the thirtieth day of November.

For more than three hours, Holck works on me, taking first all the nails from my fingers, then those of my toes. Torture is a brutal, merciless and barbaric act. But I understand why it is used. God forgive me, I have used it myself as a means to extract vital information. And, having seen it carried out on my prisoners, and now experiencing the act myself, I defy any man to retain dignity and honour when his body is forced to withstand such grievous assault. My saving grace is I have nothing to tell.

Eventually, through all of my sobs and incoherent mutterings, my torturer stops. It is past six o'clock in the evening and I have been unable to tell my captors anything different to that they already know: the plan to crown Maurice as King is still active. That is all I know. In all honesty, that is all I can testify to.

Through my blood-shot mist, I hear Holck say: "Das habe ich noch nie erlebt, mein Prinz. Ein Mann bricht normalerweise am sechsten oder siebten Nagel."

Translation: "I have never experienced this, my Prince. A man usually breaks on the sixth or seventh nail."

Maurice nods his head. He walks over to a small window that overlooks the courtyard. For several minutes he says nothing. He just stands. Silent. Brooding. Menacing.

"Release him," says the Prince in an even tone. "I am satisfied. He knows nothing more than he has told us. Pym has told him nothing."

Holck does as he is told. He pulls out a short hunting knife and cuts through the ropes binding me to the chair.

My wrists are first to be released, then my ankles. The blood that has been prevented from reaching my hands and feet suddenly explodes through my veins, and the pain I am experiencing intensifies. I groan. Once. Twice. I lose count how many times. Fresh blood pulses freely on to the carpet. And then oblivion claims me.

By the time I come round, my hands and feet have been dressed, and I have been taken out of the chair. I have been laid on a couch, from where I have a good view of my surroundings. And, for the moment at least, I am free of my shackles.

Less than fifteen feet away from me, Prince Maurice, Lady Lucy Hay and Holck are deep in conversation. They are whispering. I can make out a few words, but I have no real inkling of what they are saying. I can only assume it relates to my fate.

Lady Lucy is the first to notice I have regained my consciousness and I am watching them.

"Francis," she says soothingly, a tenderness returning to her voice. "You are awake. The castle physician has tended your wounds. He is an able doctor and has treated you well. But there will be discomfort for several weeks.

"Within a month, you should have recovered the full use of your hands and your feet. The skin will have hardened. As for your nails, they will take longer to grow back – perhaps as long as a year. I am sorry you had to endure this. But we had to be sure we were not all being ensnared in some Parliamentarian trap. More than your life is at stake."

I am confused. I am agitated. My anger is rising. And it shows.

"Francis, this could not be avoided," she continues. "Our agents in London have told us Pym and Parliament are playing games with us, that there is no intention to offer the Crown to Prince Maurice. And it appears there never really has been any true intent. At best, it was an expedition to sound out a leading member of the Royal family and test him, seeing what might come of it. At worst, it is an attempt to create division within the King's command and undermine the war effort.

"If this is the case, and Maurice is exposed, or even suspected, he is likely to face the death penalty. As will we all. It is likely Prince Rupert would also be implicated. There are many people at court would do everything in their power to see it so, and it's highly likely Pym would also stir the pot, to seize as much advantage, and create as much disharmony as possible.

"We said at the outset the stakes would be high. And they are. But we believed the approach made by Pym was sincere. You convinced the Prince and myself of this, nobody else. So that is why we have gone to these lengths to find out the real truth of the matter."

I sit up. I feel some of my strength returning. I take in the expressions on the faces of my captors. And I sense a change in the temperature, until the air is punctured once again by a clipped, harsh Germanic voice.

"Hacker, I will not apologise for what has just been inflicted on you," proclaims the Prince, with no hint of regret in his cold voice. "It was a necessary measure. You are my enemy. Your Master is seeking to dupe me and undermine the cause I serve.

"From bitter experience, we know you Roundheads like to play games. So we had no choice but to find out what you know. But you do have my word that neither you, nor your family, will be the subject of any retribution on my part.

"You have behaved honourably in this venture. And you have tried, within your means, to broker an arrangement that is for the good for all. I recognise all that you have done.

"We have intelligence that suggests this whole episode has been a ruse, nothing more. So everything ends today. It must. And we will now return to our respective sides until the outcome of the war is known, one way or another.

"But a word of warning before I take my leave of you: speak of this matter to no-one. This must remain known just by ourselves; tell others, and I will find out about it. And if it comes to my attention you can no longer be trusted, my men will find you. There will be no second chance."

The Prince picks up his hat and gloves. He rearranges his cloak. Then, with a sharp look at Holck, and a quick crack of his riding crop, both men stride out of the room, leaving me alone with Lady Lucy.

"I do not profess to understand any of this intrigue and treachery you and the Prince are entwined in," I say to the Countess. "I am a mere soldier. A simple man who takes orders from his betters, who is doing what he can in the best interests of his country. I had no say in participating in this scheme. At all times, I have done everything in my power to ensure the right things are done. And, at all times, I have spoken truthfully."

Lady Lucy looks at me. She is uncomfortable at my overt display of emotion. Her discomfort only enhances her appearance. Indeed she is a rare woman. It is easy to understand why so many men have fallen under her spell.

"That time at Banbury Castle," I say, catching her in an unguarded moment; recalling a night when temptation almost got the better of me. "I desired you. Of that there can be no doubt. But I could not betray my wife and children. I know my rejection left you feeling slighted. Insulted even. But I hope you understand the vow I swore on my Wedding Day is something that is most precious to me. I love my wife dearly. I am no betrayer, even though my flesh was sorely tempted. I could not tell you at the time, you left my chamber rather abruptly. But, my Lady, I feel I owe you this explanation and apology. My conscience has not allowed me to rest easy these past few months."

Clearly embarrassed by the intimate nature of my words and her acute discomfort at the recollection of my rejection, the Countess turns away. She looks to the ceiling in an effort to restore her composure. When she is in control of her emotions, she turns and faces me.

"Francis, you cause me no offence," she says. "I admire a man who is faithful and loyal, qualities you seem to hold in abundance. Let there be no ill feeling between us. All I ask is you remain discreet.

"I said things to you that night known only to a very small number of people. I do not know why I said the things I did; it must have been a moment of extreme weakness on my part. Unfortunately, I cannot undo what has been done.

"Whatever happens in the future, the information I shared with you must not become common knowledge. For my opponents to discover certain things about me will damage more than my reputation; many others will also be put at risk. So I need your word what was said will stay just between us. Do I have your assurance as a gentleman?"

I nod my head, confirming my assent.

I do not underestimate the implied and understated threat the Countess is making. I would be a fool to think she would not want to control me. Too much is at stake for this woman who plays both sides against each other for profit and devilment. Nonetheless, I am relieved by her words. As much as I can be, I am reassured, albeit my security, and that of my family, is now in the hands of people I cannot trust.

"Let us move on," she continues. "The past is the past. But there is much we can do to shape the future. And that is where we need to devote our energies. For I am sure we will both be needed."

Relief pulses through my body. But an involuntary movement of my left hand, which catches the armrest, quickly reminds me of the need to recover from my wounds.

The pain is excruciating. At this moment, I realise I am fit for nothing other than rest and recuperation.

"What of myself, Haselrig and Staveley?" I ask. "How long will we be held captive?"

Lady Lucy can offer no guarantees.

"I am afraid I do not know," she admits. "That is a decision for the governor, Prince Maurice and possibly the King. But I am sure you will be allowed to leave the castle once the worst of your injuries have healed.

"It is to the advantage of none of us for questions to be asked about how they were sustained. You bear all the signs of torture. It is plain to see. As far as Parliament and the court are concerned, you are one of three important figures to have been captured. No doubt you will be used as capital in some future prisoner exchange, when Royalists of rank equal to yours, need to be reunited with their comrades and families.

"Until then, I think you may have to prepare yourself for a lengthy stay at this castle. The governor, who is a good and fair man, will ensure you receive comfort and proper treatment. Your wounds will be tended to. And I will arrange for word to be sent to your wife about your welfare."

The news fuels my anger and leaves me feeling utterly helpless. But at least I am alive. It could have been so much worse. The thought of what will happen to Isabel and the children if I am not there to support them threatens to overwhelm me.

With nothing to do, other than play a waiting game, I decide now is as good a time as any to confess my sins, seek repentance from my God and take my leave.

I am certainly going to need the strength and grace of my Saviour in the weeks ahead.

"May I return to my cell?" I ask. "Thank you for your reassurances, Countess. I bid you a good day."

TWELVE

IN THE ELEVEN YEARS ISABEL and I have been man and wife, we have never been apart at Christmas. Yet, a month into my incarceration, and with no prospect of release in sight, I have been busy preparing myself for the loneliness and isolation I am certain to experience at this holiest of times.

My fingers and toes have started to heal. I no longer feel the intense pain I endured in the first week that preceded my torture.

Where my nails once were, dark scab crusts have formed. They act as a daily reminder of how close I came to meeting my Maker. For the umpteenth time, I curse under my breath and ask myself why I ever agreed to be an agent of Pym. This experience has surely demonstrated how unsuited I am to the life of a secrecy and conspiracy.

One outcome of my enforced imprisonment is that I am able to spend time in prayer and studying the Word.

The castle's chaplain, Thomas Mason, who chooses

to visit me on a regular basis, often interrupts my peace. When he isn't leading his company of horse, who we Parliamentarians have dubbed *the Fen Robbers*, Captain Mason is a rector who preaches for the royalist cause out of Ashleigh, a village located on the Leicestershire and Nottinghamshire border. By any standards, he is an insufferable man.

For reasons only known to him, he likes to visit me as often as he can, condemning and slandering my Puritan beliefs without hesitation.

Two days before Christmas proves to be no exception: today, if anything, he is more aggressive; more vocal; and more demeaning.

"You and your kind are heretics who bear false witness, Hacker," he declares to the guards and myself as he marches into my cell shortly after breakfast. "Know this, man, the Lord hates sinners like you. Mark my words he will soon strike you down, unless you are prepared to repent your evil ways. Do it, Hacker. Do it, now. Or face damnation, torment and Hades itself for an eternity."

The priest sits on my mattress. He is looking rather pleased with himself; dressed in a military uniform, and with a sword by his side. It is hardly the clothing of a man of God.

My silence only encourages him to say more.

"More of your kind will soon be meeting their Maker," he fires at me in a clipped voice, doing his best to provoke an outburst. "We are going on a raid. The governor is accompanying us. So too is our Lord, and He is going to lead us to scores of Roundheads and their spawn who are ripe for the slaughter. Who knows, we may even venture as far as Stathern."

I am unmoved. I have heard it all before.

This petulant provocation is a ritual I am forced to endure – and the rector seems to take perverse enjoyment from. Every day, since the start of my confinement, it has taken him ten minutes to realise I will not rise to the bait.

"Come on Hacker. Show me you really care about our Father," implores Mason. "Tell me of the God you serve; reveal His identity to me, sir. I would love to see if He resembles the God I love and know."

I shake my head.

"Sir, you must be conferring with the Devil, not our Father, for your words and provocations are not the teachings of any man of the true faith," I say, knowing my riposte will inflame him once again.

"Thomas, I say you are an imposter. A fraud. A malcontent. And when Parliament wins this war, and I survive the carnage you and your kind have inflicted on the common folk of England, I will make it my business to see you held to account for your evil and godless deeds."

My words strike home. They always do.

The rector's brow creases; he sucks in his cheeks; his lips turn blue as he fights to control his fiery temper. He fails.

"You will surely be sleeping in Hell soon, Hacker," he roars. "You, and other rebels like you, will soon know God's justice. You, who would rebel and seek to remove a King from his rightful throne, will find our Lord unwilling to forgive the crimes you, and your kind, have committed in His name. And I, for one, welcome the day when you receive your judgment.

"I may even seek leave to hang you myself. Now that truly would be a day for celebration."

The rector and I continue to play our harsh game until he has at last exhausted the list of insults he trades with me.

As the tirade reaches its conclusion, I realise he is more agitated than on any previous occasion. I doubt my words alone have soured his mood, for he hears my invective and counter insults every time he visits me.

No. Something else has to be the source of his discontent.

"You don't seem your usual friendly self today, rector," I say, changing the tone of the conversation. "Pray, tell me, is something troubling your soul?"

Marsh is caught off-guard.

"What do you mean, Hacker?" he enquires, wariness etched on his pockmarked face. "What are you saying? Say it plainly, braggart. Speak up. Speak up."

I say nothing more. Silence, with men like Marsh, is often a far more effective weapon than any musket, drake or pike.

"Talk, you dolt; explain yourself," he shouts. "What are you saying?"

I look at the enraged soldier cum minister, and I realise my question has struck a raw nerve. I don't know what troubles my enemy. But I rejoice at his obvious discomfort.

How I wish I could win minor victories like this every day.

It is Christmas Eve. My cell is cold and dank. Thankfully, my gaolers have given me a warm blanket, which keeps the excesses of winter at bay.

At breakfast, I become aware that the rector and the

governor left the stronghold at first light. I overhear my guards talking about a Royalist horse detachment of one hundred and forty men, led by governor Lucas, mounting raids on some of the surrounding villages in Rutlandshire.

All the targets are sympathetic towards Parliament, for the castle's pantries are almost bare and need replenishing. And, while this particular raid is carried out by Cavaliers, others will be also orchestrated in the name of Parliament against villages and towns loyal to the King. Today, homesteads and farms alike will be plundered, their provisions, livestock and valuables taken. For the victims, I fear Christmas will not bring a great deal of rejoicing and merriment: far from it.

With so many men absent, and only a skeleton force charged with defending the castle, a quietness and calm has descended. On days like these, when violence is unleashed onto folk living in the surrounding counties, I am left to my own devices. And, right now, I am increasingly aware of the inner peace that is comforting me. Only the Word, and prayer, has this kind of power. And one consequence of my imprisonment is I am fortunate enough to have the time to engage in both.

As dusk descends, and I am reading the powerful words of Paul in his letter to the Romans, there is uproar in the castle courtyard. Agitated shouts break the relative quiet. Restless and alarmed horses seek refuge. And a lone voice urges: "Call the surgeon. The governor is hurt. Make sure the gate is secured."

By dinnertime, some two hours later, the reasons for such angst are revealed to me.

I am taken to the large guardroom located on the castle's second floor. A soldier directs my escort to the adjacent gallery, where a group of men are standing around a table, listening intently to a man whose voice I recognise instantly as that of Lucas.

As soon as our footsteps on the paneled floor betray our presence, the governor says: "Thank you, gentlemen. That will be all for now. I would be grateful if you allowed me some time alone with Captain Hacker. Dismissed."

Gervase Lucas has a haunted look, the kind you get when you have looked death in the face – and survived.

I am not sure whether my chief gaoler has had a vision of Heaven or Hell. Either way, it matters little; Lucas is no longer the cheerful man he was just a few hours ago. And that is something to rejoice, for it means there is potentially could be some good news for Parliament around the corner.

The governor has a vivid slash across his face, and blood is weeping from the open wound. The castle's surgeon has tried his best to stem the flow of crimson; crude stitches pulled tight against the flesh are the telltale signs of his craft. But still the blood flows, much to the agitation of a clearly tired and irritated Gervase Lucas.

"I must look a bit of a mess?" he says as I ease myself on to a chair. "And I am sure you find my situation and discomfort somewhat amusing, eh, Hacker? So much for well-laid plans."

Despite his obvious pain, Lucas look as me, and a sardonic smile passes across his lips.

"Allow me to tell you what has happened this day: we have been bested in the field by a force roughly a third the size of our number," he confesses. "Your comrades fought hard. They were like men possessed. Captain Plunkett, one of my finest officers, and many of my men, lost their lives this day; and more than two score of our number have been taken prisoner, including one of my most senior officers.

"To my dying day, I will remember the place they call Strozby Heath! Our defeat was shameful. So enjoy the moment, Francis. For it would seem fortune is now smiling on you, Haselrig and Staveley."

The governor reaches for a cloth. He wipes the wound, wincing as the cotton catches against his raw, open flesh.

"Before I returned to the castle," he continues, "I sent a rider to my superiors in Newark urging for them to do whatever is necessary to secure the quick release of Lieutenant Colonel Sands. He is the officer your comrades have captured.

"In the last few minutes, a rider has returned ordering me to prepare for a prisoner exchange that will involve you and the other two; you are to be handed over in return for Colonel Sands and another of our faction, Sir Wingfield Beodenham. So it looks like you may all be home before the New Year."

I feel numb. This unexpected news has caught me completely by surprise. It is more than I could have hoped for.

"Thank you for telling me," I say, aware my voice is breaking. "Have you informed the others?"

Lucas shakes his head.

"No. No. You are the first to be told," he says. "Haselrig and Staveley will be informed within the hour. And then we will start to make the preparations. Now, I would be grateful if you took your leave of me, sir. As you can see, I have my own matters to attend to and I would be grateful for a few moments of privacy."

The governor rings a small bell to signal proceedings have come to a close. Two guards emerge to escort me back to my room. Lucas clicks his fingers and gestures with his right hand. I hear footsteps and then two hands grip my arms. Although there is no violence, I am acutely aware of the futility of resistance.

I allow my captors to direct my body through the labyrinth of tunnels and passages threaded through the castle until, eventually, I find myself outside my cell door.

Suddenly, as I sit at the chair that is the only piece of furniture in my cell, the magnitude of what Lucas has revealed hits me. And a combination of dread and elation grips my soul.

I will soon be free.

Although Parliament assents to a prisoner swap on Christmas Day, it takes a further three days for the two sides to conclude the necessary negotiations. Eventually, we receive the welcome news: all three of us are to be released on Monday the twenty-eighth day of December, in the early morning.

I realise my Father has been listening to my prayers all along. And I am reminded that His timescales are very different to my own!

At breakfast, Haselrig, Staveley and myself are reunited.

We have been accommodated in different parts of the castle and haven't seen each other since the end of November; a full month.

Our once well-groomed faces are now matted with

fresh, unkempt beards and, whereas my own growth is dark and lustrous, I can see that age and the ravages of prison life have been less kind to Haselrig and Staveley. Where there was a strong chin on both men only a few weeks ago, now grey beards, mottled with dark flecks of hair, disguise their features. This, I decide, ages them both by a good ten years. In Staveley's case, he is almost unrecognisable; such is his transformation. Nonetheless, both men are pleased to see me; and I, them.

We give each other a long, congratulatory hug, saying nothing for several minutes; just savouring the moment. After all, there will be plenty of time in the days ahead to visit the barber, enjoy a fulsome shave and restore our fine looks!

"Our release, how will it be done?" asks Haselrig, his nervousness audible for anyone within earshot to hear. "Is it a complicated process? Is there a risk it will not happen?"

Having carried out an exchange in East Yorkshire, shortly before the disastrous battle of Adwalton Moor, I have some knowledge of the process. So I quickly explain to the two men how matters will be conducted, and what we will all be required to do. When I finish, I see reassurance has returned to their faces and their bodies are visibly relaxed.

"Waiting for everything to happen can be the worst time of all," I say. "Minutes seem like hours. And you become convinced something will happen that will prevent the exchange taking place.

"Be assured both of you that everything will work out fine, you mark my words.

"Once both sides ratify the decision, things will proceed quickly. Providing we don't die of boredom first."

Haselrig laughs out aloud at my gentle attempt to inject some humour into the occasion, while Staveley briefly looks up and smiles. But soon we return to our private thoughts, and a state of anxiousness, as silence envelopes us while we await confirmation of our unexpected liberation.

It is eleven o'clock. We are left waiting for what feels like an age before the heavy bar that secures the guardhouse's double doors is lifted from its reinforced iron cradles.

"Time to go, gentleman," a corporal informs us. "Remember, our men will have no hesitation to hunt you down like the dogs you are should you again take up Parliament's colours. And, should you cross us once more, we will have no hesitation in finishing you, regardless of whether you are gentlemen, or not.

"But right now, in the true spirit of Christmas, please allow us to escort you to your new found freedom."

The soldier beckons us forward. Two lines of Cavaliers wait patiently, each man bearing a long barreled musket at his shoulder. We are to be accompanied by a drummer, who is busy preparing himself to lead the party.

The corporal directs us to form a third line in the centre, with just a few inches separating us from our guards. "For-ward march," he bellows. "To the gatehouse. And make haste."

We step into the winter sunshine. The brightness of the low, golden rays temporarily blinds me, and my fellow prisoners. We have become unaccustomed to the dazzling brightness of the outdoors. But, in truth, the cold air has never tasted so good.

I can feel my pulse quickening as we march closer to

the barred wooden gates. As we approach, the creaking groan of the main hinges signals movement, and soon the way is cleared for Haselrig, Staveley and myself to depart Belvoir Castle.

But before we can complete our repatriation, the corporal shouts: "Halt." As one, we come to a complete standstill. And we wait. Just wait. Five minutes pass. Then ten. Before long, the wintry air is attacking our fingers and toes, chilling them to the bone. And the pains I suffered at the hands of Holck start to return.

Fifteen minutes lapse. Then twenty.

My confidence and earlier good humour is starting to fade as pain and numbness invade my limbs.

The three of us begin to cast worried glances at each other. We are close to despair, when we suddenly hear the beat of hooves on the other side of the castle's walls. The ground shakes. I estimate there must be at least forty men and beasts less than two hundred yards away, shielded by the wall. Alas, we can see nothing.

Muffled, barked orders pierce the sterile air. Which side they are from, we do not know. Then the drum starts to beat: thud; thud; thud.

The rhythm is steady. Certain.

"You three, on your way," orders the corporal. "And let's not be seeing you again in these parts, there's good gentlemen."

The Cavaliers take a step to the side as we edge forward. Slowly. Tentatively. Soon we are clear of the gates and the walls, and we are into the extended grounds of the castle.

Coming the other way are two men. One looks every inch the soldier. Judging by his expensive clothing, the other is a civilian. We do not acknowledge each other as we pass. Instead, we focus on the kettledrum as it continues its monotonous beat. We carry on marching to its tune. Liberty. Freedom. Life. At this moment, these are our only considerations.

Slowly and surely we make our way along the track to the line of horsemen standing just a hundred yards away. Before I can recognise any of the faces awaiting us, a voice I have yearned to hear this past month, echoes across the plain.

"Francis. Francis. Is that you?"

It is the cry of my brother in arms and second-in-command, Abijah Swan.

"I see you. Merry Christmas, my friend," he roars, with heartening affection. "This is indeed a day of happiness and joy. Blessed be our Father. My prayers have been answered most truly."

We have been riding towards Stathern for almost half an hour and Abijah is struggling to hide his frustration. We are alone, only the chill of the bitter late December winds keeping us company.

The group that met us at Belvoir Castle dispersed at Long Clawson. Staveley, Haselrig and their entourages went in different directions, eager to return to their homesteads and families with all possible haste. A new year beckons and all of us wish to put the events of the last month as far behind us as possible.

Bucephalus rides like the thoroughbred he is: effortlessly, gracefully, powerfully. Never has he felt better and stronger. How I have missed my own equine king.

Yet, while I am overwhelmed to see Abijah, and I

hugged him dearly at the moment of our overdue recon-
ciliation, I find my tongue is quietened. My mind has a
hold on me. I cannot stop thinking about my torture, the
follies that put my family in peril – and what I perceive as
the recklessness of Pym. I sense the anger building within
me.

"Are you going to tell me anything?" asks my impatient friend and comrade. He is riding alongside me, gasp-
ing as the coldness catches at the back of his throat. "You
have hardly said a word since we left the castle."

I look across at the man I regard as a brother.

"My friend, do not be offended," I say. "The past
few weeks have taken their toll on me. That is all. In truth,
I am overcome with so many emotions. I was unprepared
for my release. I believed I would be held prisoner for a
considerable time. And as welcome as they are, the events
of this morning have come as a surprise.

"So forgive me if I say little at the moment. I have
much to contemplate. But be assured I will tell you everything as soon as I am able, when the time is right."

Swan knows me well enough to realise I mean what
I say. It is futile continuing with his line of questioning. He
shrugs his shoulders, nods his head in acknowledgement
and digs his heels into the side of his horse. I kick
Bucephalus. The reaction is instant. Our steeds pick up
speed and eat up the miles.

I have a lot to consider before I once again look into
the piercing eyes of my beautiful wife, and the peace of the
Rutlandshire countryside is a wonderful blessing as I contemplate our happy reunion.

My arrival at the Hall does not go unobserved.

As soon as the hooves of the horses can be heard echoing off the cobblestones of the courtyard, the shrieks and cries of my children drown out all other noise as they race from the house for our long overdue reunion.

"Father. Father," they cry in unison, as they throw themselves at my muddy and sodden torso.

Francis, my only son, leads the way. Tears are streaming from his eyes. Hot on his heels is Anne. She, too, cannot control her feelings, weeping openly as she embraces me. Then comes Isable, Elizabeth and Mary. None of my girls are wearing cloaks or scarves. If they are cold, they barely show it, such is their pure, unrestrained and unbridled joy.

Isabel follows behind. She glides towards me carrying Barbara who, at just two years of age, is the youngest of the brood.

Even though it is only a few short weeks since I last saw my family, much has happened. I am acutely aware of some subtle changes to their appearance. Francis looks as though he is grown broader and taller since he became the temporary head of the Hacker household. And my daughters look more radiant than I ever remember; their hair longer. How I have missed them all. How I have anticipated this moment: my homecoming.

Isabel moves closer. Even though she tries, my wife's near perfect smile can't hide the emotion she is feeling.

"My darling, it is so good to see you," she says, "The children have missed you so much. As have I. You must never allow us to be parted like this ever again."

With that, Isabel can no longer retain her composure. She starts sobbing uncontrollably.

"I feared the worst," she admits between deep,

ragged breaths. "We have been lost without you."

The pain I feel is unbearable.

"There isn't an hour that has gone by without you in my thoughts," I confess, my own emotions close to breaking through the practiced gentlemanly veneer my Father spent years instilling in me. "I have done much soul-searching these past few weeks. And I have not liked some of the things I have found out about myself. My love, I promise I will be a better husband and father. You all deserve this. And I will do all everything in my power to make it happen."

Suddenly a brilliant fork of lightning lights up the grey skies of the afternoon. A clap of thunder shakes the earth under our feet. We know rain is not far behind.

"Children," I say, "I think it's time for us to celebrate the birth of Christ Jesus. I appreciate I am a few days late. But I am home now. So let's go inside, eat some of the wonderful food Else has prepared, and enjoy the company of one another. What say you?"

The roar of approval tells me all I need to know.

John Pym, Parliamentarian
Known as "King Pym", John Pym was responsible, more
than most, for holding King Charles the First to account

THIRTEEN

I AM AT HOME, WITH all the comforts any man could care for. Isabel and the children have smothered me with love and affection. Much more than I deserve; my imprisonment was theirs also.

The warmth of my homecoming has been overwhelming. It has left me light-headed, happy; yet feeling wretched also.

Days become weeks and, before I know it, January has passed me by and we are midway through the bleak month of February. It is one of the coldest and darkest I can remember.

There has been little campaigning to keep myself, and the militia, busy – a thick settling of snow is keeping everyone locked indoors at Stathern and in the surrounding villages.

While I grow fat on inactivity and indulging in too much of Else's magnificent food, there is news aplenty to keep me occupied.

Since my release, I have received regular dispatches

from my superiors, informing me of the important developments in the county and wider country. From these, I learn that John Pym has finally succumbed to the cancer that has been eating away at him for the last year.

I am one of the last to learn of Pym's sad passing, for he died at the beginning of December, while I was I held captive by the Royalists. If he knew about the demise of the man we call "King Pym", Gervase Lucas chose not to tell me.

Pym's death was peaceful, and I am sure he is content in his new home, a place where he will reside for all eternity. But his loss is another grievous blow to Parliament, for he was a man who put his country first in all he did, fighting the rule of Charles for as long as any of us can remember.

The word 'great' is often attributed incorrectly to so many people. But John Pym was most certainly a great man and leader.

I consider it a privilege to have known him.

Before his demise, he reached out to the Scots, securing their support in our fight with the King. Sadly he will now never see the Scottish army march south and join cause with us as an ally. Yet, just a few short weeks after his funeral at Westminster Abbey, that is exactly what has happened: for in January, the twenty thousand men we were promised crossed the border determined to help Fairfax, Essex and Cromwell – who has been promoted to the rank of Lieutenant-General of Horse – reclaim the north and put the tyrant in his place.

As I digest this news, I thank my Maker once again for the grace he has bestowed on me to be associated with men of such caliber, integrity and faith.

Active campaigning with our Scottish allies will start when the abysmal weather, that has covered our streets and fields with snow and ice, improves. This cannot come soon enough. I have my work with the Leicester Committee to complete during the next few weeks, as the need to plug the gaps in the city's defences becomes increasingly necessary. We must make good use of the time we have been afforded while the inclement weather keeps our foe at bay, preoccupied elsewhere.

I feel refreshed, having enjoyed several weeks of recuperation with Isabel and the children.

My hands and feet have healed, albeit it will take several more months for my nails to grow back and disguise the ravages of torture. But the pain has gone and I am fully mobile once again, which is good news, as Francis and the girls have made up for lost time, encouraging me to play and indulge them with affection and attention every day since my release. This has given me the opportunity to start to make amends, and to try and make up for the many months my Militia duties have deprived my children of their father.

My one pressing concern is my friendship with Abijah.

My closest friend and comrade has become something of a stranger. We talked animatedly upon my release. Indeed, after I had become accustomed to being a free man once again, I dare say it was difficult for Abijah to stop me yapping, such was my keenness to share my fears, anxieties and hopes.

Yet for the last four weeks we have spoken little. And I know not why?

Something is clearly troubling my friend. But he

refuses to speak openly. When we are together, we talk constructively about military affairs and the welfare of the men of the Militia. And that is all. When I ask Abijah to share his innermost thoughts with me, he changes the subject and seeks to divert the conversation to something less intimate and revealing.

At first, I don't notice. I am too preoccupied with my own situation and affairs. But as the days pass, and this occurs more frequently, it dawns on me that a barrier now exists between us, one I am eager to break down, albeit, I freely confess, I do not know ho to do so..

"Has all been well with Abijah during my absence?" I ask Isabel just before we go to Church. "I sense he is troubled. And, for the last few weeks, he has been unwilling to talk to me about anything other than the militia."

My wife eyes me calmly.

"I can't say I have noticed anything out of the ordinary," she replies. "He has been everything you would have wanted him to be. He did everything he could to reassure the children and myself when you were imprisoned at the castle. This was a great source of comfort to us all. And he more than filled the void you left with the Militia. Many men commented so. And I know you wish to see Abijah progress and do not feel threatened by his relationship with the soldiery.

"So, my dear, I am afraid I can offer you nothing to shed light on your concerns. I truly have noticed… nothing… out of the ordinary…"

A deep furrow appears across Isabel's brow. Her voice trails off. I know the telltale signs. She is trying to recall something.

"What is it?" I ask. "Whatever is it, please tell me, my dear."

My wife recovers her composure. When she speaks again, she does so slowly.

"When you were captured, Abijah took it very badly," she says. "During the first few days, he was inconsolable. And he was as drunk as a Lord on at least a couple of occasions when he visited Nottingham. Now, remember we are talking about Abijah Swan. When was the last time you saw him drunk?

"Peter Harrington told me he was in a sorry state when he and Abijah visited Colonel Hutchinson at the end of November. Apparently Abijah was found drowning his sorrows at The Bell Inn, and received some very harsh words from the Colonel's wife. I never thought to speak to him about it because I just thought it was his way of coping with your imprisonment.

"I am sure there really is nothing to worry about. It's what you men do, particularly when something goes wrong and you are worried or grieving. But one thing I do recall Harrington mentioning was the description of some of the men Abijah was seen drinking with."

I look up, the remnants of my breakfast assuming secondary importance. My wife has my fullest attention.

"Don't look so startled," she says reassuringly. "Harrington simply said he didn't like the look of them. Nothing more. Nothing less. The men left an impression. That's all. What surprised Harrington, as I recall, is he got the distinct impression Abijah knew the men, yet they were some of the roughest looking rogues he had ever seen. They certainly weren't part of the Militia."

Isabel shrugs her shoulders after recounting the

events of more than a month ago.

"Anyway, there is no point worrying about things," she adds. "Abijah is probably experiencing what we all go through – a bit of the black dog. I suffer it, as do you. So let the man be and give him some space. He will be the Abijah we all know and love soon enough.

"Now, get your jacket on and make sure your boots are polished. We need to leave in a few minutes. William Norwich and Saint Guthlacs beckon. And I know how much you have eagerly awaited the chance to listen to one of his sermons once again."

I smile at my wife and nod my head appreciatively.

I get to my feet. For once, mention of the name of Norwich is unimportant to me, for my thoughts are all about the welfare of my troubled friend, so I reconcile myself to speak to Harrington as soon as possible.

It is Thursday the eighteenth day of February, in the new year of our Lord, 1644, and there is excitement in the courtyard at the most ungodly of hours. It is dark; the bedroom is dimly lit by the last remnants of a candle that has been burning for hours. Outside I can hear excited voices. And one of them I clearly recognise.

I find my robe and boots, urge a sleepy, rising Isabel to return to her slumber, and take what remains of the candle as I head down the stairwell and out of the Hall.

The cold air is bitter, it envelops my body within seconds. It can be no later than four o'clock in the morning, for Titus, the Hall's rather splendid Suffolk cockerel, is busy pacing the grounds, pecking at the snow encrusted earth in the forlorn hope of finding a tasty morsel. He hasn't yet chosen to burst into song. And everything he does is captured in the bright light of the moon, as it is suspended high in the winter sky.

"Is that you, Francis?" asks Rowland, as he strides down the path towards warmth and a comfy chair. "My goodness, it is. Brother, it is good to see you. I didn't know if you would be at home, or awake at this hour.

"I am returning to Nottingham and need to talk to you. So I come more in hope than expectation. And I figured you wouldn't want me to come in broad daylight, for all to see. So here I am; a man of the night!"

I nod. A welcoming smile flickers across my face.

We may be at war; my brother, an avowed enemy; a man I once swore I would pistol-whip because of his allegiance to the tyrant King and a stubborn refusal to turn rebel with me; but, at this moment, I am aware of just how much I miss Rowland's company and charm. It is a joy to see my brother once again, no matter the hour.

"I have important things to tell you, matters of most interest and severity," continues Rowland. "If you are prepared to offer me some modest hospitality, I will reveal to you as much as I know."

We embrace. The smell of horse sweat is overwhelming and I am acutely aware of my brother's disheveled appearance. Nonetheless, it is good to see him sounding so well, seemingly his old self once more, even though his physical appearance is in contrast to his joyful mood.

"Come inside, you rogue," I urge. "But you need to be quiet. We don't want the whole house waking, and everyone knowing my Cavalier sibling, the man who quite recently was aiding my gaolers at Belvoir Castle, making an impromptu, early morning visit. And we want Isabel stirring least of all; for my wife is in sore need of her sleep.

"So inside, if you please, my welcome guest; I think you know your way to the scullery."

When I last saw Rowland, he was angry and stricken with grief, weighed down with guilt.

The loss of Thomas had hit him hard.

On that grievous day in May, my brother had witnessed everything, but he was powerless to prevent my militiamen from cutting down Thomas on the killing fields of Nottinghamshire. The wounds he suffered were inconsequential compared to the loss of a sibling. Wounds heal. So often, grief does not.

Gervase Lucas kept us apart during my recent confinement at Belvoir Castle. Although my brother is a devout supporter of the King, quite rightly the governor did not wish to put his loyalties to the test. Therefore, remarkably, I am delighted to see the man sitting before me this morning so full of life, in stark contrast to our last meeting. Once again there is a glint of mischief in those clear blue eyes. In so many ways he is restored, ably assisted, I may add, by the restorative powers of a hearty portion of one of Else's most recent delights: rabbit pie!

"So, brother, what news have you, and, tell me, what is so important it requires you to visit us at this early hour?" I enquire in a friendly, inquisitive voice. "While I know you to be a man who will travel far and wide for a tasty morsel, or to cast your eyes on a fair maiden, I cannot believe you have come here just to benefit from our food?"

In an instant, Rowland's demeanour changes, the smile replaced by a haunted, painful look. He surveys the room, sees the door ajar, and rises. My brother takes five long strides, looks into the corridor and, satisfied nobody is skulking in the shadows, gently closes the solid block of oak.

Upon returning to the table, he says: "I believe I have nine lives, brother, for yesterday I escaped with my life, while good men all around me where either captured or perished."

I put down the glass I am holding. My brother has my fullest attention.

"I was leading a sally across the Trent into Nottingham," he says. "We were disguised, wearing the clothes of women, just as we have been many times previously. But our plans would appear to have been betrayed, for your friend, Colonel Hutchinson, was waiting for us with a large detachment of troops.

"As soon as I saw them, I knew we stood no chance. So we turned on our heels and ran for our lives. Hutchinson and his troops chased us back to the Trent, staying on our tail as, one by one, my men were cut down all around me.

"I expected a musket shot, or sword cut, in my back at any time. So, with nowhere to go and naught to lose, I threw myself into the river, as did what remained of my men. I know not what happened next. But I do know I was the only man to make it back to the garrison alive. The others are all lost, or captured.

"My brother, I feel a terrible weight of guilt, much worse than the physical pain of any torture that could afflict my body."

I can say nothing to dilute Rowland's pain. All I can do is nod in affirmation. Raw emotion has its grip on me.

Even though I am bitterly opposed to the ways of the King, and the allegiances of men like my brother, I cannot help but feel for his suffering, and that of any man, woman or child when they experience such loss.

"That's quite a day," I say. "Thank God you are alive."

"Fear not, brother, Hutchinson and his men – and even you, the infamous Captain Francis Hacker – will have to do better than that before you best me," quips Rowland, excitement and mischief still alive in his eyes. "But rest assured, I have not come to Stathern for your pity, brother. This tragedy is of my own making. And I will find a way of dealing with it and healing my own conscience.

"No, I am here to beg you to heed my warning: I fear you have a spy in your midst."

I am caught off-guard. My knuckles whiten as I grip the armchair tightly.

"Go on," I beckon. My throat is dry. "Pray, tell me more. And leave nothing spared."

Rowland pats his damp brow with a stained handkerchief.

"For the last few weeks, your capture, and those of Haselrig and Staveley, have been the talk of our garrisons at Ashby, Newark, Trent Bridge and Belvoir Castle," he continues.

"News travels fast in these times; I was aware of your imprisonment within hours of the raid on Melton Mowbray taking place. Indeed, the talk at the castle long before the governor set out on the raid, was that you were his prime target.

"Throughout your imprisonment, I remained informed about your welfare on a near daily basis, as did all the officers. There is nothing untoward, or unnatural, about any of that. You are, after all, a feared and despised enemy."

The last sentence forces Rowland to look at me directly. The smile has gone.

"I was privy to a conversation a week ago that has been worrying me sorely," he adds. "I was in the company of Gervase Lucas and a handful of other commanders, one a trusted confidante of Prince Maurice. During our meeting your name was specifically mentioned. Naturally, I said nothing, but listened intently.

"I discovered you, Isabel and the children have been under constant observation since the summer. Not only have you been under scrutiny, but my commanders seem to know where you have been – and where you are planning to be – and we are using this information to actively plan our own activities in the area."

I relax and offer a knowing smile.

"Brother, I thank you for your concern," I say as calmly as I can. "But I believe the danger has now passed. I am aware I have been watched for a considerable period. But that scrutiny is now at and end. And if you give me your solemn word, I will tell you why."

Rowland nods his head, urging me to continue. So I tell him all about my failed bid to woo Prince Maurice, and persuade him to become England's new King, at the behest of Pym; I tell him of the temptation of Lady Lucy; and I show him my mutilated hands and feet, sparing no detail of the butchery inflicted on me by Holck.

"My God, Francis, what have you been involved in?" gasps an incredulous Rowland. "This is not work for men like you and me. Why you? Why expose yourself to such risk, when you are no spy, no master of this kind of deceit? You are a simple, brave soldier. It simply doesn't make sense."

Rowland mops his brow once again. His face is a picture of concern.

"You are wrong," I say. "It makes perfect sense. For if you are Pym, and you want to achieve something without leaving a trail, you need to find a willing fool, who will put personal considerations to one side, because he is committed to doing the greater good. I am that man; that fool.

"I knew what I was entering into. And I knew the chances of success were remote. But I am fighting this war, on the side of Parliament, because I believe our cause is just and we are committed to doing the right things.

"It was only after I had agreed to embark on this futile venture that I really started to think about the consequences, particularly if things went wrong. I confess, I initially saw myself as some kind of hero figure. I was flattered to be approached by men of such stature. But that soon changed. At that moment, I realised just how dispensable, how vulnerable I am. If something went wrong, and I was exposed, or killed, it dawned on me how difficult it would be for anything to be traced back to my masters. And so it has proven. Lady Lucy will have tidied any trails I have left, and she will have done a good job. For she certainly has no desire to be exposed for what she is.

"Thankfully, I met Holck only once, and this is what he did to me."

I shiver as I show Rowland the livid scars on my hands. He struggles to keep a neutral expression.

"I have thought many times how naïve I have been – and how my actions have exposed my family," I continue. "But the Prince assured me at the castle that there is no enmity on his part, and that my family is no longer under threat. And there have been many occasions when, if we were still in danger, Maurice could have easily exacted his revenge. But we are still here. Unmolested. Alive. And no strangers have been seen in these parts. I have made many enquiries. So, be assured, I am now resting a lot easier."

My brother sips some water. He looks out of the scullery window directly at Titus, who is standing on a nearby sill and looking resplendent, proudly displaying his bright silver and red plumage as if it is a close-fitting breastplate. The cockerel has already started the recital of his daily verses as daylight starts to knife its way through the gloom. And as more strangled crowing pierces the peace of the early morning, Rowland turns back towards the table and I see agitation continues to be written all over his face.

"I am not convinced," he announces, banging the table with the flat of his hand. "You were not at this meeting. I was. And I came away believing you are still being observed and are facing a very real danger.

"Of course, there is a chance I am wrong. But I rarely am; and I am sure you are being deceived. Just because Prince Maurice says everything has ended, and you are not in danger any more, doesn't make it true.

"From what I know of the man, he cannot be trusted. He, like his elder brother, is a formidable fighter and tactician. But he is a Prince; he is no allegiance to this country; lying is second nature to him. So, my dear brother, I urge you to take precautions. For your sake, and the sake of Isabel and the children."

Just before dawn, I wave my hand in the numbing air in farewell as Rowland rides out of Stathern.

I have bid my brother a safe journey to the small garrison he now commands on the outskirts of Nottingham, where he is committed to provoking Colonel Hutchinson and his men. It has been more than six months since I last saw him; I wonder how long it will be until we are reunited once again?

I would not admit it at the time, but Rowland's talk of spies has unnerved me.

I had thought I would be able to look forward again now I am back at Stathern, occupying my time with the day-to-day hazards of mere soldiering! But, I have realised, once you become entwined in plots and intrigues of the state, such as I have, it is an impossible task to extract oneself completely from the clutches of intrigue.

A sense of dread threatens to overwhelm me. So I return to the Hall and quickly climb the stairs to the bedroom, where I find Isabel stirring.

"Where have you been?" she asks, barely coherent. "I woke up to find you gone. I heard voices in the yard, and the hooves of at least one horse, and an almighty commotion. Francis, please tell me what is going on?"

"My love, go back to sleep," I implore. "There is nothing to concern you. An over zealous messenger came to the house at a godforsaken hour. That is all. It was a dispatch from the Committee about my work in Leicester. The message could, and should, have been delivered later this morning. And I told the man so in no uncertain manner.

"The commotion you heard was him leaving to go back to the city, with a flea ringing in his ear. So go back to sleep my dearest. You need all the energy you can get to look after those children of ours who are going to be cooped up in the house all day."

Isabel yawns and turns over. She is content. My well-intentioned falsehoods are all she needs to seek a welcome return to her dreams.

But I will not get any more rest this morn.

After Rowland's visit, I have much to ponder; not least, whether I truly am the gullible and reckless fool my brother clearly thinks I am.

FOURTEEN

FOR THE NEXT FEW DAYS I am lost in my own world, trying to link things together. I see conspiracies around every corner and I am determined to leave no stone unturned in my quest to identify the potential informant: a traitor in our midst.

One minute, I perceive everyone I know is a spy; the next, they are all innocents. It is not long before realise I am torturing myself; it is beyond my capability to solve the impossible conundrum I have set.

Yet I cannot stop thinking about what Rowland has said. Only a dullard would fail to heed his warning.

My mood is sour. I am poor company. Such is my preoccupation that I leave all Militia matters to Swan and the other officers. Understandably Isabel, the children and most of the servants choose to stay away from me. My melancholy moods have most certainly returned and I am seemingly powerless to shake them off.

But rid myself I must come Wednesday morning, some six days after Rowland's surprise visit. On this day,

Stephen Harrington, Peter's son and one of the most trusted and able members of the Militia, announces his arrival at the Hall by crashing through the front door; the entire house shakes as a result of the commotion.

"What in God's name is that?" shrieks Else from the kitchen. "Somebody. Quick. See what is happening."

I am upstairs getting dressed. Isabel is at the rear of the Hall, keeping three of our girls company. As soon as I hear the noise and the alarm in Else's voice, I reach for my sword and dash down the stairs. There, in front of me, is the prostrate, curled body of Stephen. He is lying face down on the slate floor. His fists are clenched. They are beating the stones rhythmically. And he is sobbing with an intensity I have never heard emitted from another living soul.

"Stephen," I shout. "Stephen. Whatever has happened? What is wrong?"

The response is incomprehensible. His sobs echo in the hallway. I try again.

"Stephen. Why are you here? What is the problem? Tell me. Let me help?"

My pleas seem to break the spell the young man is under. He lifts his head off the cold floor and looks directly at me through bloodshot eyes.

"They're dead. They're dead," he spits out. "There has been a terrible fire. They are both dead."

I don't need to ask. Immediately, I know whom he is referring to.

"God on high," I say. "Please tell me what has happened to your Mother and Father? What of Marjorie and Peter? Tell me of the tragedy that has befallen you?"

Peter and Marjorie Harrington have been loyal to my family since before I was born.

Like my ancestors, who arrived in Leicestershire shortly after the reign of Queen Elizabeth ceased, the Harringtons' moved north from Somerset. Their home was Taunton, "a place that makes the finest cider in all of England," they have often said to me. On many occasions, Peter has promised to bring me bottles of the "potent stuff" upon his return from visiting his distant cousins. But being the devoted people they are, they have never returned to their hometown in all the years I have known them. And now, with tragedy now gripping Stathern, it seems their pledge will never be fulfilled.

The couple live in a remote cottage owned by the estate and located on the outskirts of the village. They are less than a mile away from the Hall. I have offered them better, more spacious accommodation on many occasions. To the best of my knowledge, my father also tried to get them to accept a house more befitting their status. But they always politely declined, stating they like the solitude of the property they have been occupying for more than three decades.

"We love the space and the beautiful countryside. It's God's country," Marjorie would say whenever I broached the subject of her and Peter moving. "It's just the cattle and us. And we like it this way. We have so many memories associated with the house. Our son was born and raised in this place. We have been so happy here. How can we ever leave such a wonderful home?"

Alas, it seems their wish has been granted. Now, if Stephen's fears are confirmed, they never will.

I manage to help Stephen to his feet. He is weak and

shaking. We reach the kitchen, where a clearly shocked Else has already cleared the table. Her face is ashen. I usher his despairing body into a chair and clasp one of his hands.

"Get me some water," I demand, a bit too impatiently. "Stephen. Stephen. Drink some of this. And then, in your own good time, tell me everything you know."

He reaches for the glass and gulps down the water. He coughs violently as the liquid cleanses his airways. His lungs must be full of wood smoke as he reeks of fire and destruction. Else pours more liquid from the jug. But Stephen pushes the glass away. He looks straight at me, his distorted face haunted, his eyes full of the horror he has witnessed.

"I couldn't do anything to help, Captain," he says, his blank eyes looking beyond me into nothingness. "The heat was too severe. By the time I reached the house, it was ablaze. The flames were everywhere and I couldn't reach their quarters at the back of the house. The heat beat me back every time I tried. I kept calling their names, time and again. But I couldn't hear a reply above the crackling and splintering of the wood. The fire had taken a firm hold and I was powerless.

"I don't know how long the house was ablaze before I saw the smoke. But nobody could have survived that carnage. Within a few seconds of my arrival, the roof and walls collapsed. Nothing could have lived through that inferno."

I am speechless. I look down and focus on my hands. They are shaking. I count the ageing scabs on my fingers as I attempt to find the words that will comfort this distraught and grieving young man; a man I trust and respect. And now, it seems, an orphan. My effort proves meaningless. For the words I need most at this desperate time desert me.

"Stephen, I am so sorry," is all I can say before my own sorrow makes me incoherent.

Abijah, myself and a group of farm workers from the Hall take less than ten minutes for to saddle our horses and ride to the cottage. I leave Bucephalus in the stables, preferring one of my young cobs for the short, painful journey.

The wisps of smoke are visible as soon as we pass Saint Guthlacs and start the climb up Mill Hill. Tentacles of dark grey hang in the air, clear for all to see, and the acrid smell of death is everywhere. An inquisitive Buzzard hangs low in the sky seeking out opportunity amid the chaos. There can be no doubt to anyone present that tragedy has set upon Stathern this day.

I have left Stephen with Isabel and Else. There is little they can do for him, other than offer feeble words and an uncomfortable shoulder to cry on. As for myself, I offer prayers to my Maker. For the Lord is the only comforter available to a man in these appalling circumstances.

"Jesus Christ, they will surely have stood no chance at all," says Bartholomew, one of my estate workers, upon seeing the debris and carnage. "They will be with our Father now, that is for sure. May God preserve their eternal souls."

I look across at the wiry youth.

"There is no need to blaspheme, Bartholomew," I say, aware of the hostility and sharpness in my voice. "This may be a dreadful day, and I truly appreciate you are as shocked as I am, but I must ask you to restrain yourself."

His apology is instant and heartfelt.

"I meant no insult, Captain," he says. "I just cannot comprehend what my eyes are seeing."

We canter to the brow of the hill. Before us are the smoldering ruins of Orchard Cottage, home of Peter and Marjorie Harrington. What was once a colourful, happy and tranquil home, covered in ivy and roses, is now unrecognisable; it has been transformed into a scene of ruin and pain.

As Stephen reported, the roof of the house has totally collapsed, as have two of its outer walls. Timbers are strewn across the ground. And the last remnants of the blaze continue to rage where the living quarters once stood.

It tells me all I need to know when I see the solitary Buzzard; it is the only sign of life we can see.

"Let's get to work," I say through gritted teeth. "Abijah, take Bartholomew and one other man, and draw water from the well, so we can extinguish what's left of the fire. And let's be quick about it. For all we know, there may, by some miracle, still be someone alive in there.

"Edgerton. James. You two come with me. We need to find Peter and Marjorie as quickly as we can. We also need to discover how this happened and recover as much as we can from the main building. Tread carefully – and listen out for any sound that could be a sign of life."

After less than ten minutes, all hope is extinguished.

We find the bodies, or something akin to the remains of two human beings. The combined efforts of Abijah and his small band of helpers have doused the main rump of the fire. And as the flames die, we discover a gnarled, shriveled, blackened mass of blood and gore towards the rear of the house. It is hard to believe the remains are those of our friend, a man of such vitality and zest.

The discovery proves too much for James, who spasms involuntarily and pukes the contents of his stomach onto the blistering timbers.

The youngster, who is barely a man, wipes his mouth before calling over.

"Captain Hacker, I am sure it's Peter," he says, his voice unsteady. "And I think I can see Marjorie in the rubble, just beyond."

I make my way over thatch and bricks, to an area still aglow, where the fire appears to have been at its fiercest. Here I see what is left of Peter Harrington, a man I have known all my life.

He appears to be in prayer, his hands held together, stretched out in front of him. But peace is not etched on what remains of his face; it is agony, horror and fear. I cannot begin to imagine the suffering he must have endured in his last few minutes of life, for Peter was no devout follower of Christ, with nothing to hold onto in his final moments. There will be no eternal life for him.

I start to weep uncontrollably. And I feel the bitter taste of bile rising from the pit of my stomach.

"It is definitely Marjorie lying next to him," states James. "I can clearly see her. She is not burned as badly as Peter. It looks as though the roof and walls have done for her, for she has bled heavily."

I raise my head. Anger and rage consume me. "This is a terrible day," I shout to whoever is listening. "They did not deserve this."

As I prepare to unleash another outburst, a shadow looms over me. It is Edgerton. His face is hardened.

"Come with me, Captain," he beckons, pointing in the direction of the far side of the house. "You need to see what we have found."

Edgerton has been working on the other side of the building, where the door to the cottage is located.

Incredibly, much of the wooden structure and wall remain largely intact, albeit they are badly scorched.

Abijah and the others have congregated to one side. They are staring. Nobody is speaking. Their mood is one of anger and despair. They take a pace backwards when they see me approaching.

"There," says Edgerton, pointing to the lock in the blackened, fire-ravaged door. "Look, Captain. The key is on the outside. And the door has been locked. You can see the locking bar is clearly in place. This cannot be right."

I scrutinise the scene. Just as Edgerton has stated, what remains of the key is clearly protruding from the wrong side of the door.

"And there is more," continues the farm worker. "I have been able to see the door to the chamber inside. And it's the same thing: that key is also on the outside of the door. Someone…"

"Yes. Yes. I comprehend what you are telling me," I say, realising the enormity of the discovery and trying to suppress my rage as it rises once again. "I understand the implications of what we can all see."

I swallow hard before continuing.

"Peter and Marjorie have been locked in the house," I say. "This is beginning to look as if this tragedy is no mere accident."

By the time I return to the Hall, the physician has attended to Stephen. He is sound asleep. Some balms have allowed him to claim a semblance of peace after the horrors of this tragic day. I seek out Isabel and find her bereft, her emotions seesawing from one extreme to another, unable to comprehend the scale of destruction and loss.

"Even when we are forced endure barbarous acts as part of war, I have to wonder what kind of monster would do such a thing to two gentle souls?" she asks, her deflation all too evident when I tell her about our discovery.

"They were good people, Francis, people who were liked by everyone. In all the years I have known them, I have never heard them say a bad thing about anyone, even then they were provoked. They were kindly people. So who would commit such an evil act?"

My wife can say no more. Tears overwhelm her delicate features as she digests the news that Peter and Marjorie were bound and gagged before they died.

Examination of the two bodies has confirmed their hands and feet had been tied – and traces of wool were found in both mouths. I have no doubts in my own mind: there was a clear intention to silence them and a hope the fire would destroy all evidence of the murders. Their killer was certainly leaving nothing to chance.

But not everything went according to plan, for the fire died out too early, leaving traces of the foul play.

As I continue to think about the gruesome deaths, I suddenly have a vision of a man dressed in black, who I had the misfortune of meeting quite recently. And a cold shiver runs down my spine. For I, too, was bound while held prisoner.

An inner sixth sense is linking my torture and these

two brutal deaths together. I picture Marjorie and Peter in their death throes, and I exhale loudly. But before I can think any more about the matter, my wife's voice rings in my ears. There is nothing I can do. I will have to collect my thoughts later in the day.

"They were two innocents," continues Isabel, her voice as ragged as I have ever heard it. "They didn't have an enemy in the world, and they certainly didn't own enough for someone to want to kill them for their possessions. I don't understand. Their deaths simply don't make sense."

I agree with my wife's assessment.

On the surface, these vile murders seem senseless and without motive. Yet I cannot stop thinking about everything that has happened to me these past few months. I think about Rowland's warning and the understated threats of Lady Lucy Hay; I recall the merciless cruelty in Holck's dark eyes; and I start to wonder if, somehow, my double life as an agent for Pym and Parliament may be linked to this heinous crime.

It is certainly a consideration, a plausible reason for this wicked act. And it's something I cannot ignore. Yet the more I think about it, the more I feel the grip of fear on my throat. I am scared at what I may find. For, if my instincts are proven right, I could be plunged into a pursuit where the dangers are the greatest I have ever faced.

The night is not being kind to me. I cannot sleep.

Every time I close my eyes, I see Peter's disfigured and tortured face before me. Pleading. Begging. Life extinguished. Ravaged by the flames. Grotesque. So, just before midnight, I leave Isabel and make my way to Abijah's house in the woods. I need to talk to my comrade.

A proper conversation is long overdue, for it has been several weeks since we last had an opportunity to talk openly about anything of importance.

As I approach his modest cottage, I see light in an upstairs window. The omens are good: he is awake. I pick up some small stones and throw them gently at the glass of the window I know to be his bedchamber.

Within seconds, Abijah's familiar face appears and the window opens. He peers into the gloom. For good measure, Prudence, his ever-faithful hound, barks.

"Who is out there?" he says. "Show yourself."

"Abijah, it is me, Francis," I reply. "I need to speak to you, my friend. The events of today are troubling me greatly. I will not take up much of your time, but talk to you I must. I know it is late, but please spare me some of your time. There are things of importance I need to discuss."

The house is cold. The air inside is stale. Ashes litter the fireplace and the candles have burned down to the bare wick. And Abijah's mood mirrors my own: it is as black as the night.

"I cannot stop thinking about Peter and Marjorie. The brutality of their deaths has been in my thoughts since we returned from the house," he says to me, his left hand rubbing his eyes as he pours me a glass of ruby red Port. "I keep seeing their faces. In their final minutes, they suffered most grievously."

I look at my friend. He is someone who rarely despairs. Yet this night, he is at his lowest ebb. And I begin to doubt whether I will be able to raise his spirits, or my own for that matter. But try I must.

"When I saw my brother last, he told me there was a Royalist spy in our midst; here at Stathern," I reveal while tenderly taking a sip from my glass. "I have meant to look into the claim these past few days, but circumstances have prevented me from doing so. And now this has happened.

"What if Rowland is right, and we have been infiltrated? And what if my procrastination has directly led to Peter and Marjorie being slain? I do not know why this would be the case. But the more I think about things, the more I am forced to consider they may have known something, and that knowledge may have got them killed."

Abijah drops his gaze to the floor. Tears pirouette down his cheeks.

"Peter was like a father to me," he says. "For as long as I care to remember, he encouraged me. He helped me. And, when I needed to hear it, he chastised me. He was a good man. A man I loved dearly. And if he was murdered, as you suspect, I will do all in my power to track down the killer. As God is my witness."

We stand and embrace. Raw emotion gets the better of Abijah and myself. Prudence watches from her place by the hearth, recognising it is not the time for her to be seeking her Master's attention.

Since the outbreak of war, we have endured enough pain to last a lifetime, yet I am sure we will be forced to suffer much more than this before this damned conflict with our King is won.

"We must not tell anyone about Rowland's claims," I say eventually. "For the time being, we keep this between us. Nobody else. Stealth must be our friend in the days ahead. If a spy is among us, he will make a mistake. When he does, we will have him. And then we will seek justice and retribution."

"So be it," says Abijah, laying his hand on my shoulder. "Stealth and God's grace will win the day. We will avenge the slaying of Peter and Marjorie; I swear it so."

Unfortunately I am forced to put all personal thoughts of leading the efforts to find Peter and Marjorie Harrington's killers on hold, when I receive an unexpected summons from Lieutenant-General Cromwell, ordering me to attend an urgent meeting at his farm in Ely.

According to the letter, which arrived at eleven o'clock in the morning on Thursday the twenty-fifth day of February, courtesy of an Eastern Association messenger, I have less than three days to make the journey to Cambridgeshire.

In real terms, this means there will be little time to make my preparations, brief Abijah and the other officers about the Militia's immediate priorities in my absence, and say my goodbyes to Isabel and the children.

And it will be a ride hard all the way to Cambridgeshire, of that I am sure.

Cromwell's letter, dated six days earlier, is cordial and to the point. It states:

"My dearest Francis,

"Solid progress is being made to bring the King and his supporters to heel. I wish to appraise you and other handpicked officers of such developments.

"Please join me at in Ely on the afternoon of the twenty-eighth of February. It will be good to see you again, renew our friendship and plan for victory.

"May our Lord God continue to protect everything you do in the name of Parliament and Christ Jesus.
"Your ever-faithful servant, Oliver."

I rub my forehead, grinding my mutilated fingers into my brow. I wince as a sharp pain cuts into my nailless stumps and I am reminded of my recent incarceration once again. As much as I admire and respect Oliver, and will follow him loyally and steadfastly without hesitation on the field of battle, I have to confess to dreading receipt of any orders the Lieutenant-General sends me. For recent experiences have taught me they rarely are they what they seem.

And I have less than five days to get my affairs in order and ride East.

A knock on the door forces me to look up.

Francis, my eldest son, comes into the study. His presence discomforts me and I am suddenly aware of how little I see my children, and my heart begins to tighten. I dismiss the feeling as quickly as I can.

"Hello, Francis," I say. "It is good to see you. Is Mama with you, or is this a private visit, just you and me?"

Francis shakes his head. "I wanted to see you, Papa," he says, discomfort and embarrassment etched all over his young and innocent face.

"I never spend time with you. And when you are not here at home, I worry we will never see you again. I sometimes hear Mama crying in her bedchamber. And I know she worries too. So I wanted to see you and talk to you. Can we do that, Papa?"

I look at the young man standing before me. He is barely twelve years old. Yet he is strong, intelligent and brave. He is my heir; a young man with the fine features and intelligence of his mother, and some Hacker family traits too, not least a fine mop of dark hair and a strong jawbone.

His presence makes me acutely aware of my inadequacies as a Father, for at a time when I should have been helping him to grow into a young man, I have been absorbed in war and slaughter. There has been little time for else. But, in truth, I know I could still do more.

"Come here," I say, embracing my eldest child for the first time in months. "Tell me about all the things you have been doing. It will be good to spend some time with you, my son. I can't recall when it was just you and me."

So I forget about the state of the war and the horrors that have engulfed Stathern these past few days.

All that matters at this moment is Francis. The very least I can do for my son is give him my undivided attention, for the next two or three hours at least − until I am unable to ignore Cromwell's call no more.

Prince Rupert
The Prince cut his teeth on the battlefields of Europe
and became the most feared Royalist commander

FIFTEEN

MY ANNOUNCEMENT IS GREETED WITH deafening silence. Abijah looks at the oak beams on the ceiling, tapping his fingers rhythmically on the kitchen table, his discomfort and agitation plain for all to see. Isabel has her arms crossed and her face is white, the anger rising. She is sure to vent her fury shortly.

The only member of my household who appears to be behaving normally is Else, who continues about her business as if she hasn't heard anything.

Finally, I can stand the silence no longer.

"What say you?" I ask, directing my question at my friend, rather than my wife, for fear of the strength of her reply. "Will you be able to cope while I am away – and will you have the resources and men to start a thorough investigation into the deaths of Peter and Marjorie?

"Time is of the essence. We must start our enquiries this morning and we must bring those responsible for this heinous crime to justice swiftly."

Abijah is about to reply, but Isabel beats him to it.

237

"My goodness, Francis, how can you really think about leaving Stathern at this time?" she asks. "Do Peter and Marjorie mean so little to you? Is Cromwell's business really that important that you must abandon us at this dreadful time of need? Think carefully before you speak, for I am in no mood to suffer your mealy-mouthed words this evening, husband."

I had waited until my wits had returned – and young Francis had his fill of me – to inform Isabel about my orders to ride to Ely at the earliest opportunity.

After spending the afternoon with my eldest son, I retired to the study and spent an hour working out my plans for the long journey and the measures I should take in relation to the Harrington murders. I thought I had been sensitive when I explained why I would be leaving so suddenly, and that Isabel had understood.

I interpreted her silence as understanding. How wrong I was.

"You disappoint me sorely, Francis Hacker," she continues as words elude me. "I have always believed you to be a man who practices what he preaches. You tell anyone who will listen about your desire to serve the Lord and Parliament faithfully. Well where is the Lord's and Parliament's work best done on a day like today? Is it scheming with the likes of Oliver Cromwell, or bringing the murderer of two innocent people to justice? Tell me, Francis. What have you to say on the matter?"

I look to Abijah for some support, but none is forthcoming. It is clear he is in accord with the mistress of the house. His silence is as painful as any blow to the ribs.

"My love; my friend," I say to them both. "This situation grieves me dearly. Whatever I choose to do, I will cause offence. And that is not my intention.

"I am torn between leading the search for the killers and following Cromwell's instructions. But I fear it is the latter I must obey. To ignore Cromwell's summons will cause much displeasure and lead me to face the wrath of one of the most important Parliamentarians, a man who, one day, could be the most powerful figure in the land.

"Should I choose to ignore his command, he will quite rightly hold me to account and ask me why I could not delegate the duties of Constable to Abijah, who is more than capable of carrying out the necessary enquiries and investigations. In truth, I will have no compelling argument to counter any accusations he may level. That could lead to severe consequences, as I will have failed in my duties to a superior officer and Parliament. Do you really want me to face that kind of inquisition? Do you really want our family to face the consequences that could arise from such a folly?"

I can see Isabel is not convinced; I am unsure about Abijah's views as he rarely talks openly about what he is feeling. But I am in no doubt if he did so, he would err on the side of my wife.

"Do as you see fit, Francis, and pray long and hard that the decision you make is the right one," barks Isabel, her rage openly boiling over. "Oliver Cromwell has a hold on you that I cannot rival. Your head has been turned, ever since he visited us last year. Damn this war. But if you feel you must heed this order, then go you must. But know this: I will not be happy with your decision."

I leave Stathern in the midst of a storm, the clouds a colour that reflects how I am feeling.

Isabel is nowhere to be found. Perhaps it is best I do

not see her, as I have no desire to part on bad terms. So I bid farewell to Else and Abijah, before finding the children and saying affectionate goodbyes to each of them. Francis is the last to wish me a safe journey.

"Papa, why were you arguing with Mama?" he asks as I ease my riding boots on.

"I could hear Mama shouting at you. Have you done something wrong?"

My son is looking disconsolate. Yet he is doing his utmost to prevent his fears from overwhelming him.

"Son," I say. "Fear not. Your Mother and I have simply had a disagreement about something that is relatively trivial. That is all. It is what happens between all Mothers and Fathers at times. In our case, it occurs very rarely. But when it does, your Mother doesn't refrain from telling me how she is feeling. And that is what happened this morn. But there is nothing for you to worry about.

"Now, young sir, I need you to be the squire around these parts while I am away. You need to keep all these strong-willed women, your Mother included, safe and happy. Can you do that for me?"

A smile passes across the full lips of Francis.

"Of course, Papa. Everything will be fine while you are away. And I will make sure Mama is looking forward to your return."

My pride in my son is close to bursting. I reach out and embrace the young man that stands before me, his slight frame bending as I threaten to crush him. And I believe everything he has said.

Whereas I am incapable of giving my wife and children the love and attention they need at this turbulent time, I am comforted to hear the tenderness and concern in my son's voice – and his determination to rise to the challenge of manhood.

Late February is not the time of year to be making the journey from Stathern to Ely, regardless of the importance of the matter. The cold and wet are a most inhospitable and unhelpful combination for any traveler, particularly in the midst of a bloody civil war.

Yet my trust in Bucephalus is never misplaced and I am confident my prince of horses will eat up the miles effortlessly, barely breaking sweat. He has a particular fondness for the night, which is a mercy as we have many miles to travel before dawn breaks if we are to reach our destination on time. Bucephalus loves the freedom of the countryside. Him and me: on our own.

It takes me just over two days to reach Oliver's farmhouse. He has used it little since the outbreak of war, preferring London and the field tent to home comforts.

The last time I saw him, he told me it serves his purposes well when he needs to have meetings away from the scrutiny of others in the capital. And I am sure this is one of those occasions when we will be all grateful of the solitude.

The house itself is relatively modest for a man who is becoming one of the most powerful military and political figures in the land; yet it has changed little since my last visit. Indeed, the only noticeable difference I can see is the number of men congregating in the grounds. For I count a picket of more than thirty guards stationed twenty yards apart in the grounds. I suppose it is only a fool who does not take precautions!

Bucephalus snorts as we approach our destination.

He can smell fresh hay on the breeze, food seemingly always on the mind of my steed. Ahead there is a commotion. At first, I cannot see what is going on. But as I get closer to the courtyard, I see Cromwell himself berating an unfortunate soul.

"Think yourself lucky that I am not going to take the whip to your back, young man," he shouts at the soldier. "There will be no slacking on duty by anyone who serves in the Ironsides. Do I make myself clear? Now get back to your quarters and read your Bible. And make sure you offer full repentance for the pride and sinful nature you have displayed this evening to every man here. Now be off with you."

Cromwell is about to let fly with more invective when, out of the corner of his eye, he catches sight of me.

"Why, Captain Hacker, welcome to my humble abode," he says effusively, his mood turning on the wind. "It is a joy to greet you and see you looking so well. We have much to discuss once you have stabled this fine-looking horse and been shown to your quarters for the evening."

I dismount and embrace the strong, outstretched hand of the Lieutenant-General. As ever, his vice-like grip threatens to crush my own offering. I wince and the surprise that is momentarily etched on my face doesn't go undetected.

"Forgive me, Francis," says my host, looking at my damaged fingers. "I have a habit of being over enthusiastic when a friend comes visiting. And a friend to me, and the cause of Parliament, you most certainly are.

"Several other officers are joining us tonight, for there is something I wish to share with you all that will be of great interest. And your opinion, in particular, is something I will certainly value."

I start to ask a question of Cromwell, only to be cut-off before I have mouthed a couple of words.

"Fear not, dear friend, all will be revealed shortly," he says, one step ahead of me. "Until then, find your mattress and make sure your horse is well provisioned. I will make sure one of my men is at hand to aid you until your are settled."

Short, sharp commands echo off the brickwork of the house. A trooper quickly detaches himself from a group that is congregating at the far corner of the courtyard and marches over to us.

"Saddington, this is Captain Hacker. He is an important guest of mine this evening," explains Cromwell. "Take his horse to the stables and make sure it is fed and watered. When you have done that, come back here and escort the Captain to his quarters, which are on the far side of the house. And be quick about it. I will expect you back here in five minutes."

Cromwell watches the soldier depart with Bucephalus.

"Don't be shocked at my curt manner with the men, Francis," he whispers. "My troops are highly disciplined Christian zealots. They don't always engage in small talk. They read their Bible several times every day; they pray with a passion and intensity you will not see in other regiments; and they obey orders without hesitation, because they understand the importance of obedience.

"It is some of these very things I wish to talk to you, and the others, about this evening."

Saddington is standing to attention within four minutes of receiving his command. And a broad smile passes across Cromwell's mouth.

"Francis, I look forward to seeing you at dinner," he says, dismissing me. "We dine at eight o'clock sharp."

I am the last to arrive in the main hall at the agreed hour.

Five other officers are present. And I am pleased to see Cromwell is in a jovial mood.

He sees me as soon as my shadow darkens the hall's ornately tiled floor.

"Ah, good to see you my dear Francis. Come and join us," he beckons, pointing to a large chair next to a figure I instantly recognise. "I think you are well acquainted with Colonel Rossiter?"

I shake hands with the commander of the Parliamentary garrison at Melton Mowbray and exchange pleasantries. There will be ample time to find out about everything that has happened at the garrison since my capture, although I have no desire to dwell on my imprisonment and the torture I endured. The soonest I am able to consign that particular episode to the past, the better.

Cromwell waits a minute before continuing. "The other officers you will not be so familiar with…"

In quick-fire time, I am introduced to two colonels from the Eastern Association forces, who are well acquainted with Cromwell and defer to him at every opportunity. One of them, an Edward Whalley, I have met before; he is known to be a confidante of Cromwell's. A major from the Western Association is encouraged to come forward and shake my hand.

"This is Hastings," says Cromwell, by way of introduction. "Thankfully he is no relation to the cur that causes you so much trouble in Leicestershire and the Midlands. But, even though he carries the name of a dog, he is a good man to have around in a fight.

"And lastly, please allow me to introduce you to Henry Ireton, a fine gentleman and one of the Parliamentary army's shining lights. Henry is proving himself to be a strong and reliable leader of our forces. And he, too, like all of us assembled here tonight, is passionate about the common cause we all serve."

I acknowledge all six men.

"It is a pleasure to be in your company," I say. "I am eager to make your acquaintance this evening and discuss matters of importance."

Cromwell chuckles. "Aye, there will be plenty of that, gentlemen," he says. "But before we get to business, please allow me to pour you all a glass of claret. You have had long journeys. And what kind of a host would I be if I didn't pay some attention to your needs?"

A ripple of polite laughter rings out. Cromwell quickly fills seven glasses.

"A prayer, gentlemen," he declares before any of the rouge passes our lips. We put our wine on the thickset table and close our eyes.

"Father, bless every man at this table with wisdom and a desire to carry out your will in the weeks and months ahead, as Parliament seeks an end to this bloody conflict. We give praise to you Father, for being a vigilant and loving Redeemer God; our Lord, who has forgiven us for our grievous sins. Lord, we lift up our souls to you, so you may watch over us in the coming days and guide us in a way that honours you, your son and the Holy Ghost. Amen."

As Cromwell rises and crosses the room, Rossiter

leans over to me and whispers conspiratorially

"Our Oliver's quite the preacher, isn't he?" says a man I have not spoken to for more than three years. "I am not sure he should be in the pulpit or on the battlefield, myself!

"The time is coming when I fear God may well abandon us all. We seek his forgiveness and direction – nay, even blessing – while we continue to put His flock to the slaughter. I have to confess, Francis, I struggle to see how we will atone for these sins when it is our own day of reckoning."

A sharp rap on the table draws our attention back to the business of the evening. And I make a note of the subtle scorn I have detected in Rossiter's voice.

"Gentlemen," states Cromwell, looking imperious as he assesses his audience and sounds very much the leader of this group. "If I may, I would like us to discuss a matter I consider to be of considerable importance: namely, our tactics in the field, and the readiness and ability of our armies, generals and soldiers to defeat our wily and determined foe.

"Ever since the war started, we have largely been bested by the King's men, particularly when the princes Rupert and Maurice are leading them. Our generals have, for whatever reason, been unwilling to do what is required to defeat the Cavaliers, even though we have more than enough munitions and men to do so. Discipline has been lacking almost as much as our application. This cannot be allowed to continue. And that's why I have invited you here this evening.

"Lord Fairfax and I have spoken in detail about what we must do to ensure our armies gain the upper hand, particularly now we have been reinforced by the Scots. And our considered view is we need to find a new way to wage war, a way that annihilates anyone, or anything, that dares to stand against us.

"Friends, you are here because you are regarded as some of the finest men in our armies; officers who are proven leaders; God-fearing men. And as such, we need you to play your part in developing what Fairfax and I intend to call the 'New Model Army'.

"Right now, I don't know precisely what this army of the future will look like. But I am confident that, with your help and support, we can build a force that will be invincible on the field of battle. For God will be on our side. And I know he will use you to ensure the England we rebuild is long-lasting; incorruptible; a home to all.

"What say you, gentlemen: are you with me in this venture? Do you have an appetite to help Parliament win this cursed war?"

Our passions are roused. Exhilaration is coursing through our veins. How could any of us refuse such an invitation?

"Aye. Aye," I yell until my larynx threatens to burst. My fellow guests are equally enthusiastic.

"We are with you, sir," pledges Rossiter, to my right, more enthusiastic than he was just five minutes earlier. "Tell us what you need and it will be yours."

Cromwell is silent for a moment. He closes his eyes and appears to say something to a higher authority. He then strides over to Rossiter and clasps the colonel on the shoulder.

"What I ask of you, Edward, and the rest of you, is to ready yourselves for the great adventure we are about to embark on," he declares. "We need to build a new army that works differently from anything that has come before it.

"My own regiment has challenged the status quo frequently, to our advantage and that of Parliament. As you may already know, we now boast fourteen troops of horse, some eight more than is the norm for a regiment. And that is no accident. No coincidence. It is because we know our business: the business of holy war.

"Our tactics are simple: we recruit god-fearing men who are led by god-fearing men, most of whom are not from privileged backgrounds. My men can relate to each other, regardless of their rank, and they respect each other. They pray; they sing; they eat; they live; they die. Together. They are brothers.

"Our devotion has enabled us to form of discipline that is unrivalled in our associations. My friends, it is this kind of recruitment and structure that I wish to see introduced elsewhere. If you can start doing what we are already doing in the Eastern Association, we will have no equals. And there will be no arguments of merit that will prevent us from fashioning the whole of the army in this form.

"But I urge you not to be impatient, for I realise it will take some time before we gain enough support within Parliament to bring about the changes that are so necessary. Indeed, it could take up to a year before we are ready.

"All I ask of you is you stay loyal to the cause and be prepared to meet me, and others, so we can continue our discussions, and refine our plans. Your support will be invaluable. As will your willingness to adopt new tactics and techniques in the field. For if we are to win the support of our peers, we must be able to evidence that our proposals work in practice. As we all know, there has been too much rhetoric in recent times, too many follies that have cost thousands of lives, dreamt up by men of rank, but with no commission to lead. The time has come for men like us to seize the day. So let us do so, for the sake of everything we hold most dear."

I find myself hanging on Cromwell's every word. I feel intoxicated, light-headed, even though I have not yet touched my glass of claret. Such is the power and brilliance of Cromwell's oratory. I decide, there and then, this is a man I can follow, a man we can all trust and believe in; a man with intelligence, integrity and authority, and the drive to help turn the war in Parliament's favour.

My own sufferings at the hands of Prince Maurice, which came about as a direct result of following the orders of Pym, are already a distant memory and become more so as each day passes. What is needed is a radical new way of prosecuting this damnable war. And tonight, what I have heard is something that has reignited my inner fire.

I suddenly become aware of Cromwell's hand on my own shoulder. The Lieutenant-General has moved away from Rossiter and is now bending his head towards me. I suddenly realise he is also talking to me.

"We must consign that matter to the past," I hear him say as I quickly regain my composure. "You, of everyone in this room, have a major role to play in bringing this ambition to life, Francis. I need you alongside me guiding and advising, for there is not a better cavalry officer in the land. But it will not be an easy road. We will need to convince many skeptics. And we do need to keep these conversations confidential. Only when we have the backing of others can we openly reveal our intentions."

My face feels flushed; I am conscious my cheeks may have betrayed my conceit and, dare I say it, my pride at being singled out.

"I am your man, Oliver," I say reassuringly, looking up at the ruddy face of Cromwell. "I am flattered you have sought to involve me in this important work. I will not let you down. You have my solemn word on this. But, before we discuss matters of such magnitude, I need to talk to you about recent events in Stathern, and my very real concerns that we now have an enemy agent in our midst."

Cromwell's smile does not leave his face. But there is a steely flash in his eyes revealing his thoughts.

"Let's not talk of this tonight," he says quietly. "Keep your counsel until the morrow. Let's have breakfast and talk further on this matter. Until then, mix with the others and do your best to enjoy the evening. Some merriment will do you no harm at all, my friend."

I pick up my glass, take a sip of the full-bloodied claret, and nod affirmatively.

"Until the morrow, then, sir," I agree. "I look forward to telling you all and seeking your brotherly advice and guidance."

Cromwell is full of life and vitality at seven thirty in the morning. Alas, I am afraid I am less so. My one glass of claret became four during last night's proceedings, and, as a man with no real liking or stamina for wine, my head quickly became addled by the liquor.

My weakness has ensured my head is throbbing and I will be lucky to avoid Cromwell's censure, should he become aware that my lethargy is a result of a night of revelry and drunkenness!

I sit at a table overlooking Oliver's extensive gardens. Even at this time of year, when winter is often at its most bitter, it is a picture of precision. The tree branches may be bare, but in every other respect the land is alive.

Two Robins sit within ten feet of the window, waiting patiently for prey to come within their killing range. Beautiful birds they may be. But they are also ferocious hunters. Just as the thought enters my head, the male bird makes a sudden movement and pierces a worm that has come to close to the surface of the earths crust for its own good. Close by, a red squirrel darts about, it too is seeking food.

My thoughts about nature are quickly banished when Cromwell coughs, indicating he is ready to talk.

"I trust you had a good evening?" he says. "I hope you were comfortable and slept well?"

Moving on quickly, Oliver quickly comes to the point.

"I have been informed about a couple of deaths on your estate. Have these anything to do with the subject you raised with me last night?"

He looks at me intently and pushes some cold meats and bread in my direction. I place some pork and a thick crust on a plate before speaking.

"It looks like it," I say. "An elderly couple, who were loyal to my family for more than thirty years, were murdered shortly before I received your summons. I have left my deputy in charge of the investigation. I am hopeful he will have made significant progress by the time I return. With any luck, the perpetrator will now be under lock and key.

"It was a heinous crime, with no apparent motive.

Yet, just twenty-four hours before their killing, I received information from a highly reliable source that a Royalist agent is active in my area, with my activities for Parliament of particular interest. My source also told me the Royalists have been aware of the Militia's plans for several months. These are claims I cannot ignore. And, I do not believe the two murders, for that is what they were, are not connected in some way."

Cromwell says nothing. He takes a hunk of bread and spreads a thick layer of butter over its surface. He cuts a slice of cheese. Deliberately. Concentrating. He eats slowly. Pondering. Eventually he speaks.

"Francis, I think you have every right to be concerned," he says, looking at me intently. "I would be too. You have been through a lot in recent times. You know a lot. And that means you will remain a target for Maurice and Rupert. You are one of their weaknesses.

"I am minded to speak to Sir Samuel Luke about this matter. As you know, Luke is Scoutmaster to Devereux. But he likes nothing more than to get his hands dirty poking around in the world of skullduggery. And, having heard what you have just reported, I think this is certainly something he should be told about and encouraged to look into.

"Be careful who you place your trust in for the foreseeable future. Take no chances. The tide will soon start to turn and our enemies will do everything in their power to seize the initiative. So take appropriate precautions to protect yourself, your officers and your family."

As I look at Cromwell, I am struck by his vigour and calmness. Here we are talking about matters of State, and he is able to take everything in his stride. Unflustered.

Calm. Decisive. Surely greater things await this man, who was held in such esteem by King Pym, in the months ahead? I truly hope so.

"Colonel, I thank you for your friendship and support. Be assured I will heed your advice," I say. "And thank you for taking me into your confidence about the development of our army. I am at your service. If you believe I can be of any assistance, don't hesitate to call upon me."

Cromwell clears finishes what he is eating before responding.

"My dear Francis, you are a man I can rely on. I know it," he says. "Your discretion, honour and loyalty have already been severely tested and you have proven yourself many times. Fear not. We will be talking a lot more about the needs of the army. Much needs to be done in quick time. And it can't be done without the support of men like you."

I stand and extend my hand to shake that of Cromwell. But rather than give me a cursory handshake, he leaps out of his chair and embraces me. "Francis, you are a good man," he whispers. "It is an honour to serve with you. Stay safe. Stay alert. And do everything in your power to continue taking the fight to the King."

Lady Lucy, Countess of Carlisle
Lucy was regarded as one of England's most beautiful
women. Yet few knew of the role she played in politics

SIXTEEN

IT IS THE THIRD DAY of March; a Thursday. Spring is about to return to Stathern and, as a prelude, the skies are a brilliant blue. But the darkness of recent days, brought about by the deaths of Peter and Marjorie, and Rowland's warning, is still all too evident to see.

As I ride into the village, the smiles of the villagers are in short supply. A cursory wave of the odd hand is all that is on offer to me as people continue about their business as quickly as they can, their heads weighed down while their noses gouge a trench in the cobbles.

Thankfully, Isabel's mood has thawed while I have been away – albeit there is coolness in her normally effusive welcome. Perhaps my wife would have been more unwelcoming had I not arrived looking what I was: tired, hungry and disheveled.

"Get to the kitchen forthwith, Francis," she says after planting a gentle kiss on my forehead. "Let Else feed and drink you. We can talk later. There is much for us to discuss. I will send for Abijah."

I walk the short distance to the kitchen. As usual, Else is in her prime. Several hams are roasting on a spit over an open fire. And I can smell bread baking in the ovens. The aroma makes me acutely aware of my acute hunger.

"Master Francis," exclaims the mistress of the kitchen. She strides over and plants her customary kiss on my cheek.

"What an unexpected pleasure, sir. We were not sure when we would see you again, so it's good to have you back sooner rather than later. And by the look of you, if you don't mind me saying, you would appear to have been neglecting yourself yet again."

Else points to a large chair by the table; a place has been set. Maybe our cook knew I would be in dire need of her fare?

"Sit here," she commands with her warm voice, one I am delighted to hear once again. "I will bring you some bread and a bowl of hot broth. That should tide you over until dinnertime, Master. I was just about to eat some food myself, but your need is clearly greater than mine."

Soon I am a contented soul once more.

With my stomach full, it's now time to find out what has been happening with the Militia and learn about the progress of Abijah's investigation into the murders of the Harringtons.

There is no warm embrace from Abijah as I walk into the study. Not even a handshake. His face is set. Stern. He is unwilling to look directly at me.

"It is good to see you, my friend," I say in a bid to break the silence and the mood. "I had an eventful time with Lieutenant-General Cromwell in Ely. There is much to share with you. But before I do, pray tell me, how are things with the Militia. And, in particular, what have you discovered about the killings of Marjorie and Peter? Has the killer been apprehended?"

I know the answers to my question before Abijah speaks a word. His discomfort can only mean one thing: the killer is still at liberty.

"I am sorry to have to report that my enquiries have yielded naught of any substance," he confesses. "Nobody saw anything suspicious that day. There was nothing I found at the cottage that incriminated anybody. And there isn't a soul in the village, or surrounding area, who can name any enemies Peter and Marjorie have made and who would resort to such a dastardly deed.

"I know your expectation would be that I would have caught the killer and have him ready for trial, upon your return. But the plain truth is, Francis, we know no more today than we did on the twenty fourth of February. It grieves me sorely to tell you this and to have failed you as I have."

I take my cloak and gloves off, sit down opposite Abijah and seek to reassure my second-in-command.

"Good grief, man, I do not expect you to be a miracle worker," I say. "You are my most valued friend and comrade; I trust you without hesitation. I know what Peter meant to you; and I am sure you will have done all in your power to catch the perpetrators. So please do not reproach yourself.

"I will visit you this evening and we can talk at length about everything you have done. Now I am home, we can examine everything once again. There will be a clue. I know it. We just need to employ our wits so we can find it. But do not be so harsh on yourself."

Abijah visibly brightens as he reports on the affairs of the Militia. All has been well while I have been away; the men engaged in training and general duties as the Ashby garrison largely been inactive.

"But," adds Swan, "our informers are telling us Hastings' men intend to strike Hinckley tomorrow, even though it has declared itself neutral. As many as four hundred cavalry will be raiding the town in an attempt to secure livestock and supplies – and seize members of the clergy who have signed the Covenant.

"Prior to your arrival, I sent correspondence to Lord Grey about the enemy's plans and he has ordered our troops to join him in a bid to repulse the attack.

"I have spent most of today preparing the officers and men, and getting as much information as I can about the town. From what I have been able to digest, it is vulnerable to attack from several sides, although I suspect the Cavaliers will just march in, as they usually do, via the most direct route."

I quickly absorb everything Abijah has told me and make my decision.

"We will put the investigation into the murders on hold until we have dealt with the Hastings problem," I state, to myself as much as Abijah.

"All our strength and effort must go into this venture. It is time to bloody his nose once again. So tonight, take me through everything you have agreed with Grey, for I will be joining you tomorrow in the field and I have no intention of being bested by the upstart Cavalier. It is time to strike a blow our enemy will not forget for a long, long time."

I awake early in the morning of the fourth day of March.

It is still gloomy outside with a thin mist covering the rooftops of the houses in the village, the Hall included; the Spring weather of yesterday did not last long.

Thankfully, Isabel remains sound asleep as I dress and wash and prepare myself for the excitement of the day. A strange mix of emotions take a hold of me: the thought of killing my enemy fills me with a sense of dread, albeit I have been responsible for more than my fair share of slaying; but the thought of preparing for battle, and the opportunity to out-think and out-fight the Cavaliers, makes me feel alive.

Even though there are almost three hours remaining before the Militia is due to muster, I find myself unable to relax and return to my slumber. I am alert and ready for whatever fate holds for me.

The waiting seems to last an eternity. There is too much time to contemplate the fragility of life. For a soldier, this is the worst of times.

At seven twenty five, as I expect, a trumpeter breaks the silence of the morn.

It is time to leave.

Within minutes, more than a hundred men descend on the square located just outside Saint Guthlacs. The air is still. The birds are quite.

The only sound comes from the horses, particularly those taking the opportunity to relieve themselves on the smooth cobbles. Soon a mist forms out of the steam of horse piss. The acidic cloud engulfs us, so I give a terse order to move out.

"Quietly does it," I say. "You know what your orders are: proceed with caution, at a slow canter, until visibility improves. We are scheduled to rendezvous with Grey's troop at nine o'clock. And we have more than enough time to get to our destination."

And so we begin the ride towards south Leicestershire, to a hamlet called Elmsthorpe, reputed to be the place where King Richard the Third, spent his last evening on this earth before he met his doom at Bosworth Field.

I shudder at the thought of the lonely death the last Plantagenet King must have endured; cut-off from his men and surrounded by the Tudor army's common sol-diery, and I pray to my Maker that this morning our for-tunes will be altogether different.

Thomas Grey, or to give him his full title, Lord Grey of Groby, Commander in Chief of the Midland Association forces, is a young man, almost five years my junior. He first tasted battle at Edgehill, when he was aged just nineteen.

Men react differently to being exposed to the horrors of close combat fighting and the gore and blood that flows aplenty. Some become heroes. They are the few. Most, like Grey, realise they value their lives more than anything in this world, particularly valour on the battlefield. And that stark realisation means they will do anything they can to survive.

In his Lordship's case, this has meant he has forged an unenviable reputation for himself. His superiors, men like Fairfax and Devereux, do not trust him. Cromwell, who is his unequal in terms of breeding, loathes him as much as a follower of Christ can do. But I have to endure him, for he is my commanding officer. That means my feelings for the man are mine, and mine alone.

I see Grey's standard and colours long before I hear him.

He and his men, more than one hundred and fifty of them, have ridden to the small Church, where they are now relaxing, awaiting their battle orders.

"Captain Hacker, it's good of you and your men to join us," declares Grey. "We only arrived ourselves less than fifteen minutes ago. I have sent scouts to Hinckley to assess what the enemy's strength is likely to be. Last night, our intelligence suggested as many as three hundred men are in the town. But, as you'll appreciate, we need to be as accurate as we can be. I expect the men to return within the next thirty minutes, or so. Hinckley is less than four miles away."

I look to my left and gaze west.

In the distance, above the numerous naked trees, I can see smoke rising. It would seem the people of Hinckley are wide-awake. Little do they know what awaits them!

As Grey predicted, his scouts return within half and hour. One of them has captured a Cavalier, who quickly confirms the enemy is more numerous than we originally thought. There are at least three hundred Cavaliers in the town and a further fifty dragoons, plundering whatever they can find, particularly cattle, sheep and fowl. Local Inns are being raided with ale the prime target.

One of the scouts has spoken to a well-known Parliamentarian sympathiser in the town, who reports more than thirty folk from Cosby and Leire have been rounded up by Hastings' men and detained in Saint Mary's, the parish church.

Two clergymen have also been taken, amid rumours both are to be hanged later today. Their crimes? They are among those Puritans seeking to reform the Church of England, as demanded by the Scots when they agreed to send an army south of the border in support of Parliament. And they have signed the Covenant, in contravention of the King's direct command and wishes.

Grey walks over to me when he is satisfied he has gleaned everything of importance.

"It seems our prey is fully occupied filling its boots by robbing the unsuspecting people of Hinckley of whatever they can lay their hands on," he says. "They are so sure of their superiority, there are but two men keeping watch. And it seems there is still much drunkenness in the town, with the ale that hasn't been hoarded onto carts now lining the bellies of the plunderers. So there are likely to be many sore heads, which means all augurs well for our mission, Captain."

"It seems so," I reply cautiously, less confident than my superior.

"Nonetheless, experience has taught me to be wary of traps, sir. I was caught in one at Adwalton Moor, a cursed place where I lost half my men. I have no desire to see families grieve so harshly ever again.

"If you will allow me, sir, I would like to propose a two-pronged assault on the town, thereby reducing the risk of our forces being ambushed and increasing our chances of catching the Royalists by surprise on at least one front."

Grey indicates he is happy for me to continue, so I outline the plan I have been formulating ever since Abijah told me of the intended attack. When I am finished, the Colonel nods his head in approval.

"I can see you have thought this through well, Captain Hacker," he says, with more than a hint of approval. "I could not have done any better. We will proceed as you suggest. Please brief the officers and sergeants. And make sure they know our call sign is 'God prosper us'. We don't want any unnecessary casualties.

"Let us be ready to begin our attack late in the afternoon. Your men can stand down and relax. But be sure they are ready for three o'clock. And make sure they have their wits about them."

With the light just starting to fade, we start to make our way towards Hinckley. From Elmsthorpe, we canter to a small hamlet called Barwell. Locals scurry inside their hovels when they see our column approaching. It's difficult to identify whether we are Cavaliers or Parliamentarians, so local people choose discretion over valour. They hide themselves away the best they can. For most, that means barring a wooden door and kneeling and praying. The only time we realise there is life in this barren place is when we catch a brief sight of a curious face at a window, or see shadows illuminated by candlelight.

His Lordship has taken his troop and is proceeding to the other side of the town, which is close to the old Fosse road. It's a route I know well, having used it quite recently on my travels down to Chipping Norton. So I am able to offer some advice on the best line of attack. Whether Grey is listening to me, I am not sure. We will find out in the next hour, or so.

On the outskirts of Barwell, we take a sharp turn down a lane that takes us directly to Hinckley. Dense thickets of Thornbushes, punctuated by the occasional Oak, line our way, blocking out the light.

Within a few minutes, we see a line of Cavaliers,

their muskets seemingly at the ready.

"So it begins," I say to Abijah, who is riding alongside me at the front of the column. "Disperse the men as we have agreed. And let's be about our business as quickly as we can. You know what to do. May God be with you, my friend."

Abijah gives me a rueful smile. "And with you, Captain. May He protect you too."

Puffs of smoke precede the crack of muskets recoiling. Soon the air is thick with smell of gunpowder and the screams of men fighting for their lives. The cry of 'for the King' goes up from the thin line of foe blocking our path. It is soon muted by the riposte of 'In God's name from my brothers in arms. And then all I can hear is the guttural roar of men desperate to kill and maim.

Tree trunks start to shower bark as musket balls tear into branches and trunks. Miraculously none of my men go down. A second volley, this time much closer and louder, pierces the cacophony of noise coming from both sides as they converge on each other.

Then we are among them, hacking, stabbing and cleaving at men we detest. I counted fewer than thirty of the enemy lining the path. Even if their number were tenfold, they would be no match for my troops. And so it proves; for once we are in the killing range, the slaughter and carnage begins.

I see the enemy's commanding officer stagger backwards and fall, blood spurting from a neck wound opened up by a powerful lunge from Smith. The melodious roar of our very own minstrel, whose blood lust is in full flow, drowns out the Cavalier's death rattle. Two more swings of his razor sharp cleaver yield similar results against two hapless and terrified enemy soldiers. I smile as they crumple and their dying bodies twitch, the life oozing rapidly out of the terrible wounds that have been inflicted on them.

It is a similar story all around me.

Cavaliers are littered on the ground. They are either dead, or badly wounded and begging for their lives.

"What say you, Captain, shall I finish him off?" yells Huckerby, the tip of his sword pointed at the throat of one of the vanquished.

"Nay, Nathan," I respond. "We are soldiers not a band of cut-throats. The Cavaliers may have no honour. But we are better men. And we are doing God's business. Remember that."

It has taken less than five minutes to complete the rout.

Not one of my men has been lost. Eight enemy soldiers lie prostrate in pools of blood, with a further twenty suffering some form of serious injury.

By the time my wits fully return, the Cavaliers have been herded into a circle. Fear and pain are imprinted clearly on the faces of the survivors.

"Abijah," I yell as loudly as I can. "On me."

My second-in-command quickly falls into place by my side. He is unflustered by the skirmish, even though his white blouse and leather jerkin is spattered in blood.

"Nobody has been killed, or injured," he reports. "I think Smith terrified them all on his own. Not one of their muskets hit home; the worst wound was a nick on the cheek. Against such overwhelming odds, it is a miracle. When they saw how impotent they were against us, it's little wonder they capitulated as quickly as they did."

"Well done," I say appreciatively. "The men have

exceeded my expectations. They couldn't have executed their orders any better. But we need to make haste. Lord Grey will be breaking through on the far side of the town as we speak. And we still have two miles to go before we reach him.

"Leave the prisoners here with a guard of ten men. If we are able, tend to their wounds. But tell the guards to help only those who have a chance of living, for I fear several will be joining their comrades in the grave before the night is out, such is the severity of their wounds. You have got five minutes before we need to be on our way."

Abijah quickly organises a detachment to take care of the Cavalier prisoners. Then we are back in the saddle, galloping towards the market square, located in the centre of the town, to rendezvous with Grey's detachment.

The noise of battle greets us less than half a mile away from Hinckley's centre.

The tower of the parish church rises above the roofs of scores of dwellings and shops. In the gloom, we hear steel clashing against steel, muskets being unleashed and the anguished and pained profanities of men.

I turn and address the column.

"This is as far as we go with the horses," I shout as loudly as I dare. "Dismount and make yourself ready to march the rest of the way. Bring your muskets and flint-locks and as much powder as you can carry. And be quick about it."

As one, the men leap out of their saddles and lead their animals to the side of the road, where there is grass aplenty.

"Smith," I shout. "Take ten men and look after the

horses. You have earned the right to rest a while and I need a good man in charge, someone I trust. Take good care of them. The rest of us will go and finish off Hastings' force and relieve Lord Grey."

We reach the Market Square within fifteen minutes.

On one side, taking up a position close to the church, is the main group of Cavaliers. They are firing indiscriminately and erratically at the smaller Parliamentarian squadron, which has dispersed itself a little more than a hundred yards away, shielded by many of the town's main shops and buildings.

Rather than take the fight to the Cavaliers, Grey seems to be content to wait for my arrival. This could prove a fatal mistake if the Royalists muster their strength and mount a coordinated counterattack.

Thankfully, I cannot see any obvious signs that the enemy is gathering its superior number. Like Grey, Hastings' men also seem content to fight at a distance.

I quickly instruct Abijah and my other officers to carry out the second phase of the plan. "It looks like it is down to us to make the breach," I say. "May God protect you all."

As moonlight descends on this small market town, a hundred and ten of my finest men stream out of Castle Street, discharging their flintlocks in the direction of Saint Mary's. There are two waves, each comprising an equal number. The effect is to create a curtain of never-ending leaden death and noise. And it works.

Dense clouds of gun smoke hang in the air as my men quickly eat up the open ground. The plumes emitted from their guns cling to the air, forming a screen that cloaks their advance.

Such is our speed that before they can rally, we are upon our enemy.

Unlike many of my men, I do not rejoice in the death of my enemies. But, on occasion, I can forget I am a follower of Christ Jesus, a cruder side of my character coming to the fore.

In Hinckley, on this fourth eve of March, I forget who I am; hacking indiscriminately at anything that blocks my path. My survival instinct cuts in. I shout 'In God's name' as loudly as I can, in a bid to protect myself from a misplaced thrust from one of my own soldiers.

I don't have a care in the world. My only goal is to live, and see my men emerge victorious from this bloody madness. Nothing more; nothing less.

I am not sure how long the fighting lasts. Ten minutes? Maybe fifteen? It matters little. For we win the day. I soon hear Cavaliers begging for mercy all around me. At first it's the odd voice. Then a defeated choir strikes up, pleading for their lives.

We have prevailed; our nemesis, Henry Hastings, has had his nose bloodied once more; and I start to weep tears of joy.

I am allowed a few, fleeting moments of tranquility before a soldier's voice calls out

"Captain Hacker! Lord Grey! Sirs, you are needed," comes the cry. "At the Church..."

I fail to recognise the man. He tries again: "Captain Hacker. Lord Grey. You are needed at the Church."

I reach the large wooden doors just ahead of Grey.

Saint Mary's is an unremarkable place of worship, like so many Churches of its kind. It dominates this small Leicestershire town, it's grey stone a stark contrast to the whitewashed walls of the nearby houses. Inside we see a mass of people standing at the far end of the hall. Their hands are bound. These must be the folk from Cosby and Leire who have been detained by Hastings' men?

Just in front of the crowd is a hastily erected scaffold; two ropes have been strung. Nobody needs to explain what its intended purpose is. The two Puritan ministers are sitting nearby, their hands and feet have been tightly bound.

"It looks like we have arrived in the nick of time to save these two poor souls," exclaims Grey as he surveys the scene. "To use God's house in such a way is sacrilege. Find the man who ordered this and bring him to me, Captain Hacker. He has some questions to answer."

I speak to the prisoners. Several offer up the name of a Royalist officer called Captain Mainwaring.

"Where is he?" I demand. "Can you identify this man? I need to speak to him, urgently."

One of the prisoners spits out a sardonic laugh.

"With respect, I think he may be beyond conversing with you, sir," he says. "If you look outside, you'll see his body in the square. He was the first man to be killed when your men broke into the town. Where he has gone, he will have to explain his actions to a far greater authority than thee or me."

My face remains neutral as I digest the news. I merely nod my head in the direction of the Cavalier in acknowledgement of the news.

"Aye, I suspect he will," I say to myself. "Praise be to God for our deliverance. For our Father has certainly protected his flock this day."

By eleven o'clock in the evening we have been able to tally

the final reckoning. Thirty enemy soldiers – including Mainwaring – are buried in a communal grave. A further forty of their number are now held as prisoners, many of them wounded in the fight. Some will never be able to hold a musket or sword again; such is the extent of their wounds. Only two of the men we hold are officers. We have also seized almost a hundred horses and significant amounts of ammunition and arms, which we have distributed among our men, much to their delight. In contrast, just four of our men were wounded. None were slain.

Unlike our foe, we do not permit plundering. Our reward for victory is the simple taste of life after the battle's end, knowing God is on our side. And how sweet the air tastes knowing this.

Unfortunately, a quicky tally reveals Hastings was not among the vanquished.

The prisoners have told us he has been absent from Ashby for at least two weeks, basing himself at the Newark garrison, where he is no doubt plotting the King's victory and our demise. They also tell us he has also suffered greatly in recent months after losing an eye at the skirmish in Bagworth.

So although the victory is soured a little for Grey and myself, knowing our foe is still at large, I am content to hear of his discomfort.

For our men, the victory is another sign the Militia is maturing into a fine fighting force. And, quite rightly, they now fill the hostelries that remain open in this freshly liberated town, enjoying a sip, or two, of the ales that, only hours before, were destined for the likes of Ashby, Newark and Belvoir Castle.

I am on my own in the graveyard of Saint Mary's, looking down at the stilled town. I seek peace and solitude.

The only noise I can hear is the laughter of some of the Parliamentarian troops, who are reveling in their sweet victory.

It is a cool evening, yet I feel inner warmth. I find myself contemplating. Assessing. After a while, I confess to feeling an overwhelming sense of elation, for the tactics we employed won the day.

Cromwell will be pleased.

The Lieutenant-General proposed them at the clandestine meeting I attended in Ely only a few days earlier. And the evidence is clear for all to see: greater discipline, firepower and mobility in the field wins the day. I make some notes in the diary I carry with me everywhere; I will inform Oliver of our victory and the role his tactics played as soon as I return to Stathern.

Thoughts of home force me to think about what awaits when I return. And there is only one thing that matters: pursuing the investigation into the deaths of Peter and Marjorie with my fullest vigour.

Every day that passes means our chances of catching the killer are reduced.

I have sworn I will find those responsible and bring them to justice. It matters little whether it this exacted by my own sword arm or the hangman's noose: all that is important is the perpetrator must be caught and pay the appropriate price of their crime; death the only outcome that is possible.

The lack of progress in finding the killer of the Harringtons leaves me feeling melancholic. Tears well up. I am aware of a stabbing pain. My vision is blurred temporarily. Thankfully the dark of the evening masks my emotions. My men will remain unaware of my weakness.

To my left, I hear footsteps. "Who goes there?" I call.

"So here you are," replies Grey, emerging out of the gloom. "I have been looking for you. I have found a fine bottle of port. Come and share a glass with me. I wish to discuss the events of today with you."

It is a rare invitation. Thomas Grey – the Lord of Loughborough and son of the Earl of Stamford – is from a vastly different section of society to myself. His family is one of the most powerful in Leicestershire, if not the whole of the Midlands, only rivaled by that of the infamous Hastings and his brood.

My own family hails from less privileged stock. When we are not at war, the Hackers live a comfortable life tending the land and investing in small business ventures. We go about our lives unobserved and are rarely called upon by the state. But Grey and his kind strut the corridors of Whitehall and Parliament with relish and purpose, seeking out opportunity wherever it lies.

I dare not refuse his request, even though I confess I am in no mood for socialising with a man whom I struggle to respect.

"It will be a pleasure, my Lord," I say. "Please, lead the way. It will be a delight and honour to share a glass with you and spend some time in your company."

Prince Maurice
A formidable fighter in his own right, Maurice often lived
in the shadows of his popular brother, Prince Rupert

SEVENTEEN

THOUGHTS OF THE ROUT AT Hinckley are rapidly replaced by the continued frustrations of drawing a blank in the pursuit of the killer of Peter and Marjorie.

I have to bring this matter to a conclusion quickly, for the sake of my own sanity, and that of justice. So I decide to press Abijah about the matter, with a view to gathering all the information we have at our fingertips.

"Explain to me precisely how you have conducted the investigation?" I say earnestly to Abijah. "I am not questioning your methods or thoroughness, I just need to understand what has, and hasn't, been done in this matter. That is all."

For the first time, I see my friend looking like a defeated man. Abijah can barely look me in the eye as he responds.

"From Stephen to everyone in the village, I have spoken at length to all potential witnesses," he says. "And there is nothing. Nobody can tell me anything about Peter and Marjorie's last moments. It's not that people don't want to help. It's simply that they have no knowledge that sheds a light on their last moments.

"The cottage is out of the village. Exposed. Out of the eye-line of the other dwellings. Nobody can remember seeing anything unusual. And no strangers have been sighted in the local area for several months. The only sighting we did have came in October, when one of the farm hands saw a man acting suspiciously. But that has nothing to do with the matters we are looking into."

I tap my fingers on my desk. I am in the study. Two days have passed since we returned from Hinckley.

Abijah has pulled up a chair and is sitting opposite me. Through the open door, across the hallway, I can see Else in the kitchen, busy preparing today's meals. She looks up. I give a stifled wave and then quickly avert my gaze and refocus on the matter in hand. I can sense my impatience and frustration rising.

"What about the cottage, did you find anything unusual there?" I press. "In their chamber, where the bodies were found, did you find anything that struck you as being unusual? Or was there anything that seemed to be missing?"

I realise I am more likely to be agitating Abijah rather than taking the inquiry forward. But I need to be confident my second-in-command has been diligent and meticulous.

The awkward silence that greets my question tells me something is awry. "Pray, tell me you have been back to the cottage and examined the ruins?" I ask, rather more aggressively than I intended.

Abijah refuses to lift his head up.

"No," he confesses. "It is something I intended to do

at an opportune moment. But I was called to Nottingham while you were away in Ely. And the Militia's affairs just took over when I returned. Do you really think there could be something important we missed at the cottage? We examined things pretty thoroughly on the day."

I am shocked by friend's tardiness.

Had Cromwell been sitting in on the conversation, he would regard Abijah's conduct as a case of abject neglect. Isabel, too, feels this way and tells me I am too lenient with my trusted second-in-command. But I know Abijah's heart – and I am convinced he will have done everything in his power to expose the killer. So I do my best to conceal my irritation. "There were large parts of the house we couldn't access because of the heat coming from the burning embers," I say as kindly as I can. "It's these we need to be looking at. With luck nobody will have visited the ruins, so any clues that do exist may still be there. But we need to proceed with haste."

Abijah nods his assent cautiously.

Through the hallway, I can see Else is standing still, listening intently to the conversation. I stand and walk over to the door.

"Else, can you please bring some ale into the study for Abijah and myself. And a crust, or two, of bread would also be most welcome."

Before she can reply, I close the door.

I had planned to take Abijah with me on the short journey to the brow of Mill Hill. But, unable to trust my tongue or emotions, I choose to travel the short distance on my own.

It is just two weeks since the deaths of the Harringtons, yet numerous black scars, where flames scorched the earth around the base of the cottage, still dominate the landscape. Bricks and timbers are strewn across the ground. The stench of destruction hangs in the air. And where there was once a happy home, a ruined carcass now stands in its place.

In this exposed place, a wind is blowing eastwards. A chill quickly claims all feeling in my hands. I look at them and I wince. They are white, all except the tips, which have remained blackened these past months. Alas, there is still no sign of my nails returning to fill the void created by Holck's cruel pliers.

A bead of cold sweat trickles down my spine and I shudder involuntarily.

I find myself consumed with grief as I begin the job of clearing the site in pursuit of the truth.

While I was visiting Cromwell at his Ely farm, Peter and Marjorie were laid to rest at Saint Guthlacs. I am told many tears were shed that day. The tortured souls of Stephen, their son, and others who knew the couple well, were at their rawest. Yet where was I when I was needed most? The truth is something I have difficulty digesting, just as my wife predicted I would.

Simple, fire-damaged furniture, made by Peter's own hands; an array of clothing; and broken ornaments; these are little to show materially for a lifetime on this cruel, unforgiving earth. It is only when death takes us that we see what a life without faith has to offer. And judging by what I see before me, trodden into the dirt of Mill Hill, it didn't amount to much.

An hour passes quickly and there is little left for me to examine. I am now in the area that would have been the bedchamber. In truth, there is nothing left that is recognisable: the bed is gnarled, distorted and blackened, its metal frame having melted in part due to the heat of the blaze. Two large chests have also been gutted, their ruined, naked drawers emphasising the violence that shattered the peace and tranquility of this once happy homestead.

I decide it is time to leave.

As I move, I notice something gleaming in the late afternoon sunshine. It is only by chance that I see it: resplendent; regal; so inviting. I bend down. It is a brooch, and it is remarkably intact, showing little sign of the fires that devoured everything else.

Wiping mud and grime of the gemstones with my cuff, I discover it is a beautiful pageant of diamonds and emeralds, set in gold with an ornate clasp. I cannot recall ever seeing Marjorie wear this item. Indeed, knowing how much the couple gets paid by the estate, I cannot believe she would have been able to afford such a wonderful piece of craftsmanship. But what do I know about women? They are the strangest creatures I have ever encountered! If they want something, they most surely find a way of getting it.

I put the jewel in my pocket. I will return it to Stephen at the earliest opportunity.

When I arrive at the Hall, Isabel is waiting for me.

"How did you fare at the cottage?" she enquires, her face a picture of hope. "Did you find anything that explains what may have happened?"

I shrug my shoulders. "Nay," I say. "I have been discovered naught. I fear the trail is now cold. I think we need to start accepting we may never discover who was responsible for the slayings and why Marjorie and Peter were killed.

"I intend to visit Stephen tomorrow. But I fear I will have nothing new to tell him, nothing to offer him that will dull his pain. I am loathe to admit it, but I am starting to think this whole matter may now be beyond my capability."

Isabel slumps in her chair. She stares blindly into the blue flames of the fire. When she speaks, it is a fragile whisper.

"So, that's it then. There is nothing to be done, is that what you are telling me?"

My face betrays my thoughts far more than mere words ever can. And, with her suspicions confirmed, the sobs take firm hold of my wife's body.

I reach into my pocket for my handkerchief. As I retrieve it, the brooch I recovered from the cottage tumbles onto the slate floor of the kitchen. I quickly reach down, check it is intact, and hand it over to my wife.

"As I was leaving, I found this in the remains of the bedchamber," I explain. "It is a fine-looking piece. I have brought it back to give to Stephen. It's his inheritance, the only thing of any value he will have to remember his mother and father by."

Isabel leans forward, her interest in the jewel taking her thoughts away from death and murder.

"This is a lovely and precious item," she says, before pausing and giving the brooch a thorough examination.

"Francis, I am sure I have seen it before," she says after several minutes have passed. "If my memory serves me right, I have seen this on several occasions. But I am sure Marjorie was not its owner. It belonged to someone else."

I look at my wife with an intensity that clearly shocks her. She recoils as my pain and anger rise to the surface.

"If not Marjorie, then who, Isabel," I demand rather too harshly. "Who is the owner of this jewel. Think, wife. Who?"

Isabel stands and walks over to the window. She gazes at the lawns, as the last strands of daylight are eaten by the onrush of night.

Beyond the lush laws, the Vale, in all it beauty, beckons. But rather than act as a soothing balm, it leaves Isabel facing more torment. She turns around and addresses me directly.

"That's a problem," she says. "Right now, I cannot remember. I can picture the jewel; I see it on someone we know. But their face remains a mystery to me.

"All I can say with absolute certainty is it is someone we know. I just can't name them. It is so frustrating. My brain is addled by all this intrigue and tragedy."

I offer a tired smile.

"Fear not," I say encouragingly. "In the scheme of things, this mystery pales into insignificance compared to everything else we need to find answers for. But I will still visit Stephen the morrow. I just won't tell him about my find. There's no need to trouble him unnecessarily."

The shadows on the walls of the kitchen, created by the flickering flames of the candles, reveal the lateness of the day. It is almost six o'clock and I am famished.

"Are we dining together this evening?" I ask Isabel, changing the subject. "I am in sore need of sustenance."

Isabel tilts her head to one side. "Else?" she calls gently to the far side of the scullery. "When you are ready, can you please serve dinner? The Master is in need of your finest game pie. And so do I, for that matter."

The response is instant.

"Everything is ready, Mistress," replies the Hall's ever-reliable cook. "I will start serving immediately."

EIGHTEEN

THREE EVENTS OCCUR ON MONDAY the seventh day of March, in the year of our Lord, 1644, that are to have a profound effect on my fate – and the fortunes of some of the people I hold most dear.

It is an unseasonably warm morning.

Isabel and I are taking breakfast with the children, when a messenger arrives at the Hall. He is carrying a dispatch from Staveley, my fellow Committee member in Leicester.

Although it is several months since I drew up comprehensive plans for the renewal of the city's woeful defences, and there have been many positive developments during the intervening period elsewhere in the county and wider region, Leicester continues to be a sore for Parliament.

The safety of its citizens, merchants and gentry is becoming a source of anxiety for all concerned, with the exception of Mayor, Thomas Rudyard, and many of his self-serving aldermen, who appear to be dragging their heels at every opportunity when called upon to do what is needed. At the moment, Leicester cannot be defended in the face of a sustained Royalist attack. Its walls and ramparts are broken down in too many places, and little, or no attempt, has been made to effect repairs.

The garrison continues to be of major strategic importance to Parliament. From here, the Cavaliers' activities in Ashby and Newark are frequently disrupted, making it a significant inconvenience for the likes of Hastings and Prince Rupert. Yet, despite receiving numerous warnings and pleas from Parliament and Committee members like me for more than twelve months, the city remains highly vulnerable. And the King's men will come. As sure as winter follows autumn, it is only a matter of time before the Ravens enjoy their feast.

Since we were freed, Haselrig and Staveley have been doing their utmost to unite the thirty, or so, committeemen deemed wise enough to look after Leicester's affairs. Their goal has been to get the Mayor to see sense, so a programme of rebuilding works can commence as quickly as possible.

The problem is the cost: Rudyard is refusing to countenance the works on the basis that "Leicester cannot afford the exorbitant amount" of seven hundred pounds! Instead he would rather welcome death and destruction.

Alas, it now falls largely on the shoulders of Staveley to win the day for the men of reason, as Haselrig has now chosen to earn a reputation in the field, pressing Parliament's cause as an officer, having sacrificed the Guildhall for garrison life.

Deteriorating working relations with Lord Grey of Groby proved to be the last straw for Thomas. In his last note to me, before he withdrew from the Committee, he claimed it was "an impotent body". Of particular frustration was the way in which its valid pleas to Parliament's principal officer in the region are ignored, or meekly acted upon.

"I pray daily that this gross incompetence and negligence will be overcome," he added. "But I live in hope rather than expectation. And it is now for better men than me to try and persuade his Lordship to do his duty".

Dispatched yesterday, the doughty Staveley's correspondence reveals similar frustrations. His letter addresses the scale of the continuing impasse with the Committee. He writes:

"My dearest Captain Hacker.

"Forgive me. I have been a poor servant these past few months. Since our incarceration at the hands of Gervase Lucas, I have been detained attempting to convince the Mayor of the need to act decisively in relation to the defences of the city. Alas, I fear my best efforts have failed.

"As agreed with Thomas Haselrig, I presented the outline of the new line of walls, trenches and sites for drakes, as was devised October last. There was initial enthusiasm at these proposals. But as soon as the costs of such a venture were discussed, the committee's vigour waned. Within less than a week, the issues that have plagued the Committee since the onset of the war neutered any opportunity there may have been to achieve a positive outcome. Therefore, I regret to report there has been little progress in implementing your plans to strengthen the fortification. The stalemate has lasted these past two months and, unless something can be done about the situation, I fear it will remain unresolved.

"I fear we will not be successful until we are able to influ-

ence some of the key men. To this aim, I feel it right that we convene, so we can reassess our plans and, where it is appropriate to do so, revise any costs associated with the venture. It may also be prudent to speak to some of the other committee members privately, so we have the best possible chance of securing their confidence.

"Please be assured I remain committed to achieving a positive outcome for the City and Parliament in this critical matter.

"Your trusted servant, Arthur Staveley."

I read Staveley's words again, to make sure I have absorbed everything of import. When I am finished, I throw the paper onto the table. If I could throttle the Mayor with my own bare hands, thereby hastening his departure from this world, I fear I would. Such is the anger I feel at this unnecessary and potentially costly prevarication. I can feel my head starting to throb and my heartbeat getting faster. The signs of agitation are once again taking their hold.

"Whatever is the matter, husband?" asks Isabel. "You look as though you have received untimely and most unwelcome news."

I pick up the letter, crush it into a ball and throw it in the direction of Isabel. It narrowly misses her head, drawing a justifiable scowl in response.

"Read it for yourself, my dear," I shout ungraciously, my frustrations boiling over. "Why am I forced to work alongside imbeciles like Thomas Rudyard? Why? How can these fools on the Committee not see sense and bring him to heel, instead of behaving like craven children who pander to his whims?"

Isabel walks around the table, ignoring Staveley's

carefully crafted prose, and places her hand on my shoulder. She runs her other hand through my hair. I find myself calming down, the red mist dissolving. Of course, this is my good wife's intention. How well she knows me. How easily she can manipulate my affections and mood.

"Tell me, Francis," she says. "Why do you take things so personally?"

So I tell the woman I love, who I seek to protect, about the perils that await the folk of Leicester, and the wider county. I spare no detail and I am forthright in my views about the negligence of the Mayor and the one score and ten men who control the city in the name of Parliament.

When I am blown, she uncorks a bottle and pours me a glass of port. It is not yet ten thirty in the morning, but I am grateful for the comfort it brings.

"Drink this," she instructs. "You need it. You will feel better for it. And when you are ready, we can discuss what actions you are going to take to get those buffoons to reconsider. For I fear it is you Francis who must persuade Rudyard and the Committee, and help them see the very real threat that is posed by Rupert and his kind.

"I am afraid this is not work for men like Staveley. It is beholden on you to convince them to do the right things. And I do not underestimate the difficulties this task will impose on you."

It is well into the afternoon before Isabel and I emerge from the kitchen, my reply to Staveley already penned and ready for dispatch. And when we do, I feel a weight has been lifted.

If Leicester were to fall, it would be a significant setback. Charles would control the heart of England, and Parliament's supply lines would be cut in half; the siege of Newark would be threatened; and the Royalists' ability to strengthen their hold on the north would be greatly improved.

So it cannot be allowed to happen.

My wife is an astute woman and she understands this predicament. More often than not, when I am close to despair, all I need do is look into her opal eyes, explain the dilemmas I am facing and allow her do the thinking.

In the early years of our marriage, I would never countenance doing such a thing. My pride would not allow me to confide in any woman. Yet age and war can have a dramatic effect on the way one views the world. Prayers take on a different meaning; there is a greater depth, honesty and integrity to them. And this applies also to relationships; particularly with those we care about and respect the most.

I now realise certain matters may be my ultimate responsibility, but I would be a dullard if I did not utilise the superior wit that is available to me, regardless of gender. Experience has taught me that finding the right answer is all that matters; how you do it is of little consequence. As a result of Isabel's interventions, pragmatic and appropriate solutions to seemingly unsolvable problems materialise. They are timely reminders of how blessed I am.

As walk into the Hall, the weight of the Leicester conundrum momentarily lifted from my shoulders, I see Abijah Swan waiting by the main door.

"Hello, my friend," I say jovially in welcome.

"What brings you here this afternoon? I hope that

whatever it is, you bring good tidings?""

I see Abijah smile for the first time in a long while, such has been the melancholy that has consumed him since Peter and Marjorie's deaths. He looks better in himself and, judging by the state of his clothing, he has at last cleaned his breeches.

"While you and Isabel were talking, a messenger from the Eastern Association arrived," he says. "It is the usual rider, Isaac Threadmorton. I have seen to it that he is escorted to the stables and is able to feed his horse while some of the men prepare a meal for him. But he insisted you are given this message at the earliest opportunity."

Abijah hands me a small letter. I recognise the hand and wax seal immediately: they are those of Cromwell. The correspondence carries yesterday's date, so Threadmorton's visit suggests there is some urgency.

I quickly read the Lieutenant-General's hastily written note. It concerns a matter that has been the talk of the nation for almost four years – the impeachment of Archbishop Laud, the head of the Church of England and the scourge of all non-conformists; a foresworn enemy of men like me.

Laud was arrested a week before Christmas Day some four years ago, when the King still had ample opportunity to avert the confrontation that has engulfed our nation in barbarity and conflict. The archbishop is a hated man who has no friends, except Charles and the Devil. Since his impeachment, he has been imprisoned in the Tower, where he has become a forgotten figure, such has been the need for every able bodied man to get behind the war effort and devote his time to the cause.

As a man of Christ Jesus, I should not revel in another man's suffering. But I do. As do so many of us as far as the archbishop is concerned.

Laud has been forced to endure much for his sins these past few years. And he will experience more pain before his days are at an end. Parliament will see to it, just as it did for that other rogue and despot, the Earl of Strafford. We had Pym to thank for bringing Thomas Wentworth – the man we called 'black Tom Tyrant' – to account. And many, like me, will shed tears of joy when Laud treads the same path and suffers the same fate on the scaffold.

If I need to, I will repent afterwards.

"What has Cromwell got to say for himself, then?" enquires Abijah. "Is he full of the joys of spring?"

I cough, a little taken aback by Abijah's boldness.

"You could say that," I spit out, attempting to suppress a smile. "The Lieutenant-General has informed me that Archbishop Laud is to be tried for High Treason. The trial will take place on Saturday the twelfth of March. Cromwell says all the preparations are in place for it to be a decisive prosecution. He believes the court will have little difficulty in finding the archbishop guilty. The trial is likely to be the source of a lot of jubilation across the country, so he is asking us to start informing ministers with known sympathies to Parliament, so they can prepare their sermons for the weeks ahead."

My weakness gets the better of me. I laugh aloud. It takes me a moment to regain control of my senses.

"I am sorry, my friend," I continue. "But at a time when the Militia is seeing action on a regular basis, overall victory is far from assured and treachery, Typhus and the plague are rife in our villages and towns, Lieutenant-

General Cromwell is the only senior officer who would think spiritual matters are of equal importance to the wider concerns that trouble us so. He is certainly the only man I know who would send a rider more than one hundred miles to deliver the news. And for that, he has my esteem and respect."

Abijah doesn't respond immediately to my jest. He is wary whenever the Cromwell's name is mentioned as his religious zeal perturbs him. In fairness to my friend, Cromwell intimidates a great many, such is his intelligence, forthrightness and commitment to the Lord.

After reflecting on my words, Abijah asks: "Do you wish to speak to Isaac before he departs?"

I think for a minute.

"Yes. Escort him through," I say. "I have a dispatch I need to write and I would like him to deliver it in person to Cromwell upon his return."

As Abijah walks to the stables, I quickly go to the library and start penning a note to the man I have pledged my loyalty and allegiance to. I tell him of the Leicestershire Militia's recent triumph at Hinckley, confirming the successful use of the new battlefield tactics we discussed at the recent Ely conference. And I promise him my continued vigilance and support in the weeks ahead. This is in specific response to his plea to be at the ready as "major confrontations loom in the north of the country".

I chose to say nothing to Abijah about this particular matter as I relay to him the general contents and good wishes of the letter. When it comes to military planning, I am under strict orders to say nothing to my subordinates. I agree with this policy.

For the time being, the less men like Swan know of

developments in the field, the better. Far too much is at stake.

After he has had time to digest his breakfast and stretch his aching limbs, Threadmorton emerges from the stables. He appears in good spirits, the result, perhaps, of some fine Leicestershire bacon and sausage. It is hard to believe he has just endured a long journey, for he walks with real vigour and purpose. I rise and go outside to greet this ever-faithful servant of Cromwell and Parliament.

"It is good to see you again, Isaac," I call out as I cross the courtyard and greet this likeable and earnest youth. "I trust all is well with the Lieutenant-General and the affairs of the Eastern Association?"

As he approaches, Threadmorton salutes and smiles.

"All is good, thank you, Captain Hacker," he responds. "Parliament's cause grows on a near daily basis, and has done so since I last saw you. I see it everywhere I ride: where there was once despondency and fear, hope and purpose abounds. God is blessing everyone who is taking the fight to the tyrant King, and none more so than Lieutenant-General Cromwell."

I shake my head approvingly.

"That is good to hear, my young friend," I say. "Let us pray our common cause continues to flourish and an end to bloodshed is not far away. As for your Master, I would ask you to hand him this message in person. And please tell him the Militia thrives in these parts. We look forward to joining forces with him in the weeks to come and taking the fight to curs like Hastings and Lucas."

Threadmorton takes the envelope I place in his hands and carefully seals it in the leather satchel secured around his shoulders. "You can be sure, Captain, that I will do so. May God bless you and your men."

I shake the young man's hand and wish him a safe journey to the east and the relative safety of Ely. I leave him with Abijah, who will escort him to the gates of the Hall, then return to the library to reflect on the letter I have written to Staveley, reiterating the steps and tactics that must be taken to ensure the continued security of Leicester, the result of my lengthy conversation with Isabel.

I do not realise it at the time, but I will never see Isaac Threadmorton again. The cruel hand of fate has already got a firm grip on his destiny and my own.

My unusual day is further interrupted just before dinner-time.

I am in the midst of reading the latest edition of *Mercurius Civicus*, a pamphlet printed in London in support of Parliament, when I hear animated voices in the hallway. One of them belongs to Samuel Hibbert, the estate's long-serving shepherd.

Samuel has been away from Stathern driving a large flock of sheep to Pool, a major town in Montgomeryshire. Samuel has been taking our sheep to the town's market, where they are sold for meat and wool, for as long as I can remember. He is a popular figure in Pool, a town he visits at least twice a year, and he is a larger than life figure in these parts too.

But I have never heard his voice raised like it is this evening.

I stand and walk away from the table. My desire to reacquaint myself with the likeable shepherd is far greater than the lure of reading the latest newssheet that takes great pleasure in revealing the latest trials and tribulations of our despotic King, but isn't always truthful. As I approach the door, a flustered Else rushes into the room.

"It's Samuel, sir," she announces excitedly. "He's in a most distressed state. He wishes to speak to you directly. I have tried to find out what he wants to tell you, but he is unwilling to say. The only thing I can get from him is he has some important information he must relay to you in person. What would you like me to do?"

"Why, please show him in, Else," I say reassuringly. I am excited at the prospect of spending some time with a man who has been loyal to my family for more than forty years. Whatever it is he wishes to discuss, I am sure the conversation will be worthwhile.

"If you are able, please bring us some ale and bread," I add as Else scurries away. "I haven't seen Samuel for what seems like an age, so once I have found out what is troubling him, I may seek to delay his departure for quite a while as we will certainly catch up on other matters."

I listen as Else attempts to talk to Samuel in an orderly manner, confirming that I am delighted to see him. But her voice soon tails off. In its place I hear brusque footsteps walking down the hallway. Suddenly the door is pushed open and I find Samuel standing before me. His face is flushed, pain and anguish written all over his weather-beaten features. It certainly doesn't look as though a jovial conversation is on his mind.

"Master Francis," he declares, with no attempt at niceties or small talk. "In all conscience, I must talk to you about the murders of Peter and Marjorie Harrington. For I may know something of significance."

I fix my gaze on Samuel and usher him into an armchair. I attempt to clear my head. My enthusiasm for our reunion has now been replaced with a sense of dread. "Tell me all you know," I say, my throat dry. "This is a grievous matter I am most committed to resolving. And any assistance you can give me will be greatly appreciated."

Samuel looks around the room and sees the door is ajar. He rises and walks over to the entrance. He looks into the hall before retreating into the library, closing the door firmly behind him. He appears satisfied we cannot be overheard.

"Shortly before I left for Pool, Peter came to see me," he reveals once he has sat down and regained his composure. "He was in a sore state, Captain, deeply concerned about something Marjorie had witnessed some days yonder.

"In all the time I have known him, I had never seen Peter like this. He was troubled; concerned; so fearful. So I asked what was ailing him and his good lady. He told me Marjorie had been visiting Saint Guthlacs on the evening of the twenty second of February, when she had seen a person known to this family perpetrating what she perceived to be some ill-gotten business. I don't know if it was thieving, or if it was something else.

"He refused to name the person concerned or what Marjorie's suspicions were, for he did not want to be the bearer of malicious gossip. But he did tell me the Mistress would be told about everything at the earliest convenience.

"Master Francis, do you know if Marjorie did this?"

I shake my head. "Nay, Samuel," I state. "Marjorie did not speak to the Mistress about this matter, of that I am sure. If she had, I would know about it."

My heart is beating wildly. My breathing is rushed. I am desperately trying to comprehend everything that is pulsing out of Samuel's mouth. I know it is important. I am just not sure why.

"And there's something else," he says. "Peter said Marjorie had some evidence that would prove the truth of her claims. As I said at the outset, I do not know what it is Marjorie saw, but I am sure it was something of real importance. Peter would not have troubled me with trivialities.

"I only found out what fate had decreed for the Harringtons when I returned to the village a couple of hours ago. The first I knew of the tragedy was when I saw the ruins of the cottage – and then I learned that Peter and Marjorie had been killed most foully. So I had to come and speak to you, sir."

I close my eyes in a bid to gain control of my thoughts. As much as I try, I cannot stop thinking about the ominous words my brother uttered on the evening of the seventeenth of February: "You have a spy in your midst!"

At the time, I did take the threat seriously. I do so now. But, with no evidence to back up Rowland's claim, I have had little opportunity to investigate this matter, beyond asking the odd question and, where I can, improving security. I just don't know where to start or who to speak to. Yet the murders, coming when they did and committed so cold heartedly, have left me with much to ponder.

The time has come for me to find out whether there is a credible link between Rowland's warning and Samuel's worrying revelations. And I have to do this quickly.

"You have done the right thing, my friend," I reassure the shepherd. "I thank you for coming here and telling me what you know. Do not speak to anyone other than myself about this matter. If you do, our chances of apprehending the killer may be lost. And you may put yourself at risk. Do you understand?"

Samuel nods his head in assent.

"Aye, Master, I will speak to nobody about this," he confirms. "All I wish is to see the man responsible for the deaths of the Peter and Marjorie Harrington brought to justice swiftly. And I will do everything in my means to help you make this a reality."

It is nine o'clock in the evening. Isabel and the children have enjoyed a hearty dinner of braised beef, prepared by Else's expert hands. Unfortunately, I have only been able to pick at the meat on my plate, despite my hunger.

My distraction is absolute; I cannot eat.

Away from the kitchen table there has been much to digest. Thankfully, I have been able to mask my true emotions and thoughts for much of the night. And now the girls and young Francis have gone to their beds, I have the opportunity to disclose to my wife everything Samuel Hibbert has revealed.

After listening to me patiently as I set out all I know, Isabel is emphatic in her view.

"This is the breakthrough you have been seeking," she says, her voice unsteady, as she comprehends the scale of deceit and the potential dangers that could lie ahead. Undeterred, she continues: "Surely it is plain to see: Marjorie was slain because she knew something of importance and the killer needed to be sure that knowledge would never be revealed. It was no chance killing. It was deliberate and calculated.

"It beggars belief that such people could be caught up in something so heinous. And, God willing, we will soon find out what it is. But, Francis, be under no illusions: there are risks for all of us until those responsible are apprehended."

I shake my head. I am unconvinced, much to the irritation of Isabel.

"Samuel's testimony has given me much to consider – and it does take my enquiries forward," I admit. "But, at this moment, I am struggling to see what my next step is. I have already been forced to look at the conduct and allegiances of everyone living here at Stathern. I have found nothing. Abijah's enquiries found nothing. We have been clutching at straws these past weeks. Without more precise evidence, I fear I will not able to move things forward at all. Everyone, in the purest sense, remains under suspicion, even you and me. But there is no path to follow. The killer did his work well."

My wife looks alarmed. "You cannot be serious?" she says, her voice revealing her surprise.

"It is time for you to use the brains our Lord has blessed you with, my dearest husband. And, while you are at it, you need to open your eyes.

"Have no doubts, you have moved forward. Samuel's testimony has given you an insight you haven't had thus far. It takes you out of the abyss you had found yourself in. It is plain for all to see. For you are now aware when Marjorie made her discovery. You also know the graveyard is somewhere that is a vital place of focus.

"Just as importantly, you have been told that

Marjorie was much troubled – and that Peter was filled with angst. This suggests the person we are looking for may be someone who is known in these parts. If this is not so, why would a stranger have bothered to kill them at all? For two days, they were alive. That suggests their slayings needed to be planned. There needed to be a degree of thought applied."

Isabel never ceases to surprise me. On occasion, she can be wrong. But more often than not, my wife is unerringly accurate in her assessment. And my senses tell me this is another one of those occasions. How frustrating it must be sometimes to be a woman like my wife, living in a world dominated by inferior men.

"So where should I be looking?" I plead, eager for some guidance to help me overcome my uncertainties and doubts. "What step do I take next?"

"Francis, you will not like what I am going to say to you. But say it I must" she responds. "Do you remember the conversation we had about Abijah several weeks ago?"

Suddenly I feel pensive. Guarded. I nod my head, confirming I do recollect the words we exchanged on the matter. I realise I do not want to hear what is about to come.

"Do you recall Peter seeing Abijah drinking heavily with some men in Nottingham while you were imprisoned at Belvoir Castle? Peter did not know the men that Abijah chose to get himself blindingly drunk with. Peter thought them most odd fellows for Abijah to be associating with," continues Isabel, aware of my discomfort. "Ever since your release, Abijah, your trusted friend, has been a different man. Secretive. Uncommunicative. Aloof. Behaving oddly. You have said so yourself, when you lost your temper about his recent efforts to uncover the identity of the killer – efforts you called 'lamentable'. You also said you were deeply disappointed in Abijah and how you felt his enquiries could be deemed to be bordering on the negligent."

Isabel looks at me directly. She is challenging my view of the world and the protection I am affording my friend. She can feel my caged anger, for I am barely concealing it. So she chooses to adopt a more conciliatory tone.

"Do not misinterpret what I am saying, husband," she says. "I am not suggesting Abijah is guilty of anything. I certainly do not believe him to be. But I am saying you should be looking closely at his conduct, not ignoring it. For anyone charged with investigating such deaths, it is an obvious place to start.

"This enquiry has been going on long enough. It has cast a dark shadow over our village and it has undermined your authority. Your obligation is to Peter and Marjorie. You also have a duty to Stephen. He needs answers, as do we all."

Of course, my wife is right. I know it. And I am irked by her words because I know what she says is true. I am a soldier, not a detective. I am used to order and routine, not being required to live off my instincts. And I have a major weakness: I like to trust people.

Five minutes pass and, as my mood mellows, I think about what Cromwell would do faced with this kind of situation. Would he prevaricate and dither like I have done? Would he discount certain lines of enquiry because of the relationship he enjoys with particular people? Or would he simply be committed to doing the right things?

The answer is all too obvious.

"My love, thank you. Once again, you have opened my limited and weary mind," I say, my humour returning. I move closer to her and kiss her affectionately on the cheek. "I am thankful you continue to be my conscience and guardian angel. You have my word, I will start work in the morning and leave no stone unturned until I find the truth, whatever the cost."

Little do I realise it, but these will prove to be prophetic words.

NINETEEN

I AM ALWAYS AT MY best before breakfast. There are few distractions – and I am always in awe as God's Kingdom awakens. It's beauty, even in these cruel times, never diminishes. So it is a joy to witness a Green Woodpecker hopping through the sky as this fine Tuesday morn comes alive.

My quill has been busy. I have listed twenty-three people I must interview about the deaths of the Harrington's – and Abijah is the first person I will be formally questioning.

I promised Isabel I would start work with real vigour, energy and intensity. And so I have. Her barb about my authority being undermined really stung.

By nine o'clock, I am ready to have a frank, honest and long overdue conversation with Abijah. Thirty minutes earlier, I sent a guard to his cottage, ordering him to attend on me with immediate effect. Unusually, I gave no details about the matters I wish to discuss.

"What's this all about, Francis?" asks Abijah as he

enters the library, his boots smeared with the mud and filth of yesterday, his shirt hanging out of his breeches. I can see my abrupt summons is not welcome. "This is very early for you. We don't normally go over the Militia's strength and impending activities until midday."

I motion for him to sit down at the main table. It is large and it is bare, deliberately emphasising the distance between the interrogator and the interrogated.

We will be talking about two capital offences, and possibly more; this is not meant to be a pleasurable experience. To emphasise this, an armed Dragoon stands guard vigilantly outside the room. And I have a note taker present to record everything that is said.

"Good morning, Abijah," I say rather more officiously than I intend. "Please don't be offended by what I am going to say to you this morning, for no offence or slight is intended.

"Yesterday, new information about the deaths of Peter and Marjorie Harrington came into my possession. I am afraid I am not at liberty to tell you what this information is. But, because of what I now know, I must ask you formally to answer some questions about your conduct in relation to this matter. Are you willing to cooperate?"

Abijah is afflicted with many of the same weaknesses as me, one of them being his inability to conceal his raw emotions. It's one of the reasons we have such a bond. Right now he is bewildered, off-guard and wary. And very quickly, I recognise the signs of his mounting anger and frustration.

"How dare you," he says as calmly as he can. "You may be my superior officer, and my friend, but you have no right to do this; to ask questions of me.

"You know what they meant to me, particularly Peter, and yet you speak to me in this way, as if I was somehow complicit in their deaths. You know me to be a loyal man, someone who you have deemed good enough to be your deputy for the duration of the war. I am no cutthroat killer of old women and men. You know that to be true."

Isabel warned me of Abijah's likely reaction to this kind of questioning. And she was right. But press on I must, regardless of the turbulence I am likely to create. Justice demands it.

"I am accusing you of nothing," I say as reassuringly as I can. "You are my trusted friend and a damned fine soldier. But I cannot ignore certain things, particularly the new evidence that has just come to light. My job is to find the truth, not be feckless and incompetent. It is as simple as that. So I must ask you about your actions in seeking to bring the killer to justice – and I must also seek information about an acquaintance you have with some men in Nottingham; strangers you have been fraternising with to the point of excess?"

So begins my lengthy interrogation of Abijah Swan.

By the time the questioning is finished, Abijah and myself are spent. We have endured every conceivable emotion. And many a harsh word has been said. I suspect it will take time for our relationship to return to normal.

"Is that all you require of me, Captain?" he asks icily as I indicate the meeting is now at an end.

"There is nothing more I can add," continues Abijah. " You now know everything: all my failures, weaknesses and vices – and the contempt I have for myself at being unable to find Peter and Marjorie's killer. Are you satisfied, sir? Can I now go and get on with my duties?"

How I wish I could take my friend into my confidence, to offer him an assurance that I believe everything he has told me. But that would not be the right thing. To do so would be a gross dereliction of my duty as an officer of the Parliamentarian army and the man charged with keeping law and order in these parts. Right now, I only have Abijah's word he is telling the truth. I have no corroboration. Not yet. Therefore, the law dictates he is to receive the same, respectful treatment as everyone else involved in this investigation.

At this difficult time, all that matters is I uncover the truth, in whatever form it manifests itself. That a few eggs are broken, as Isabel reminded me yesterday, is of little consequence, providing I remain fair and open-minded at all times.

Yet the thought I must put a further twenty-two men and women, many whom I have known most of my life, through the same examination as I have just imposed on Abijah is akin to torture. And, if I am dissatisfied with their answers, I am duty-bound to arrest them and then question them further. The perceived privilege of social rank is laughable. Right now, how I wish I could be anyone other than me.

"Am I free to go?" repeats an anguished Abijah, breaking the spell of my inner thoughts and turmoil.

Such is the discontent I feel I cannot look at him.

"Of course you can go," I say to the man who has saved my life on the battlefield so many times. My protector. "You are quite free to return to your normal duties."

Over the course of the next seven days, I speak to everyone on my list, with the exception of Else. I am forced to abandon this meeting when I receive more correspondence from Staveley about yet more problems with the Leicester Committee. Unfortunately, the rider requires an immediate response, so I will have to find time to speak to our good lady cook at a later date. For everyone else, it has been a demanding, but necessary, experience.

The interrogations were not pleasant affairs, even though I tried my utmost to explain I am merely re-evaluating certain things after looking at all the evidence I now possess about the slayings; and I stress that nobody, at the present time, is suspected of being the perpetrator of these vile crimes.

Despite my best efforts, my reassurances fail. The mood at Stathern gets bleaker by the day. Whenever I pass someone in the street, they can barely bring themselves to acknowledge me. Even members of the Militia keep their heads down for fear of coming under the scrutiny of the man now dubbed 'the Inquisitor'.

On Friday, I make a long overdue visit to the home of Stephen Harrington. It is more than two weeks since I last saw him. Much to my shame and distress, I have been unable to make the short journey to Harby, where he lives, such has been the amount of work I have been required to undertake.

Since I last saw him, Stephen has buried his mother and father, tried to come to terms with everything that has happened and recently returned to his military duties. Thankfully, as he opens the dark door that keeps the ills of the world at an arms length, he looks far stronger and resilient than when I last saw him on the twenty fourth of February, prostrate on the slate floor of the Hall.

It is a day I will never forget.

Stephen is surprised to see me standing on the doorstep of the modest cottage he shares with his pretty wife. Harby is a village that is less than a ten-minute ride from Stathern. Like so many similar places, it is vulnerable to raids from the roaming bands of Royalists that regularly strike out from the stronghold controlled by Gervase Lucas. Livestock, vegetables and hay are frequently plundered, fuelling a growing hatred of the King's men in these parts.

Conveniently, the abode is within walking distance of The Nags Head, an inn Stephen regularly frequented with his father. If I find him in good humour, maybe Stephen and I will take a stroll to the hostelry and enjoy a tankard of ale, or two!

"Captain! Welcome. I wasn't expecting you," he says. "Please come in. It is a wonder to see you again."

I am shown into the main room and beckoned to sit by the hearth.

"I was just getting ready to take some of the men out to Colston Bassett," reports Stephen, quashing any thoughts I may have had about retiring to the inn. "We are regularly patrolling that area now the Cavaliers are becoming more active again."

Talk of the village, where I own a small house, brings back memories of my late Royalist brother, Thomas, who was killed there in a skirmish while fighting against my own men. It is almost a year since his passing. But time is meaningless; every day I grieve and pray for his soul.

"Stephen," I say as reassuringly as I can.

"I need to talk to you about some recent events concerning your Mother and Father. Is it convenient to do so now?"

A bow of the head gives me the assent I require. So I inform Stephen of everything I know, on the strict understanding he will not disclose anything without my express permission.

"I thank thee most humbly for everything you are doing, Captain Hacker," he says when I have told him all. "But I am afraid I am not in any position to help you. I am unaware of the events Samuel has brought to your attention. My mother did not confide in me. It was only my father she shared things with. I fear she may have taken everything she knew with her to the grave."

When I return home, I find Else hard at work in the kitchen. "How are you, Master Francis?" she enquires. "You look exhausted and famished. Would you care for a slice, or two, of mutton and a tankard of ale?"

I am hungry and it is midday.

As well as being a superb cook, Else also appears to be an accomplished reader of minds! So I thank her and sit down ready to receive my fare graciously. I relax. I have nothing that requires my immediate attention. And the food looks inviting.

"Else," I say, in between mouthfuls. "We were unable to talk the other day about Peter and Marjorie Harrington. Can we do so now, while I am eating my food?"

Our hard working cook looks at me. For a moment she seems uncomfortable at the prospect. But she then noticeably relaxes before replying: "Of course, Master. I am happy to do so. I was close to them both and had known them all the time I have been at the Hall, for they arrived here three years before your father offered to bring me to Stathern. And that was in the year of our Lord, 1617, during the reign of King James. Their passing has caused me considerable pain. But be assured, I will help you any way I can."

I talk to Else for the next hour, gentling probing. She answers my questions as fully as she can. There is no need for a note to be made. Her answers seemingly confirm she knows nothing about the horrific events of the twenty second of February, a day that cast such a shadow over Stathern.

Almost as an after thought, I say: "There's something I would like you to take a look at. Do you mind?" Before she can answer, I rise from my chair and leave the room. I walk upstairs to the bedchamber I share with Isabel and I find the hidden chest where my wife and I place trinkets, jewels, documents and other items of value. From this box, I extract a small pouch. I then return to the kitchen where Else is waiting for me.

"Is everything alright, Master Francis?" Else asks.

I smile reassuringly. "All is fine, Else," I say. "There is nothing to worry about."

From the small bag, I retrieve the emerald and diamond brooch I discovered in the ruins of the Harrington's cottage. Its brilliance shimmers as the rays of the bright sun beat through the window on to the kitchen table. I pass the jewel to Else. It is a magnificent object.

"Do you know what this is and who it may belong to? Have you ever seen it before?" I enquire.

For a fleeting moment, I think I see shock register on Else's face. Then her features return to normal.

She holds the jewel between her thumb and forefinger, looking intently at its craftsmanship. Eventually, she reaches for the jug of water that is on the table and fills a glass. She drinks the liquid slowly. Deliberately. When she is ready, she says: "It is beautiful, sir; a wonderful gem. It must be worth a Duke's ransom, for this is an item of the rarest quality? Even I can see that. But, alas, I am afraid I cannot help you; I have never seen it before. If I had, I would certainly have no difficulty in recalling it."

I scrutinise Else for a while, not saying a word.

For the first time in my life, I find myself not believing what she is saying to me. I am surprised at my reaction. I am not quite sure why I feel as I do. Something just does not ring true. A feral, gut instinct tells me Else is uttering falsehoods. She does know something, of that I am sure.

I don't know how. But I do know I have no option: I must find a way of pressing her further.

"Else, your reaction suggests the brooch may have jarred a distant memory," I state flatly; my voice neutral. "Can you please look at it again, just to be sure; I really need to know if you have ever seen this brooch before. It is of the utmost importance."

Her voice adopts a defiant edge as she speaks.

"Master Francis," she says. "What you say is true. The brooch reminds me of a wonderful piece of jewelry my mother used to wear. It brought back some distant memories I thought were lost forever. But all that has happened is my emotions have been played with. That is all, sir. I have never seen it before.

"My mother meant a lot to me. She passed away when I was but fourteen. And even though I was meant to inherit all she had, in the end I received nothing. For children like me are not deserving souls, particularly when it is time for the possessions of the deceased to be shared among family members. We are a reminder of the sins, lusts and weaknesses that exist in all our lives. At these times, when the niceties are at an end and all that is left is to distribute the spoils of death, people like me discover our true worth. And I certainly found out my value."

Never before have I heard the bitterness that flows so freely from Else's tongue. Hitherto, her past has been a taboo subject. Today's outburst is a revelation. We all have pasts. And many of us are forced to hold on to things that will torment us for a lifetime. And that is what my questions seem to have triggered within her, as she unveils a deep, tormented anguish that disfigures her fine features.

And there is something else: a hardness I do not recognise.

I suddenly realise there is so much I do not know about Else. And I am acutely aware I may have underestimated her.

"Don't look shocked, Master Francis," she says after a lengthy, embarrassed silence. "The memories I speak of are from a long time ago, more than thirty years. Seeing that item of jewelry has simply brought back things I would prefer to forget, including a childhood of bitter regrets. That is all. Nothing more."

It is time to end the questioning for now. I believe I have gained everything I can from the conversation. Else cannot assist the murder investigation. She claims knows nothing of relevance or value. But, I am not totally satisfied.

For some reason, I am convinced she is lying to me about the brooch. Why she should do so, I do not know. I cannot make sense of it. But at some point in the very near future I will seek to find out what connects her to this valuable item – and why she is so determined to deceive me.

At dinnertime I discover Else is nowhere to be found.

A search of the Hall reveals she is missing. It is only when I ask Abijah if he knows where she may be that I am informed she has travelled to Long Clawson to visit an acquaintance.

"Isabel and myself know nothing of this," I say. "Who agreed to this, and why did Else need to make such a journey?"

Abijah is still bruised and prickly after our formal conversation about the Harringtons. He is distant and clearly doesn't wish to engage in a protracted conversation with me.

"She came to my cottage just after one thirty this afternoon and said she needed to visit someone," he recalls. "She said it was an important journey. I asked if everything was in order, and she said it was. On that basis, I said she could take her leave of the Hall. One of the men has taken a carriage and is escorting her as we speak. I don't expect her back until later this evening."

I am already feeling uneasy, but this latest news heightens the anxiety I am feeling, although I do everything in my power keep my feelings under a semblance of control.

"Do we know where exactly in Long Clawson she has gone?" I ask. "Do we have a name and an address?"

No response is forthcoming from Swan.

"I will take your silence to mean 'no'," I say curtly. "This really is not good enough, Abijah. Please take steps to ensured I am informed as soon as Else returns. I need to have a word with her about a matter of some sensitivity. And ask Sergeant Farndon to report to me in thirty minutes. You are dismissed."

I make my way out of the Hall and into the garden, where my wife is busily entertaining the children. Laughter and merriment lead me to where the small group is listening to one of Isabel's enthralling homespun fables. It is about the forces of good and evil and how the righteous always prevails. How I wish it were so.

"You look as though you are having a troubled time, husband?" my wife says, looking up and detecting my all too obvious unease. "Is there anything I can help you with?"

I nod my head, smiling at young Francis as I do so. My son stands up and runs over to me, throwing his body at my midrift. "Papa, have you come to listen to Mama's story," he enquires, the hope that I will say 'yes' so evident in his strong, vibrant voice.

"You ruffian. Be easy on your old Papa," I say, as the force of my son rocks me back on my heels. I give him an impromptu hug and ruffle his hair.

"I am afraid that must wait. As much as I love listening to your mother's wonderful tales, I am afraid there is something I must discuss with her that is of equal importance. So, as a favour to me, would you mind taking your sisters to the corner of the garden and looking after them for a few minutes? You would do me a great service if you did."

With the girls under the supervision of their protective brother, I turn to Isabel.

"Something is not right," I state. "I fear deceit is rife

in Stathern. I can feel it. Something is unraveling, but I don't know what it is."

Isabel looks confused.

"Francis, you are not making any sense," she says. "You are being rather dramatic, my love. Start at the beginning, talk slowly and tell me what is causing you such unease."

I take a deep breath and move under the branches of one of the resident beech trees that encroach on the forest. I make sure we are alone before I start to articulate my thoughts and suspicions as accurately as I can. By the time I stop speaking, my wife's joyful face has adopted a sobriety and gravity that mirrors my own.

"You are right to be troubled by these matters," Isabel confirms. "On their own, I suspect they could easily be dismissed. But in the context of the murders and the wider struggles, I believe there is chance they could be of great significance. You must act with speed and decisiveness. It is far better you act appropriately, and these suspicions are ultimately proven to be groundless, than you do nothing at all. The risks are too great for impotence to take hold of you."

I make to leave the room, resolved to act decisively.

"Francis," calls Isabel. "Wait. Before you leave, there is something else I need to tell you. It is highly relevant to what we have just been discussing. Please sit down."

I find myself unable to concentrate on anything else than this most pressing of matters.

Panic is not a feeling I am familiar with. So to feel as I do is discomforting. It forces also me to consider whether I am fit to be in charge of this rapidly developing situation, such has been the scale of my potential misjudgment.

The library becomes my refuge. Its paintings and books of bygone times are my solace. A knock on the door shatters my peace. In steps Farndon; he is on time.

"Thank you, Sergeant," I say. "I need you take six men and start searching the cottage Else resides in. You are looking for anything that is not as it should be, particularly correspondence.

"Do not be kind to the house, if you need to cut into walls or remove the floor, then do so. Bricks and mortar can be repaired easily enough. All that matters is you find what I suspect to be there. Any questions?"

Farndon shakes his head.

"That's good," I say. "Be on your way, Sergeant. If you find anything, make sure you tell nobody other than me."

With Farndon organising a search detail, I give orders to be left alone in my sanctuary unless the evening, unless there is an emergency. And, even then, I expect my Militia subordinates to do their utmost best to deal with any military matters that arise – unless I am explicitly required to prevent the imminent demise of Parliament! I make it clear there will be serious consequences for anyone who does not follow this order.

I need time to think.

At the heart of my troubles is my latest conversation with Isabel. It has flushed out a long-lost memory she has been carrying, something so ordinary that it should not be of any importance at all. It is a miracle she has recalled it at all. Yet what Isabel has remembered is potentially so vital that I am deeply unnerved, as is she.

The events of recent weeks have put a strain on us

all. Yet I must quickly reconcile my emotions in order to have the best possible opportunity to get to the truth. For the moment, nothing matters more than addressing the anomalies that have left Stathern in turmoil and cloaked in fear. And I resolve to do so.

At six o'clock, there is a knock on the library door. I am expecting the intrusion. As Milas Farndon enters the room, I feel noticeably relaxed. But apprehension still grips me.

It is two hours since the Sergeant's last visit, when he reported a cache of papers had been found in a secret compartment located under the floorboards. It was in the scullery, the last place to be searched, that the discovery was made. How appropriate for Else she should hide her illicit treasure in the room that is her domain.

"The carriage has been spotted, Captain," reports the sergeant, his voice steady and formal, betraying no hint of emotion. "It is less than a mile away. Everything you have requested is at the ready."

I dismiss Farndon, thanking him for his diligence; I find myself looking out of the library's large window. A murmuring of Starlings paints an incredible picture in the early evening skies. Back and forth they fly in near perfect unison. A black mass, no apparent leader, yet all playing a leading role. I find their maneouvres reminding me of Cromwell and the conversation I had with him about the tactics he wants a future New Model Army to adopt. I dwell on these thoughts for a moment before returning to reality. It will be dusk in just over an hour. By then, there will be no opportunity to turn back from the decisions I am about to take.

I drop to my knees. Only my God can help me now. I pray He deems me worthy to be His servant and helps me find the truth I so desperately require.

The carriage rolls into the village at precisely six thirty. As soon as it reaches the Hall, a squad of dragoons surrounds it, Sergeant Farndon marshalling the cordon. There will be no escape for the occupants. All twelve Militiamen have their swords drawn. A further group of six have their flint-locks primed and ready to fire, should there be any attempt to flee the scene.

When Farndon is satisfied all is secure, I approach the carriage. The two horses are being released from their harnesses, to be led away to the stables. They are nervous at the scene being played out before them. So am I.

Sitting on the raised dais of the carriage are two people – a man I recognise as Nicholas Rowse, one of the Militia's regulars, and Else, who is staring ahead. No words of protest, or surprise, have passed her mouth since the troops emerged and surrounded her. She just sits there. Still.

I am the first to break the uncomfortable silence.

"Can you please dismount and accompany Sergeant Farndon to the guard room," I say as calmly as I can. "Everything will be explained to you in a few minutes. And fear not, you will have ample opportunity to speak."

Else opens her mouth as if to utter something. But no noise emerges. She looks at the scene being played out around her, raises herself off the crude wooden bench and descends. As she reached the cobbles of the courtyard, she stumbles, fear betraying her weakness. Two dragoons seize her arms and escort her away.

Even though she passes within three yards of where I am standing, the woman I have known for almost three decades refuses to look in my direction. And she says absolutely nothing. Racked with contrasting emotions, I am as contented as I can be under the circumstances.

"Sergeant Farndon, is there anything else I need to know before I speak to the prisoner?" I ask.

The veteran, who fought in the Bishops Wars for the King before joining the Militia, approaches me and speaks quietly.

"We are continuing to search the cottage, Captain," he confirms. "My men are finalising things as we speak. You can be sure we will be thorough. If there is anything more to find, the men will uncover it. They know their business."

War brings out the best in the people you are closest to. In equal measure, their very worst traits are also revealed. Nobody stays the same. And on this Friday evening, with the Ides of March just four days away, I believe I am about to discover things that will define my character for years to come.

As I enter the guardroom where Else is being held, I feel a mixture of anger, pity and revulsion.

The building is located in one of the houses close to Saint Guthlacs that has been commandeered for Militia business. It is small and ordinary, with just a single room downstairs and two bedchambers on the first floor. None of the rooms have locks on the doors, for this is the first time we have been required to hold a prisoner. In the past, when the Militia has apprehended Cavaliers, we have held them in barns, or taken them directly to the dungeons of Leicester.

Thankfully, Farndon is unperturbed by the unexpected turn in events. He has placed an armed sentry at the top of the stairs and by the main door. He has also increased the number of men on guard duty. While we don't expect any trouble this evening, it is wise not to take any chances.

And the evidence against our cook continues to mount.

Isabel has recalled an occasion, some years past, that links Else directly to the brooch found at the Harrington's home. This revelation, which I learned about just after lunchtime, forced me to order the search of Else's cottage while she was in Long Clawson.

As a result, my men have now uncovered a locked strongbox, hidden under the kitchen hearth, containing covertly coded correspondence. Spies from both sides are known to communicate with each other using the juice of onions to write down their secrets and treachery; it is invisible to the human eye when it dries. It is the essential ingredient that aids them as they compile hidden messages that can only be read when the parchment is held over the flame of a candle.

It appears all of the letters contained in the horde found at Else's cottage have been composed this way, so some of Sergeant Farndon's men are now busy decoding the communiqués. And there are many of them.

The results will be brought to me just as soon as they are ready.

Since her arrest, Else has been left on her own for more than two hours. She has not been offered food or water. And she remains unaware why she is being detained under armed guard. This is all part of the plan. I am hoping the tactics will loosen her tongue when the interrogation begins, which will be in ten minutes time. At nine o'clock.

But I am troubled. Events are developing so quickly. Only this morning Else was our trusted cook, with no hint of suspicion attached to her name. She was our friend; a confidante, loved by us all. Now she is appears to be deeply implicated in the deaths of the Harringtons. And, if Farndon's efforts deliver what I expect they will, I fear she will confirmed as the spy in our midst that Rowland warned me about all those weeks ago.

War may have scarred me and hardened my heart in so many respects. But at this moment, it is hard to reconcile myself with the searing, physical pain I feel as I prepare to condemn Else as a traitor.

"Before I ask you some questions, is there anything you might like to tell me, Else?" I say to the prisoner, as I confront her for the first time. "It may aid your cause greatly if you choose to talk to me freely about what you have done and what you know. There may be things I can do to ease the sentence you receive."

I am disappointed: silence greets my conciliatory offer.

"I will ask you a second time. Else, is there anything you wish to say to me of a voluntary nature? Something that sheds some light on the things me men have discovered this day?"

For the briefest moment, a nervous twitch in the left eye of the prisoner is the only movement in the room. Then I see her looking around wildly, seeking something to focus on, something that will mute the effects of my interrogation; another classic trait of the spy. And still no words of confession are forthcoming.

"That is most unfortunate," I say, meaning it. "I was hoping you would be able to explain all the abnormalities that have come to my attention these past few hours. For I have no desire to see you held like this unless there is just reason and cause to do so. But your silence leaves me with no choice. Having given you the opportunity to tell me what you know, and your failure to utter a single word in your defence, I must assume a level of guilt on your part. Therefore, I am now going to interview you as someone I consider to have played a part in the deaths of Peter and Marjorie Harrington. How say you to this?"

Again, Else's silence is deafening.

Without waiting further, I list my concerns about her conduct: I tell her that I believe she lied to me about the brooch before leaving Stathern and making the surprise and irregular visit to Long Clawson; I tell her of Isabel recollecting she saw Else wearing the jewel several years prior, at a family christening; and I tell her, for the first time, that my men have found a cache of letters in her cottage that have been decoded. In truth, I do not know precisely what the correspondence contains. But the reports I have received from Farndon, detailing some of the evidence he is amassing, is already damning. It reveals Else has been in league with the Royalists for a considerable time and leaves the reader in no doubt of her allegiance to our enemies.

"I hope you appreciate I need to hear what you have to say about these matters." My voice is tetchy. Impatient. Angry. "Be in no doubt, the punishment for Treason and Murder is death. If you are found guilty, you will be drawn to the gallows and there burned alive for these crimes. And it looks bleak for you right now. So, unless you are a willing spy and killer, I urge you to confess all as freely as you can."

Else is shaken. Her hands are unsteady and she bites on her lower lip to prevent her fears from escaping. Tears start to trickle down her left cheek. At first it is just the odd droplet. Isolated. Alone. Then, with her eyes blinking, a flood begins. She is gripping the side of the table so tightly, the blood from her fingernails stops flowing. And then, with her head lowered in defeat, at last, she speaks.

"Master Francis," she pleads in a breaking voice. "I have much to contemplate and much to say. I wish to tell you all I know. But I am in no state to do so this evening. Exhausted I am. My head is spinning. Can you please give me the rest of the night to compose myself and recall the events of the past few months? I wish to confess and not be a hindrance. If you are able to give me a few, short hours, I will repay your kindness with all I know in the morning."

I look at her. Her words are unambiguous; they confirm her guilt. In a few short sentences, she has condemned herself: a traitor. All I need to establish is the scale of her crimes and whether she had willing accomplices.

I look at my pocket watch. It is past ten o'clock. It has been a long and emotional day. So I accede to Else's request. A good night's sleep will benefit us all. The morrow, we can get to the bottom of these evil events once and for all.

"I will grant you your wish," I confirm. "But be in no doubt, I require you to tell me all you know. The truth. Nothing else. You will give me names, dates and times. And you will tell me why. I want to know everything you have in your possession that is material to the matters I am pursuing. You are well acquainted with the detail, so I expect no tricks. There will be no more lying. If there is, I will turn you over to Lord Grey's torturers, who will not hesitate to rip you apart in the pursuit of getting the facts out of you. Do you understand me? Can you perceive the agonies that await if you fail to cooperate?"

Talk of torture makes me recoil. I remember my own ordeal as if it were yesterday, and I escaped relatively lightly, just losing my finger and toe nails, and suffering the odd broken bone. For a spy and murderess, there can be no respite. The suffering will be total. Their body will be savaged. And, at the end, death will be a welcome release.

Else understands these things and her response is barely audible. "Yes, Master," she whispers. "I know what you speak of. I will pray to God between now and the morning."

I leave the cell, slamming the door behind me. I tell the guard to stay vigilant and ask him to feed Else as soon as he can. Even though I now recognise her as my enemy, I will not succumb to the temptations of the barbarian. The morning sun will soon rise. And when it does, I need my prisoner to talk fulsomely. When she does, I will learn the truth about her betrayal and discover why the Harringtons were brutally killed.

And once I know it all, then justice can be meted out.

Archbishop Laud
A key part of the King's inner circle, Laud introduced
unpopular changes to religious practices in England

TWENTY

I HAVE BEEN ASLEEP FOR barely four hours when I am awoken. It is just after three o'clock in the morning on Saturday the twelfth day of March, in the year of our Lord, 1644.

I sit upright, my ears straining to hear the noise that roused me from my deep slumber. I remain motionless for several moments, my eyes straining to cut through the darkness, my ears trying to recognise the source of my agitation. Then I hear it again: the sound of swords clashing and men fighting for their lives. And I am wide-awake, ready to enter the fray.

My heart is beating erratically. I cannot comprehend what is happening at this early hour. But I know death has come to Stathern.

Isabel stirs as I quickly put on my breeches, boots and doublet and strap my sword and knife to my side.

"What is wrong, my dear?" asks my wife, barely awake. "Why are you getting up so early?"

I lean over and kiss her, striving to hide my alarm. "I

am needed in the guardhouse, my love. There is a minor disturbance. Concern yourself not. I will be back before you know it. Now get back to sleep."

As I walk down the stairs of the Hall, a couple of candles guiding me to the railing and enabling me to descend untroubled, I quickly calculate how many members of the Militia are on guard duty. I recall the strength returns submitted yesterday and realise only eight men are actively patrolling the streets and surrounding areas of Stathern. After the excitement of last night, and Else's arrest, a further three men are stationed at the guardhouse. I feel my chest tighten. Despite the precautions I have taken, I am suddenly aware of how vulnerable we are.

As I close the door to the Hall, a muffled scream cuts through the thick fog that cloaks the rooftops of the village. It is an unnatural sound often heard on the battlefield: it is the reaper's lament.

I run towards the noise; partially sighted; feeling my way along the street. I make slow progress as blade parries blade. As I pass close to the church, I see a still body. It is one of my men. In the dim light, I can see blood is oozing from a deep slash across the unfortunate wretch's neck. The main artery has been severed. There is nothing I can do for him. All the vital signs of life are shutting down as the victim's blood continues to course out of his veins, like red-hot lava spewing out of an erupting volcano.

A hundred yards on, at the back of Saint Guthlacs, two more of my men lie prostrate. Such is the speed and precision of their attackers they have departed this world without unsheathing their swords. This time, I recognise the fallen: Henry Gibbing and William Walker; married men. I say a brief prayer for their souls before moving cautiously on.

A similar picture of carnage awaits me when I arrive at the guardhouse. The sentry charged with patrolling the main door has a knife protruding out of his back. Gabriel Caunt, the son of the local mill owner, has collapsed at the foot of the stairs. His lifeless eyes stare at me, the shock of his violent final seconds on this earth captured vividly in his contorted features.

I look to the left. The main chamber is empty, with the exception of Sergeant Farndon, who is rooted to his desk. He looks as though he is in a deep slumber, sitting at his station. Parchments are scattered all around him. His head is tilted backwards; his mouth is wide open. If I didn't know better, I would swear he is about to snore. But the crimson stain on his tunic means there will be no awakening for this most trusted and reliable of men. Like Gibbing and Walker, he has been dispatched to paradise far too soon.

Panic threatens to overwhelm me. I start to despair. I take a step towards Farndon's body. And then the blackness of oblivion claims me.

I don't know how long I am unconscious. Minutes? Hours? It matters little. When I awake, all I know is I have a throbbing ache at the back of my head, I am bound to a wooden chair – and I am alive. For the moment, at least!

"Hör auf zu reden. Er kommt herum," a familiar voice barks out. "Ich werde mit ihm sprechen. Geh und überprüfe, ob draußen keine Wachen mehr lauern."

Translation: "Stop talking. He is coming around. I will speak to him. Go and check there are no more guards lurking outside."

A face that has been the source of my nightmares these past four months looms into the corner of my blurred vision.

"Ah, Captain Hacker," laughs Gustav Holck. "It is a pleasure to renew our acquaintance. Please accept my apologies if you are suffering a slight headache. One of my men doesn't know his own strength!"

I groan aloud. "Holck? You? What are you…?"

The Bohemian, a man I last saw in the company of Prince Maurice at Belvoir Castle, clears his throat. As he does, my fingers and toes start to ache. Using his crude, guttural English, he says: "No doubt you are wondering why I am here tonight? What my purpose is? Why I have made such efforts to enter your den?"

I am unable to say anything. Stabbing pains kneed the base of my skull and make it hard to concentrate; my eyes are unable to focus.

Holck looks up as a well-built fighter enters the room. "Was ist es?" he enquires. "Haben Sie gefunden, wonach wir suchen?"

Translation: "What is it? Have you found what we are looking for?"

The soldier looks discomforted. "Nein, mein Kapitä n," he replies. "Wir haben das Haus und den Wachraum durchsucht und nichts gefunden."

Translation: "No, my Captain. We have searched the house and the guardroom and we have found nothing."

A flash of irritation passes across Holck's dark, battle-hardened features. It is gone in an instant. "Danke Kamerad," he responds. "Es sieht so aus, als müssten wir Hacker drücken, bis er aufgibt, was wir brauchen. Du bist entlassen."

Translation: "Thank you, comrade. It looks as though we will need to press Hacker until he gives up what we need. You are dismissed."

The powerful Holck wipes his forehead. He is sweating. Is he over-exerted by the fighting, or is this a sign that everything is not well in the enemy camp? Whatever the truth, I am likely to be the last person to find out.

"Are you going to be a good fellow and give me what I need?" he says, grinding the edge of one of his heel into the toes of my right foot. "The correspondence and the brooch, Hacker. Where have you hidden them?"

The shock on my face prompts Holck to start laughing. "You look surprised, Captain?" he declares. "But I forget, you are such a simple man. No? Wasn't that your defence when we last met? Aren't you a soldier who does as he's ordered and doesn't ask questions? A man who likes to keep it simple? A man who obeys his superiors, to the letter? In my country, we call such men fools!

"Do yourself a favour and tell me where the parchments are you took from the cook's quarters. I also require the notes your Sergeant made and the brooch. Don't test my patience. Tell me where they are. Now."

Holck starts to pace the room. His polished boots echo on the wooden boards. His face is bloated. He is troubled.

"Try the Hall. He keeps everything of value and importance at the big house." The voice is Else's, freshly released from her confinement. Her words are laced with a mixture of contempt, bitterness and righteousness.

"Judas, Else. You are a Judas," I cry once I have been released from the shock. "You were our friend. You were part of our family. And this is how you now choose to repay us. Your betrayal is putting Isabel and the children in the gravest danger. May God forgive you, for I will not."

I struggle to release myself from the bonds practiced hands have fastened. I know it is futile, but I have to try.

"Don't try that, fool," shouts Holck. "It is pointless. Give me what I need and I will release you and your family will remain unharmed. We will leave this place as soon as we can. Stay quiet and you will die where you sit. And I will ensure your wife and children suffer before they perish. Do not doubt me, Captain Hacker. You know from experience that I mean what I say. So. Decide quickly what you wish your fate to be."

To have refused to cooperate would result in one thing – my death and the slaying of the people I love the most. For I do not doubt the sincerity of Holck's threat. Death is his trade and he revels in it. Man, woman or child, it matters little; all are fair game to this killer, who cut his teeth on the battlegrounds of Europe. So, without hesitation, I agree to show him where the documents and brooch are hidden.

I need to buy time.

Less than twenty members of the Militia reside in Stathern. These are the men most likely to be able to aid me tonight. Help from six of them I can discount immediately: five are away in Nottingham on Committee business; and I am held prisoner. A further eleven have been killed by Holck and his assassins, leaving just three who are at liberty and able to mount a rescue attempt. Among them are Abijah and Smith, the killer who possesses the singing voice of an angel. If I were to pin my hopes of survival on anyone, it would be these two warriors. I can only pray the distinctive sounds of battle has awoken them and, right now, they are drawing up a plan to bloody the enemy's nose and free me.

It is a remote possibility, but I have to live in hope.

"I will be with you in a few minutes," says Holck, his voice full of the confidence and cruelty he displayed while ruining my hands and feet. "I have something to attend to before we visit your home. We will make our way there upon my return."

His smile fades as he turns to one of his men and says in English: "Kill him if he gives you any trouble."

With Holck gone, the room is stilled. The two Royalist guards that remain sit at the far end, their feet on the table; their eyes closed; their hands firmly on the hilts of their swords. The only movement comes from the flickering candles that continue to light up this scene of brutality and death.

A creaking floorboard betrays Else's approach. No longer looking like the vanquished woman she was only a few hours before, she is now composed, in control, basking in her newly found superiority. She stops a few feet away, close enough for me to see the contempt gleaming from her eyes.

"It seems our fortunes have been reversed, Master Francis," she says mockingly. "Lord Grey's torturers will be disappointed."

I try my best to assume the posture of a man unperturbed by his predicament. It is not an easy task, particularly when I am also seeking answers that explain all this madness.

"Why? Why have you betrayed us so, Else? Tell me, for it does not make any sense." I cannot help asking, almost begging my tormentor. I must know what has turned this woman into a cold bloodied traitor. "Have you been offered riches by Holck and his kind?"

She laughs, her scorn all too visible. This is not the woman I know.

"You really are clueless, aren't you, Captain?" she says. "You have been so engrossed in your own world of playing the country squire and the Parliamentarian soldier to take account of the people around you. Had you done so, you would have realised a long time ago I am a Leal subject, who abhors this rebellion and all it stands for. But you and the Mistress have never asked me what I think. You assumed I was one of you. But you have taken so much for granted.

"For years in the kitchen I have heard you talking so openly about your plans for the Militia, your frustrations and Parliament's military strengths and weaknesses. You have even spoken to me on occasion, seeking my advice! It has been so easy to record what has been said and relay it to my masters at Newark. Your trust in me has been absolute and tonight it is likely to be your undoing."

I see it all now. How right Else is; my naivety is my ruin.

For longer than I care to remember, Isabel has warned me that my desire to believe in people of all classes, and trust them unreservedly, would be my undoing. And it appears my failure to heed this caution has put me, once again, in an extremely perilous situation.

Despite my parlous situation, I continue to probe, desperate to uncover more of the truth.

"Else, you have been a part of our family," I say, seeking answers. "I must ask you again: why have you turned against us? Isabel is your friend. I am your friend.

Our children adore you. Why abandon us for a tyrant King and men like Holck?"

Else sits down in front of me, close enough so she can be heard with little difficulty, and far enough away to ensure I cannot molest her.

"Captain Hacker, I have worked for your family for twenty seven years," she states. "Before coming to Stathern, I was raised in London. At Whitehall, my mother served King James and then his son, Charles. She was a loyal subject. As am I. Had you ever really talked to me, on those many occasions I fed you in the kitchen, you would have discovered this.

"I didn't set out to betray you, sir. Circumstance dictated my fate; that is all. When the war broke out, I was contacted by one of the King's officers at Newark Castle; I had been overheard revealing my thoughts when visiting Stamford. Before I knew it, I was being asked to provide information about known Parliamentarians. You were one of the men I was asked to monitor. And I did so willingly.

"As the struggles continued, and you became a prominent member of the Militia and the Leicester Committee, the King's cause has required more information about you and your activities, particularly this past year. So I have supplied it. And I have naught regrets. For you and your kind are rebels, would-be usurpers playing the power game for your own ends. You seek change for your own advancement, not because you oppose the right of Kings to rule. You are hypocrites. And that is why I have chosen to do what I have done."

There comes a point in everyone when shock affects your sense of reality and perspective. Your head starts spinning; a fog descends; and despair is all consuming.

As Else vents her spleen, I am aware of how helpless and lost I feel. Yet I sense there is more Else wishes to tell me. So I try to press on.

"Did you pass on details of any Parliamentary army plans you may have heard about the confrontation at Edgehill?" I ask.

The response is instant: "Yes I did."

"Did you provide the information that helped Gervase Lucas capture me and the other Committee members at Melton Mowbray?" I demand.

Her words are unambiguous: "Of course. It was my duty."

"And what about the slaying of Peter and Marjorie. Are you responsible for these senseless murders as well? Did you kill them?" I ask.

Suddenly, the arrogant mask Else has been wearing these past few minutes is cast off. In its place, I see the torment that is etched on Else's face as she struggles to find adequate words to answer my question. Her eyes start to water and large tears trickle down her cheekbones. "I told Holck where they lived," she hisses. "But I did not know they would be killed. It is not what I wanted. It was never the intention. This is the truth. Their deaths will haunt me until the day I die."

I find myself staring at my damaged fingernails, the results of Holck's handiwork. "I never realised you had such malice and evil in you, Else," I say. "Your betrayals have led to the deaths of innocents, my own brother included; for your intelligence has directly influenced Royalist activities in this area. What you told your Masters, cast doubt on the loyalties of Thomas and Rowland. They ordered my brothers to resume patrols in Colston Bassett.

And we all know how it ended.

"Yet I would never have guessed you would be capable of such disloyalty. On the surface, you appeared true; dedicated. Yet you have consorted with Lucifer himself and you are now an agent of the Devil. And, if I have any influence at all, I will see to it you will burn in Hell for your misdeeds."

I quickly bite on my tongue. I fear have said too much. But my outburst has an impact: it uncorks a wave of emotion in Else that at last helps me understand why killing the Harringtons was absolutely necessary. They had to be silenced.

"Marjorie saw me leave something for Holck in the graveyard at Saint Guthlacs," confesses Else. "She thought it odd, so continued to watch the place I used. After a while, she saw a stranger go to the tree and retrieve the dispatch I had left, placing a message for me, from Holck, in its place.

"Marjorie was completely unaware of the kind of adventure I was embroiled in. The stupid, meddling woman thought I was stealing foods from the Hall and selling them to some local unworthies. She confronted me, saying she was going to tell the Mistress everything she knew.

"She took the message sent to me by Holck, which, to the naked eye, was nothing more than a plain sheet of parchment. I would have been done for if she had she known how to read it. She would have taken it straight to you, not confronted me with her misguided accusations. Unfortunately for her, she also found my brooch, which had fallen from my cape at the graveside plot. This is the jewel you now have in your possession. It is something that means a lot to me, as it is the only thing I own that belonged to my mother. It was a gift to her from my father."

I say nothing at these revelations. I wish I could, but there is simply too much to absorb and comprehend. Thankfully, Else needs little encouragement to continue as she seeks to cleanse her soul.

"After Marjorie confronted me, I panicked," she admits. "I contacted Holck through the network I have used these past couple of years and told him I needed urgent help. Within twenty-four hours everything had been agreed. He promised me he would retrieve the letter and the brooch, and ensure the Harringtons stayed quiet about the matter.

"At no time did he tell me he would be killing them. Had he done so, I would not have cooperated with him. And that is the truth. But he allowed me to think he would merely be frightening them. And I believed him. So I told Holck where they lived, much to my eternal regret and shame. And I was as shocked as anyone when Stephen burst into the Hall and reported the fire. It was not what was agreed."

It is now my turn to spit out a mouthful of contempt and ire. At the outset of my enquiries, I had told myself I would remain neutral if I were to discover the reasons behind the deaths. But I find myself unable to keep my composure.

"Hear me," I say. "You are as guilty as anyone for the deaths of these innocents. Do not seek forgiveness and understanding from me, for none will be forthcoming. You have chosen to deal with Holck and his kind. He is a killer, nothing more. And you are no better. Your words condemn you. You seek to justify your actions, which led to the deaths of two people I care about. But you are a betrayer. A traitor. And, if I can, I will do all I can to ensure your punishment befits the magnitude of your devilry."

At that moment, as Else comprehends my threat, Holck returns. He has been absent for almost fifteen minutes. Thankfully, he appears not to have heard any of our conversation. But his breathing is heavy; his mood suggests danger is in the air.

"It is time to go," he says brusquely. "We have little time. I need the correspondence and the brooch. Now take me to them, Captain."

The Hall has been a place of safety for me for as long as I can remember. Here I am contented and happy. Danger is something I have never countenanced, until this morning.

When we arrive at the Hall, I hear Isabel's raised voice. "Get your hands off my son," she is shouting. "Leave him alone."

As I attempt to force my way forward, Holck places a crushing hand on my shoulder and presses the blade of his knife a little harder into the base of my spine. "Go in," he commands, pointing in the direction of the kitchen. "Calm your wife down and ensure your children remain quiet. Do it. And do it quickly. When all is quiet, get me what we came here for."

I am not prepared for the scene that confronts me.

My family is huddled in the far corner, away from the window and doors. One of Holck's men is physically restraining Isabel, his hand around the back of her neck. I can see the man enjoys the cruel game he is inflicting on the defenceless.

All of my children are crying. And Francis is lying on the floor, a red welt covering his right eye and cheek.

"What in God's name is going on?" I shout. "Leave my wife alone, cur. She is not your quarry. Try someone your own size who has the will and strength to fight back."

I receive a blow to the back of my head. I fall. Stunned. I hear the cries of my children. And then I come to, with Holck's face staring into my own, his corrupted breath polluting my airways.

"Get to your feet, fool," he shouts. "And do as you are told. The next time I won't be so gentle."

Isabel is disconsolate as I attempt to calm her down.

"These men seek some items of value. That is all," I try to explain. "Please do not worry. Providing I do as they instruct, you will all be safe."

Six men have accompanied Holck to the Hall. All of them look every inch what they are: formidable, accomplished killers. And like their commander, they all appear to be Bohemian.

"Beobachte die Familie," says Holck to the closest soldier. "Bring sie zum Schweigen, wenn sie ein Geräusch machen."

Translation: "Watch the family. Silence them if they make a noise."

With his left hand gripping my neck, Holck prods his dagger in the direction of the door. "Move," he commands. "Let's get on with it."

My captor accompanies me to the bedchamber. The door is ajar. Clothes, garments, jewelry and linen are scattered all over the floor. Our captors have clearly attempted to find the objects they came here for prior to my arrival. I glance over to the spot concealing the secret chamber. Remarkably, it is intact.

"Where are they hidden?" he demands. "My men couldn't find them, despite their best efforts. You have had some good fortune, for they were just starting to work on your family when we arrived. Your presence has ensured they are spared. For now; as long as you deliver what you have promised."

I look fiercely at the Royalist mercenary. Only on a few rare occasions have I felt malevolence in the field; at places like Adwalton Moor, when my blood lust is raised and I have unleashed myself on the enemy, despite the hopelessness of the situation. I have this sensation right now, albeit for very different reasons.

"I am aware of exactly how you might be feeling," says Holck, perceptively. "And that is okay, Roundhead. But if you step out of line you and your family will perish. Remember that as you do what is required. Now get on with it. Schnell."

I do as I am told.

I go to the main window and open the shutters. Moving quickly, I find the small clasp that is hidden underneath the sill. I unclip it, freeing the heavy wooden ledge. It slides easily out of its frame, exposing the chamber underneath. It contains one item – a large leather case. I remove this object with both hands, placing it on the frame of the overturned bed I share with Isabel. I quickly find the appropriate key, retrieve it from my pocket chain and open both locks. Only then does Holck make his approach, allowing me to reveal the contents to him.

"Ingenious," he says, as he peers into the small darkened vault that concealed the case. "Not quite big enough to hide a priest, but ample enough for precious items. I am appreciative of the skills of your carpenter and stonemason, Hacker. You are certainly a man of many surprises. Now give me everything I need."

I do as I am instructed. After close examination, Holck is satisfied. The items are quickly put in the satchel he is carrying. It bears the emblem of Prince Rupert. Once he is satisfied everything is secure, he signals it is time to leave, beckoning me to march ahead. With the sharp knife pressing into my flesh and drawing blood, we begin the short journey back to the kitchen.

When we return, I am relieved to see Isabel is sitting down and the girls are all within her protective embrace. Francis is perched next to her. His face is a picture of hostility and anger towards the intruders. There is no sign of fear. My brave boy continues to confound and grow in stature.

Handing the satchel to one of his subordinates, Holck says: "Nimm drei Männer. Bereite die Pferde vor. Wir fahren in fünf Minuten."

Translation: "Take three men. Get the horses ready. We ride in five minutes."

The two other mercenaries position themselves carefully: one behind Isabel and the children, the other in front of me. Both have their swords drawn.

"Now," says Holck. "There is the small matter of…"

Suddenly the quiet of the early morning is shattered by the sound of men shouting "In God's name!" followed by the clash of cold steel. A musket is discharged. Somewhere close by there is an agonized scream. And the shouts get louder. "In God's name" reverberates in the streets of Stathern, punctured by the torments of men preparing to meet a sudden and unexpected doom.

Holck draws his sword and waits patiently. He is silent; still; poised to strike. A sense of elation fills my soul. The veins in my forehead throb. I forget the dull ache at the base of my neck and a nervous tension starts to release itself as I realise liberation is close at hand.

"In God's name" is the cry of Parliament. The Militia is here.

Within a few minutes the sound of the conflict dies away. Peace replaces the cacophony of slaughter. I hear voices outside; close by. I recognise at least one of them.

If Holck is surprised by his reversal of fortune, he doesn't show it. I presume he has survived equally precarious situations in his home country, when the Spanish overran it. He quickly barks out an order to his men: "Wä hle zwei der Kinder aus. Sichere sie. Dann bring sie zu mir."

Translation: "Pick two of the children. Secure them. Then bring them to me."

Before I know what is happening, two of my daughters have been forcibly extracted from my wife's safe clutches. Isable is just six-years-old, Barbara not yet four. Their hands are quickly bound as Isabel starts to throw herself at our persecutors once again in a bid to secure their release. She receives a stunning blow to her face. I am unable to intervene, as Holck has drawn his Flintlock and is aiming its muzzle directly at me. All I can do is urge her to remain calm and sit down. There is nothing more to be done if we want to survive.

Now he has regained a semblance of control, Holck sheaths his weapon and addresses me. "I need insurance, Captain Hacker," he explains, pointing at my children. "I have no intention of becoming a prisoner. I know what fate awaits me should I ever lose my liberty to the forces of Parliament. So I am taking two of your daughters as hostages. Should you, or your men attempt to apprehend me on my journey, I will have no hesitation in killing them. Am I making myself clear?"

At that very moment, Abijah and Smith walk into the room. If they expected to see the enemy defeated, they are going to be sorely disappointed. Sure enough, their victorious smiles are soon replaced with the painful looks of men who know a wily opponent has outfoxed them.

More than thirty elated members of the Militia stand outside the Hall. They have been roused from the villages of Harby, Hose, Plungar and Langar by the concerted efforts of Swan and Smith. All live less than a twenty-minute ride away. All have played a part in routing the enemy.

Quite rightly, they await the anticipated surrender of Holck and what remains of his force of cutthroats. Their surprise is total when the painful reality makes itself known to them.

I emerge from the house and speak to my men, leaving no detail spared. Their grim expressions tell me more than any words ever could.

"I now need you to move back to the guardhouse," I command. "Collect any bodies you find in the streets, ours and theirs, and wait for me. I will not be long. I will issue orders as soon as I get to you."

Turning to two of the men closest to the Hall, I add: "Nixe. Jeruis. Find three of their horses and bring them here. Make sure they are fit, large enough for two riders on each and are fit enough get to Newark unimpeded. And please make haste."

I return to the kitchen, where young Isable and Barbara are doing their best to stay resolute, but their uncontrollable grief betrays their terrors and anxieties. The rest of my family sit in stunned silence, struggling to understand what is being played out in front of their very eyes.

"Fear not, my darlings," I implore them both. "No harm is going to come to you. Papa is going to make sure everything is okay."

Pointing directly at Holck, I add: "This man and his comrades are going to take you on a short ride. Do not worry. There is no reason to be frightened. I will make sure you will soon be back at home with Mama, your brother and your sisters. Just make sure you do everything he tells you."

Both attempt to break free from the clutches of Holck's mercenary. But he has a firm hold and easily thwarts their attempts.

"Where will you release them?" I ask Holck, fighting hard to control my anger and thirst for revenge.

He thinks for a moment before responding.

"Be in the grounds of All Saints in Elston at four o'clock this evening. It is an hour's ride from here. Providing you stay true to your word, your girls will be waiting for you. Lie to me and you know what the outcome will be."

Charles the First of England
The King believed he was only answerable to God – no
living man had the authority to tell him what to do

TWENTY-ONE

CHILDREN SHOULD NOT BE USED as pawns in warfare. They are innocents, who should be protected from the slash of a sword thrust or the agony of the red-hot pain a musket ball inflicts. Yet many thousands have already perished in this gruesome struggle. And many more will join them in the grave before it is all over; casualties of our King's desire for power at any price.

To my cost, I now know what it feels like when your child is placed in mortal danger. It becomes impossible for you to function normally; you will do anything to ensure their safety, happily laying down your own life to preserve theirs. So, when Abijah tells me Else is in the safe custody of the Militia, it has very little meaning to me. She is no longer a priority; securing the release of Isable and Barbara is only one thing that matters.

"Ensure she is guarded; take all precautions that are necessary," I tell my second-in-command. "Send a messenger to Lord Grey, informing him of the situation. Let him know a further dispatch will follow shortly. Triple the number of men on duty until we know we are sure we are all safe.

"Make sure all duties are organised so they accommodate our heightened state of alert. If we have to maintain this level of readiness for several weeks, then so be it. We must never be caught off-guard again."

More than twenty-four men perished during the early morning carnage that came to Stathern. Eleven of the fallen are my brothers-in-arms; men I have laughed and cried with these past months; men I respected and loved, as a brother in Christ loves another; men who survived Adwalton Moor. The other bodies are those of the mercenaries who rode with Holck. A further nine men of the Militia received wounds. But I am relatively unconcerned about their injuries. None are serious. In good time, they will all heal.

I write the second dispatch to Grey, informing him of the attack on Stathern and details about the kidnapping of my daughters. A rider leaves immediately for Bradgate House, where his Lordship resides. I ask him to suspend patrols in the Newark area for the next twelve hours; this will enable me to honour my promise to Holck and secure the safe release of Isable and Barbara.

I also reveal details of the capture of Else, her treachery and the information she holds. I have no doubts my cook will now suffer at the hands of the Militia's harshest, cruelest men. Grey will see to it. And this time, there will be no second chances.

Abijah is making reassuring noises to Isabel when I return to the library. She has noticeably calmed down – but I know her fears, like my own, will be bubbling very close to the surface. There is no doubt the events of today will leave a deep scar for a long time, particulalry among our children.

"I have been talking things through with Isabel," says Abijah. "I have told her everything is usually a formality in these situations, and explaining why the Cavaliers can be trusted to keep their word."

Under the circumstances, I try to look as confident as I can be. I approach the table where my distraught wife is sitting. Francis and the girls are close by. All four of them are muted. Lost. Struggling to understand what has happened, why violence has errupted in their home and two of their siblings have been taken hostage. In turn, I kiss each of them. I offer comforting words and embrace them, as a Father should. But I know it all counts for naught until I return home with Isable and Barbara.

With Francis taking charge of the girls, I approach Isabel. Her cheeks are flushed, her eyes bloodshot. A red mark on her neck is stark evidence of her struggles less than two hours before.

"Abijah is right, my love," I say. "Holck will do as he has pledged. He has nothing to gain by doing anything else. While I make the journey to Elston, you are best employed looking after Ann, Elizabeth, Mary and Francis. They need the strength of their Mother to return."

Isabel reaches out and clasps my hand. Our fingers entwine. I feel her physical pain, desperation and loss.

"Bring them home," she pleads. "Promise me you won't let those monsters harm our Barbara and Isable."

Abijah, Smith, myself and three other men set out from Stathern at two o'clock in the afternoon. I have been itching to leave the confines of the village for the last few hours. I have been trapped, unable to do anything of merit. I need to be with my men, astride Bucephalus. I am tormented and will continue to be so until I have rescued my daughters.

We pass through the villages of Granby and Aslockton as we gently set about covering the seventeen miles between Stathern and Elston. Bucephalus cuts a frustrated figure as I refuse to allow him to stretch his legs fully and eat up the land. Today, his job is to serve my cause, and that alone; nothing else. He need have no fear. After today, he will be able to indulge himself once again, the rolling fields of Leicestershire and Rutlandshire his theatre.

At a quarter to three, we arrive at St Mary and All Saints in Hawksworth. It is just four miles away from Elston. The church's starkness is fitting of the gravity of the situation in which we find ourselves; it is also a welcome diversion, as I am weighed down by the need to pray and cleanse my heart of the sins and dark thoughts that have consumed me for several days.

This particular House of God will serve my needs perfectly as I repent and seek my Lord's forgiveness.

"Let the men relax for half an hour," I call out to Abijah as I enter the Church. "Allow the horses to graze on the pastureland. Get your prayer books out and prepare yourselves for what is to come. Hopefully, we will be home for dinner, with everything once again as it should be. Now excuse me, my friend. I need to make my own peace with my Maker."

I am deep in prayer when the doors of the Church are thrown open and my peace I have sought is brought to an abrupt end. Abijah is standing at the entrance.

"Francis. Francis," he calls, the urgency in his voice undeniable. "Francis, you must come. We may have a serious problem."

I emerge from the darkness and solitude of St Mary and All Saints to be greeted by my own troop and another group of armed men on horseback. There are no more than twenty of them. I recognise the man closest to me, looking down from his lofty perch.

"Captain Babington," I say in recognition. "This is a coincidence. What are you doing in these parts?"

Thomas Babington is an active member of the Leicestershire Militia. He is part of the gentry in Rothley, a village close to Loughborough, and is a man of the highest repute. Like myself, he reports to Lord Grey. But he is rarely found in these parts, preferring to be active in the garrison at Leicester, far away from the range of the cannons of Newark!

Babington looks distressed.

"I fear I may have some worrying news for you, my friend," he says. "For I am just returning to Newark, where my company is due to bolster the siege. We left Copt Oak this morning and have been completing routine visits to the outlying villages and towns as we make our progress.

"Just under two hours ago, my scouts were involved in a skirmish with some Cavaliers. I really thought nothing of it at the time. It's only when we were riding through here that I saw Swan and your men and they told me of your vital mission this day. That's why, in all urgency, I feel you should know about this matter."

My legs feel weak; nausea grips my stomach; I feel my heart beating quickly against my chest.

"Tell me, Thomas," I ask my fellow officer. "Where

did you encounter these cavaliers and how many where there?"

Babington calls over to one of his men. When the dragoon is within earshot, he adds: "Pray, William, tell Captain Hacker of your encounter with the Cavalier horsemen this day. Describe all you saw."

As soon as the young soldier begins to describe the men he pursued, dread takes a hold of me. There can be little doubt; the picture he paints is that of Holck and his two mercenaries driving their horses towards Elston.

"Two of the horses seemed to be riding at a reduced speed," adds Barke. "They appeared to be carrying something that was slowing them down. We were too far away to identify the men or their cargoes. And, for the most part, we were following them, so we only saw them from the rear. They certainly would not know who we were, of that I am sure."

Barke becomes aware of my distress. "Are you alright, sir? Have I said something out of turn?"

I shake my head. "No, soldier, you have not. Rest easy. But please tell me the extent of the skirmish. How intensive was the fighting you and the men engaged in?"

The young rider points to the side of his saddle, where his musket is housed. "We fired these, sir. That is all. In all probability, six riders discharged no more than twelve rounds. And the enemy did not respond. As far as I could tell, we did not hit any of them. In truth, they were too far away. They just kept riding. They were outnumbered and had no desire to engage in fight with us."

I thank the soldier and walk back into the church. It takes all the energy I can muster to reach the doorway. The gargoyles lining the inner walls appear to be laughing at me as I reach the chancellery. I close my eyes; I am spent; powerless. All I can now do is pray Holck takes pity on my beautiful daughters.

Bucephalus starts to blow just as we sight Elston.

The village, recorded in the Doomsday Book of William the Conqueror some six hundred years ago, is just four miles away from Hawksworth. But the pace I have set has been unrelenting and it is little wonder he is tiring.

I look behind and see Abijah, Smith and the other three Militiamen trailing far behind. Their steeds are strong, but they are not the equals of my thoroughbred.

A large oak tree is to my left. Its bare branches remind me of the bones of the dead, after the crows have stripped the flesh. I have seen it at the plague pits that litter our land and I shudder at the thought. I dismount, eager to shake off my melancholy state of mind. I watch as my comrades get closer, saying another prayer for Isable and Barbara as I await their arrival. Whatever fate has in store for me, I will surely need my Father and my men by my side.

Thankfully, it doesn't take long for Swan to catch up and rein his horse in beside my own. He is aware of my bleakness.

"Stay strong, Francis," he says when he is close enough. "All will be well. They will be here; we will soon be on our way back to Stathern. You mark my words."

I do not share my deputy's confidence.

My despair is complete.

"It is out of my hands," I say. "God's will has been done. I know not what awaits; I only know I am consumed with dread and fear."

I have no more appetite for talk. I walk away, signaling I wish to be on my own for a moment. I need to pull myself together, albeit my heart aches so.

When the six of us have come together, we cautiously approach All Saints. It is a simple church building, the sort of place where a Puritan like myself would be happy to participate in communion.

Today, seeing its red bricks glimmering in the early evening sunshine, the bile starts rise in my stomach once again. I cannot go any further. I am terrified of what I am about to find.

"Come now," says Abijah, taking hold of the reins and steering Bucephalus the last few yards. "Let's find them and be on our way."

I walk by the side of my horse. I can find no words.

My men dismount. They tether their horses and fan out. Two of them, James Harward and Robert Whittell, enter the church building and start looking among the benches and antechambers; Abijah and John Mantell, a hard-working and diligent farm hand, go to the left, scanning the far corners of the graveyard. Smith accompanies me as we comb a large section of land to the right.

"The church is empty," shouts Whittell, emerging into the sunlight. It has taken him and Harward less than five minutes to check the Church and its outbuildings. "There is nothing here, no sign of them. They must be elsewhere in the grounds."

Ahead of me, I hear Abijah calling out their names.

"Barbara, where are you?" his voice chimes. "Isable, come out and find me. It is Abijah, I have come to take you home."

At my rear, Smith's harmonious voice now enters the

fray. Surely, with the voice of an angel aiding our quest, they must be able to hear us now?

"Francis, I think I can see them," yells Abijah excitedly. "Come. Come quickly. They are here. We have found them."

I turn and run. I hit a wall and feel no pain as my thigh is opened just above the knee. I brush past Smith, who hasn't heard Swan's call and is still sweeping through the tree-lined hedge; and I find myself required to sidestep row after row of unmarked graves as I burst into the burial area.

I am running as fast as I can. My legs are buckling. I am fit to drop; yet I somehow find myself standing next to Abijah. He is silent. Quite still. He raises his arm, his fingers pointing to somewhere in the distance. He is shaking. And grief is pouring out of him.

I look to where his hand is directing me. I see a lone tablestone some hundred yards away: the resting place of a local member of the gentry, a marker commemorating another precious life cut short. Sitting there is Barbara; her dark curls fluttering on the gentle breeze. She appears to be soundly asleep, her head resting against the monument. Alongside her is Isable. She too is motionless; and she is clutching something in her right hand. Both look to be at peace with the world.

What appear to be red necklaces are adorning their pale white, tender necks.

I call out to them, but neither of them hears me. I call again, louder this time. As I do, I feel Abijah's strong arms wrap themselves around my waist. I look at my friend. His cheeks are wet, moistened by the tears freely flowing from both eyes. His voice is slurred. I am struggling to understand what he is saying.

Suddenly Smith is with them, at their place of rest. He bends down and holds their wrists. He moves his fingers to their necks. Five. Ten. Fifteen long seconds pass by. Then he strikes the tablestone with all the violence he can muster.

He looks up and shakes his head. It's at that moment his words cut deep into my trance:

"They are done for," he says. "There is nothing I can do for them."

And then the enormity of the moment consumes me.

TWENTY-TWO

GRIEF DESTROYS MEN AND WOMEN in different ways. For some, it leads to unrestrained and unbridled anger, when thoughts of retribution dominate the waking hours. Others become trapped in an unedifying cycle of depression and woe. They become shadows. Loners. Forgotten beings. In truth, I do not know what I have become. But I fear it, whatever it is.

It is three weeks since Isable and Barbara were murdered. Their throats had been sliced open by an expert hand. Clenched in Isable's lifeless hand was a note, written in Germanic. The message consisted of one word: *"Trottel."* I am told it means "fool"; the name Holck called me at the Hall.

The physician who attended the scene on that dreadful day assured me the girls would not have suffered; they would have known little about what was happening to them.

"Their deaths," he said, "would be just like entering a deep sleep".

I remember looking at the Doctor, scrutinising his hawkish face as he waited expectantly for his fee. Somehow his puerile words were supposed to make me feel better, to help me dull my guilt and pain?

Well they didn't. Only God's grace has that power; and I seem to be lost to our Maker at the present time.

For Isabel, the last few weeks have been a period of unmerciless torment and pain. Two of our beloved infants have been snatched away. Children that grew inside her; the flesh she nurtured and loved for so long. All for naught, it would seem.

I promised I would defend the girls with my life and bring them home safely. But I lied. I didn't fulfil my promise and Isabel is now lost. And I don't know when, or if ever, her soul will be found.

In private, we weep every hour of every day. And we will for a lifetime. We will not forget the departed. But right now, the only things we both live for are our surviving children: Francis, Ann, Elizabeth and Mary.

The funeral services for Isable and Barbara take place on Friday the eighteenth day of March.

More than three hundred members of the Militia attend, as does my estranged Father, who grows frailer by the day. I have not seen him for many months: due to my Parliamentarian allegiances, he has disowned me. It is two years, at least, since he came to Stathern; when there was only talk of war, not the daily killings we now endure. But there's nothing like a tragic death, or two, to flush out the lost. Rowland cannot come, for obvious reasons. But he sends Isabel and myself a moving note he has penned while overseeing the Trent Bridge garrison. In it he expresses his deepest regrets for not being able to provide more substantive information about Else's treacherous activities.

"My dearest brother and sister," he writes. "The identity of informants is closely guarded. As God is my witness, I have never heard any names mentioned that could have identified the spy. And, had I been pressed, Else would have been the last person I would have pointed an accusatory finger at. She played the Judas so well: the perfect spy.

"Even so, I feel I should have done more. I hope you will be able to forgive me one day."

My brother has no reason for regrets, or for seeking our forgiveness. He was not culpable in any way for the loss of our daughters, far from it. Indeed, he did all he could to help us flush out the viper in our nest. But he could not compromise his position in the King's army any more than he did, for I know he is closely watched.

The renewal of our loving relationship has been one of the good things to come out of the debris of recent months. A Cavalier and a Roundhead reunited: the healing power of our God at work. I will be sure to tell him of the regard I hold him in the next time we see each other. And I will continue to do so every time we meet.

William Norwich, a Minister with a deep love for our King and little time for me, conducted both funeral services at Saint Guthlacs. They were quiet, tearful affairs: respectful and deeply sad. Thankfully, my wife enjoys cordial relations with the churchman, so she found his words comforting and soothing, even if he spoke, in large part, a popist doctrine I refuse to recognise. Nonetheless, I made a point of thanking him for helping Isabel start the process of healing. I realise it will take a long time. But she has started to move forward. And, in this regard, Norwich has an important role to play in the weeks and months ahead.

Isabel knows what I think of our Minister and what I would willingly allow to be done to him if I had my way, backed by the will of Parliament.

She is a much more devoted and obedient servant than I can ever be. Her interventions have meant I have defied the Leicester Committee on several important occasions, failing to hold Norwich to account for preaching a false gospel.

If Parliament and the Committee had their way, the errant Norwich and his family would be living on the streets by now. How long I can continue to protect him I do not know, particularly while I am in my present state of mind; when vengeance is the only thing that occupies my waking hours.

It is Sunday the third day of April and I have risen early, as I have done most days these past three weeks.

A church sermon out of the mouth of the Reverend Norwich beckons – and I must do all I can to still my own tongue, should he stray into his popery ways. So I am praying to the Lord, seeking forbearance and an end to the pain my wife and I are suffering.

Unlike Lord Grey, from whom I have received no correspondence since tragedy struck, Cromwell has written to me on several occasions. He has been informed of the news about Barbara and Isable, and I know his condolences are sincere. Oliver has a brood of children himself; Richard is his most prominent son, but Bridget, his eldest child, is the apple of his eye. And although military and

Parliamentary affairs consume most of his time, he has a real affection for all of his offspring. So I know he relates to the acute loss Isabel and myself are experiencing.

As well as wishing me well, and checking on my health, Oliver also sends me news about the war. And, while I have been mourning, there have been some significant events.

In a dispatch sent on Monday the fourteenth day of March, the Lieutenant-General appears to be in a jovial mood while relaying the news that Archbishop Laud's trial has started in London. Cromwell expects it to be a lengthy affair, and he remains confident he will be found guilty as charged.

I rub my brow, contemplating the likely fate that awaits such a man. I find myself unable to find any pity in my heart for Laud. For surely only the most terrible of deaths can be the only just outcome for a man who has sought to corrupt God's Word so vilely?

Cromwell's letter of the twenty-second day of March is less ebullient.

In the dispatch, he reports Prince Rupert has relieved the siege of Newark, and urges me to talk to Lord Grey and see what the Midlands Association can do to exert pressure on the King's nephew. I know something of this matter, living as close as I do to this key Royalist stronghold. But I am not sure Grey will be prepared to mobilise his men and march them to the Trent. Experience tells me he will do his utmost to find a way of weaseling out of any request. But try I will. For Rupert's untimely intervention is a setback to Parliament's cause and could affect future campaign plans in the north of England if a serious challenge is not forthcoming.

Meanwhile, a messenger arrived from Ely only yesterday. It was not Threadmorton, our usual rider, who made the journey. The new rider reveals Isaac was killed as he rode back to Cambridgeshire the last time he visited Stathern. He was the victim of an attack by an opportunist band of Royalist brigands from Belvoir Castle, under the command of Captain Thomas Mason, one of the Devil's very own disciples; a man I recall vividly from my period of incarceration.

I learn Threadmorton was slain while riding near Corby.

My mind recalls the conversations I had with Else and I cannot stop wondering if her benign influence led to the untimely demise of this fine young man? It matters little, for I know Grey's torturers are already be having their fun with the woman I once trusted; and her agonies will be a small degree of atonement for the cruel betrayals she perpetrated.

Thankfully, Cromwell's new rider, a likeable fellow called Hugh Walker, also brings some positive news, which dulls the pain of Isaac's passing: it reveals details of a glorious military victory for Parliament in Hampshire on Tuesday the twenty ninth day of March, seventy-two hours hence.

For more than eighteen long months, Parliament's armies have been seeking to check the fortunes of the rampant Cavaliers, who have been in the ascendency in large parts of the country.

With the exception of Edgehill, at the outset of the war, which ended with neither side a clear winner, there have been no opportunities for a decisive victory in the Midlands. But in the South it is now a different story, for

General Waller's Southern Association has turned the tide at a place called Cheriton, where the Royalist Lords Hopton and Forth have experienced a crushing defeat.

According to the lengthy dispatch, Parliament's forces eventually secured a much-needed victory after several days' of fighting, culminating in a major encounter in Cheriton Wood. Only sixty of Waller's men fell in the battle, with the King's army losing more than three hundred of their number. Among those who perished were Lord John Stuart, the Lieutenant-General of Horse; Sir John Smith, Major General of Horse; Henry Sandys of the Vyne; and Sir Edward Stowell. These men had proven reputations in the field, won bravely against our cannon, muskets and swords, and the King will feel their loss most grievously.

"I appreciate this continues to be a time of great personal sadness and you are both in my prayers," adds the Lieutenant-General. "I hope you will forgive me for intruding. But once you have been able to accept this most painful of losses, an important role awaits when you are able to renew your service to Parliament and God. And be assured I will do all I can to see you and your family restored to your former happiness and prosperity."

The dispatch is signed: "Your loving and devoted friend, Oliver Cromwell".

Seven days after Cromwell's letter arrives, Isabel finds me yet again in a state of utter despair. I do not know what has triggered the state of my present mind; perhaps it is a consequence of so many things, including the events of recent weeks? Nonetheless, I find myself increasingly behaving irrationally; and feeling listless, with a burning rage within that I can barely suppress. I am occasionally prone to bouts of the 'Black Dog' and, initially, I believed this was just another short-term episode. But as I sink lower into my pit, and withdraw further, I realise it is something far worse. And, alas, Isabel and the children are forced to bear the brunt of my volatile moods.

"Leave me alone, woman," I yell at her, as she enquires yet again about my welfare. "I do not need you to show me any concern. I will do as I see fit. And I do not need your approval for anything I do."

It is a Friday, and recent days seem to have blended into one long period of semi-consciousness. Once again, I start drinking Port in the kitchen just after the breakfast dishes have been cleared away.

Since Else's betrayal, the Hall has been without a cook. Isabel has taken charge at meal times. When we are done, my wife makes herself scarce and I reach for the bottle, and I quickly lose count of the times I refill my glass. I don't know how this has happened, or why I have succumbed to such weakness; I just know the pain I feel has been diluted, albeit my temper is running on a very short fuse.

I have discovered the taste of a fine Ruby agrees with me. And it has been like this for the last five days.

"Francis. Husband. This is not you talking," says Isabel, refusing to be intimidated by my latest outburst. "Drowning your sorrows in a bottle of Port is not an effective way of coping with your grief. It is the road to ruin, a path to more grievous and damaging pain.

"Do you really believe you are the only person suffering torment and anguish at the moment? The children are distraught. They have lost their two sisters in the harshest of ways; enemy soldiers have ransacked their home; they have seen their mother beaten; and now they see their Father, a man they love most dearly, lost to a weakness, stupor and anger he cannot control.

"I need you to come back to me, Francis. The children need you to be their Father once again. We must grieve together. That way, we will emerge stronger and be able to put these events behind us. And the Militia needs you, for you have been of little use to Abijah and the other officers these past few weeks. So, for God's sake, come back to us."

I hear everything my wife has said. Yet I care little for her pleadings.

I am lost. Consumed with thoughts of nothing other than an acute awareness of my own powerlessness, and my own grief. I have visions; I see Cromwell, Holck, Lady Lucy Hay, Barbara and Isable and Prince Maurice; they are mocking me; taunting me; playing me for the fool I have become. They have manipulated me, to my family's cost.

When I started on this ill-fated quest, after being wooed by Cromwell and Pym's flattery, I swore I would keep my wife and children safe. But I couldn't. It was beyond me. And that knowledge will torment me until the day I die.

"You don't understand," I shout in Isabel's general direction, my words slow, unrefined. "How could you? You lead a protected and privileged life while men like me get our hands dirty.

"I try to protect you all, to keep the vile corruption of the world away from your front door. But it is all to no avail. And, as all have witnessed, I am not man enough to be equal to the task. Barbara and Isable died because I expected a Royalist assassin to keep his word. That man, Holck, always maintained I was too trusting; that I was a fool. And he was right: I am.

"My weakness cost our children their lives. How can I reconcile myself to the reality of that? Tell me, woman, how can I do that?"

Isabel doesn't respond.

She moves to the fireplace and picks up the iron poker. She prods the remnants of the coals that have blackened the hearth's bricks and tiles. She reaches out with her left arm, using the mantelpiece to prop herself up, her gaze never diverting from the floor. All of a sudden, her body spasms: once; twice; I lose count how many times. She drops the poker on the tiles; the noise startles me. I watch as Isabel stands there, on her own; weeping uncontrollably.

I reach for my glass and take a sip of the deep red liquid. I don't feel inclined to get up and comfort her. Why should I? Her grief can be no greater than my own. And who in this house is comforting me?

Eventually, she turns around. She looks haunted. Her eyes reveal it all. Where pronounced cheekbones illuminated a happy and attractive face just a few weeks ago, all I see are the dark, deep bags that disfigure her immense beauty. And I feel emptied.

"You could do nothing to help our daughters and that realisation is crushing you," she says. "It is sucking the life out of you. Husband, you must not blame yourself.

"Right now, you are lost, Francis. Lost. My pain is just as real as your own. It is eating away at me too. I can feel it as much as you can. But I am the one who is alone;

the one who is comforting our children every hour, every day. I have not forgotten my duty. A bottle has not become my crutch!"

Her last remark ignites a flame within my heart. I reach for the Port and hurl it towards the fireplace. It misses Isabel. But it shatters on the bricks, showering the floor with broken glass and whatever is left of its contents.

Isabel lets out a stifled scream. The door to the kitchen bursts open. Abijah stands there. Statuesque. Brooding.

"What in heaven's name are you doing, Francis?" he demands. "This is no way to behave, man. You can be heard all over the Hall. Your harsh words have reduced your children to tears. Francis is at his wits end. So I urge you to pull yourself together and stop this selfish nonsense."

I barely hear my deputy. His voice is clear enough. But I am staring at the hearth and the broken glass. Isabel is still standing there, crying. And I am failing to comprehend what I have just done.

"Please leave us alone, Isabel," commands Abijah, misreading my state of mind. "I will deal with Francis. You must attend to the children. They need their Mother; their comforter."

With Isabel out of the kitchen, Abijah approaches me. His concern of previous days has been replaced with an obvious agitation and wariness.

I reach out to him. He pulls away. I try grabbing hold of Abijah's tunic again, a bit more forcefully this time. The next thing I am aware of is a numbing pain on the side of my jaw. I look up; I seem to have fallen to the floor. Abijah is standing over me, his fists clenched.

"You have had that coming for several days," he bellows. "Your self pity and self-loathing is ruining you, Francis; and it is damaging your faithful wife. And you have no right to behave this way."

And then I remember nothing.

I am lost to the world for several days. Bedridden. Cursed. Left to my own devices to confront the demons polluting my heart and soul.

Occasionally I sense a cool touch on my forehead and some murmured words. Then I drift away, reclaimed by the darkness that has a hold on me. I am unaware of how long I am left to drift between consciousness and oblivion. All I know is, after many troubled days and nights, I awaken. My fever has broken and my head has cleared.

Although noticeably weaker, I am aware of the inner force burning within. I flex my joints and feel sure I can stand without much difficulty; as I do, sunlight bursts through the bedchamber's locked shutters.

It is ten o'clock in the morning on Thursday the twenty first day of April. Abijah and Isabel are close at hand. My wife is the first to break the silence.

"How are you feeling, Francis?" she asks. "You have had some difficult times these past nine days."

I rub my chin; I am no longer clean-shaven, a thick bristle covers my jaw.

"I have felt better," I say. "My head is throbbing. Otherwise, I feel fine, a little bit weak perhaps. How long have I been confined to my mattress?"

My two nursemaids look at each other. Abijah is the first to speak.

"It's been nine days," he says. "You caught a fever, and at one stage we thought we had detected the onset of pneumonia. Thankfully this wasn't the case. It was a false alarm. But all the drink you consumed certainly did not aid your recovery.

"You have been delirious. And you have also been quite obnoxious to many of the people who have been keeping a watchful eye on you. Most of all, however, you owe your heartfelt thanks to Isabel. She has not left your side these past nine days. It is because of her that you got through the worst."

I look at my wife; she is smiling. But she has the appearance of a woman who hasn't slept for an age.

"Now, if you can manage it, you have an important visitor, someone who is desperate to see you," adds Abijah. "Do you have enough strength to see him, or shall I send him away?"

I look at Swan, my face a picture of confusion.

"There is no need to worry," he says reassuringly. "Your visitor is happy to wait until you are strong enough to see him. My only concern is whether your mood will allow you to meet a man whose sole objective is to persuade you to return to your military duties as quickly as possible. What do you think, are you willing to receive him this afternoon?"

I look to Isabel for guidance. She smiles, her eyes shining brightly despite her obvious fatigue.

"You have been missed," she says. "By me, the children – and the Militia. It seems we all need a healthy Francis Hacker back in our lives."

I try to smile, but I find I can't. I remember, with absolute clarity, the conduct that led to my period of hospitalisation, and I can barely look at my wife and my loyal friend. With that knowledge comes a deep sense of shame and a realisation that I do not deserve the love being bestowed on me. Yet here Isabel is, standing before me: loyal, loving and true.

After digesting Abijah's words, I say: "In principal, I would be delighted to receive a visitor. Tell me, whom will I have the pleasure of greeting?"

Abijah approaches the mattress.

"It is a man who, these past two weeks, has been seeking information about your wellbeing on a near daily basis," he replies.

"It's your friend, Oliver. Oliver Cromwell."

TWENTY-THREE

I MUST HAVE FALLEN INTO a deep sleep, for when I awake it is dusk. Candles are burning brightly in the chamber I share with Isabel. Sitting close by is Cromwell, his head bowed. He is reading my Bible.

"Oliver," I say after a couple of minutes of observing a man I hold in the highest of esteem. "It is wonderful to see you. How long have you been here? Why was I not awoken and told of your arrival?"

Cromwell looks up.

I laugh inwardly; one of Parliament's leading figures, a man charged with finding new and better ways of taking the fight to the enemy, is immersed in the King James translation of the good book. It is from here that he finds his inspiration.

Oliver smiles warmly; the irony not lost on him. He puts the book down carefully and rises from the chair. He quickly straightens his clothing before approaching my mattress, hand outstretched.

"Worry not, Francis, I told Isabel I would happily

wait for you to awaken," he says while shaking my hand vigorously. "It is always a joy to find precious moments when I can study the Word. They are far too infrequent these days. So to find you resting was blessing, for I needed to spend time with the Lord. And to have you rested, and now awake, is a blessing also. I am delighted to see you well.

"But enough of this small talk, I didn't come here to exchange niceties; we have much to say and discuss."

It is a welcome surprise to find Cromwell in Stathern once again. Since he last visited my home, his fortunes have continued to soar. Many who know him have always believed Oliver will be a major figure in the advancement of Parliament's cause. But few of us predicted his progress would be so rapid. He is effectively second in command of the Eastern Association's army; he is working closely with Fairfax to find ways to out-think and out-fight our foe; and his influence in London is growing, much as the late John Pym had predicted and hoped for.

With so much to consider and the weight of responsibility bearing down on his shoulders, he has chosen to spend much of his day with me. And I don't know why?

"I can see how your mind is working, young man," he says, catching me by surprise. "I should tell you there are several reasons why I am choosing to invest a considerable amount of time and resource in you. I will have no hesitation in disclosing all in due course. But before I do, please allow me to appraise you of everything that is going on."

Preparations for the creation of the New Model Army continue to gather pace, albeit in continued secrecy. Many Parliamentarians still need to be convinced about the radical plan. Nonetheless, Cromwell was delighted to hear of the Militia's victory in Hinckley, which was largely achieved using the tactics he espoused at the secret meeting in Ely. He tells me he has shared details of the success with other commanders, including Fairfax. And he reports the news has been greeted with widespread acclaim.

Confidence is continuing to soar among the militias aligned to the Southern Association. The Royalist defeat at Cheriton means Parliament believes its forces can now claim the whole of the region in the weeks ahead.

"The defeat of Hopton and Forth's army is a catalyst for a major change in the balance of power," claims the Lieutenant-General. "Mark my words, the King is finished in the South West. It is merely a matter of time."

I greet the news with delight, but I am sure there is more to come. And I don't have long to wait.

"Yesterday," says Cromwell, with added gravitas. "A Parliamentary and Scottish army besieged York. The city is now cut off from the rest of the King's forces and it is only a matter of time before it surrenders, or there is a decisive battle in the north. Whatever the outcome, I am confident we will prevail. I can honestly see no other outcome than a success for Parliament. If it were not so, I would say freely."

I find myself smiling. It is something I have been unable to do these past weeks. But Cromwell's news is truly heartening and helps me forgot my own woes.

Oliver is restless. He gets up and paces the room, eventually settling on the very windowsill from which Holck forced me to yield the brooch and secret papers.

I wonder if I will ever be able to forget that fateful day? I try to dispel my thoughts by probing Oliver's motives for his visit.

"Lieutenant-General," I say respectfully. "Thank you for updating me on these important matters. But I am surprised you felt breaking this news to me necessitated a trip of such a distance. While I am grateful for your company, I am sure you could have told me all in a dispatch, sir."

Cromwell is quick to reply, wagging his finger as he does.

"I am in these parts because the Eastern Association is moving its troops and armaments into Lincolnshire," he says. "We will soon be laying siege to Lincoln, in a bid to rid the city of the malignant Cavaliers. And when we have done this, our goal is to move to the west and join the Northern Association at York, thereby strengthening the siege.

"Much is now starting to unfold, Francis, as I predicted it would. But we need our finest men leading our militias; and you are one of these men.

"You are needed, my friend. A bedchamber is no place for a man of your talents and capabilities. So I am officially here to discover how long it will it be before you are able to lead the Leicester companies of horse and dragoons once again?"

I suspected as much; I knew there was a less altruistic reason Cromwell would be willing to devote so much of his time to one person! As for returning to active service, the truth is I have mixed feelings: on one hand, I want to play an active part in the war effort against the King by leading the Militia. Yet I cannot forget Holck, a man who has deprived my family of so much. Until he is brought to justice, whether it is by the sword or the noose, I will not be able to rest. And I tell Cromwell so.

I spend the next two hours talking to Oliver. We discuss the challenges that lie ahead, beyond ending the Royalist hold on York, and we agree on some significant points, not least our joint belief that the weakness of Parliament's armies has yet to be addressed, particularly the suitability and effectiveness of our generals.

Both of us have witnessed decision-making that has been more about self-interest than winning the day. And many of our contempories drawn from the gentry and merchant classes, good officers, solid God-fearing men, have also been left shaking their heads in despair. With the tide turning in our favour, we are reaching a critical point where we cannot allow things to continue this way.

"In all matters, I am forced to be subordinate to the Earl of Manchester," confides Cromwell, his anger plain to see. "He is not fit to lead an army that is serious about taking the fight to many of his friends on the King's side. Like so many, he forgets sometimes which side he is on. These men are undermining Parliament and blunting the sharpness of our swords. The New Model Army will change all. The nobility's impotent influence will end; men of ability will be given authority and rank."

It stirs my blood to hear talk of change. But the path Cromwell is advocating is dangerous. There will be opposition. Some of it could be violent. I am not opposed to it all. But care needs to be taken, and I tell my superior officer so.

"You are quite right. Caution is a necessity," he admits. "And such an approach slows down the speed of change. So there will be no immediate change, even though there is a pressing need for radicalism in our thinking and application. The New Model Army is some months away from being more than an idea. But every day that passes brings more people round to our way of thinking. And that is a blessing, Francis: a true blessing.

"My friend, I value our friendship and the contribu-tion you will undoubtedly make as part of the army's van-guard in the months ahead. And, Francis, I look forward to us defeating our enemy and uniting our country."

Cromwell is everything I would wish to be as an ora-tor. His words have power and substance; they inspire and enthuse; critically I believe them. But before I can move on to the glorious future Oliver anticipates, and is actively devising, I need to reconcile the recent past. So I break the Lieutenant-General's spell by changing the subject of our conversation to my nemesis: Gustav Holck.

"Oliver, I need your help," I say. "I need you to sup-port an application I intend to make to Lord Grey, to give me leave of absence from the Militia for the next few weeks. I cannot sit by idly. If I do, I will be fit for nothing. I must pursue Holck; I must hold him to account for his actions. I need you to help me secure a temporary release from my military commitments. Can I count on you?"

For more than thirty minutes, Cromwell keeps his own counsel. He listens to my petition. He asks a number of questions. And he now paces the floor of my bedchamber. Contemplating. Thinking. Seeking guidance. After a while, he reaches again for my King James Bible.

A renowned and fiery preacher, Cromwell thumbs through the pages he knows so well, breathing in the Word as if it is life-giving oxygen. He flicks one-way and then the other, back and forth, until his hand stops. At last, he has found what he is looking for.

"I have something of interest to share with you," he declares. "I am reading from the Book of Samuel in the Old Testament; chapter twenty-two, verses thirty-eight to forty-three. It says thus:

'I pursued my enemies and crushed them; I did not turn back till they were destroyed. I crushed them completely, and they could not rise; they fell beneath my feet. You armed me with strength for battle; you humbled my adversaries before me. You made my enemies turn their backs in flight, and I destroyed my foes. They cried for help, but there was no one to save them... I beat them as fine as the dust of the earth; I pounded and trampled them like mud in the streets.'

"And if you need further affirmation, there is the Book of Ezekiel, chapter thirty-three, verses eight and nine, which states:

'When I state to the wicked, 'You wicked person, you will surely die' and you do not speak out to dissuade them from their ways, that wicked person will die for their sin, and I will hold you accountable for their blood. But if you do warn the wicked person to turn from their ways and they do not do so, they will die for their sin, though you yourself will be saved.'

Cromwell puts down the Book, running his finger over the crucifix on the cover as he does so.

He looks directly at me once again.

"We all interpret the Word of the Lord in different ways, Francis," he says, not as my teacher or superior officer, but as my friend. "This quest you are set on is fraught with danger. Holck and his associates are dangerous, ungodly men. He has bested you on two previous occasions. What makes you think he will not prevail a third time? You have lived thus far. You may not be so lucky the next time. If that were to happen, what will the future hold for Isabel; what will the future hold for your children? And what about your men; who will lead them into battle?

"I, too, need you, young friend. I do not spend such

lengthy periods of time here to flatter you: far from it. I recognise the important role you must play in our military affairs. I have done so ever since you undertook the assignment with Prince Rupert and his brother.

"One day, sometime soon, I believe you will be the foremost Colonel in the Parliamentary army. I would go as far as saying it has been predetermined. Nothing must jeopardise this. I say these things, Francis, because I understand what it is like to have an inner despair; a fire that will not go out until you have sated your thirst; until righteous vengeance has corrected a heinous wrong.

"The Bible gives men of faith authority to root out evil in God's name; in His strength, not their own. Holck is certainly an evil man. He may, indeed, be the spawn of Lucifer. What you have told me, what I know of my own volition, confirms that. But the taking of a man's life, as an act of pure, lustful revenge, is clearly against God's wishes. Only our Father can sanction such a course of action."

Oliver climbs from the chair once again, stretching his legs as he does.

He walks to the window and gazes into the darkness. The candles shimmer in the draught his movement creates as he turns around one last time to address me.

"I will contact Grey on your behalf, if that is your wish," he adds. "But if you choose to take this path, make sure your conscience is clear and you are pursuing this man because God has truly put this matter on your heart.

"I implore you to explore your inner self before you decide on any course of action, for you face eternal damnation if you merely seek revenge in the names of Barbara and Isable."

The escort that accompanies the Lieutenant-General everywhere is assembled and ready to depart Stathern.

Sitting astride their chestnut stallions, they are a striking picture of precision and discipline; they look every inch the feared "Ironsides" Cromwell's men have now been dubbed by the Cavaliers. All have enjoyed as hearty a breakfast as could be afforded them. So has Cromwell. As he walks towards Black Jack, the renowned horse that is as dark as Whitby's precious Jet stone, Oliver turns to me, his arms outstretched. We embrace one last time.

"Think hard on what we talked about last night, my friend," he reiterates.

"You are good man, a loyal follower of Christ Jesus. So never succumb to temptation. Be the beacon you are called to be, understanding at all times there will be many personal sacrifices you are asked to give along the way. You have already experienced some of these. But there will be more. And how we behave at these times defines us as men of God.

"I have written a dispatch to Lord Grey, requesting permission for you to be granted leave. I have suggested he allow you to return to duties on the first of July. This request will only become valid if you formally seek leave of absence. It is invalid if you don't. So think long and hard before you decide on what you choose to do. Whether Grey heeds my plea, only time will tell. But don't raise your hopes: I think the man is a buffoon and contemptible. His personal view of me is equally uncomplimentary."

Black Jack paws the ground with his huge hooves. He is almost the equal of Bucephalus, but I am sure my steed has the edge. Just.

Cromwell breaks away from me after bidding his

goodbyes and mounts the huge beast. Unlike the men he is travelling with, who are wearing an array of heavy lobster helmets, Oliver prefers to ride bareheaded; his thinning dark locks trailing behind him.

"Take care, Captain Hacker," bids Cromwell from the saddle. "Whatever course you choose in the weeks ahead, I look forward to seeing you again in July. May our Lord protect you."

Abijah and Isabel support me as I stand and watch this remarkable man canter out of the Hall's grounds and join the road that leads to Nottingham and, ultimately, the killing fields of Lincolnshire. He has an aura unlike any man I know. And there is no doubt: with him on our side, anything is possible.

I am ready to leave Stathern on the morning of Monday the eighteenth day of April.

Many tears have been shed: by Isabel, the children and myself. And after a lot of praying and discussion, my family is united behind the decision I have made.

Details of my journey remain secret, particularly my destination and ultimate quest. Only my immediate family, Cromwell, Grey and Abijah know why I will be absent from my duties with the Militia for the next seven weeks.

The ride will take no more than three hours. I am travelling to a village calling Coddington, located some three miles outside of Newark, where I am to meet a Parliamentarian agent called Edmund Goodyeare. I will reside at his home for the foreseeable future, until I return home at the end of June.

Thanks to the assistance of the Lieutenant-General and some of his associates, I have discovered Holck frequents several inns in the Newark area. According to the information I now possess, which came into my possession late last night, via one of Cromwell's couriers, the man I am pursuing has been seen regularly these past two weeks drinking with some of his associates. A list of the inns was included with the dispatch. Now I am fit again in body and mind, it will be at these hostelries that my search for justice begins.

It will be tomorrow that I start my quest in earnest; today is all about departing on good terms with the people whom mean the most to me in this turbulent world.

One by one, Anne, Elizabeth and Mary come to the front of the Hall and say tearful goodbyes. I embrace them dearly and tell them they will be in my thoughts every day until I return. Without fail, I tell them of my love for them, their mother and our family. I receive a precious peck on the cheek from them all as a token of their affection.

Francis is the last of my children to bid me farewell.

My son refuses to look at me as I hold out my arms, beckoning him to me. His face is taut as he attempts to mask the deep emotions raging within. I know he is angry, he has told me so on several occasions. I have done my utmost to explain my reasoning. But Francis has not listened. He simply extends his hand.

"Goodbye, Papa," he says. "Come home soon."

Then the young man who fills my heart with so much pride and joy is gone.

Isabel beckons all four of the children inside. As she does, Abijah leads Bucephalus by the nose towards the place where I stand. My horse's ears are raised; he is aware he is about to embark on an adventure and I can tell the prospect is to his liking. There is an exaggerated swagger as he walks the short distance from the stables.

He bows his head as we greet each other yet again, a sure sign my reliable steed is aware of the importance of my mission. And immediately my spirits start to improve.

To my left, Abijah approaches, clasping my arm strongly; it is a sure sign of the strength of emotion he is feeling.

"Make sure you do nothing reckless," he urges as he hands over the reins. "I understand why you must do this thing. And I wish you God's speed. But do not be foolhardy. You are entering the lion's den. Take no risks. Do all in your power to ensure you come back to us."

My beloved wife stands at the main window of the Hall. The children are clinging on to her like four lonely limpets stuck on the rocks. She puts her hand to her mouth and blows me a kiss.

We said all that was needed prior to my departure. This includes my long overdue confession about the encounter I had with Lady Lucy Hay at Banbury Castle all those weeks ago.

I have been mute for too long on this matter, never quite having the courage to raise the subject; the guilt I have felt about my own conduct has been eating at my innards; distorting my emotions; placing guilt on my heart. Yet my wife dismissed the matter; not quite out of hand, but more brusquely than I could dare have hoped for.

Isabel said the telling factor was not that I was tempted by another woman, but I had not succumbed to my impulses. To me, there is no difference; I lusted after another woman who was not my wife. The sin was plain. Yet Isabel sees things very differently.

I fear I will never be able to comprehend women.

"Francis, you are a husband who doesn't understand the wily ways of vixens like the Countess," was Isabel's forthright reaction to my confession. "The fact you are telling me this, when you could have easily said naught, speaks volumes about you and your character.

"I know you are a true man and father. We all sin, my dearest, even you. If it is as you have said, and I believe it so, then you have nothing to reproach yourself about. You offered the Lady no encouragement and you dealt with the matter in a way that emphasises your absolute integrity and honour.

"The shame, if shame is the right word, is that you have felt unable to tell me of this until now, on the day you are leaving us. How I wish you could have spoken to me about this earlier; how I wish you hadn't been forced to carry this guilt.

"For weeks I have known of your torment; I know you have been consumed with remorse. I assumed it was something to do with your imprisonment and torture. And, in a sense, it was. But be assured, my love, there is nothing to forgive on my part. You have acted properly at all times, as I know you always will."

To be able to leave Stathern with my wife's blessing and love is more than I could have hoped for. It means everything.

Isabel is fearful that I won't return, as am I. And, echoing Cromwell, she can't understand why I would put myself at such risk after everything I have endured these past months.

The truth is my wife didn't discover Isable's and Barbara's bodies; she didn't experience the cruelty of Holck at Belvoir Castle; and she really doesn't comprehend why this killer has to be stopped at all costs, even if that means I may have to surrender everything that is mine to give.

In time, I pray she will understand and extend her forgiveness once again, if I fail to come home.

I take one last look at my family before easing onto the padded saddle that will hopefully help me stave-off the sores that so often accompany a long ride.

Coinciding with my ascent, the sun bursts through the low-lying clouds that have been blanketing the Vale hitherto, golden light eclipsing the gloom. From some-where, the lone bell of Saint Guthlacs starts to ring out; its metallic, single note bolstering the optimism I feel, filling me with renewed hope.

I look to the skies and then reach for my pocket watch: the time is ten minutes past ten. How can this be so? The bell is always so punctual!

My heels dig into the flanks of Bucephalus and we ease out of the courtyard.

As we pass the charred remains of the Harrington's cottage, I marvel at such impeccable timing; and I have no doubt my Maker is blessing me, giving me the answer Cromwell urged me to seek.

A gentle trot becomes a canter. Soon my horse is in full stride, eating up the lush grasslands that stretch out before me, mile after mile.

In the days and weeks to come, I will miss my home and the wife and children I love. But with God at my side, I will return soon enough.

Of that I am sure…

THE END

Lieutenant-General Oliver Cromwell
The rising star of the Parliamentarian army, Francis
Hacker became a staunch supporter of Cromwell's

FRANCIS HACKER
1618-1660

THE STORY OF FRANCIS HACKER has been waiting to be told ever since his untimely death, by public hanging, on the nineteenth day of October, 1660.

He was forty-two years old at the time of his demise.

In life, Francis was an extraordinary figure. A respected and talented military commander, and a loving husband and father, he was a man of immense faith, who believed he had a duty to uphold the teachings of the Bible – and hold to account those who he believed supported popery and false teachings. This included Charles the First of England and some of the most trusted members of the King's inner circle – men like Archbishop Laud.

During the three civil wars that scarred England for so long, Francis was a staunch supporter of Oliver Cromwell, who from 1643 was a rising army officer, a man noted for his strategic brilliance and the firm disciplinary hand he exercised on Parliament's Eastern Association army.

He would remain a firm ally and friend of Cromwell

until the Lord Protector's death on Friday the third day of September, 1658.

Francis was the only member of his family to support the Parliamentarian faction; his brothers, Thomas and Rowland, were officers in the King's army, waging war against the Leicestershire and Nottinghamshire Militias from the Royalist garrisons of Trent Bridge, Ashby Castle and Belvoir Castle. His father, John, was also a staunch Royalist; it is not known what political views Anne, his sister, held.

He married Isabel (nee Brunts) at Saint Peter's Church in East Bridgford on the fifth day of July, 1632. At the time of their wedding, the couple were incredibly young: Francis was just fourteen years of age; Isabel was twenty.

They were to be together for twenty-eight years.

Six children would be the product of this largely happy union: Francis (born 26 May 1633); Anne (born: 25 March 1634), Isable (born: 24 January 1638); Elizabeth (christened: 9 October 1637); Mary (christened: 8 March 1639); and Barbara (christened: 18 July 1641).

Little is known generally about Francis's life.

Even though he was to become a prominent figure in Parliament's military machine, and one of the men who signed the decree condemning Charles the First to death, Francis is one of the forgotten men of this cruel conflict. *Rebellion* attempts to fill the void, through accurate accounts of the time and, where there are gaps, my own embellishments and fantasy.

I will leave you, the reader, to discover the ultimate truth, should you wish to go on such a journey?

As for any factual mistakes, these are of my own making. Please accept my unresrved apologies if you unearth anything that proves to be erroneous. I hope it doesn't detract from the overall story I am telling, which is of a man who dearly loved his wife, children and God – and did his utmost to serve the cause he believed in.

Francis will return in *Redemption*, the second book in The Hacker Chronicles series.

WITH GRATITUDE

AMONG THE PRINCIPAL SOURCES I have used while researching this book are: Cobbett's *Complete Collection of State Trials and Proceedings for High Treason and other Crimes and Misdemeanors* (Volume Five), printed in 1810, which offers access to eye witness accounts of the court hearings of King Charles (1648) and the regicides (October 1660); Lucy Hutchinson's *The Memoirs of Colonel Hutchinson*, published in the late seventeenth century, chronicling the life of her husband, John, when he was the Parliamentarian Governor of Nottingham; *The History of Leicester during the Great Civil War*, published in 1833 by JF Hollings, detailing the period leading up to the siege of the city in 1645; Ian Payne's *A Keeper of the Magazine Identify'd*, chronicling the many allegations of atrocities in the siege of Leicester; and *The Civil War in Leicestershire and Rutland*, a truly excellent treasure trove of wonderful facts and information, written by the talented and thorough Phillip Andrew Scaysbook.

In addition, I have read the works of accomplished

authors Peter Akroyd, Charles Spencer, Dianne Purkiss and Geoffrey Robertson. Akroyd's *Civil War* and Spencer's *Killers of the King* I wholeheartedly recommend to anyone studying the civil war period. Thanks to these writers, I was able to think more creatively than I would ever have dared.

Online resources have also been invaluable. And I would like to thank the authoritative BCW Project, which offers writers and researchers access to a feast of detailed materia from the period, and the British History Online digital platform. In researching *Rebellion*, I accessed more than a hundred and forty different online resources. All offered me important information and insights that enabled me to dig deeper into the seventeenth century and make this book possible.

The staff at the Public Records Offices in Leicester and Nottingham offered enthusiastic support, granting access to original documentation that I have used faithfully in this book. The Library team at the University of Leicester has also been most helpful – particularly archivist, Ian Swirles, who enabled me to access the large collection of seventeenth century engravings and pictures that make up the fabulous Fairclough Collection. As you will have seen, some of these images have been reproduced in this novel.

I would also like to thank Kevin Winter for allowing me to spend time with him at the National Civil War Museum in Newark. Kevin's observations and guidance were incredibly helpful. Being able to handle the swords of the period, lobster helmets, leaden shot, armour and an array of other items, was highly illuminating and thought provoking. Anyone wishing to find out about this critical period in English history need look no further than Kevin and his colleagues at this wonderful national treasure.

Last but not least, my heartfelt thanks go to my good friend, Janique Helson, for convincing me to write a book and commit my thoughts to print; my tennis partner, Keith Potter, for his unstinting support and appetite for proof-reading; my old school friend, Dean Yates-Smith, for his passion for the story and his invaluable printing expertise; and to my wife, Julie, for her ever-lasting love, enthusiasm, and positivity.

THE AUTHOR

PHILIP YORKE (KNOWN AS "TONY") has always had a special interest in history – and loves reading intelligent, multi-layered plots and well-told stories.

He is a former Fleet Street reporter who has worked for several national newspapers. After leaving the media, he has advised a number of UK businesses – and been the co-owner of a public relations and marketing agency. He currently works in the Third Sector and is an active church-goer.

Married to Julie, with whom he has five children, he enjoys relaxing to classical music; reading the works of Nigel Tranter, Bernard Cornwell, Conn Iggulden, Robyn Young, Jan Guillou, Simon Scarrow and CJ Sansom; and supporting Hull City AFC and Leicester Tigers rugby club.

Today, he lives in Leicestershire, England.

To keep up-to-date with all future book releases, blogs and articles, please visit: **www.philipyorke.org**

mashiach  publishing

Read an excerpt from

Redemption

By Philip Yorke

Book Two of the Hacker Chronicles

MARSTON MOOR

THE SECOND DAY OF JULY in the year of our Lord, 1644, will be remembered long after my flesh is no more and my bones have been reduced to dust.

It is close to seven o'clock in the evening. It is a Saturday, a time when husbands should be at home with their families; when sons should be working with their fathers; on farms; in forges; anywhere but this cursed place: the moorlands of Marston, some eight miles outside the great city of York.

As torrential rain lashes the land and lightening illuminates the grey and foreboding sky, more than forty thousand men silently await their doom.

At this late hour, the armies of the King and Parliament are preparing to unleash themselves upon each other. They have been waiting for most of the day. Patiently; silently; nervously; eager not to show their hand too early, lest it gives the other side an unassailable advantage.

And the stench of their fear is overpowering.

Every man fears death before he marches into battle. Sometimes it is visible; sometimes, it is not. But it is there, seeping from every pore, just as surely as pus oozes from a corrupted, fetid wound.

At these times, nerves are tested and, as men, we discover who we are and what we stand for. As we prepare to meet our Maker, most of us realise glory is not what we seek; it has never been so. The simple preservation of life itself is what we wish for – and to be reunited with the ones we love.

Bravado cannot disguise the sense of powerlessness that grips a man's soul. On the battlefield, he has nowhere to run, no place to hide. The only available pathway will, in all likelihood, lead to his painful extinction – at a place where axes, swords and muskets bite into flesh and reap a rich harvest; at a place where all destinies are fulfilled.

In a bid to find inner peace, men like me kneel and pray; we sing psalms, hoping the Lord will accept our repentance and forgive us for a lifetime of sin. For others, it is a moment of torment and angst; of bleakness; it is a time of pleading to whoever will listen, begging to be spared.

Alas, nobody escapes the torture the final minutes bring, when the silence is deafening and when we have time to dwell on the many ills we have perpetrated in this vile civil war and our increasingly meaningless life. Long before the cries of *"In God's name"* or *"For the King"* strike up, shattering the peace and sending cold pulses racing down the spines of every man who still possesses a conscience.

Many are affected, their rank and social class meaningless at a time that makes all men equal.

Fear consumes almost every one of us. It doesn't discriminate. Regardless of our breeding, we cannot control our bowels and bladders, so we soil our breeches where we stand. For men of war are meant to be humiliated when the rivers of blood start to flow over our rich and verdant lands.

In the gloom that shrouds this cursed place, brave, godly men fill the Royalist ranks and look down from the ridge on the massed ranks of the Parliamentarian army. They, like my comrades and I, are sodden, such has been the intensity of the deluge.

As I watch my foe through the narrow slits that are protecting my eyes from the lashing storm, I cannot understand how committed followers of Christ Jesus continue to pledge their fealty to a Sovereign who does not deserve their loyalty. A deceiver who believes his rule is by divine appointment. Prince Rupert of the Palatinate and the Earl of Newcastle, commanders of the Cavalier army, are also undeserving of the support they receive, for they are brutal, reckless and selfish men.

Our King has been in the ascendency since this damnable and bloody conflict started in August 1642. Parliament has lost many battles thus far. And men like me are deemed to be "rebels" because we choose to stand up to the tyrant and try to force him to rescind his Catholic ways, rule justly and accept the will of his people.

Edgehill, in the county of Warwickshire, is the one exception. We fought Charles here, bringing our massed army to this quiet, unassuming place. Unfortunately, we achieved naught, only a stalemate. On that bleak day, thousands died. There were no winners, only losers. Men went to their grave for no compelling reason.

And it has been the same ever thus.

Now allied forces, comprising soldiers loyal to Parliament, led by the Earl of Manchester and his deputy,

Lieutenant-General Oliver Cromwell, and Scots soldiers from the Covenant army, sent south of the border under the command of the Earl of Leven, have an opportunity to deliver a telling blow against the King's northern regiments. These are the wily foxes that just twelve months ago decimated Fairfax's northern armies at Adwalton Moor. I remember our capitulation well; forty-nine of my best, most committed men died that fateful day.

Soon we will know whether Parliament has learned lessons from so many painful defeats: swords are being drawn from their scabbards, our many cannons are being loaded with grape shot; men are continuing to pray, and all around me the blood lust is rising.

And this damnable rain, that turns the firm ground into merciless, unyielding mud, continues to hammer down.

I look at myself; I am in a sore state. The realisation makes me laugh aloud and recall a memory from long ago about my old Latin tutor. Whenever he needed spiritual guidance or sought to draw strength from his Faith, Erasmus Woodbridge would quietly whisper to himself: *"In deo speramus."*

It is an apt expression. Even though I know very little Latin, this is something I have remembered for more than twenty years. And it is so true. For who can we trust if it is not God?

Hell will be unleashed once the Parliamentarian army has filled its belly and the men of the York garrison, who have swelled our number, are given their battle orders. Their arrival takes the strength of the army to just under twenty-five thousand men.

We are more numerous than the enemy, and our fifty

drakes and many mortars will wreak death and carnage when they are brought to bear on the foolhardy and arrogant King's men. I am confident, for as the day grows longer the omens and conditions become more favourable.

For some reason, Rupert chose not to attack us when we were at our weakest: that was in the morn when we first arrived and our command lines had yet to be established, our men were hungry, and our armies were of equal strength. As the day has worn on, we have grown stronger and more confident by the hour, not least because reinforcements have continued to arrive and Cromwell has had us singing psalms most of the afternoon.

He knows only too well how these precious words always give us the lift we need before the fighting starts.

It is now seven-thirty in the evening, and the Royalists are in the midst of retiring when the slaughter begins. They are surprised and unprepared for what is to come.

Leading the fight for Parliament is Cromwell. His Ironsides slice through the King's men, like water bursting through a dam. Such is the ferocity of the Lieutenant-General's perfectly timed charge, and the courage displayed by the infantry on the left, that Prince Rupert's finest men are powerless to resist our violent advance. They buckle. And that is all the encouragement we need.

The sound of the death rattle is everywhere. The steel of thousands of sabres flash in the gloom; gunpowder turns the air grey as muskets are fired indiscriminately; and men from both sides fall from their horses, their warm blood eagerly consumed by the ravenous Yorkshire meadowlands.

Death is stalking many a soul, all because Charles, the tyrant King, refuses to yield to the will of his people.

In the thick of battle, as Cromwell's force clashes with Lord Byron's men, the Lieutenant General lurches to his side. Crimson flows from his neck; a well-aimed musket ball has left its painful mark this day.

"Drive them back," he yells to whoever will listen, barely noticing the stinging sensation pulsing down the left side of his body and the blood that is now flowing freely onto his leather jerkin. "Send these curs to Hades. Show them whose side God is on."

As Cromwell leaves the field to have his wound dressed, a huge cry goes up. His men are driving the enemy backwards, angered by the injury to their commander; their very own Alexander the Great. As the pressure intensifies, our foe struggles to keep their footholds in the mud; the spilt blood, intestines and guts of their comrades adding to their acute difficulties. And all the time, Parliament's forces press forward, a relentless, disciplined and unstoppable phalanx.

For many, it is too much. Facing overwhelming odds, hundreds of Byron's troops surrender in the face of the onslaught.

I survey the wondrous scenes. Almost everywhere, it is a similar story: Parliament is winning the day.

As the battle reaches its conclusion, it is becoming evident the King's army was grossly unprepared for the assault. Afterwards, we will learn that many troops had left their positions in a bid to find food to fill their ravenous bellies, believing hostilities would not commence until the following day, the Sabbath. Their underestimation of Parliament's resolve is their fatal mistake.

It is surprising just how little the likes of Rupert and the Earl of Essex know us. They have been fighting our forces for the last two years – besting us on so many occasions. Surely they should know our armies are filled with thousands of God-fearing, zealous men who have no desire to draw blood on the Sabbath. Give them the chance to fight in the rain on a Saturday, albeit every inch of them will be soaked through to the skin, and they will take it gladly. For Sundays should always be a day of rest and prayer.

While Cromwell is being attended to by the field-surgeon, Prince Rupert's famed squadrons of horse continue to be pressed in the centre of the Royalist formation.

In just over an hour, the fourteen thousand-strong Scottish covenanters, led by Lord Leven, have succeeded in bludgeoning their way through to the most famed troops in the King's army. No quarter is given. Many of the Prince's men die where they sit. They are hacked. They are mutilated. The Scots have a point to prove and a bounty to earn.

On the right flank of the allied line, Fairfax's men are engaged in a far more even struggle. It is only when he breaks free of the struggle and rides to Cromwell, alerting the newly stitched-up Lieutenant General to his plight, that the tide turns.

Cromwell quickly gains control of his men and, as a disciplined wedge, they plough into the foe, shattering the tenuous advantage the Royalists hold over Fairfax's brave and steadfast men. Hundreds die as they come under sustained assault from Parliament's most formidable fighting force. The sickening sound of swords and axes being hammered into flesh and bone can be heard all along the line, as can the screams of the dying. It doesn't take long before the Cavaliers seek to take flight, the need for survival so much stronger than any other instinct.

And so the slaughter becomes a rout.

By thirty minutes past nine in the evening, with the skies continuing to emit tears of unbridled joy, the fighting is at an end and more than four thousand Royalists have been slain. A further two thousand enemy soldiers are captives and all of the King's artillery is in the possession of Parliament.

The battle is over.

The tide of the war is turning.

Printed in Great Britain
by Amazon